War Co

Betty Firth grew up in rural West Yorkshire in the UK, right in the heart of Brontë country... and she's still there. After graduating from Durham University with a degree in English Literature, she dallied with living in cities including London, Nottingham and Cambridge, but eventually came back with her own romantic hero in tow to her beloved Dales. Betty Firth also writes romantic comedies under the pen name Mary Jayne Baker and Lisa Swift, and wrote *Edie's Home for Strays* as Gracie Taylor.

Also by Betty Firth

Made in Yorkshire

A New Home in the Dales
War Comes to the Dales

Betty Firth

War Comes
to the Dales

hera

First published in the United Kingdom in 2023 by

Hera Books
Unit 9 (Canelo), 5th Floor
Cargo Works, 1–2 Hatfields
London SE1 9PG
United Kingdom

A CIP catalogue record for this book is available from the British Library.

Print ISBN 978 1 80436 192 4
Ebook ISBN 978 1 80436 191 7

Look for more great books at www.herabooks.com

Printed and bound in Great Britain by Clays Ltd, Elcograf S.p.A.

I

I'd like to dedicate this book to the Polish aircrew of the Vickers Wellington that crashed on Buckden Pike, North Yorkshire, on 30th January 1942. Five members of the six-man crew died in the crash or as a result of injuries sustained.

Flight Lieutenant Czesław Kujawa

Pilot Officer Jerzy Polczyk

Flying Officer Tadeusz Jan Biegański

Sergeant Jan Sadowski

Sergeant Jan Andrzej Tokarzewski

Sergeant Józef Fuśniak

Dialect glossary

Afore = before
Allus = always
Any road = anyhow
Aye = yes
Badly = ill
Bairn = child
Beck = stream
Bonny = pretty
A brew = pot/cup of tea
Canny = sensible
Capped = pleased
Clout = a slap (or a cloth/item of clothing)
Dale = valley
Favver = father
Fell = hill or mountain
Fettle = to fix or put in order
Flayed = afraid
Frame = to work hard
Frame thissen = get to work
Gang = go
Gimmer = young female sheep
Grand = excellent
Lad = boy/man
Happen = perhaps; possibly
Herssen = herself

Hissen = himself
Laiking = playing
Lass = girl/woman
Lish = nimble, strong
Mam = mother
Mardy = grumpy
Missen = myself
Mourngy = sulky or miserable
Mun = must
Nay = no
Nithered = feeling the cold
Noan = not/none
Nobbut = nothing but; only
Nowt = nothing
O' = of
Oss = horse
Owd = old
Owt = anything
Shearling = young sheep before its first shearing
Shippon = cowshed
Sin = since
Sithee = goodbye/look here
Snicket = a small path or alley between buildings
Spice = sweets/candy
Summat = something
Sup = drink
T' = the
Tha/thee = you
Thi/thy = your
Thine = yours
Think on = watch what you're doing; be careful
Thissen = yourself
Thrang = busy

Tup = stud ram
Tyke = someone from Yorkshire
Us = our
Wi' = with
Yon = yonder/over there
Yourn = yours
Yoursen = yourself
Yow = ewe

Chapter 1

April 1941

It was all over Silverdale by suppertime. A telegram had come. Ida Wilcox had got a telegram. *The* telegram.

Bobby Bancroft was in the Golden Hart, buying herself a drink to warm up after a chilly shift at the ARP shelter on the village green, when she heard the news.

'You'll know all about it, I reckon,' said the landlady, Lizzie, as she poured Bobby a half of brown ale.

'All about what?'

'Have you not heard? I thought you'd be first to get news, you being from t' paper.'

It always amused Bobby, the way the Silverdale folk saw no difference between their own little magazine about the Dales – *The Tyke* – and national newspapers such as *The Times* or *The Daily Telegraph*. But the landlady had an earnest expression on her face, so Bobby suppressed her smiles.

'There's been talk of nowt else in here all night,' Lizzie said as she pushed the brown ale across the bar. Bobby rummaged in her tunic pocket for sixpence.

'Beer keeps getting weaker, but price of a pint keeps going up,' a man at the end of the bar observed mournfully as he watched Bobby pay for her drink. 'Every ounce o' water they put in adds another farthing. Bloody Germans.'

Bobby nodded in sympathy before turning her attention back to Lizzie.

'Is there some war news?' she asked. 'I've been on duty, so I haven't listened to the wireless tonight. Something good, I hope.'

'Nay, summat bad. The worst sort o' bad.' Lizzie lowered her voice. 'Ida Wilcox's youngest. Billy, as went for the merchant navy.'

'Oh no. He isn't—'

'Missing, but they don't have much hope. Ship went down. One o' them U-boats, they say. And him nobbut nineteen – a bairn, I call that.'

'What an awful thing to happen,' Bobby said with feeling. 'Poor Ida.'

'That's three village lads now as won't be coming home. Tell you what, I could wish this business over tomorrow – even if it meant a Swastika flying up the flagpole on the green.'

Bobby shook her head. 'You don't mean that.'

Lizzie sighed. 'Well, happen you're right. I'm angry, that's all. Them lads deserved better. They all do.'

'How's Ida bearing up?'

'She were out milking her little goat when I went over with a packet o' dripping for her supper. Putting a brave face on, as she does, but white as white. Hit her hard, that's my feeling.'

'I'll go over this weekend with Mary and take her something. We've a block of new cheese in the larder. I'm sure the Athertons would want to make her a present of it. Lord knows I'd be hard pressed to muster energy to feed myself after a shock like that.'

Lizzie smiled. 'That's Silverdale way, right enough. When we can't bring comfort any other road, we can allus help out with a square meal. You mun be going native, Miss.'

'I hope you're right.' Bobby took her drink, then hesitated. 'Um, has my father been in tonight?'

'Aye, he were in an hour or two sin. Laiking at dominoes wi' Pete Dixon.'

'Did he stay long?'

'Nobbut an hour, I reckon. Why?'

'No reason. I was just wondering if he'd left the house today.'

Lizzie took up a cloth and started wiping down the bar. 'Does him good to get out, I should say.'

'Yes. I suppose so.'

Bobby went to claim a seat by the fire where she could warm up. She took off her felt ARP hat, put it down on the table and eyed it meditatively.

Silverdale felt so far away from the war that it was easy to forget – when you were walking through the sleepy meadows with their carpets of many-coloured wild flowers or relishing the untamed, open freedom of the fells – that somewhere not very far away the bombs were falling. It gave Bobby a jolt, sometimes, when she picked up a newspaper and was reminded of the chaos raging elsewhere around the globe. The cinema newsreels made it look like it was the end of the world. Perhaps it was. But the end of the world never could feel quite real here – not in Silverdale.

Nevertheless, the war was out there. Words that had been unheard of just a few years since – words such as blitz, evacuee, ersatz – were now part of everyday vocabulary on the Home Front. Overseas, men were dying every day – men like poor Billy Wilcox, who were little more than boys. With two brothers in the army, a sister in the Wrens

3

and a… well, Bobby wasn't quite sure what the right word for Charlie was, but for now she supposed 'sweetheart' would have to do – a sweetheart about to leave for training with the RAF, Bobby had felt it was high time she was doing her bit for the war effort too. When Silverdale's elderly chief warden, Amos Horsely, had hung up his whistle last month, it was Bobby who volunteered to fill the empty place on the three-man team that monitored the village's air raid precautions in shifts every evening.

Bobby had been on duty tonight since six. It was half past eight when she handed over her whistle and wooden rattle to the next warden on the rota. By that time, she was stiff, achy and numb with cold. She was hoping the beer would help to get her blood circulating again.

Not that there was much for an air raid warden to do around here. No bombs were going to fall on Silverdale. Three or four times a week when Bobby had finished her work for *The Tyke* magazine, she donned her denim bluette uniform and overcoat and spent most of the evening sitting in the dark, damp, draughty little hut on the village green, sipping lukewarm cups of weak cocoa from her flask and humming dance tunes to herself as she tried to knit by the dim light of the ARP oil lamp. Every half an hour she would go out and patrol the village to check for blackout infractions, but there was rarely anything worse than an inadequately dimmed bicycle lamp to contend with.

Nevertheless, she felt better for doing something, small though it was. Yes, the war felt far away from the Yorkshire Dales – farther away than it ever had at home in Bradford, with uniformed folk on every street corner and the aftermath of the city's bombing raid the previous year still very much in evidence – and yet she could feel its hand

4

on her shoulder. War seemed to be creeping ever closer as 1941 progressed, shattering the centuries-old peace even of Silverdale. Ida Wilcox must be feeling tonight that the war was something very real and very near indeed, and she wouldn't be the only one.

Bobby glanced around the pub. It was still largely a man's realm, as it had been when she arrived in the village, although the Silverdale natives had grown used to seeing the city girl who lived in their midst make an occasional foray inside. But the regulars who drank from their pewter pint pots seemed older now than they had the first time she'd entered the Golden Hart back in the autumn. As with so many places, the war had stripped Silverdale of young, fit males. And some of them, like Billy, wouldn't ever find their way to home and safety again.

One of them still remained, however, to help cheer Bobby's nights and chase away gloomy thoughts.

'What're you doing over here by the fire?' Charlie Atherton – handsome and boyish as ever, with an expression of lazy fun in his brown eyes – pulled up a chair and sat down beside her. 'I've been waiting for you in the snug this half an hour.'

She smiled warmly at him. 'Charlie. I'm glad to see you.'

He frowned. 'Anything wrong?'

'Why do you ask that?'

'Well, it's rare that you confess you're glad to see me. Although I know you're only being coy and it secretly sets your girlish heart aflutter whenever I stride into view.' He took out a Woodbine and lit it. 'Did you forget our date?'

'We didn't make a date.'

'Of course we did. We've got an arrangement, remember? Today's Thursday. And since you've

5

deliberately avoided me all day, that means I've been waiting here for the chance to make my regular Thursday proposal.'

Bobby couldn't help smiling. 'Must you keep asking?'

'I'll stop as soon as you like. All it takes is a yes.' He removed the cigarette from his mouth and smiled his hard-to-resist smile at her. 'How about it, Bobby? I can get down on one knee if it'll help.'

'You know I can't. You're going off to the RAF, I've got my work… Let's just stay as we are for a while. It's the best way.'

'For how long?'

'Until… I suppose until things are settled. One way or the other.'

Charlie reached out to turn her face towards him.

'You look worried,' he said in a gentler tone. 'Did something happen during your shift? I fret about you out there on your own.'

She sighed. 'Lizzie just told me the news, that's all. Billy Wilcox.'

Charlie took a long drag on his cigarette. 'Isn't it dreadful? I knew Billy all his life. I don't know why that should make it harder to believe that he's gone, but it does.'

Bobby reached out to press his hand. 'You will be careful out there, Charlie, won't you? You will… you will come back?'

He smiled. 'I don't think I can promise that until you offer me something worth coming back to. A wife would be just the thing.'

'Don't joke, please. Not about this. Just promise me.'

'All right,' he said softly, leaning over to kiss her cheek. 'For you, Roberta, I promise.'

Bobby shuffled away

the pub.

'You shouldn't kiss me,

here. Someone might tell R

'No they won't. Dalesmen

own business.'

'I mean it, Charlie.'

'If you weren't so conscientious,

rotten little ARP hut so we could hav   ddle

while you're on duty.'

Bobby laughed. 'And if Hitler invades Silverdale while I'm letting you distract me with your wandering hands, what then?'

'Oh, then he'd really be in trouble. It's very bad form to interrupt an Englishman when he's courting.' He nodded to her drink. 'It's high time I had you all to myself. Finish that and I'll let you take advantage of me on the walk back to Moorside.'

'All right. I mean, you can walk me home – my dad will worry if I'm out too much longer. But I'm far too much of a lady to take advantage of young men in the blackout.'

Charlie sighed with mock tragedy. 'I know, more's the pity. Sup up then.'

Bobby finished her drink while Charlie put his cigarette out, then she stood up and let him help her put her coat on.

Chapter 2

It was nine o'clock and the sun was sinking beneath the ridge of the mossy limestone crags that surrounded them, casting a pink glow over the rolling landscape. Bobby breathed deeply as she and Charlie sauntered at a leisurely pace back towards Moorside Farm. For a little while there was a comfortable silence between them while they drank in the late-April evening.

Bobby had soon learned that seasons worked differently out here in the Dales than they did in the city. Rather than the traditional four of winter, spring, summer and autumn, Dalesfolk tied the weather to the changes in the landscape around them, and to the jobs that needed to be done on the farms where they earned their livelihood. Hay time in the summer often crossed over with clipping time, when hired men appeared on the farms to shear the hardy sheep that roamed the fields and fells. At 'backend', as the autumn months were known, root crops and oats were gathered in, ready for the inclement weather of winter. Rather than having a specific start or finish, seasons began and ended whenever the weather or the tasks to be done dictated they should begin and end.

Currently, they were seeing out the season known as lambing time. This had begun with the appearance of the first lamb of spring in March and would soon give way to the most beautiful of Dales seasons, which they now approached as April tiptoed towards May: cuckoo time. This was when wild primroses clustered together on the banks of the village beck, the woods were redolent with the scent of kingcups and lilies of the valley, and the cuckoo called out from every tree. Charlie's lyrical descriptions of the season had not been wasted on Bobby, who looked forward to experiencing her first spring and summer in the countryside.

'I'm glad I shall get to see the cuckoo time one last time before I go,' Charlie said quietly, as if reading her thoughts.

Bobby shook her head. 'Don't say that.'

'Why?'

'Because it's bad luck. You make it sound like you believe you won't come home to see another.'

Charlie looked at her. 'You're very superstitious today. A chap might feel quite morbid if he had to listen to this sort of thing all the evening.'

She sighed. 'Sorry. It all just seems more real suddenly, after the news about Billy.' Bobby stopped walking to observe a vibrant cluster of bluebells on the roadside, highlighted in the pink-gold light of the setting sun. 'It can feel so safe and protected in the countryside. The war feels like a story here. Then someone you know gets the telegram and it reminds you it could come to any one of us. I hate to think of it. I hate to think of what might happen if we lose.'

'It'll be all right.'

'You don't know that. No one does.' Bobby looked up, her expression unguarded for once as she let her concern for him show through. 'Do you have to go, Charlie? After all, vets are reserved. Maybe it's not too late to change your mind.'

He looked away. 'And what sort of man would that make me?'

'You're entitled. Vets do valuable work for the war effort too, helping to keep the farms running and people fed. I'm sure everyone would still respect you.'

'But I wouldn't.'

'You might at least have volunteered for ground crew. You didn't have to fly.'

'It's too late, Bobby. I've made a commitment and I know it's the right one for me.' He pointed to the bank of the beck, where a mallard and his mate were snuggled contentedly among the weeds. 'Mr and Mrs Duck seem to have the right idea. I'd like to try a little of that myself. Will you sit with me a while?'

'My dad…'

'He won't miss you for ten minutes more. It isn't quite dark yet.'

Relenting, Bobby allowed him to guide her to the bank. Charlie took off his overcoat and laid it down so they could sit.

'You're not going to propose again, are you?' she said, trying to lighten an atmosphere that seemed to have become rather sombre. 'Remember what we agreed. Only once a week and a bonus proposal on bank holidays.'

Charlie didn't smile, however.

'You won't object if I put my arm around you?' he asked.

'I won't object.'

He did so, and Bobby shuffled closer to him.

'So that's the trick, is it?' Charlie murmured, half to himself.

'Pardon?'

'I never know from one day to the next whether you're going to push me away or throw yourself into my arms. But it seems I'm most likely to get a cuddle from you when you're in fear for my life.' He turned to look at her. 'What are we, Bobby?'

She dropped her eyes. 'We're… friends. Good friends.'

'Friends.' He fell silent, his gaze following the silvery ribbon of the beck as it weaved its way down from a still snow-capped Great Bowside, the highest of the peaks that loomed over the village. The last of the mellow evening sunlight was fading and the pale light of the moon had started to take over. 'Suppose I told you I wanted to be more?'

'How can we be?' She looked up at him. 'There are things I want to do with my life, Charlie. You know that. My work on *The Tyke*, with your brother… perhaps it doesn't seem important to you, but it is to me. You're a man. You've always known you could do anything you wanted with your life.'

'I'm not sure that's true.'

'You can't see it because you were born to it, but it's the way things are. It isn't the same for me as it is for you. There's only ever been one thing I was expected to do with my life, and I'm sorry but I can't be satisfied with that.' She leaned forward and kissed him softly. 'I'm fond of you, Charlie. I'd like to be with you, always. If that was all there was to it… but I can't help feeling I'm going to be forced to make a choice, and it's one I really don't want to make.'

'I wouldn't ask you to give up your work on the magazine. Not if you didn't want to.'

'Wouldn't you? A lot of husbands would worry it made them seem less of a man, having people think they couldn't keep their wives.'

Charlie shook his head. 'I wouldn't be that stuffy, old-fashioned sort. One of those husbands who expects his wife to be nothing except his wife. You know me better than that.'

'You say so now. Marriage changes things.' Bobby sighed. 'Even if you didn't ask me, it would be expected by others. Married women aren't expected to work when their husbands can keep them. Mothers certainly aren't, and the one will usually follow the other. I know your brother wouldn't approve.'

'We can persuade him. Mary would take our side.'

'And how would we manage when a baby came along?'

'We can cross that bridge when we come to it.'

Bobby was silent, gazing at the moon above the little humpbacked bridge. The silhouette of a dipper bobbed on a rock underneath, alert for food in the bubbling waters of the beck. She rested her head on Charlie's shoulder. If only this moment was all there was – all there ever needed to be. Just her, Charlie and the moon, with the beck chattering past their feet and the pastel-blossom scent of a Dales springtime in the air…

But there was always life. Work and marriage, family and duty, and of course there was the war. There was everything that was expected of Charlie as a man and her as a woman, casting a shadow over the time they spent in each other's company even as their feelings deepened.

As much as she cared for him, the thing Bobby dreaded most was finding herself trapped in the sort of life she knew she couldn't bear. She wouldn't give up her dreams. She wouldn't lose her own self; see her identity, her soul, her very essence, swallowed up by wifehood and motherhood. She'd seen too many of her peers – once bright, eager girls with their whole lives ahead of them – become walking shadows, lost to the cares of domestic life. She couldn't risk that, even for Charlie Atherton.

'Besides, he'll be leaving me soon,' she murmured to herself.

'All the more reason to make it official before he does,' Charlie said, giving her a squeeze that snapped her out of her reverie. 'That could be the thing that keeps me going when it gets hairy out there, couldn't it? I can carry a lock of your hair with me and boast to the other boys about my girl back home.'

'Don't joke.'

'I'm not joking. Not really.' All of a sudden, he sounded earnest. He dipped his head to look into her face. 'I won't ask again if it's going to make you unhappy. You know what I want. I love you, Bobby, and I want to plan a future with you. I want to know that's what I'll be coming back to when this madness is over. I wouldn't ask you to choose between me and that damned magazine of my brother's you care so much for, but I can't keep on forever in limbo, neither one thing nor the other. It isn't fair – not on either of us.'

Bobby turned away. 'It's dark. We'd better go before my dad starts to wonder where I am.'

He sighed. 'All right. If that's what you want.'

He removed his arm from her shoulders, and Bobby experienced a sudden, deep panic at the withdrawal of his touch; a sinking feeling of dread in her stomach, as if she'd been left bereft and alone.

'Charlie.' She put a hand on his wrist. 'Don't get up yet. Wait a moment.'

13

'What is it?'

'Here. Come here.'

She took his face between her hands and planted a lingering kiss on his lips.

This wasn't like the chaste pecks she allowed Charlie to give her when they went on dates to the dance halls in town. Nor was it like the kisses she sometimes permitted on the rare occasions they could be alone together, in the cottage when her father wasn't at home or on the back row of the cinema in Settle. Those were the kisses that nice girls weren't supposed to allow but were too good not to, once in a while – kisses that were hot, needy and dangerous; delicious, wrong and right all at the same time. But this… this was a kiss where she tried to convey everything she felt and thought and feared. All that she hoped for, all that she dreaded, and every flutter and thump of her heart that somehow went hand in hand with her feelings for Charlie Atherton. Charlie's eyes closed as he took her in his arms and pressed her tightly against him. For perhaps the first time, Bobby dropped her guard entirely, threw any worries about who might be watching to the wind and gave all of herself to the kiss. It seemed like hours had passed when they eventually separated again.

'Well that was… new.' Charlie was flushed and breathless. His creamy brown eyes seemed huge in the moonlight. 'What brought that on? You never kissed me that way before. I mean, don't think that I'm complaining.'

'I just wanted you to know. To understand.' She held his gaze for a moment. 'I'm sorry I can't give you the answer you want. I do love you, Charlie. Just… come back to me, that's all. Come back to me and somehow, maybe, it'll all be all right.'

Chapter 3

Charlie walked Bobby the rest of the way home in silence. The unexpected warmth and urgency of their kiss seemed to have rather knocked him for six, and he floated along beside her as if in a dream. It wasn't long before they descended the dirt track that led to Moorside Farm, which constituted both the offices of *The Tyke* magazine and the home of its editor Reg Atherton, Charlie's older brother, and his wife Mary.

A large converted barn in the grounds, known to its residents as Cow House Cottage, had been both Charlie's veterinary practice and his home until the month before, when he'd moved into the main house with his brother and sister-in-law so that Bobby and her dad could make a home there. There was a faint outline of light around one of the blocked-up slits in the wall, which told Bobby that her father hadn't yet retired for the night.

'The plaster must be starting to crumble if the light's showing through,' she observed to Charlie. 'I'd better ask Dad to repair it, before I scandalise the neighbourhood by having to fine myself.'

Charlie still seemed to be in a world of his own, however, gazing into the distance.

'Goodnight then,' Bobby said, tapping his arm to wake him up. 'You'd better not linger. I'm sure either Reg or my father are listening out for us.'

'Hmm?' Charlie seemed to rouse himself. 'Oh. Yes. When will I see you again?'

Bobby laughed. 'You live twenty yards away, Charlie. I'll see you tomorrow at breakfast, I should think.'

'I mean, when will I see you alone?' He smiled, looking a bit more like his usual self. 'You're not allowed to kiss a man like that and then start playing hard to get, you know.'

'Perhaps we ought to wait a few days.' What Bobby felt she badly needed, after tonight, was a little time out of Charlie's company so she could think. So she could feel, and work out what she was allowed to feel.

'We don't have long. I'll be leaving in six weeks.'

'Yes. Yes, I know.'

'Come to the pictures with me tomorrow.'

She hesitated.

'Let's just have these last six weeks, Bobby. Me and you, doing what young people are supposed to do together, and to hell with the bloody war. If you can't give me a yes just yet, at least give me some memories to take with me.'

His voice was back to its usual teasing tone, but there was an undercurrent of something else. Emotion. Need. It wasn't like Charlie to swear in the company of women.

Bobby smiled, trying to lighten the mood. 'I'm not sure I trust you at the pictures after the last time. Mabs Jessop asked me the next day how I liked the film and I was forced to confess I couldn't remember a thing that happened.'

'I'll be good.' He paused. 'Fairly good. Will you come?'

'I can't. I'm on duty.' She met his eyes, and as so often happened, quickly found herself giving in to temptation. 'Saturday, all right?'

He grinned. 'I knew you couldn't resist me.'

'Don't let it go to your head.'

'So, is it a pact? Six weeks of no proposals, no war talk – just us?'

'It's a pact,' she said with a smile. 'Goodnight, Charlie.'

There were definitely curtains twitching over at Moorside Farm now. Bobby turned her back on her suitor and entered the barn-cottage she shared with her father.

There was no illumination in the parlour, but a faint light was coming from under the door of her father's room.

'Dad?' she called, flicking the switch to turn on the parlour light.

Her father peered around the door. He was in his pyjamas with a book under one arm, evidently getting ready to settle for the night. Bobby sagged with relief, as she always did on coming home to find him safe and sober, then instantly tried to hide it.

'You've taken your time coming home,' he greeted her in his usual gruff way. 'Where've you been for t' last hour?'

'I stopped in at the pub after my patrol to warm up by the fire.'

'Hmm. Not sure as I like you drinking in that place on your own.'

'I didn't have much choice, Dad. I couldn't feel my fingers. It's freezing in that little hut.' She went to plant a kiss on his bald crown. 'Besides, I wasn't alone – at least, not for long. Charlie was there. He walked me back.'

'Huh. Even worse.' But there was a half-smile on his lips. Her father disapproved of Charlie because he felt it was his job to disapprove of young men who spent too much time hanging around his daughters, but Bobby knew he couldn't help liking the man for all that. It was mildly irritating to Bobby that everybody did like Charlie, even when he wasn't trying – especially women.

'I'm home safe and sound now, aren't I?' She took off her ARP coat and hat and flung them on to a chair. 'I suppose you'll have heard the news in the village. Lizzie said you'd stopped in.'

'Aye, I heard. Another young lad gone.' Her dad's expression darkened. 'Shame. Bloody shame. Throwing their lives away, and for what? It'll make no difference in the long run. Made none last time.'

'This time it will,' Bobby said firmly. 'It has to. Otherwise it would all feel so... unfair.'

'That's war. Nowt fair about it.'

'Well, let's talk about something else. I'm sick of thinking about the damn war.' She glanced at her father. 'Did you stay for a few pints in the pub?'

'Nobbut two or three.'

Bobby knew 'two or three' could easily mean 'three or four' according to her dad's method of accounting – or even five or six or seven. He'd seemed better since the move to the country, but it was hard to keep tabs on his drinking when she was working all day and patrolling several nights a week. And yet she knew that making him feel he was being spied on would have exactly the opposite effect to the one she wanted, sending him back to the bottle in a fit of wounded masculine pride. Still, at least it was only the Hart's weak beer he was drinking these days. It had been weeks since he'd asked her for a glass of the whisky she now kept locked in one of the cabinets in Charlie's veterinary surgery, which adjoined the main cottage.

'I'm glad you've made a new friend here anyhow,' she said, although she wasn't sure a rogue like Pete Dixon was the best sort of friend for her dad, who was still battling the demons created during his time in the trenches. The man was a known poacher, and Bobby had heard he was operating other fiddles on the wrong side of the law too. Still, at least it was company for him. The worst thing for her dad right now would be too much time alone, and she couldn't be with him herself every second of the day.

'Couple of letters on t' table,' he said, nodding to them.

'Letters?' Bobby seized on the envelopes at once. 'Bad news?'

'Nay, nowt to worry about. One from Jake addressed to us both and one from your sister to you. I read our Jake's but I didn't open yours from Lil.'

Reassured, Bobby took her youngest brother's letter from its envelope. It was short and to the point, as Jake's letters always tended to be – or the few letters they'd had from him since he'd left home to start his army training.

> *Dear Dad and Bob,*
>
> *Everything all right here. Prefer army life to Butterfield's, though all the marching's a bugger. Good bunch of lads too. Been getting along pretty well and Sergeant says I might make lance-corporal if I keep it up. Some of the lads who'd finished their training shipped out last week. Makes you think, that, I reckon. Hope everything's fine your end. Should get some leave Bowling Tide week. Eddie wrote that he's fitted a new exhaust pipe to the bike – dying to see it. Going to take Nessie Tate out for a ride just as soon as I get back. Don't know where I'll stay. I'll work it out some way.*
>
> *Love to both,*
> *Jake*

The letter made Bobby smile, for all the little there was of it. Of course it was his precious Triumph motorcycle her brother was dying to see when he came home, closely followed by his girl. If he could fit in his family as well, that would be a pleasant but optional bonus.

She'd have to arrange somewhere respectable for him to stay though. The ever-impractical Jake was only likely to forget. Lodgings would book up quickly for Bowling Tide week, which meant her brother would probably end up sleeping rough in some friend's air raid shelter or on a bench in the park. The family's little terraced house on Southampton Street in Bradford was being let out as a billet for trainee soldiers, which was a good thing as it meant her father had a small private income from the rent despite being out of work. However, Bobby's city-dwelling siblings seemed reluctant to spend their precious leave time ensconced in Cow House Cottage, many miles from what they considered to be civilisation.

Bobby's gaze lingered over one sentence in Jake's letter. *Makes you think, that, I reckon*. Nineteen-year-old boys weren't known for their articulacy, particularly in writing, but Bobby could read between the lines. Jake was fearful about what might be waiting for him when he completed his training and went out to join the fight. It made her think again of Billy Wilcox, no older than her brother, whose body now lay lifeless on the ocean bed. The mental image made her shudder.

'What's the matter?' her dad asked, noticing her expression. 'He sounded well enough to me.'

'Nothing.' She forced her frown to lift. 'Sorry. I was thinking about something else.'

She opened the letter from Lilian and glanced over the contents. In contrast with Jake's short letter, her twin sister's small, neat writing covered several sides of paper. Bobby could see that Lil had plenty to tell her about the new friends she'd made down in Greenwich, and new beaus too, of course. The first paragraph was about plans for her leave in August. The first word of the second paragraph was *NFDE* – an old code from childhood that stood for Not For Dad's Eyes. This, Bobby knew, meant that everything after the first paragraph was intended for her alone.

'Owt to tell us, has she?' her dad asked.

'It's mostly just about parties and girls' things. Nothing you'd care about,' Bobby informed him airily. 'But she has got some leave in August, same as our Jake. I'll read what she says.'

Bobby read out the first paragraph: the one that Lilian had deemed suitable for a father's ears.

> *I'll be coming home the week of the 9th. The house is still full of soldiers, I suppose, so I've arranged to lodge with Clara Stockwell. Why don't we make a holiday of it, if you can take time off from work? You and Dad can come over for Bowling Tide and take a room with Clara for the festival week. It'll be just like old times, and we won't allow even a single mention of the war for the whole seven days. Write back and say yes at once, or I'll be very cross indeed.*

'What do you think, Dad?' Bobby said. 'Would you like to go home for Bowling Tide? It would be nice to have all the family together again and catch up with old friends.'

She half-expected him to say no. Her dad had never been one for a party and, left to himself, would probably hardly leave the house except to visit a pub. He nodded, however, with something like enthusiasm in his eyes.

'Aye, I could fancy a visit home,' he said. 'Funny. You spend your life packed in wi' all that smoke and muck, working every hour God sends, wishing you could be in some place like this instead. But you can't help missing it once you're gone, all t' same. Suppose it's in the blood.'

'I know. I feel the same way.' Bobby patted his arm. 'Now go to bed and I'll bring you some hot milk before I turn in.'

He treated her to a rare smile. 'Well, you're a good lass. Just watch yoursen wi' them young men, that's all. Not right for a girl to be wandering around at night on her own.'

'It's war, Dad. We all have to do our bit. Besides, I can take care of myself. This is Silverdale, not Bradford.'

When her father had retired to his bedroom, Bobby made two mugs of hot milk, diluted with water to make it go further. She brought her dad's in to him, then took herself off to bed so she could enjoy the rest of Lilian's letter in private.

Bobby couldn't help but feel a pang of envy as she read about her sister's exploits among her new friends in Greenwich. What she was allowed to say about their work made it sound difficult but interesting, and Lilian quickly seemed to have built up a camaraderie with the girls in her billet – 'even the toffee-noses from down south aren't so bad when you get to know them', she wrote. The Wrens' evenings were spent going out to dances with the hand-some naval officers they mixed with in the course of their work or the soldiers from a nearby barracks, although most of the girls preferred to stick to their own service when it came to courting. Lilian, of course, had several boyfriends anxious for her favours: turning boys' heads was a skill she had mastered in their schooldays. However,

Lil wrote that she was starting to grow rather weary of going out on dates with different boys. Now she was on the hunt for something more serious – a man who might make her a good husband.

Bobby was rather surprised to learn this. Her twin loved to be admired, particularly by men in uniform, and although Lilian adored the idea of being in love – the sort of love she saw in the films – she had always enjoyed the company of admiring boyfriends far too much to settle into anything steady for very long. But, of course, she was getting older – they both were – and perhaps it wasn't surprising that at nearly twenty-four, Lilian's thoughts had turned to settling down.

Bobby wished her sister was here, so they could talk through their feelings properly. It did feel as though their carefree days were slipping into the past. Growing older, husbands, babies – these were new and scary things that deserved a deeper conversation than could be had by letter.

Bobby tucked the letter under her pillow and tried to settle down to sleep, letting the low bleats of the sheep, and muffled hoots of the owls and other night prowlers, lull her as they usually did. And yet sleep wouldn't come. Lilian's letter, the suggestion she might be entertaining thoughts of marriage with a suitable man, were fresh in Bobby's mind. That, combined with the drone of a plane flying overhead, led her inevitably to thoughts of Charlie.

Six weeks, then he'd be gone. What would happen to the two of them then?

Bobby couldn't help being angry at herself when she reflected on what had happened between them earlier. She tried so hard to keep Charlie at a little distance, in spite of her feelings for him. Not because she wanted to go on dates with other boys or anything of that nature. She never had been much interested in that sort of thing, until Charlie had turned up and shaken her resolve not to get entangled with any man. Now that he was in her life, there was an understanding that they were reserved for one another, even without any official engagement. Charlie had even managed to stop flirting with every woman he met – or at least, he'd tried to. Charlie Atherton flirted like other men breathed, Bobby reflected wryly. It seemed to happen instinctively, without any input from his brain.

Nevertheless, Bobby tried to be at least a little aloof with him. Some days she might greet her lover with kisses, other days with coolness, just so he wouldn't make any assumptions about where their relationship was headed. She never had told Charlie, until tonight, what her real feelings towards him were. Although he'd said it to her on several occasions, the words 'I love you' had never escaped her lips. But this evening, with thoughts of Ida Wilcox's loss fresh in her mind, she hadn't been able to help telling him – and showing him, through the kiss she'd given all of herself to – exactly how she felt.

She knew she was trying to have her cake and eat it when it came to Charlie. She knew it wasn't fair to keep him hanging on while she dithered over marriage. It was all so confusing! She wanted to be with him. She couldn't bear the idea of not having him in her life. But there were other things she wanted to do too – important, meaningful things that mattered deeply, at least as much as Charlie himself. She wanted to make a success of her career as a country reporter and help Reg turn *The Tyke* into the sort of magazine that might one day be described as an institution, chronicling the lives of the people here so they wouldn't be forgotten. She wanted to live her own life. She loved Charlie, in a way she felt she never would be able to love any other man, but wives and mothers were wives and mothers. They couldn't be anything else. Motherhood was the highest calling a woman could aspire to, according to an old saying – the problem was that once it happened to you, it was also the only calling you could aspire to.

This was usually the point in her musings when Bobby started to develop a headache. It wasn't that she didn't want to be a wife, or a mother either. She and Lilian had stepped into that role for their two younger brothers at the tender age of fourteen when their own mother had died. Bobby got on well with children and doted on her two young nieces: Susie and Rose, her brother Raymond's daughters. It was just that once you became a mother, society refused to allow you to be anything else. Why must men be so free and women so restricted, when they had so many talents outside of the home? It felt so unfair! But she couldn't change the way the world was, as much as she may want to. All she could do was to make what choices she could, and try to forge a path that belonged to who she was and not what she was constantly being told she'd been born to do.

And that had seemed easy – until Charlie had come along. Now Bobby couldn't work out what she ought to do. She wanted to be with him, but when it came to marriage, it felt that the sacrifice she was being asked to make was just too big. They tried to be discreet in their relationship, or at least Bobby did – especially around her father and Reg, who were wont to disapprove – but it wasn't exactly a secret they were walking out together. The residents of the village whispered confidently to one another that Charlie Atherton – Silverdale's most eligible, and most notorious, bachelor – and the 'lass from t' paper' would be altar-bound before backend was upon them. Bobby didn't know which she feared more: that they were wrong, or that they might just be right.

So now they had six weeks. Six weeks to live and love and be together before he left her – perhaps forever. And that, the idea she might lose him irrevocably… that was the most unbearable idea of all.

Chapter 4

Bobby was arranging her hair when there was a knock at the cottage door early the next morning.

Washing and dressing were always a challenge in the spartan environs of Cow House Cottage, which meant an early start for Bobby on workdays. Although it had been used as a human habitation for probably about a century, the place still felt more like a barn than a home.

The occupant before Charlie – whoever that might have been – had made some modernisations to the place, including the addition of stone partition walls to create two bedrooms, a parlour and a kitchen from what had previously been a single large room. Apart from the surgery in an attached side building, all the rooms shared the same high-beamed ceiling – rather like animal stalls. There was also the outhouse, a separate structure that they shared with Moorside Farm.

Charlie had added some home comforts during his residency too. Cow House Cottage now had mains electricity, which meant Bobby and her father could listen to the wireless without the need for a heavy accumulator battery that would have to be driven into town for recharging once a fortnight, and there was a telephone in the surgery that could be used in an emergency. The cold was a constant problem, however. No matter how many layers of clothing Bobby wore to bed, she always woke up with numb fingers and toes.

Her first job was to get the fire in the parlour lit before her father woke up, which helped to take the chill out of the air. Then she boiled some water so she could tackle the ice that had formed on her mirror overnight and started preparing herself for work. She was halfway through removing her curlers when the knock came. Hastily, she wrapped her hair in a headscarf and went to answer it.

'Morning.' Charlie removed his hat. 'Sorry to turn up so early. I've got Fred Midgeley bringing one of his dogs in at half past seven and I need to get the surgery ready. I'd have told you last night, but he didn't telephone until late.'

'That's all right. Um… do you want tea or anything?'

'Don't worry about me. You go finish doing whatever it is you need to do to your hair. I've been a bachelor long enough to know how to boil a kettle.'

He looked awkward, clutching his hat in his hands as they talked – a very un-Charlie-like attitude. Bobby felt awkward too. She wondered why. Was it the kiss they'd shared last night? The pact they'd made? Or could he sense that she'd spent an almost sleepless night worrying about their future together – if they had one?

'Who's there, Bobby?' her dad called from his room.

'It's only Charlie, Dad!' Bobby called back. 'He's got an early appointment in the surgery. I'm just showing him through.'

'Aye, well. Tell him to make sure that's all he's here to see to, that's all.'

Charlie smiled at her.

'Your old man thinks I'm sneaking in early in the hope of catching you in your frillies,' he whispered.

That seemed to lighten the atmosphere a little. Bobby smiled too.

'Well, are you?' she asked, raising an eyebrow.

'Would an Atherton stoop to such low tricks? I don't know how you can think it of me, Miss Bancroft.' He glanced down at her dressing gown. 'What are you wearing under there?'

'A woollen nightgown, some impenetrable winter drawers and several jumpers, if you must know.'

He laughed. 'Good old Cow House Cottage. I feel terribly guilty at night, all warm and snug in my bed at the farmhouse. Mary always makes me a hot water bottle.'

'There's no need to rub it in, you know.' She tapped his arm. 'Off you go and mix up your dog drugs, or whatever you have to do. I need to finish getting ready, and I wouldn't want to drive you mad with desire at the sight of me in my woolly knickers.'

'You could drive me mad with desire in a siren suit.' He glanced quickly behind him to make sure her father hadn't emerged before stealing the opportunity to give her a kiss. 'I'll see you later, Bobby.'

Bobby went back to her room to finish getting ready, smiling to herself. The short encounter had cheered her up a little and seemed to have restored the balance to where it ought to be. She tried to push aside her worries about Charlie, the future and the war as she prepared for another day of work at *The Tyke*.

–

Usually, she and her father joined Reg and Mary for breakfast, but her conversation with Charlie had made her late. By the time they entered the kitchen at Moorside, Reg had disappeared, and Mary was washing up their plates.

'Ah, there you both are,' she said in her usual warm way, giving Bobby's arm a squeeze of welcome. 'I hope you don't mind us not waiting. Reg was as hungry as a hunter, he said, and you know how men get when they aren't fed on time. I've kept it warm for you.'

'Sorry we're late,' Bobby said as she took a seat. 'Charlie came over early needing access to the surgery and started talking nonsense to me as usual, so it was really all his fault.'

Mary smiled knowingly. 'Was it indeed?'

'Can you pass the eggs, Dad?' Bobby said, hastily changing the subject before he picked up on the suggestiveness in Mary's tone.

Mary ran her gaze over the sparse offering on the table and sighed.

'It's not much of a breakfast, is it?' she said. 'I never thought the war shortages would hit us so hard out here. Never thought I'd see the day you couldn't at least get mutton and milk for the asking in farming country. Seems you've to account for every bite and drop these days, and the Ministry of Food would fine a shopkeeper soon as look at them if they put a toe wrong.'

'Better than we got at home,' Bobby's dad said as he helped himself to a sausage. 'Us country folk don't know how lucky we are.'

Mary smiled. '"Us country folk" indeed. Well, Rob, I'm glad to hear you think of yourself as one of us now.'

He smiled at her. 'Aye, when the sausages are this good, I reckon I'm willing to be adopted.'

'Still, wartime's no time to be a housewife.' Mary, who'd always prided herself on keeping a good table, eyed the few strips of stringy bacon and loaf of gritty brown bread glumly. 'Meat ration of a shilling apiece since they dropped it again last month. How can I keep three grown men fed on that, I ask you? And cheese rationing will be starting next month. I wouldn't wonder if they rationed milk next, it's getting that hard to lay your hands on. The sooner this war is won, the better.'

'But your food's just as delicious as ever, Mary,' Bobby said as she cut herself a thin slice of bread. It was a white lie, of course, which she thought must be permissible to spare her friend's feelings. 'And if there's a little less of it, I suppose that's a hardship we can bear when there's men out there fighting.'

'Well, happen you're right. Our troubles aren't so big compared to some. I shouldn't be ungrateful. It's only that it makes it all seem more real — the war, I mean.'

'I heard in t' village that there's a batch of evacuees from London being sent here for billeting,' Robert observed as he tucked into a sausage.

'I heard the same. Poor loves, who knows what horrors they must have seen down there? It does feel as though this war that felt so far away is finally arriving on our doorstep.' Mary turned back to her washing-up. 'You'll both have heard about Ida's boy Billy, I suppose.'

Bobby nodded. 'Lizzie told me in the Hart last night. Will you go to see her?'

'Aye, of course. Ida and I were at school together — not that that makes any matter. A neighbour in need would always be due a visit. I'll go tomorrow afternoon.'

'Not today?'

'No, she'll be busy receiving family. I'm told she's expecting her daughter and the bairns over from Burnsall. Young ones in the house ought to do her a power of good.'

'I'll keep you company if I won't be intruding. I'd like to pay my respects too, on behalf of me and Dad. Could we take her a little cheese or can't you spare it?'

Mary brightened. 'That's an idea. I can bake it up into a cheese pudding for her. I've some stale bread from yesterday that can be turned into breadcrumbs, and a couple of eggs need using up.'

More cheerful now there was the prospect of providing solace to a troubled soul through the medium of cooking, Mary started gathering the ingredients for the pudding together, humming to herself as she did so.

'What are your plans for today while I'm working?' Bobby asked her father as they finished their breakfasts. 'I'll be straight out on patrol after work, so you'll need to warm up your own tea, I'm afraid. There's the remains of yesterday's shepherd's pie in the pantry.'

'I'm meeting Pete in the woods up near Cockcroft's Gill,' her dad said, helping himself to another rasher of bacon. Both his appetite and his temper had improved greatly after six weeks of country living.

'Oh. Well, if you're going walking then you can take your dinner with you. It's corned beef sandwiches. You know where the spare flask is for some tea.' Bobby paused. 'Is that the plan? You and Pete are going walking?'

'Aye, walking. Mainly walking. Might bring you and Mary back a rabbit for tomorrow's supper.'

Bobby shook her head. 'It's private property, Dad. Lady Sumner-Walsh owns that land. I wish you wouldn't.'

'She'll not miss a brace of rabbits, with all her fine food.' Her dad wiped his mouth then stood up. 'You go to your work, Bobby, and leave me to mine. I don't feel right unless I'm putting something on the table. I'll see you tonight.' He fixed her with a stern look. 'And no dawdling at the pub with young Charlie either. Thanks for breakfast, Mary.'

Bobby watched him leave.

'You're worried,' Mary observed as she collected Robert's plate and teacup to put in the sink.

'Well, it's poaching, isn't it? And Topsy Sumner-Walsh is a friend of mine too. I feel dreadful, knowing he's taking game from her land without permission.'

'He's right though, she won't miss a couple of rabbits. Your dad needs to feel like he's doing summat, Bobby. It makes a man feel weak when he's forced to let his women support him. Foolishness, I know, but we can't change how God made them.'

'It does help with his... his problems,' Bobby said, flushing slightly. 'He can't abide feeling useless; it depresses him awfully. But it's illegal, isn't it?'

'We all bend the rules occasionally. You've had your share of off-the-ration butter, haven't you?'

'Yes, but that was yours that you churned and gave to me. It wasn't stolen butter. Besides, the Ministry of Food is so much stricter about that sort of thing these days. I want my dad to be happy here, but I don't want him to get into trouble.'

'Oh, Topsy would cover for him and Pete if they ever did get caught, no doubt. She's a decent sort despite her funny ways. I'm sure she'd make you a gift of some rabbits if you told her you wanted them, although I don't suppose that would be much of a balm for your father's pride.'

'Perhaps, but what if it starts to go further than poached game? I know Pete Dixon's got bigger fiddles than rabbits going on and Dad's desperate to be doing some sort of work.'

'Rob wouldn't let himself be dragged into anything really dangerous. He's a sensible body. Besides, Pete's a rogue but he's not a bad man. He wouldn't get a friend into trouble if he could take all the blame on himself.'

Mary was a good friend, but if she had one flaw as a confidante, it was in her stolid determination to see only the best in everyone. As much as Bobby would like to believe her dad's new friend had his best interests at heart, her inner cynic – the one that sounded a lot like her friend Don Sykes – couldn't help whispering that there might be danger in the association.

Chapter 5

Mary lowered her voice and tapped Bobby's shoulder confidentially. 'So, now that we're alone. I understand our Charlie walked you home again last night.'

'Who told you that?'

'Got eyes, haven't I? I spotted you outside, whispering sweet nothings to one another on the barn steps for a good ten minutes. I hope he wasn't making improper suggestions to you.'

'Very likely, being Charlie.' Bobby sighed. 'But it's the highly proper suggestion he keeps making that's been keeping me awake at night.'

'You still haven't given him a yes? Perhaps it's a foster mother's bias but I do believe he'd make you a good husband, in spite of his reputation. He's ever so fond of you, Bobby. I've not seen him this way with a lass before, although he's walked out with plenty in his time.'

'How could I say yes? Maybe when things are settled, but it's only six weeks we've been walking out and...' Bobby dropped her gaze. 'I'm so afraid, Mary,' she said quietly. 'Of what might happen to him after he goes. Of the war. Of the future.'

'I know.' Mary took Bobby's dad's vacant chair and put an arm around her. 'Seems like there's a lot of future to fear right at the moment. But love doesn't just stop, does it? Not even for war.'

'It isn't only the war.' Bobby looked up at her. 'Did Reg want you to stop painting after you married?'

'He never said so, but I'd less time for it then, especially after Nancy was born and Reg lost the use of his leg. And then there was Charlie – he needed a mother badly after he lost his own, and even before that. Violet was a flighty sort, not much taken with motherhood or homemaking, so as a little lad he naturally looked to me. I didn't have a lot of time for myself.'

'Did you mind giving it up?'

'I missed it, and I made time for it when I could, but it felt like a fair trade all in all. I'd rather have my Reg than a gallery's worth of watercolours.' Mary examined Bobby's face. 'Happen you don't feel the same way about our Charlie.'

'No, I… I care about him. I love him, even. But the work I do on the magazine isn't just a hobby for me, it's… I don't know how to describe it. I need it. I need it for my life to be mine – so I'm not just someone who exists for other people but a person in my own right.' Bobby gave a bashful laugh. 'I suppose that sounds like foolishness to you, doesn't it? What sort of woman wants a job over a husband?'

'No, I can see the sense in what you say. It isn't only about the work; it's about you. Your independence.'

Bobby smiled gratefully to find her friend so understanding. 'Yes. That's exactly it.'

'Women are asked to give up a lot for their men,' Mary observed. 'And sad to say, I've met plenty of husbands who were never worth the price. I was one of the lucky ones.'

'The thing is, I know Charlie's a good man in his heart. I know that if it isn't him I marry then it probably won't

36

be anyone. I suppose I just haven't decided if any man's worth the price, for me.'

Mary looked a little concerned. 'Independence is a fine thing when you're young, Bobby, but it's cold company as you grow older. Are you not at all afraid to be alone? To be an old maid?'

'Not so afraid as I am of losing myself. If I could just be with Charlie the way we were last night, sitting on the bridge...' She sighed. 'But life doesn't work that way, does it? Children come along, there are chores to be done, homes to keep. Once life is filled with domestic cares, ideas like romance and love probably become rather silly.'

Mary looked away. 'For some folk, perhaps. Not for all.'

Bobby reached for her hand and pressed it. 'I'm sorry, Mary,' she said softly. 'I should have thought before I talked about children. I didn't mean to upset you.'

'Well, bairns change things; there's no getting away from that. But love's never silly, even if it feels different after thirty years together than it did when we were nobbut twenty. I don't suppose what Reg and I have looks like much to a young thing like you, but it's love all the same. Aye, it changed through having a child, and even more through losing one, but it weathered and was all the stronger for it.'

'Charlie isn't Reg though.'

'No, but he's not as different from his brother as he likes to think he is, in spite of the twenty years between them. You watch and see. One day our Charlie will grow up and stop laiking about, and then I reckon he'll surprise us all.'

Bobby smiled. 'I fell in love with him the way he is though – rather against my better judgement, I have to say.'

'I was surprised by that, I must confess,' Mary said. 'You always seem such a sensible body, and Charlie's... well, Charlie.'

'Perhaps that's why I fell for him – because we are so different,' Bobby said. 'My sister always says that it isn't good for me to be sensible all the time and what I really need is to let my hair down with the wrong sort of boy. I doubt she pictured me falling in love with him at the same time though.'

'Is Charlie the wrong sort of boy?'

'I might have thought so when I first knew him, but... no. No he isn't. Still, I can't picture him as a father. He's far too fond of enjoying himself for that sort of responsibility.' Bobby pushed her fingers up into her hair. 'I wish I knew the best thing to do. I can't expect Charlie to hang around forever, waiting for me to make up my mind. I was awake most of the night fretting about it.'

'That's something for you to puzzle out yourself, Bobby. No one knows your heart but you, and you'll have plenty of time to delve around in there when Charlie's gone. But if you need to talk about it with someone then you know where I am.'

'Yes. Thanks, Mary.'

After breakfast, Bobby joined Reg in the parlour for another day's work on *The Tyke*.

The first two hours of her day involved filling envelopes with past numbers of the magazine to be sent out to names and addresses copied from the telephone directory. It was the one part of Bobby's job that never changed. Reg had observed to her that he wouldn't be happy until there were copies of the little magazine in every home, public library, doctor's waiting room and dentist's surgery in the county. If Bobby hadn't known him as well as she did, she might have believed he was joking, but when it came to his ambitions for *The Tyke*, Reg was always deadly serious. His biggest enemy now was the wartime paper rationing, which meant they were struggling to accommodate even their current rate of growth. Reg seemed confident that the war would be over before too long, however, and doggedly pursued his plans for world – or at least, Yorkshire – domination despite the shortages, building a list of potential subscribers for the days when paper would once again be plentiful.

Once the envelopes had been filled and taken to the post office, the actual reporter part of Bobby's job began. Since returning to work at *The Tyke*, she had written ten articles and helped with the research for many others. Pieces as diverse as 'The Terrible Knitters of Dent', 'Door Knockers in an Old Yorkshire Village', 'Memories of "Sandstone Jack"' and 'The Habits of Dales Foxes' would all proudly bear her byline when they appeared in the magazine.

Her job for this afternoon was to select, correct and type up the readers' letters that would be suitable for inclusion in the next number. A couple of elderly shepherds were having a lively debate on the letters page as to the correct method of counting sheep in the Dales, with one swearing the counting system began 'yan, tan, tether, pathas, pimp', while the other claimed the only correct way was the one that began 'yan, tan, tethera, pethera, pip'. Bobby had asked Reg which was correct, and he'd laughed and said that depended on whether you were counting your sheep in Borrowdale or Wharfedale.

But it was the sort of thing their readers liked, so he was willing to let the two old gents fight it out.

There were letters that made Bobby smile while she sorted through them, and even some that brought a tear to her eye. A woman in Hull wrote asking to purchase repeat copies of every number of the magazine to date, as her collection had been destroyed along with most of her possessions when her home had been bombed out in a heavy blitz. A soldier serving overseas contacted them to thank the little magazine for giving him a link to the Yorkshire countryside he loved and missed so dearly, telling them that he and his Yorkshire comrades read and reread their copies until the ink faded and the pages fell out. The monthly taste of home reminded him exactly what they were out there fighting for, he said. A pair of young lovers wrote a joint letter requesting that their two subscriptions be merged into one, 'as a wedding was soon to take place'. Bobby could sometimes feel that her work on *The Tyke* was trivial or foolish when she was traipsing around Dales villages making sketches of door knockers or reading about the mating habits of foxes, but working on the letters always gave her mood a boost. The stories she wrote might seem small in the general scheme of things, but they brought a lot of pleasure and comfort to people at a time when pleasure and comfort, like the meagre butter ration, were spread very thin indeed.

Reg still seemed reluctant to send his young reporter out into the thick of things, however. Most frequently, he assigned Bobby pieces that she could research from the farmhouse, or at least without interacting with too many of the Dalesfolk. If there was an important event to write about or an interview to conduct, Reg almost always sent a freelance writer out or covered it himself. He'd deny it if she were ever to suggest it, Bobby knew, but she could tell he was still embarrassed about the girl from the city he'd been forced to employ in the absence of suitable males. She muffled a sigh as she carefully copied a rough sketch of an ornate brass door knocker into 'best' for one of her features.

'Reg?' she said as she shaded in some of the detail.

'Hmm?'

'Are you in a good mood today?'

'I don't have good moods. I'd have thought you'd know that by now.' He looked up from the copy he was correcting. 'What are you after this time? Not Kiltford Show again? I told you, it takes someone with farming knowledge for that. I'll cover it myself.'

'I wasn't going to ask about reporting on the show. I just wanted to ask… would I be able to have some time off in August?'

Reg laughed. 'Time off? You only came back to work six week ago.'

'I know, but it's Bowling Tide in Bradford the second week in August – our Wakes Week, you know – and my brother and sister are coming home on leave. It would be nice to spend some time with them, and my father too. If you like, I'll work over Christmas to make it up.'

Reg sighed. 'No need for that. Go on, take the week. Make sure you work all the harder the rest of the month, that's all.'

Bobby beamed. 'I will. Thank you. And if you did change your mind about me covering the show, I mean if your leg was too painful or something—'

Reg shook his head. 'You're very keen on that. I'm not sure what you're expecting to find there. It'll be nobbut cows' backsides and farmers getting drunk on cheap ale.'

'But everyone goes, don't they? Charlie told me it's the highlight of both the farming and the social calendar around here. I'd love to see it.'

'And you're welcome to go on your own time, but it'll be me as writes it up,' he said firmly. 'It won't be a patch on the usual shows this year any road. We're lucky to be getting it at all when so many of the big shows have been stopped for the duration, but folk kicked up such a stink when they talked about cancelling that they said it could go ahead if it were cut back from the usual. Farmers still need to sell their beasts, after all.'

'Still, it's an important event even if it is smaller than usual, isn't it? Charlie says so.'

'Huh. It'll be nowt but a glorified auction mart this year, I reckon. Worth half a page in the mag at most.' He gave her a sharp look. 'You know, you'd do well to pay a bit less mind to what that good-for-nothing brother of mine whispers in your ear in the moonlight and a bit more to your work.'

Bobby flushed. 'This is about my work. I thought it would be useful for me to see what it's all about. The show's important to the farming communities around here and I want to get a better understanding of what makes them tick.'

'Young lady, you might live in a barn but it don't make you a horse. I bet you wouldn't know a shearling from a sapling.'

'I would. I've been reading up. One's a young sheep and the other's a young tree.'

Reg laughed. 'Oh well, I can see you're an expert. Listen, Bobby, all you'll get for your trouble if I send you to the show is laughed at, and your bottom pinched by gangs of drunken old men who ought to know better.

I'll not send a young lass like you into that dissipated mob. Covering the show's a man's job and that's an end of the matter.' He softened slightly when he saw her disappointed expression. 'Now, don't go into a pet about it. It's for your own good. I'll tell you what, you can write the walk for next month's number. How about that, eh?'

'OK,' Bobby said, trying not to sound too subdued. Reg knew she enjoyed writing the walks, but she really had set her heart on covering the big show. 'If you want me to.'

'Aye, you've a fair turn of phrase for a townie – maybe even because of it. It's a while since we did a local one. Strap on your boots next week and take an afternoon's paid time out on the fells.' He picked up his pencil to get back to work. 'You might even get that layabout brother of mine to go with you. He could do with the exercise.'

Bobby blinked. It wasn't like Reg to encourage her to spend time with Charlie. Was he starting to come around to the idea of the two of them together at last?

'Um, all right,' she said. 'Thanks, Reg.'

Chapter 6

Saturday afternoons, when Bobby had finished her morning's work on the magazine and her time was her own, had become what she called her village afternoons. It had taken a long time for the Silverdale folk to accept her presence there, but they had finally welcomed her as a member of the community. Not quite as one of them – she and her father were still very much seen as the 'off-comed-'uns' from the city. However, these days the villagers smiled and nodded when they encountered Bobby in the village, and many of them stopped now to pass the time of day with her. She was a Silverdalian by adoption, at least, and she didn't intend to lose that hard-won status. That was why Saturday afternoons were dedicated to seeing the few friends she'd made in the area, and occasionally going visiting with Mary.

She and her father weren't the only off-comed-'uns in Silverdale these days. With seaside resorts and other pleasure grounds closed for the duration of the war, the countryside was starting to see a deluge of visitors from towns and cities as the weather grew warmer. It was evident who these aspiring cyclists and walkers were, in their brand-new outdoor clothing and with expressions of wondering admiration on their faces as they experienced the charms of the Dales for the first time. The villagers regarded them with a detached amusement, although the more enterprising Silverdalians had thought up ways to earn some additional income from these comparatively wealthy tourists. Signs had started to appear in cottage windows proclaiming, 'teas a penny each', 'fresh vegetables', or 'bed and breakfast – rooms available'. Quick-thinking farmers had turned their sheep out on to the fells to offer some of their fields as camping sites, and tents had started to pop out like measles on the grass around the village.

Bobby spotted one such visitor as she approached Newby Top, the farmhouse where her elderly friend Andy Jessop lived with his new wife, Ginny. The farm was somewhat remote, a challenging ramble over rough moorland, but for the new visitors to the Dales that seemed to be half the appeal. Bobby found Andy outside the front door in an easy chair that had been placed there for him, smoking his pipe with his old dog Shep at his feet. Assorted metal items were piled up next to him for some reason. A rather pompous-looking young man with shining pink cheeks and round spectacles, dressed in the attire of a rambler, was standing talking with the old farmer while he smoked.

'What air you have here!' the man was saying to Andy. 'I do envy you, Mr Jessop. I imagine people rarely die here, do they?'

'Nay,' Andy replied mildly. 'Nobbut once.'

'I'm surprised you don't have folk from the cities rushing here to buy up your quaint little cottages so they can have a slice of paradise for themselves,' the visitor continued obliviously.

'It's a place, Mr Soames, that's all. Same as any other, only happen colder and wetter than many.'

'Oh, no, it's so much more. That air!' Mr Soames took in a deep lungful. 'What a wonderful life you must have had here, sir.'

Bobby, who knew that Andy's life – like so many Dalesfolk who had lived through the agricultural depression of the late 1800s – had been marked by poverty, hunger and heavy loss, chose this moment to hail her friend and halt the conversation.

'Good afternoon!' she called as she approached, waving to him.

'Ah, now here's a visitor I'm right glad to see,' Andy said, flashing her a genuine smile. 'Now then, young man. Here's a name tha'll know, right enough. This here is Miss Roberta Bancroft.'

Bobby laughed, both flattered and amused by the evident pride in his voice. 'You talk as though I'm Dorothy Sayers or somebody, Mr Jessop.'

'She another lady writer, is she?'

'Yes, she's very famous. You'll have heard her stories on the wireless.' Bobby nodded a greeting to the young hiker, who was regarding her in a puzzled sort of way. 'I must apologise for my friend. He thinks I'm far more of a celebrity than I am. I'm really only a humble journalist.'

Mr Soames raised an eyebrow. 'You're a journalist?'

'I know, it's hard to believe they have them even out here. I work for a magazine.'

'Ah, I see.' The man smiled indulgently, looking as though he was back on familiar ground. 'You write for one of those women's magazines. I thought for a moment... very foolish of me.'

Bobby tried to hide her annoyance. 'No, not a women's magazine. I work for *The Tyke*. It's a country publication about Yorkshire and the Dales.'

'Aye, and a good one at that,' Andy said, glaring at Mr Soames as if daring him to disagree. 'She don't just write recipes and that neither. Never one like her for words. Me and t' missus are right proud to know her.'

'Oh, I'm sorry. I didn't mean any offence. I'm sure it's a charming publication.' Mr Soames gave Bobby a patronising smile. 'My wife used to do a bit of scribbling in that vein herself, when she was single. Short stories, articles, poems, that sort of thing. You might have seen her work in the *Reader's Digest*. Her maiden name was Penhaligon – Ivy Penhaligon.'

'Ivy Penhaligon,' Bobby repeated slowly. 'Yes, I remember reading some of her stories. Great flair for description. She's a very talented woman, Mr Soames.'

He shrugged, as if it was no concern of his whether his wife was talented or not. 'Perhaps. I've never read her stories myself.'

'Does she still write?'

'No, she gave it up after we married. Well, we hardly needed the income.' He puffed himself up. 'I'm the assistant manager for a bank, you know.'

'She could still write for her own enjoyment. It's a shame to waste natural talent.'

'There was no time for foolish pastimes after the children were born. I daresay Ivy was happy enough to let it go once she had her babies to attend to. Women always are.' He glanced at her ringless wedding finger as she removed her gloves. 'You'll feel the same way yourself once you marry and become a mother, Miss Bancroft.'

Bobby tried not to glare. 'I don't believe I will.'

'Oh, you will. Take it from someone who's seen rather more of the world than you have. It's in a woman's nature – instinct takes hold, and her husband and children become her whole world. As they ought to be, of course.' He nudged Andy. 'A good thing for us chaps, eh, old man? Lord knows where we'd be if these little girls got it into their heads to leave us to our own devices. I'm sure I'd have burned the house down long ago if I'd lived alone as a bachelor.' He laughed uproariously, as if the idea was absurd.

'Where is your wife?' Bobby asked, barely managing to keep the coolness out of her tone.

'At home with the children, naturally. Sometimes a hard-working man needs a little holiday to himself.' His gaze flickered again to her left hand, and he smiled slightly. 'Perhaps we might see more of one another while I'm here. I've booked for a full week. I noticed a shabby sort of little pub in the village – I don't know if you frequent?'

'Occasionally,' Bobby said coldly. 'My young man usually escorts me.'

Mr Soames didn't seem perturbed by the rebuff. Bobby had seen enough of life to know that men like him rarely were.

'Well, if you're short of an escort any evening then I'd be glad to join you for a drink,' he said. 'I must be pushing on, or my landlady will have me locked out by the time I get back to my lodgings. Goodbye, Mr Jessop. Miss Bancroft. I shall be sure to purchase a copy of your little magazine if I see one on the newsstand.'

'Young streak o' nowt,' Andy muttered as the man walked away. 'Tha sees why I warn thee about lads, Miss Bancroft. I've seen too many a clever lass ruined by a husband who believed he were more than he was. Don't let that young fiancé o' thine take thee for granted neither.'

'He's not my fiancé yet,' Bobby said absently, watching the annoying Mr Soames stride away. 'Besides, Charlie isn't like that.'

'Don't believe it, lass. They'll offer thee t' moon, till they get what they want from thee.'

They were interrupted by Ginny bustling out of the farmhouse with a couple of saucepans in her hands and an old tin chamberpot under her arm.

'Oh. Miss Bancroft,' the old lady said, with a slightly flustered smile. 'I never heard you arrive. Now let me just finish sorting through this metal for salvage, then you can sit along of Andy and I'll get young Mabs to bring you out a pot of tea. It's too nice a day to be inside.'

Andy laughed at the selection of metal items his new wife was holding. He nodded to the chamberpot. 'Now then, our lass. Tha's noan after giving away that old po for scrap?'

Ginny put the chamberpot and pans on the pile with the other metal items. 'Well, and why not? It's tin, isn't it?'

Andy laughed again. 'Would tha credit it, eh, Miss Bancroft? Twenty year that were under my bed, till Ginny moved in and made me buy a new one. Seems this time next month, it'll be t' tail of a Spitfire.'

'You ought to dictate me a letter to the magazine about it,' Bobby said, smiling. 'That's bound to tickle our readers, if Reg isn't too much of a prude to put it in.' She turned her attention to Ginny. 'Are you having a spring clean, Mrs Jessop?'

'Bride's prerogative,' Ginny said, smiling back. 'There's pans in Andy's cupboards that mun go back to when t' owd queen were a lass. Besides, I like to feel we're doing our bit for the war effort. Might as well send this stuff for salvage as have it sitting unused in cupboards.'

Andy gazed meditatively at the pile of metal.

'You look thoughtful, Mr Jessop,' Bobby said.

'I were just thinking about way things have changed this last couple o' year,' he said soberly. 'I've never had much brass to spare, Miss Bancroft, but when I'd a bob or two loose in my pocket and our Mabs read us from t' paper that they were after donations for Boots for Bairns, I'd allus send in what I could afford, like. I remember what it were to see in winter wi' your soles worn through to t' ground so tha could feel muck and snow getting in. Now all papers are full of is that Spitfire Fund and others like it. Folk sending off their hard-earned brass so powers that be can build bigger, more deadly machines for men to destroy each other. And what happens to t' bairns whose parents can't afford shoes now, eh? They gang barefoot, I reckon. I'm not what might be called a pacifist but that don't seem right to me. Happen tha might like to write about that in thy little paper.'

It was this stoical compassion that had first drawn Bobby to Andy Jessop, and indeed seemed to be a trait of Dalesfolk in general. They were wary and cautious, slow to warm to strangers, but they were fair-minded and, above all, they hated to witness cruelty or injustice. Outsiders might think them sluggish of brain, but Bobby knew this was not the case. It wasn't stupidity that gave the impression of slow thinking, but rather a determination to weigh up all sides of a point before forming and offering an opinion.

'We'd be called unpatriotic if we printed anything of that nature, I'm afraid,' she told Andy. 'I know what you mean though. It feels as though the war's taken over everything. People forget that all the problems the world had before are still there, war or not. Poverty and hunger haven't gone away, even if they're rarely in the newspapers any more.'

'Aye, there's some truth in that,' Ginny said. 'Still, it's right that we should do our bit, I reckon. After all, there is a war on, and now our Davy's gone for a soldier...'

'Your grandson?'

'That's right, my middle daughter's eldest.' She looked sombre. 'I remember when his grandad went. The last war, I'm talking about. I didn't know, when I said goodbye to him that day... well, let's hope this time things will be different.'

Andy stood up to put his arm around her waist and there was silence between them for a moment. Bobby maintained a respectful silence too. She hadn't realised Ginny Jessop's first husband had been killed in the last war, but so many people had lost loved ones during that conflict that it was hardly a surprise.

After a little time, Ginny roused herself.

'Well, this standing about isn't getting much done, is it?' she said, back to her usual briskness. 'You sit down, Andy. I'll bring a chair for Miss Bancroft and she can read our paper to you while you drink your tea. You'll have brought us new one, I suppose, Miss Bancroft?'

Bobby smiled as she produced the latest number of *The Tyke* from her handbag. 'I never come without it.'

Chapter 7

After Bobby had finished catching up with Andy and his family, she walked back into the village, mounted the old bicycle she had left leaning against the post office wall there and pedalled in the direction of Sumner House. One advantage of the longer spring evenings was that she could make the most of her visiting time, before the darkness of the blackout set in to curtail her activities.

When she reached the cottage in the grounds where Topsy Sumner-Walsh lived with her old nanny, Maimie Hobbes, Bobby found her friend on her hands and knees in the little vegetable patch in the front garden. Topsy always had to have a project or several on the go, and her current obsession was trying to dig her way to victory by creating a kitchen garden. The problem was, Topsy had little natural aptitude as a gardener and no patience to learn. All she'd managed to grow so far was a small patch of cress, of which she was inordinately proud. Bobby had never seen such satisfaction on her friend's face as she had when Topsy had presented her with an egg sandwich '*avec garnir*', as she described it. Bobby had made sure she smacked her lips appreciatively after eating the meagre feast, and Topsy had looked as pleased as punch.

Bobby felt a fluttering of guilt. Her dad had come back from his 'walk' with Pete Dixon the day before swinging a dead rabbit from one fist, as he'd promised he would.

He'd looked so proud to feel he was helping to support the family that Bobby didn't have the heart to take him to task about it. After what had happened in the winter, when his spirits had sunk so low following the loss of his job at Butterfield's Mill that he'd attempted to take his own life, his daughter knew how important the small contributions he was making to the household were in helping him to feel like the head of the family still – like someone who mattered. Still, she hated feeling that her meal of rabbit pie later this evening would be at the expense of stealing from her friend.

Topsy appeared to be planting some seeds, a little trowel grasped delicately in her perfect white fingers. Mrs Hobbes's pet goose – a cantankerous and rather smug animal called Norman – was lying comfortably in a bed of green leaves, watching her.

'You needn't look so clever at me, you know, Norman,' Topsy could be heard saying to him as Bobby approached. 'I don't suppose you could grow a marrow even if you tried. Could you, you lazy animal?' She glanced up at Bobby. 'Honestly, he does infuriate me. Did you ever meet such a beastly waterfowl? Such an expression of superiority as he always has. Be a darling and hold this seed packet for me, will you?'

Bobby, who was used to the speed with which her friend's mind could jump from one topic to another, obediently crouched down to hold the packet while Topsy poked little holes in the soil with the point of her trowel. Bobby was relatively certain it wasn't yet the season for planting marrows, but since her friend would likely be devastated on being informed her gardening efforts had all been in vain, she decided to keep quiet on the subject.

'You didn't bring Charlie with you,' Topsy said in an accusatory tone. 'And I had such news for him too. I've told you, Birdy, there's really no need to be jealous about him.'

Topsy, who delighted in thinking up nicknames for her close friends, had triumphantly rechristened Bobby as Birdy to celebrate her return to Silverdale six weeks previously. She claimed the name suited Bobby's perpetual expression of curiosity and the way she cocked her head to one side like a budgerigar listening intently for his master's voice. Bobby wasn't sure whether she ought to be gratified at this testament of her friend's regard – Topsy only issued nicknames to her most intimate pals – or offended by the comparison to a budgerigar. Generally, though, the name made her smile.

'I'm not jealous,' Bobby said. She wasn't sure why she bothered protesting, because Topsy was about as likely to listen to her as Norman was.

'Of course Charlie had his little pash for me but that's the most ancient of history. Honestly, darling, it's up there with the Romans and the Hebrews and all that rot from school. You really don't need to keep him from me. I would never steal a man from a girlfriend, unless she deserved it, but then if she did she wouldn't really be a proper girlfriend at all, would she?'

'Charlie's at work, vaccinating on one of the farms.' Bobby judged it best for her own sake to pick a topic of conversation from the myriad Topsy was tossing about and try to stick to it. 'What news did you have for him? Was it about Billy Wilcox?'

'Billy Wilcox?' Topsy said, frowning. 'I don't think I know him. Is he one of the St Ives Wilcoxes?'

Lady Honoria 'Topsy' Sumner-Walsh liked to think of herself as a woman of the people. She even made some rather grand socialist claims about her intention to one day marry a poor man and pursue a life as the wife of a lighthouse keeper or something similar. This didn't change the fact, however, that her intimate circle was rather different from Bobby's. Topsy was certainly a part of life in Silverdale, but with her title, her film-star charm, her extensive lands and her grand house, she was very much set on a pedestal by the ordinary village folk.

This made Bobby think of an old saying of her mother's. She couldn't help smiling as she remembered it. *Never put folk on a pedestal, our Bobby. They'll nobbut want dusting.*

Topsy threw down her trowel and put her hands on her hips. 'Now Birdy, are you laughing at me? I must say, I think that's too much. I'm sure I'm doing it just as it said in the book old Fletcher, the head gardener, gave me.'

'I wasn't laughing at you.' Bobby forced her lips straight. 'Sorry. You just reminded me of something my mother used to say when she was alive. No, Billy Wilcox is the son of a widow lady from the village. He was reported missing in action two days ago. I thought that might be the news you'd heard. Everyone's been talking about it.'

'Oh. No, I didn't hear about that.' Topsy's eyes took on a faraway expression. 'I say, that's rather hard luck on his mother. Ought I to send something for her? That's the sort of thing my father used to do when he was the squire here.'

'I'm sure she'd be very grateful. She isn't wealthy, and I suppose there'll be a lot to arrange.' Bobby held out the seed packet for Topsy to take another handful. 'What was your news?'

'I probably shouldn't tell, but I'm going to all the same because it's been so deadly dull around here since all the children left.'

When Bobby had first met Topsy five months ago, Sumner House was being used by the government as a boarding school for evacuees. The school had been forced to close, however, following the discovery that the head-mistress was neglecting the welfare of children in her care. Nevertheless, the powers that be had refused to return it to its rightful owner, and Topsy continued to live in the cottage with her old nanny.

'Are they reopening the school?' Bobby asked. 'I suppose the government must be planning to do something for the war effort with your house since they've refused to give it back to you.'

'They are. You'll never guess.' Topsy's eyes took on a gleeful sparkle, as if she had something of great interest to impart. 'Sumner House is going to be a hospital for airmen. I knew Charlie would be interested in that, when he's so close to becoming one himself. And I'm going to be a nurse there, how about that?'

'You're going to nurse?' Bobby found it hard to keep the disbelief from her tone. She couldn't imagine fluttery, fun-loving Topsy in the calm and collected role of nurse.

'That's right. I volunteered for the VAD. I'm still waiting to be invited for an interview but I'm sure I'll be accepted. They must be desperate for nurses and I know I'd be darling at it. Wrapping bandages, mopping brows and all that, just like Florence Nightingale. Besides, the chairman of the British Red Cross is an old friend of Father's.'

'Will you not find it rather... gruesome?'

'Oh, I'm sure I can stand the sight of blood if it's in the name of duty, as ghastly as it is. Of course I've never been tested, but if other women do it then I don't see why I shouldn't be able to.'

Bobby decided to remain silent about her doubts on this point. 'When will the hospital open?'

'They started moving in beds and things this week. I'm not sure when the first patients are going to arrive – when the Germans have shot a few more of them down, I suppose. Sumner House isn't much of a country seat, but I should think it could house thirty wounded men – perhaps more.'

Bobby flinched. 'Must you talk about men being shot down so casually?'

'Oh, now don't think it's because I don't care. Of course I do. That's why I offered myself as a nurse. It's only my silly way of talking.' Topsy brushed off her skirt and stood up. 'Let me wash this beastly muck off myself and we'll have some tea.'

They left Norman snoozing in his bed of weeds and went inside the cottage. Bobby followed her friend to the kitchen, where Topsy washed the dirt of the garden from her hands.

'Now where do you suppose the tea things might be?' she said, glancing vaguely around the kitchen. 'I'm always at sixes and sevens when Maimie goes out.'

She looked at Bobby expectantly, who took the hint.

'You go and sit down in the parlour,' she said. 'I'm sure I can find everything. I'll bring the tea through when it's brewed.'

'I couldn't let you do that. You're my guest.'

'Honestly, I insist.' Bobby smiled. 'I'm very particular about how I take my tea. You'd better let me do it if you want me to visit again.'

'Well, if you really insist. You're just an absolute angel, Birdy.' Topsy floated out of the room – she always did seem to float rather than walk – leaving Bobby to hunt around in the cupboards for the kettle, cups and a tin of tea.

To be honest, Bobby was rather glad to have a break from Topsy's company for a short while. Conversations with her friend could feel a little like being on a speeding train with your head poking out of the window.

The news about the airmen's hospital had interested her. The decision to locate it here must have as much to do with the presence of a new RAF training school some ten miles away as it did the restorative power of the Dales air, she supposed. The sound of planes flying overhead had been unnerving at first, particularly for her father, who still suffered flashbacks of the trenches. However, both Bobby and her dad had now become used to the familiar sound of the Wellingtons and Halifaxes used in the airmen's training humming above them at night. She wondered what difference the hospital would make to their sleepy lives here, and how the airmen would find Silverdale. Even more than that, she wondered how her vivacious, scatter-brained friend was going to get along as a nurse.

–

Bobby's last appointment of the day – apart from her date with Charlie at the pictures in Settle that evening – was with Mary, who had agreed that Bobby could accompany her on a visit to poor grieving Ida Wilcox.

Bobby left Topsy's cottage as she always did: exhausted by her friend's fast-paced and somewhat demanding conversation, and a little homesick. Bobby had become genuinely fond of Topsy in spite of her foibles, but as nice as it was to have a lively, fun girlfriend of her own age in Silverdale to spend time with, she did find herself missing Lilian whenever they were together. Topsy was a good friend in her way, but she was no substitute for the twin sister who had, until recently, shared every aspect of Bobby's life since they'd lain side by side in their cradle. It made Bobby sad – or at least wistful – to think of her sister down in Greenwich, forming new friendships and living a whole new life that didn't involve her twin at all.

Bobby felt guilty, too, about the fact that she hadn't been as honest with Lilian about her feelings for Charlie as she might have been – her twin had no idea about his regular proposals, for one thing. It was harder to share those things by letter, but nevertheless, Bobby resolved to write to Lilian as soon as she got back to Cow House Cottage and lay any secrets she'd have kept back at her feet. It was horrible to think the new, very different lives they were now leading might drive a wedge between them.

She'd invite Lil to visit again too, when she could get a day or two of leave. Lilian was reluctant to spend her precious time off in what she saw as the dull and closeted countryside, but Bobby was certain this was only because her sister had never experienced the Dales. She'd felt the same way herself before she'd moved here. Once Lilian saw the beauty of the region for herself, she'd fall in love with it just as Bobby had.

Bobby met Mary in the village. She dismounted from her bike and they walked to Ida Wilcox's cottage side by side, Mary holding a covered dish containing the freshly baked cheese pudding in front of her like a talisman to ward off evil.

'I hope I won't be intruding,' Bobby said to Mary as she rested her bicycle against the wall and pushed open the gate to Ida's humble stone cottage. 'I don't know the family like you and Reg do, but I felt I ought to pay my respects on behalf of me and Dad.'

'Oh, nonsense. You belong to Silverdale now. Ida will be very grateful to know you're thinking of her, I'm sure.'

Bobby patted her pocket, where she'd stashed a paper bag containing half her week's tea ration. It wasn't much to console someone for the loss of their boy, but it was all she had to offer.

She wasn't sure what to expect when they called on Ida. Would the grieving mother have taken herself to her bed, perhaps? Would she fall into hysterics? When Bobby tried to imagine how she might feel if it was her loss – one of her brothers, God forbid, or even Charlie – her brain and heart quickly rebelled against such monstrous daydreams. In fact they found Ida in a cobbled yard to the side of the house, engaged in the very unhysterical activity of pegging out her washing while a couple of merry girls played with a skipping rope nearby. Her little nanny goat Strawberry lay placidly watching the play of the children.

The tiny widow turned to them with a smile, putting down her basket. 'Well, is it Polly Atherton? And young Miss Bancroft too. I'm sorry, you've caught me in the middle of washing day. Our Jenny's bairns make more washing for me than a troop of soldiers, I'm sure.'

Mary smiled. 'Afternoon, Ida. It's good to hear that old nickname again. I reckon you must be the last one round here still uses it.'

'I didn't know you were ever a Polly,' Bobby said.

'Aye, when I was a bairn it was always Polly for short.' Mary sighed. 'Long time since our schooldays.'

'You're not wrong,' Ida said wistfully. 'I find myself forgetting sometimes just how long ago them days were.'

Mary held out her pudding. 'We brought a little summat for your supper.'

Ida lifted the lid and shook her head. 'Nay, I can't take this. That mun be half yours and Reg's cheese for the week, Poll.'

'Now don't you be daft. We can spare it for a friend.'

'You'll let me pay you.'

'I'll do no such thing and I'd thank you not to insult me by suggesting it. You've more important things to spend your brass on than cheese puddings.' Mary took her arm. 'If you want to make payment, a cup of tea will do me just as well. Your washing will keep.'

Ida smiled. 'Come on inside then.'

Ida's whitewashed cottage was typical of those occupied by the poorer folk of Silverdale: small, cramped and old-fashioned, but built to last with thick stone walls that kept out the weather. A single room functioned as both kitchen and parlour. Ida set the kettle on the fire to boil while Mary busied herself putting out mugs for their tea.

'Um, I brought this for you, Mrs Wilcox,' Bobby said shyly, producing the packet of tea. 'I'm sorry, it isn't much.'

'Oh, now, isn't that kind?' Ida said, beaming at her. 'You're a good lass; I've always said so. I'm sure I never believed talk about city folk being excessive proud and the like.'

Bobby smiled at the peculiar compliment. 'Can I help make the tea?'

'Aye, that you can.' Ida pointed to the breadbasket. 'There's a bread knife in t' drawer and butter's in the pantry.'

When a tray had been loaded with a plate of bread and butter and a steaming pot of tea, Ida ushered them into seats around a little table. There were only two armchairs, so Bobby perched on a low stool that she assumed was usually occupied by one of Ida's grandchildren.

'Any more news?' Mary asked, helping herself to a slice of bread and butter. Bobby was surprised at the way her friend broached the subject of Ida's loss so directly – she'd have opened the conversation with some general small talk first. Ida didn't seem upset by the question, however.

'Some officer sort sent me a letter,' Ida said, sounding bitter towards this bearer of bad tidings. 'The words was fancy but I knew what they meant, right enough. Until this morning there was still that tiny bit of hope, I suppose. Then it was there, set down in black and white.'

Ida's expression didn't change, but her hands shook as she picked up the milk jug. Wordlessly, Mary took it from her, added a little milk to Ida's mug of tea and stirred it for her.

'What happens now?' she asked quietly.

'They said… they said we can make arrangements. We might never have Bill's body back to bury him, but I'm to speak wi' parson tomorrow morning about funeral.' Ida's mouth flickered. 'He's not coming home, Poll.'

'I know, love. I know.'

'When we were told he were missing, I thought that meant we had hope. But it don't. Our Billy's just as dead as if it had been printed right there on that telegram. All it means is I'll never get my boy back for a proper Christian burial. To think of him at bottom of the sea, left there like chucked rubbish...'

Ida looked away, her face working with emotion. Mary reached for her friend's hand and there was silence for a time; nothing but the click of Ida's throat as she fought against tears. Bobby, touched by the woman's grief and a little embarrassed at being present to witness it, bowed her head.

After a moment, Ida dabbed her eyes with her sleeve. When she looked back again, she appeared as calm and composed as ever.

'Well, there's nowt to be done,' she said quietly. 'Whether there's wars or whether there's not, death happens. Always has, always will – you know that as well as I do, Poll. Nowt for those left behind to do but the job that's in front of them, and that's putting Billy to rest as best we can.'

'Can I help?' Mary asked. 'Give me a task, Ida, for God's sake.'

Ida patted her arm gratefully. 'I'll need help wi' t' wake, if you don't mind. Lot of people to feed.'

'Of course. Can't see your Billy off without a do, can we?'

'I could arrange the flowers,' Bobby said, anxious to contribute something. 'Lady Sumner-Walsh told me today that she'd like to do something in memory of Billy. I'm sure she'd be happy to contribute from her gardens.'

'Thank you,' Ida said earnestly. 'You're very kind. Everyone's been... very kind. Now if you'll excuse me, I must go look out at the bairns.'

–

Bobby was quiet on her date with Charlie that evening. They kept to their bargain that there'd be no war talk, and she changed the subject whenever he tried to tease from her what was tying her tongue. Nevertheless, she saw very little of the film he'd taken her to see. She was haunted all the evening by Ida Wilcox's eyes, wet with the quiet devastation that came from knowing her child would never again come home. In the darkness of the cinema, Bobby held on to her lover extra tightly, her heart whispering a silent prayer that his loved ones, at least, might never know such a loss.

Chapter 8

The following Thursday, Bobby met Charlie in the village, where he'd been attending to a sick sheepdog of Myrtle Barraclough's. Bobby was dressed in the slacks and boots she wore for roaming the fells, paired with a thick jumper and coat – no matter what the season, winter clothes were always needed on the tops.

She tried to ignore Mrs Barraclough's suggestive raised eyebrow when she met Charlie at the old lady's front gate. Together they took the footpath that would lead them out of the village and up on to the moors. Charlie, who had a sweet tooth and was usually carrying a bag of what Yorkshire folk called 'spice' in his pocket, offered her an aniseed ball to suck while he smoked a cigarette.

'It's nice to be allowed to see you in the daytime,' he said when they were out of sight of the village, stamping out his cigarette so he could slip an arm around her waist. 'Where are we going on our date?'

Bobby wriggled free of his arm. 'The shepherd's hut on Bowside, and it isn't a date. You're not to forget I'm on the magazine's time just because Reg gave me permission to invite you. No cuddling, no kissing and definitely no proposals, all right?'

'I've been a good boy, haven't I?'

She couldn't help smiling. 'I'm not sure I ought to answer that.'

'I haven't proposed to you for over a week, at any rate. That ought to count for something.' He glanced behind him to make sure they weren't being observed, then leaned over to kiss her cheek. 'We don't have to go walking. We could hitch Boxer up to the trap and go to the pictures instead. You know the way to the shepherd's hut well enough without traipsing all the way up there.'

'We've seen everything at the pictures. Besides, I can't afford to go that many times in a week.'

'I was hardly going to let you pay, was I?' He lowered his voice to a suggestive whisper as he brought his mouth close to her ear. 'It doesn't bother me if we've seen the film before. I just want to get you alone in the dark.'

Bobby felt her stomach flutter at the idea, but she fought against it. She stopped walking and turned to her sweetheart with a stern expression worthy of a particularly strict schoolmistress.

'This is my work, Charlie,' she told him with as much firmness as she could muster. 'I'm glad to have your company today but your brother's given me a job to do. If I ever want him to take me seriously as a reporter then my reputation depends on me doing the work he sets me, all right?'

Charlie kicked at a rock with his boot. 'Yes, Miss.'

'Oh, don't sulk,' Bobby said as she resumed walking. 'We spend far too much time at the pictures as it is. People are starting to talk. Besides, it's perfectly possible for us to have a nice time together in full daylight.'

'Not as nice a time as we could have with the lights out.' He nudged her. 'Come on, Mistress Sensible, play truant with me for once in your life. You know you could write directions to the shepherd's hut with your eyes closed.

Why waste time walking there when we could be out enjoying ourselves?'

'It isn't just about the directions.' Bobby looked out over the limestone-studded expanse of the moor, the face of Great Bowside looming dark and imperious in the distance against an iron-grey sky. 'Most of the people who read the walks in *The Tyke* will never do them. It's about writing them in a way that evokes the landscape and the journey, so they feel they're with you in spirit even whilst sitting in their armchairs. Making a story of it. Your brother says I've a flair for that sort of writing,' she added, somewhat proudly.

Charlie sighed. 'Well, he is right. You do have a talent for making a man feel he's there on the spot. I suppose I can forgo fun in the dark for the sake of your career, since it's so important to you.'

She smiled and rewarded him with a quick kiss, to the dignified shock of a nursing ewe nearby. Peace was restored, and this time Bobby didn't object when Charlie slipped his arm around her waist while they walked.

'I've got a theory about why my brother is suddenly so keen for us to spend time together,' Charlie told her after a few minutes of comfortable silence.

'What's your theory?'

'Reggie's finally realised you're not just another ship that passes in the night. He's noticed how mad I am about you and given us his blessing. He always approved of you far more than he ever did of me. I'll bet he thinks you're just the sort of girl I need to settle me down and turn me into the pipe-smoking, watch chain-wearing pillar of the community he's always wanted me to be. What do you think?'

'That's how Mary feels about it, I'm certain. I know she believes it's long past time you were settled, and she's very keen to reassure me you wouldn't be such a dreadful husband in spite of appearances to the contrary.'

He laughed. 'Glowing praise for her darling foster son.'

'She thinks better of you than you probably deserve,' Bobby said, raising an eyebrow in his direction.

'I know she does.' He glanced at her. 'So you'll have to marry me, won't you? Reggie and Mary will be so disappointed if they can't have you for a sister-in-law now that they're counting on it.'

Bobby shook her head. 'Remember our pact. No proposals allowed.'

'I wasn't proposing. Simply stating a fact.'

'Sorry, but I'm afraid I can't support your precious theory. It seems to me that Reg is far less interested in our love lives than he is in *The Tyke*.' She looked up at him. 'If you ask me, this is a test.'

'A test of what?'

'Of whether I can spend the afternoon with you without letting you distract me from my work. He wants to see how committed I am.'

'That does sound like Reggie,' Charlie conceded. 'He certainly thinks a lot more of that magazine than he does of his little brother.'

'No he doesn't. Not really. Reg is very proud of you, Charlie.'

'Huh. If he is, he's been hiding it well for the past twenty-six years.'

'Honestly, I know he is. He'll show you one day, wait and see.'

There was silence for a while as they walked on, both lost in their separate thoughts. Bobby chose her footsteps carefully as she dodged flat, slippery patches of limestone, jagged lichen-covered rocks that threatened to send her tumbling, and the treacherous peat bogs that were so well disguised by the heath you could easily lose a boot to one before you realised it was there. Charlie, of course, was a native and could navigate the moors almost without thinking. Nervous, half-wild sheep and their lambs skittered away in the wake of these peculiar two-legged creatures.

The abandoned shepherd's hut that served as a landmark in an otherwise barren stretch of landscape was visible in the distance now: a little grey dot about two-thirds of the way up the face of Great Bowside. The ramshackle building was about three miles from the village and, while no longer employed for its original purpose, it was occasionally put to use as a shelter by hikers who found themselves caught on the mountain in dangerous weather conditions.

'Have you ever been to the summit?' Charlie asked, nodding to the impressive peak of Great Bowside.

Bobby shook her head. 'No farther than the hut. It didn't feel safe in the winter months, while there was still snow on the tops. I should like to make it up there now the cuckoo time is coming.'

'I've been up and down this mountain a dozen times to tend to injured animals who'd got themselves stuck,' Charlie said in a dreamy voice. 'I hope the new assistant vet at Smeltham who'll be covering my practice is a fit, active sort. You need to be to work land like this, but so many of the young vets and farmers have gone to war now that the old men left behind are struggling to cope.' He glanced at Bobby. 'Sorry. I know we agreed not to talk about the war until—'

'—until we have to talk about it,' Bobby finished for him. 'Will you take me, before you go? To the summit, I mean.'

'Yes, there ought to be plenty of daylight when double summertime begins next week. I'd like to see it again before I leave. The walk isn't what I'd call a good time, but the view... you can see the whole dale from up there. It's quite beautiful, especially at sunset.'

'I should love to see it.'

'I'd like to see it with you.' He gave her waist a squeeze. 'It'll make it new for me again. Everything feels like the first time with you.'

She smiled. 'That's nice, Charlie.'

A few heavy drops of rain fell from a sky that was fast turning black. The wind was picking up and there was a faint smell of sulphur in the air. Bobby pulled her coat tighter around her.

'Did you walk by the village green on your way to meet me?' Charlie asked her.

'No. Is there something happening there?'

He nodded. 'It might be almost comical if it wasn't so heartbreaking. The evacuees from London who've been shipped here are all there, being distributed to the families roped in as hosts.'

'How many were there?'

'Two dozen or so. This scary-looking WVS billeting officer had them all lined up outside, labels round their necks like unclaimed packages, while the village women browsed among them, picking out those they best liked the look of. It reminded me of when I was sent away to school. The children looked fair flayed wi' it all, as our friend Mr Jessop might say.' For once, Charlie seemed serious. 'The faces on some of these kids, Bobby. Their eyes. It made me think of…'

'Of what?'

'Of your father,' he said in a low voice. 'And of Reggie. Those men who saw the things they saw in the last war. Things are bad down in London. The newsreels, the wireless, the papers – they're only telling us half the story, I'm certain of it.'

Bobby thought back to her time working for the *Bradford Courier* and the strictly controlled information they were allowed to give about the progress of the war. 'I think you're right. Are there homes for them all?'

'That's what worries me – the sort of homes they're likely to find when they're standing about waiting to be claimed,' Charlie said, scowling. 'Mildred Shackleton was poking and prodding at them like cattle at market. She's meaner than a miser, that woman, and her husband's no better. If they're giving a home to bairns that aren't theirs, it's not for any Christian reason. They'll expect them to work, and they won't be the only ones.'

'She wouldn't be unkind to them, would she?'

'She won't be unkind, but the Shackletons never do anything for anyone unless they think there'll be a return on their investment. The children I'm really worried about are those too sickly or tiny to work though. People here aren't cruel, but they have to work to survive. Graft at an early age is a normal part of life. They don't want to be saddled with outsiders who can't bring anything into the household.'

'I thought families had to take them if they had space.'

'Well, yes, they can be fined if they refuse, but I've a feeling there are some who would rather take a few quid fine over a child.'

Bobby sighed. 'I wish we could offer to have one. But the cottage is so small and cold, and my dad… The sort of nightmares he has would terrify a bairn. When he wakes up screaming… No, I couldn't bring a young one into a home like ours.'

'Does your father still suffer?'

'Not so much as he did in Bradford, but he'll never be cured.'

'No. I don't suppose any of them will.' Charlie looked at her. 'You know I'd take care of him too, don't you? If you said yes, I mean. I'd make sure you were both looked after.'

'He'd hate to feel he was being supported by any other man. He's got his pride, Charlie.'

'Then we'd make sure he never knew it.' The rain was driving thick and fast now in the strong hilltop wind, blinding them as they slid this way and that in the mud. Charlie pointed to the hut, now no more than two hundred yards away. 'Come on. We can shelter inside until this squall blows over.'

Bobby hung back. Charlie turned to look at her.

'What's wrong, Bobby?'

She wasn't sure what to say. They'd never been completely alone before in a place as isolated as this. Charlie wasn't one of those men who feigned deafness when a woman told them no. She did trust him, but… could she trust herself to say no if the time came?

'Well, a girl has her reputation to think about,' she said lightly, attempting to make a joke of the situation.

'We can't go back down in this. It isn't safe. I can barely see my hand in front of my face.' He nudged her. 'I won't tell if you don't, all right? Your precious reputation will be safe with me.'

The rain really was bad, and a distant rumble of thunder had broken out. Unable to think of further arguments, Bobby followed Charlie to the hut.

Chapter 9

The hut's door was wedged slightly ajar, stuck in thick mud, and Charlie had to heave it fully open with his shoulder before they could get in. Inside was a small stone bunk, with little else present but a ewe and lamb who had wandered in to seek shelter from the elements. The young mother humphed at the human intruders before trotting out with her little one.

The sheep left a smell behind them that Bobby would once upon a time have found unbearable, but now, after months of country living, she found it to be rather comforting. It wasn't a pleasant smell, but it was pungent, earthy and real, and it belonged to the Dales. As long as she was somewhere that smelled like the old hut did – of earth and dung, and fresh rain and wet sheep – Bobby knew she was safe.

Charlie wrinkled his nose at the smell. 'You see? Hardly a seducer's lair, is it?'

She smiled. 'I suppose not. I feel guilty for depriving the sheep of their shelter though.'

Above them, they heard the low drone of a bomber from the airbase.

'Sounds like a Halifax,' Charlie said. 'I don't envy those boys flying in this weather. I wonder they haven't been grounded until it blows over. Still, I don't suppose the

German bombers stop for wet playtimes, do they? I'll be up there myself soon enough.'

Bobby sighed. 'I know you will.'

Charlie glanced out of the glassless square that served as a window, watching the thick blobs of rain pelting the moor from the black cloud overhead. 'The thunder seems to have stopped, but this rain might take a while to clear. Get as comfortable as you can, Bobby. I'll take the first watch.'

He took off his coat and laid it on the stone bed for her, then went to stand by the door like a sentinel.

'Won't you be cold?' Bobby asked, removing her soaked headscarf so she could wring it out.

'Me, cold?' He struck a heroic pose, making her laugh. 'I'm a mountain man born and raised, lass. Yorkshire's own Hopalong Cassidy.'

Bobby sat down and huddled into his thick greatcoat. 'And what are you watching for, Mr Cassidy? Is there an Indian raiding party on the horizon?'

'You never know what might be roaming the moors. Marauding sheep. Invading Germans. Spectral hounds.' He glanced at her. 'Besides, I saw that look in your eye before. Since you're worried I'll find it hard to behave like a gentleman while I'm alone in the desert wastes with you, perhaps it's better if I keep my distance.'

'When in your life did you ever behave like a gentleman?'

Bobby expected him to laugh, but he didn't. Instead, he turned away to look out of the door. The atmosphere seemed to have changed suddenly and she wasn't sure why.

'Did I say something wrong?' she asked, frowning. 'I was only teasing, Charlie.'

'I know,' he said. 'It's only… never mind. Forget I said anything.'

'Charlie, what is it? If I've offended you, tell me why.'

For a moment, he didn't answer. When he spoke again, his voice was choked.

'Bobby, you have no idea.'

'No idea about what?'

'About how it feels, having to see you every day and hardly ever being allowed to touch you. Do you know what that's like?'

She frowned. 'Are you being serious now?'

He laughed bleakly. 'Deadly, I assure you.'

Bobby had heard speeches like this from boys before. They only ever happened when men got you alone, and they were usually the prelude to increasingly urgent pleading, cajoling and even threatening as they tried to convince you that their inflamed state was entirely your fault and it was up to you to put it right. She knew the right time to extricate yourself from such situations was as soon as possible, before they started pressing for what they wanted with more than mere words. But she thought she knew Charlie well enough by now to know he'd never push her to do anything she didn't want to. Besides, he didn't sound like those boys did. He sounded pained and a little sad – not at all like his usual teasing self.

'I know what people say about me and women,' he went on. 'I know what they think – what you think too, probably. But I don't… I'm not… oh, hang it!'

He turned back to her, and the expression that had appeared on his face did make her feel a little afraid. Bobby had never seen Charlie's usually merry eyes so filled with fire, or his brow knit into such a determined frown. This was a different man from the one she knew. She felt like she was suddenly alone with a stranger.

'You really don't know how tough this is for me, do you?' he said in the same choked voice.

'I don't…'

'I love you, Bobby. I want you. And damn it, I respect you – too much to press you to be with me until I know you're really mine. Do you think because I tease and I joke that it isn't real?'

'I never thought that.'

'I don't want a mistress. I wouldn't insult you by expecting you to be anything less than my wife, and I honestly don't know how much longer I can wait for you to decide that's what you want to be. Every time I ask and you say no, I make a joke of it because…' He swallowed, and the fire that had been in his eyes fizzled out in an instant. 'Because I hope you won't see how every time it breaks my heart a little bit.'

Bobby wasn't afraid now; she was only filled with pity, and with guilt for the 'yes' she still hadn't given him. She beckoned to him and he went to sit by her on the stone bed, looking limp and defeated after his outburst. Bobby took him in her arms.

'I wish I could say yes,' she whispered, stroking his hair. 'You don't know how much I want to.'

'Then do,' he whispered back, nuzzling into her neck. 'Nothing bad will happen, Bobby. We'll be together, that's all.'

'For now, perhaps.'

'What are you so afraid of?'

'That the world and all it expects of us will kill how we feel about each other now. That I'll be forced to give up the job I love to be with the man I love. That I'll fail you as a wife and our children as a mother, because I can't be content with being only those things. And that…' She swallowed. 'That I'll lose you. That having had you, I'll be forced to face life without you – me and our children, perhaps.'

'Maybe none of those things will happen. Maybe we'll live our lives together as Reggie and Mary have, still loving each other when we're old and grey. Why shouldn't it be that as well as the other?'

'Because of me and who I am, and you and who you are. Because of the war.'

'You won't give a man who's off to war something worth fighting for? Worth dying for?' His voice was soft, as soft as his lips on her skin, and she could feel herself weakening. 'We don't have to marry right away, darling. We can wait until the war is over, if that's what you want. I don't mind waiting for you if I know you'll be mine at the finish. All I want from you now is a promise.'

Bobby shuddered, and Charlie looked up from her neck. 'What is it?'

'Please don't talk about dying.' The tear she'd been holding back slid down her cheek. 'I… can't bear it.'

'I'm sorry.'

'Don't ask me any more, please. Just let me think. I need time to think it over.'

'But you'll give me an answer? Before I go, you'll give me your real, final answer?'

'Yes.' She took a deep breath. 'Yes, I owe you at least that.'

He looked out of the window. 'It's still raining hard. I hope it lets up before dark. You get some sleep if you like. I'll keep watch and wake you when it stops.'

Bobby could already feel her eyes closing. Their conversation had drained the last of her energy, and she was having to fight her body to stay awake.

'Charlie?' she murmured.

'What is it?'

'I do love you.' She pressed a kiss to his lips. 'I hope you know... whatever answer I give, that's how I feel. I always will.'

'I'll never understand you if I live to be a hundred,' he said gently, smiling as he brushed her damp hair away from her face. 'Perhaps that's why I've always found you so hard to resist. There's no one quite like you, Bobby Bancroft.' He kissed her forehead. 'I'll see you when you wake up.'

–

When Bobby awoke, the rain had died down to a drizzle and the sun was glowing weakly through the grey clouds. She could see at once that Charlie had failed to keep his promise to stay awake. He was sleeping at her side, one arm over her body and with a little corner of the greatcoat she'd been using as a blanket pulled over him for warmth.

Bobby was about to wake him, but she couldn't help pausing a moment to look at him as he slept. His mouth was open, the brown curls still damp from the rain sticking to his forehead. He looked young and boyish – too young to be risking his life in the skies. And yet she knew, in her heart, that Charlie could never like or respect himself if he didn't do what he saw as his duty. She couldn't wrap him in cotton wool because he was hers, no matter how much she wanted to. If all English women behaved so with their men, Hitler's war would be won – and then where would humanity be? But as much as she respected Charlie for doing what he believed was right – as much as she herself felt it to be right – she wished it didn't have to be that way.

For a moment she stroked his hair, watching him sleep. Bobby had spent many sleepless nights agonising over what answer to give Charlie, but she had given very little thought to what their actual married life might be like. For the first time since he'd started proposing to her, she realised that waking up every morning with Charlie Atherton sleeping beside her, safe and content in his arms, was something she could heartily wish for. She bent to wake him with a kiss.

'Charlie,' she whispered. 'Time to wake up.'

'An angel speaks my name.' He blinked his eyes open and grinned drowsily up at her. 'I must have died in my sleep and gone to heaven. Reggie will be pleased. He's been warning me for years that I was bound for the other place.'

Bobby tapped his nose with her fingertip. 'You weren't supposed to be sleeping at all. It looks like the rain stopped ages ago. We'll have to hurry down before it starts up again – there's still an angry sky up there. You'd better stop flirting with me and get up.'

'You're right.' He reclaimed his coat and sat up to put it on. 'You will think about it properly, though, won't you, Bobby? I mean, before you give me an answer.'

'I will, Charlie. I promise.'

Chapter 10

They walked home in almost perfect silence. Charlie looked like he was a thousand miles away, frowning as he pondered whatever was preying on his mind, and Bobby's thoughts were whirling too. Her brain was full of so many things: the odd little scene with Charlie in the hut, when he'd finally shared his full and unguarded thoughts with her; waking up in his arms, almost as if she was his wife already; the huge, life-changing decision she now had a mere month to make. Of course, it was only fair that she gave Charlie his final answer one way or another and let him leave for the RAF as either an engaged man or a free one. But every time she tried to think about it, her brain rebelled against what felt like an impossible choice.

She wished Lilian were here to advise her. In Bobby's last letter, she'd begged her sister to visit if she possibly could, hinting she had big secrets to share that only a twin could understand. She was hopeful there might be a reply waiting for her today when she arrived back at Cow House Cottage.

'What are you up to this evening?' Bobby asked Charlie as they crossed the old packhorse bridge into the village, breaking a silence that had begun to feel rather gloomy.

'Hmm?' Charlie roused himself. 'I don't know. I might stop in at the Hart, perhaps. Gil Capstick will be in and he owes me a pint. I suppose you'll be on duty in that horrible little ARP hut, won't you?'

'No, I don't have a shift tonight. Mary asked if Dad and I would like to spend the evening with them in the farm-house. Reg bought her some new gramophone records last time he went into town.' She looked up at him. 'Will you stay in too?'

He smiled, looking a little like his old self again. 'Sit in the farmhouse all night with Reggie and your father glaring at me if I so much as glance in your pure and chaste direction? I'd rather have you to myself somewhere, thanks all the same.'

'I'll bet you would,' she said, smiling too. 'But stay in with us, though, please. I know it probably seems beyond dull to you, but I love those nights when we all sit together by the parlour fire. It does my dad good, and it feels… I suppose like we're a little family.'

He glanced at her. 'I never knew you felt that way about it.'

'Nor did I, until I thought about it just now. Will you stay at home? For me? We don't have many nights left to be cosy by the fireside all together.'

'If it means that much to you, I suppose I can bear the disapproving frowns of our respective father figures. Perhaps I might even convince them I'm husband material after all, playing records and smoking with the real men while the womenfolk darn our socks. Your dad doesn't know you've been out with me today, I suppose?'

'No, he's gone fishing with Pete Dixon. He'd blow up if he knew about the shepherd's hut.'

'I won't tell if you don't.' He squinted as they descended the track to Moorside Farm. 'Hullo. What's going on down there?'

Outside the farmhouse, there appeared to be strange things afoot. Piles and piles of back numbers of *The Tyke* stood out in the rain on a table, half-covered by an inadequately weighted tarpaulin that was flapping about in the wind. A little piano with the legs removed, a baby's cot and an old tin bathtub lay about looking sorry for themselves.

'Could Mary be spring cleaning?' Bobby suggested as they approached the odd collection of bric-a-brac. 'Maybe this is all to go for salvage.'

'My brother would have her guts for garters if she gave away his precious magazines for scrap.' Charlie shifted the tarpaulin so it covered the piles of magazines, protecting them from the drizzle. 'And I doubt she'd ever part with Nancy's cot.'

'Then why is this stuff out here getting wet?'

The door to the farmhouse opened and Mary herself appeared, more junk in her arms. She looked flustered as she dumped it with the rest, and faintly guilty.

'Oh,' she said. 'It's only you two. I thought Reg might be home. He's driven the car over to the printer's in Settle.'

'What's going on, Mary?' Bobby asked. 'Why is all this stuff out here?'

'I've been clearing out the attic.'

'You managed to get all this down from the attic by yourself?' Charlie said. 'You ought to have waited until I was back.'

Mary avoided his gaze. 'No time for that. It had to be sorted out this afternoon.'

'You're looking decidedly furtive, you know, Mother. Are you trying to smuggle Reggie's stash of magazines away while he's out? Because if so, I'd like to make myself scarce before the ensuing explosion.'

'I'll find somewhere else for them. The attic's needed for other purposes.'

'What other purposes?' Bobby asked. 'Are you moving me and Reg up there?' It was Mary's favourite complaint: the fact that her parlour had been almost entirely taken over to be *The Tyke*'s unofficial office.

'No. There's an old mattress in there I'm making up.'

'Have you got visitors coming?'

'You might say that.' She sighed. 'Reg is going to play heck when he finds out. Still, it's too late now.' She flashed Bobby a defiant look, as if daring a challenge. 'Besides, what would have happened to them if I hadn't, I should like to know?'

'To whom?' Charlie asked. 'You're not making any sense, Mary.'

'Well, it happened this way. I dropped in on Ida to talk about the arrangements for Sunday – Billy's funeral – and on my way back through the village... oh, come and look for yourselves. They're in the kitchen.'

Charlie looked as bewildered as Bobby felt. He gave her a 'your guess is as good as mine' shrug as they followed Mary into the house. She led the pair of them into the kitchen.

In there were two small, pale, red-headed girls, standing in their slips by the fire next to a rack of clothes. Both had the sallow complexion that came from spending too much time out of the sunlight, and bags under their eyes from lack of sleep. The younger child was cautiously stroking Winnie, one of Reg's huge but placid wolf-hounds, who was curled up with her brother Barney in front of the blaze.

'They were soaked through,' Mary said, shaking her head. 'I had to get them out of their wet things right away before they caught their deaths. Being made to stand out in the rain like they're at a butcher's market while half the village prodded and poked at them! Disgusting, I call it.'

Charlie glanced at a pile of suitcases and gas mask boxes dumped in one corner of the room. A couple of large labels threaded on string sat on top. 'They're evacuees?'

'From London. The Docklands, where I'm told the worst of the bombing is. Poor things, they were the last ones left. Too little and scrawny for domestic work, I suppose, so no one would take them in.' Mary shot him a look of challenge. 'Well, I couldn't just leave them there, could I? We have enough space with some shuffling, so I volunteered us as a host family for them.'

Bobby shot a worried look at Charlie before dropping to her knees to talk to the girls. They looked terrified – not so much by where they were, she suspected, but by what they'd seen before they arrived there. Charlie was right; there was a haunted look in their eyes that reminded Bobby powerfully of her father when he awoke from one of his nightmares about the trenches. No child should look like that.

'What are your names, my loves?' she asked gently.

'Florence Parry, Miss,' whispered the elder girl. She was softly spoken, with the nasal accent of London's East End. 'My little sister's Jessica… Jessie.'

The younger girl smiled shyly but didn't show any inclination to speak.

'Well, it's a great honour to meet you, Florence and Jessica Parry. Charles Atherton, at your service.' Charlie bent down and held out his hand to Jessica with a manly frankness that was quite comical, and the child let out an involuntary laugh that for a moment made her look like a normal, happy little girl instead of the fearful ghost created by nearly eight months of constant bombing. After hesitating a moment, she shook his hand.

'Now then, I'll bet I can use my mind-reading powers to find out how old you both are,' he said when he'd shaken Florence's hand too.

Florence giggled. 'You can't read minds.'

'Can't I indeed? Then how do I know you're thinking about how good an aniseed ball would taste right at this moment?'

'No I weren't.'

'Oh, well. Then you won't want one of these,' Charlie said airily, taking the now rather sticky paper bag from his trouser pocket.

'I was thinking that,' Jessie piped up, clearly an intelligent child who had already worked out on which side her bread was buttered. Charlie smiled and held out the bag for both girls to take a sweet.

'Now. Your ages.' He put his fingers to his temples and adopted a comical expression of earnest concentration. 'Florence Parry... Florence Parry... could that be the Florence Parry who's ten years old? And her little sister Jessica, seven years and eight months this May?'

Jessica's eyes widened, and she turned to her sister with an expression of wonder. 'Florrie, he can really do it!'

'How'd you know how old we are, Mr Atherton?' asked the more sceptical older child.

'I'm a close personal friend of Father Christmas. Don't worry, I know you've both been good this year – at least, so far.'

Bobby smiled. The children's birthdates were written on the labels they must have been wearing when Mary brought them home, sitting there on top of their cases right where Charlie could see them, but it was a good

86

trick all the same. While Charlie was amusing the girls, who had started chatting to him now like old friends, she took Mary aside for a talk.

'He's surprisingly good with them, isn't he?' Mary said with a fond glance at Charlie. 'I don't think you need be worried on that score, Bobby.'

'Never mind about Charlie.' She lowered her voice. 'I take it Reg doesn't know you were planning to take in some evacuees.'

'Of course he doesn't. He'd say we didn't have the room, what with that damned magazine taking up every spare corner of the house. But the poor little bodies have to live somewhere, don't they? It's high time we did our bit for the war, same as everyone else.' She sighed. 'There'll be fireworks when he gets home though.'

'He might send them away again.'

'Send bairns away when they've no home to go back to? He'd do nothing so cruel – not my Reg. He's too good a man.' Mary glanced at the children. 'Still, I'll have a job of work to convince the stubborn old goat it was a good idea. I'd appreciate some support from you and Charlie.'

Bobby turned to look at Charlie, who was making the girls laugh as he told them a story about one of his regular patients – a mischievous cocker spaniel called Bruno who was forever getting into scrapes – complete with impressions of the foolish beast chasing its own tail around the surgery. 'You can count on us.'

'Thank you. I knew I could.'

'Are you sure we'll be able to talk him round though? Reg is… set in his ways. There's his leg too – you know how grumpy he can get when it's giving him pain. I can't imagine how he'll cope with two small children in the house.'

'He'll cope. He was a father once, don't forget – a fonder one than you might imagine, knowing him now. Besides, it will do him good to be reminded that the whole world doesn't revolve around Reginald Atherton and that magazine of his.' Mary looked at the two evacuees laughing with Charlie and smiled. 'It'll certainly be something to have bairns around the place. It's a long time since we heard the laughter of children at Moorside.'

Chapter 11

It was an hour later when the three of them heard Reg's battered black Wolseley pulling up outside the farmhouse. Mary had finished furnishing the attic for the two evacuees, and Florence and Jessica were now upstairs in their new room in dry clothes and with a mug of hot milk each. The adults had tried to keep from them their fear of a scene when the man of the house arrived home, but the Parry girls were quick-witted little things and seemed to have picked up on the general air of anxiety. They had readily agreed to go and play in the attic until Mary summoned them down for their evening meal.

Most of the clutter from outside had been rehomed – Bobby and Charlie had dragged the little piano to Cow House Cottage, Nancy's old cradle was in the kitchen, and the back numbers of *The Tyke* had been piled up in any corner of the house currently unoccupied. There were still a couple of chairs and a woodworm-infested table out there, however. Mary had asked Charlie to break them up for firewood just as soon as they'd explained things to Reg.

Charlie peeped through the net curtains to watch his brother getting out of the car.

'How does he look, Charlie?' Mary asked nervously. 'Is he scowling?'

'No, he's whistling. He must have had a useful meeting with the printer.'

'If he's in a good mood, that ought to help,' Bobby said.

'All right, troops, to your stations,' Charlie said. 'Mary, you meet him at the door with his slippers. Bobby, make a pot of tea for us all.'

'Was Gil able to sell you some tobacco?'

Charlie patted his pocket. 'Reggie's favourite Gold Flake. I'll fill his pipe for him now.' There was the sound of Reg's key in the side door – no Dalesman would use the front door of his home unless there was a bride to carry through it or a corpse to carry out. 'Let's go.'

Bobby headed to the kitchen to boil the kettle while Mary went to greet her husband, but she kept her ears open for any snatches of conversation. Despite Mary's assurances he could be talked round, Bobby couldn't help worrying that Reg was going to be difficult about the two little girls. And yet it would be so good for him to have children around the place. It would give him something to enrich his life that wasn't *The Tyke*, which Mary worried he focused on rather too obsessively to be entirely healthy. It might also smooth away some of the rough edges that had developed through years of grief, pain and brooding. Bobby knew the Athertons had never recovered from the loss of Nancy, their one child, at the age of two. The Parry sisters could be just what was needed to help heal that wound at last.

'Now then, our lass, what's all that junk doing outside?' she heard Reg say to Mary as he entered the house, his walking stick thudding heavily on the hall flagstones. He sounded quite jovial, at least for Reg – hopefully that was a good omen.

'I took it down from the attic while I was cleaning,' Mary answered. 'Young Charlie's going to break it up for firewood. Here are your slippers, dear, all warmed by the fire.'

'The best of wives.' There was a pause, which Bobby thought must mean Reg was giving his wife a kiss. She had long had her suspicions that her stern, taciturn employer was a fond, perhaps even downright demonstrative husband when there was no one around to observe him.

'What are all these papers doing lying around the place?' he asked next.

'I told you, I was clearing out the attic. Never mind about them. Come into the kitchen and have a cup of tea – Bobby's in there making a pot for us. Your brother's filling your pipe in the parlour. He came back from the village earlier with some of your favourite tobacco.'

The pair of them appeared in the kitchen a moment later, Reg looking somewhat perplexed at the attentions being inexplicably heaped on him by his nearest and dearest. He glanced at Nancy's old cot in the corner and frowned.

'What's that doing here?'

'I brought it down from the attic,' Mary said. 'I was worried it might be getting swollen with damp, so I put it in here by the fire to dry out.'

'Good evening, Reg,' Bobby said brightly. 'I hope you don't mind, but Mary invited me and Dad over this evening to listen to those new records you bought her. I thought I'd come early to see if I could make myself useful around the place. The tea's just brewing.'

Reg was still holding the slippers in one hand, as if he'd forgotten they were there. 'Hmm. There's something going on around here. What is it then?'

'Now don't be daft,' Mary said, managing to recover something of her usual no-nonsense tone. 'Sit down, take your boots off and have a cup of tea whilst I tell you about my day.'

'There must be some womanish conspiracy going on if I'm greeted with warmed slippers and hot tea when I'm barely through the door.' But Reg was half-smiling as he rested his stick against the fireplace and sat down at the table. 'Well, Mary, let me hear what you've got to tell me. You two have heard some village gossip you're desperate to pass on, no doubt.'

They were interrupted by Charlie, who entered bearing Reg's pipe before him as if it was a royal sceptre.

'Here we go, Reggie,' he said. 'I know you don't usually smoke before supper but as you've no doubt had a long, cold trip into town, I think you might make an exception today. I got you your favourite Gold Flake for a treat.'

'Not you as well,' Reg said, shaking his head. 'What is going on around here? I'm getting the distinct impression that an attempt is being made to butter me up. And if you're in on it as well as the women, Charlie, then that really is something to worry about.'

'Can't a man bring his only brother a gift once in a while without being suspected of underhanded motives?' Charlie glanced at Mary. 'Although we did have some news to tell you.'

'Ah. Now we get to the point.' Reg looked suspiciously from Charlie to Bobby. 'I hope this news isn't anything to do with the pair of you. If it is, then you'd better let me know the worst straight away.'

'It isn't about me and Charlie.' Bobby nodded to his wife. 'It's Mary who has something to tell you.'

Mary went to rest a conciliatory hand on his shoulder. 'Now Reg, you mustn't explode. After all, the attic was sitting empty apart from some old rubbish we could easily part with, and they've got to go somewhere.'

'They? What *they* do you mean?'

'The children, Reg. The poor loves were bombed out of their home, and they've no mother. Well, I mean to say. How could I have walked on by and still called myself a Christian? You remember your scripture: "For I was hungry, and you gave me meat. I was thirsty, and you gave me drink. I was a stranger, and you took me in."'

Mary's voice had taken on a pleading quality, but Reg didn't say anything. He just stared straight ahead as the truth began to dawn, his brow knitting into a scowl. Bobby shot a helpless look at Charlie.

'Pass me my stick,' Reg said quietly after a short time had passed.

'Now, Reg, I hope you aren't going to—'

'Pass me my stick, Mary.'

With a worried expression, Mary handed it to him. He got slowly to his feet and left the room. A moment later, they heard him climbing the stairs to the attic.

'What do you think he's going to do?' Bobby whispered. 'He wouldn't turn them out?'

'Of course he wouldn't. He's a kind heart, for all his grumbling.' But Mary didn't sound quite as self-assured as she had earlier in the day.

Reg reappeared a moment later with an expression like thunder.

'So. You've all been conspiring against me, have you?'

'We haven't, honestly,' Bobby said. 'Mary offered to have them on the spur of the moment because they were getting wet in the storm and no one else wanted them.

Charlie and I didn't know a thing about it until we came home from our walk.'

Charlie nodded. 'There's no conspiracy, Reggie. You just married a kind-hearted woman who hates to see little ones suffer, as I'm sure you know. You wouldn't really be angry with her for it, would you?'

Reg's expression softened a fractional amount, but he refused to look at Mary.

'They can't stay,' he muttered. 'This is a working establishment. I can't produce a magazine and mind a pair of bairns at the same time. Besides, there's no room.'

'I'll do all the minding of them,' Mary said. 'You'll hardly know they're here. Poor motherless little things. It'll do them a power of good to be out in this good clean air, away from the city and those awful bombs.'

He folded his arms stubbornly. 'This is my home and I expect to be consulted about who's invited to share it.'

'It's my home too, Reg.'

Reg rested his stick against the fireplace again before sitting down at the table, placing his hands flat on the surface and glaring at them. 'Nevertheless, they go tomorrow. The attic can't be spared. I need it for storage.'

'Go where? No one else wanted them.'

'The WVS can find a place for them. It's for them to worry about, not us.'

'But they might split them up if they can't find someone who'll take them together.'

Reg remained silent, sullenly avoiding her eye.

'They'll fine us if we turn them out now they know we have the room,' Mary said, sounding increasingly desperate.

'Let them fine us then. I'd rather pay the fiver than be lumbered with uninvited guests for the rest of the war.'

'Reg, please.' Mary's voice cracked a little and she rested a hand on his arm. 'Children, here at Moorside. Do you know how long… How much I've always wished… For me, dear.'

'It can't be done, Mary. It just isn't feasible when I've a magazine to get out.'

Mary drew herself up and put her hands on her hips. 'Reg Atherton, I've been married to you for a quarter of a century. I've cooked your meals, borne your child, put up with that magazine of yourn taking over every inch of my home and I've never once asked you for anything. Well, I'm asking now. I'm begging, even. Please, let the girls stay.'

Reg laughed. 'Never asked me for owt? Did I want to employ some slip of a city girl to work out here in a man's country? No, but I knew you'd never stop nagging me about it until I agreed to take her on. Did I want to put Charlie up when he could have found more appropriate lodgings for a bachelor in the village? No, but you begged me to let him have the spare room until he went off to the war.'

'Those were for your own good,' Mary said stoutly. 'And so is this. Stop being a stubborn old fool and listen to your heart, Reg. Do what you know is right.'

Reg didn't speak. He just continued to glare at the backs of his hands as if they'd done him a terrible wrong.

Bobby, sensing it was the man's pride that had been hurt more than anything else, decided to try another tactic.

'Perhaps they could stay with Dad and me in Cow House Cottage instead,' she suggested. 'I know there isn't much room, but I could put a mattress on the parlour floor for them.'

Reg looked at her sharply. 'Bairns, living in that draughty old shippon? The pair of them look sickly enough as it is.'

'They have to stay somewhere. And if you can't find the space for them here…'

Reg stared moodily into the fire.

'Your dad still troubled with them nightmares of his, is he?' he asked after a bit.

'They're better than they were, but… yes,' Bobby said quietly. 'Once a week, perhaps, he'll wake up thinking he's back in the trenches.'

'Aye, I've heard him. Lashes out, I imagine?'

Bobby lowered her gaze. 'He… he sometimes breaks things. Not on purpose, but he can get quite… distraught. Sleeping powder and whisky will usually chase it away, until the next time.'

Reg fell silent again, frowning as if in deep thought. Charlie, obviously sensing they were making progress, pushed the pipe into his brother's unresisting hand and took out a match to light it for him.

There was a faint little tap at the kitchen door, and a moment later, Florence's red curls appeared around it. She was holding a tin mug in her hand.

'We finished our milk, Mrs Atherton,' she said. 'Jessie said we ought to bring the cups down, in case you ain't got enough for your tea.' Jessie peeped around her sister and nodded, looking rather pleased with herself for the suggestion.

'That was very thoughtful of you, my loves.' Mary took the mugs from them and put them in the sink. 'And there's to be none of this "Mrs Atherton" nonsense. You may call me Mary while you're staying here.'

Jessica shot a worried glance at Reg, who was looking them up and down with a stern expression on his face. 'What are we to call you, please, sir?'

Reg didn't answer, but continued to examine the girls.

'You don't look like you eat much,' he observed at last. 'Don't they feed you down in London?'

Jessie looked at Florence, unsure what she ought to say.

'Dad buys us what he can afford,' the older girl said. 'But we could eat twice as much, couldn't we, Jessie? It's not good to say so though. He gets upset he can't buy us more, and it's worse now 'cause of the war.'

'Poor, are you?'

'We didn't used to be, Dad says, but now I suppose we must be...' The girl looked as though it would pain her to say the word, perhaps through a pride instilled by her father. 'I suppose we might be... not so rich. I don't remember when we had more money than now. It must've been a long time ago.'

'Where is your father?'

'Gone to the war.' Florence puffed herself up. 'He's a soldier. The best one in the whole army.'

'I don't doubt it. And your mother's dead?'

Florence nodded. 'She died when Jessie were a baby.'

'Who takes care of you then?'

'Our Aunt Sadie, only she don't take much care. I don't think she's bothered about what we do. She leaves us on our own most night-times to go dancing with her boyfriends because Uncle Jack's off fighting. She makes us go to school, though, but only to get us out of the house all day – when we still had a house.'

'Your home was bombed, was it?'

Florence lowered her eyes. 'S'right. We come up from the shelter after the all-clear and there was only... only stones and dust and broken furniture left. And all our toys and books and clothes, and my ma's picture what we kept by our bed… That's when Aunt Sadie went home and we got sent away here.' The child looked suddenly ferocious. 'I hate those old Germans. What have they got to drop bombs on people's houses for? I hope my dad kills every single German that there is. I'd go to the war too if they'd let me.'

Reg smoked his pipe, watching the pale, skinny child as she clenched her little fists and vowed to take on the entire Third Reich by herself. His mouth twitched.

'You can call me Reg, to answer your question,' he said. 'I hope you'll both be good children while you stay here. Eat up all your meals, learn your lessons, say your prayers, mind Mary and play in the outdoors as much as you can. I'm afraid it might be some time until you can be with your dad again.'

Florence nodded solemnly. 'We'll be good, Mr Reg.'

He laughed, and it suddenly dawned on Bobby what an unfamiliar sound Reg's laughter was to her. 'Well, plain Reg will do.'

Mary, smiling, bent to plant a soft kiss on his cheek. 'Thank you,' Bobby heard her whisper. 'You won't be sorry, Reg.'

Chapter 12

The arrival of the Parry sisters on that rainy May afternoon seemed to mark a new era for the inhabitants of Moorside Farm. The two girls soon lost their shyness under Mary's motherly care, growing rosy-cheeked and plump through the solicitous application of solid, nutritious food, fresh air and vigorous play. Their eyes, too, lost some of their haunted look as – away from the shriek and thunder of the London Blitz – they started to feel safe once again. However, they would still cling to Mary or Bobby whenever they heard one of the bombers from the nearby airbase flying overhead.

Charlie – Uncle Charlie, as he quickly became – was a firm favourite with them from the day they arrived, finding himself constantly badgered to be a participant in their larks and games whenever he wasn't at work. He was a fun and patient playmate, letting the girls dress him up and push him around according to whichever of the endless worlds of make-believe they wanted him to be a part of that day. In the warm, mellow evenings of the cuckoo time, the two little girls would spend hours playing in the farmhouse garden with Charlie, and with Barney and Winnie, Reg and Mary's dogs. Bobby joined them whenever she could, relishing being a part of the girls' healthy, hearty play. Even her father would carry out his chair so he could sit and watch their games, looking every inch the fond patriarch. Bobby had long felt that the Moorside residents were a sort of family, but she hadn't known they were an incomplete one until the two little girls had come to fill a hole she hadn't recognised was there.

The girls' father, they learned over the course of their first fortnight in the farmhouse, was Captain George Parry: a soldier who had been with the British Expeditionary Force at Dunkirk. His children were inordinately proud of him, as well they might be.

A letter to his daughters' hosts thanking them for their hospitality revealed a little more about the family and the change in their fortunes hinted at by Florence. In civilian life, George Parry had been a master tailor and at one time the keeper of a successful gentlemen's outfitters. The family had led a comfortable existence until a crisis some seven years previously had forced him to sell his establishment. The money earned from the sale had quickly disappeared, and the family had never quite recovered from the loss. Although Captain Parry didn't say in his letter what the crisis had been, Mary had surmised that it must have been connected to his wife's decline in health and ultimate death following Jessie's birth. On reading Captain Parry's letter, she had immediately given each girl a hug and ninepence each for some 'spice' from the village shop, earning grumbles from Reg about them becoming quite spoiled in their temporary home.

The surly editor – set in his ways and disliking changes to his routine – had been a tougher nut to crack than the rest of the household. Of course, the way to his heart had proved, as always, to be through his magazine.

Bobby was at her desk in the parlour one afternoon, typing up the Bowside walk she'd done with Charlie, when Reg approached to see how she was getting on.

'Nearly done, are you?' he asked, looking over her shoulder.

'Almost. Another ten minutes and it'll be ready for you to sub.'

'Happen you made it to the hut that afternoon then?'

Bobby fought back a smile. 'Did you doubt I would?'

'I knew my no-good brother would do his best to lead you astray. I wouldn't try to defend him if I were you. I know what he's like all too well.'

'He might have suggested cutting the walk short. There was a storm brewing, so I don't think you ought to be too hard on him for that. Anyhow, I stood my ground and insisted we keep going until we reached the hut.'

'Glad to hear it.' There was the faintest flicker of a smile. 'Since you managed to pass my little test, I might be persuaded to let you cover Kiltford Show with me after all.'

She looked up at him. 'Oh gosh, would you really?'

'Well. I know you've had your heart set on it, for some reason. If we're separated, just be sure to watch yourself round the beer tent. The farmers around here are a respectable lot 364 days of the year, but when the ale flows on show day then young ladies need to watch themselves.'

'Thanks, Reg. You won't be sorry.'

'See that I'm not.'

She smiled. 'You know, sometimes I think you might be almost glad you let Mary talk you into employing me.'

'Let's not get carried away,' he said with a rare smile. 'Still, you're not bad for a lass – I doubt I could've done better. Good brain, fair turn of phrase and not afraid of hard work. I don't know why you want to be hanging about with a bone-idle ne'er-do-well like our Charlie.'

It was unusual for Reg to give her praise worded any more strongly than 'aye, that'll do'. Bobby looked up at him, sensing an opportunity to build bridges between the two Atherton brothers while he was in a communicative mood.

'Do you really think that?' she asked. 'Surely you can't believe all the bad things you say about your brother.'

He shrugged. 'Sometimes I do. Then again, sometimes I don't. Depends what he's been up to.'

'I would have thought you'd be proud. He didn't have to join up but he did. He's conscientious in his job, even if he does like a good time outside of work. Everyone in the village likes him.'

'Aye. A bit too much, if we're talking about some of the lasses.'

'And he's been a wonder helping Florrie and Jessie settle in,' Bobby went on, ignoring that remark. 'They think the world of him.'

'That's the thing, isn't it?' Reg said, looking away. 'Charlie's got a lot to him, scapegrace that he is. Strong brain. Good heart when he stops thinking about himself for five minutes. He's got courage too, and a conscience of sorts, but he's lazy and juvenile. Doesn't care enough about what people think of him – takes after his mother in that respect. Charlie's too fond of enjoying himself when he ought to be improving himself, and he drags others down with him.'

'If it's me you mean, you needn't worry. I feel like we balance each other out, Charlie and I. I'm too much inclined to overwork, him to overplay. I suppose that's what makes us… friends.' She met his eyes. 'He never says so, but it hurts him that he thinks he doesn't have your approval. He looks up to you as a father, Reg.'

'What do you know of it?'

'More than you might think. I'm a reporter, aren't I? I notice things. It'd mean the world if you told him just once how much he's done to make you proud.'

'Huh. I go hard on him because I want to see him get on in life,' Reg muttered. 'I hate to see him wasting his talents while he's out chasing women or knocking back pints at the pub, having everyone in the village whispering about what a rum lad he is. They might like him but they don't respect him. Why should they? He's done nowt to earn their respect.'

'He's been better lately.'

'Happen,' Reg said noncommittally. 'Still. If I don't tell him he can do better, who else is there to make him try? Mary spoils the boy, and like you say, I'm the closest he's got to a father.'

'But he isn't a boy, Reg. He's a man – a man about to go to war. I know how much it would mean to him to know you're proud of him for what he's doing. Think about it. Please.'

He looked at her curiously for a moment. 'And what about ye two then? Still courting?'

Bobby flushed. 'I… yes. At the moment.'

'Has he asked you about being wed? I reckon I'm entitled to know, as his brother.'

'He's asked – lots of times – but I haven't given him an answer yet. I'm… still deciding what to do for the best.'

'My missus thinks you might be just the wife our Charlie needs to finally make him respectable.'

'And what do you think?'

'I think she might be right. Then again she might be wrong, and I don't want to see someone else whose welfare I care about dragged down by him. My brother isn't a bad man at heart, but it'd be a fool who ever relied on him for anything.' He paused. 'Be cautious, lass, that's all. The thing about marriage is that there's no way back if you make the wrong choice.'

'I know. Thanks for the advice, Reg.'

They were interrupted by a tap at the door. Reg called for whoever was there to come in, and Florence appeared with her sister.

Reg frowned. 'You pair ought to be at school.'

'There's a half-day holiday today,' Florence said. 'Mary told us to ask if you want some tea making.'

'We're *helping*,' Jessie announced importantly, placing significant emphasis on the last word.

Bobby laughed. 'Helping or hindering?'

'Honest, Bobby, we are helping,' Florence said. 'I hung out the washing. Mary let me stand on a chair and do it.'

'I peeled the potatoes for dinner,' Jessie informed them eagerly. 'Mary says if we're good, we can help bake the bread too.'

'Aye, tell Mary I could manage a brew.' Reg hobbled back to his own desk and sat down. 'Hop along then, you two. You know you're not to bother us in here when we're working.'

Jessie had wandered over to Bobby's desk, however, and was looking at her notes with fascination.

'Is it code?' she asked.

'I suppose it's a sort of code, yes,' Bobby said.

'Ooh! For sending messages to spies and things?'

'I'm afraid not,' she answered with a smile. 'It's called shorthand. It helps me to write faster, and it keeps things secret too. Only Reg and I are able to read it.'

The little girl's eyes sparkled. 'I love secret codes. I know lots of codes and spy tricks, like where you use lemon juice to write and it's invisible till you put it over a candle, and the one where you make a wheel to swap the letters so only your friends with the same wheel can read what it says. Can you teach me this one too?'

'I could teach you a little of it, if you've the patience to learn.'

'Hooray!' She turned to grin at her sister. 'If she teaches us, we can play Spy School, Florrie.'

Bobby smiled. 'We'll all play later, shall we? I have to work now. You go back to Mary and let her know about the tea.'

Jessie nodded and went out, but Florence hung back. She was looking shyly at Reg.

'Reg, are you writing things for your magazine?' she asked.

'I am,' he said, not looking up from his typewriter.

'What are you writing?'

'Book review.'

'What's the book please?'

'Historical novel. Load of rubbish.' He looked up. 'Nowt to interest a bairn.'

'Am I a bairn?'

'Aye, that you are. A naughty one as doesn't do what she's told first time.'

Bobby smiled to herself as she carried on with her work. Reg was doing his best to keep up his irascible tone, but she could tell he was amused. Ever since Florence had told him on the day she arrived that she'd gladly take on the entire German army single-handedly, Bobby had noticed a certain affection for the girl – although, of course, Reg always did his best not to show it.

Florence scuffed her shoe against the carpet. Reg waited, but she didn't speak.

'Well?' he said. 'Am I to be left in peace today or not, Florence Parry?'

'It's a good magazine, your magazine,' the little girl said.

Reg laughed. 'Read it, have you?'

'Some. I'm good at reading for my age, Miss Reed says.' Miss Reed was Florence's teacher at the village school, where the two girls had been enrolled along with their fellow evacuees.

Reg looked amused now. 'What parts do you read then, Little Miss Good-at-Reading?'

'I like the bits about what animals do and the comics. I like the stories too. Even the scary ones, like the one about the ghost dog, if I don't read them before bedtime. But I don't understand the bits where all the spelling goes funny.'

'That's our dialect here – dialect means the way that folk speak. When you've been in Yorkshire long enough, you'll be able to understand it. You need to listen to how we talk, that's all.' He went back to his work.

'Reg?' Florence said, somewhat hesitantly.

He looked up. 'Are you still here?'

'I wrote a story. For your magazine.' She puffed herself up. 'It's about an owl called Owly and her sister who get sent to live in Yorkshire because of the bombs.'

'Sounds familiar.'

'Uncle Charlie read it and he said that if you put it in then it'd be one of the best stories he'd ever read in *The Tyke*.'

'Huh. Did he indeed?'

'Will you read it and see if it's good?' She scuffed her foot again. 'It probably ain't good enough for your magazine. But I want you to read it anyhow. I wrote it for you to read.'

Bobby looked up from her work. 'You know, Reg, that isn't a bad idea. I've thought before that we ought to have a page or two for children. Puzzles and comics and so forth. They could write to us with their jokes and stories too. Why not?'

'Why not? Because there's a war on, lass, that's why not. I had to cut four pages last month thanks to the paper ration. We've no room for the scribblings of bairns.' He looked at Florence's hopeful face and sighed. 'All right, let's see this story then.'

The little girl clapped her hands and ran up to the attic to get it for him.

She came back with a sheet of scrap paper filled with small, painstakingly neat writing, as if the story had been drafted roughly and then copied into best for Reg's benefit. She handed it to him shyly.

'I'll go see if our tea's ready yet,' Bobby said, judging it wise to leave them together for a few moments.

Mary was kneading bread in the kitchen with Jessie. The child was arranging a couple of mugs, a milk jug and sugar bowl on a tray with the pompous air of a new housewife proud of a job well done.

'What's to do then?' Mary asked, looking up in surprise when she entered. Bobby rarely left the parlour during the working day, except at midday, when she went home to make herself and her father their dinner.

'Nothing's wrong.' Bobby smiled. 'Florence wrote a story for the magazine. I left her and Reg alone while he read it. He'll be less embarrassed saying kind things about it without me there.'

'That was good thinking.'

Bobby waited for the tea to brew, then carried in the pot while Jessie brought the tray through. The little girl had been adamant she could manage the pot as well, but Mary had wisely judged that seven-year-old children and boiling water oughtn't to be mixed.

Bobby couldn't help smiling when she re-entered the parlour. Florence was kneeling on a little stool she'd pulled over to Reg's desk, watching with awe while he showed her how to work his typewriter. Jessie skipped over to join them.

'Can I try?' she asked.

'All right,' Reg said. 'Hop up on the stool and see if you can type your name. You need a good, strong tap to make an impression.'

Florence got down from the stool so her sister could climb up. Bobby pretended not to pay attention while she poured out the tea, knowing Reg would be embarrassed at being caught without his usual protective shield of feigned curmudgeonliness.

'I'd like to learn how to make a magazine,' Florence announced.

'Well, happen you can stay with us and learn some tricks of the trade,' Reg said, avoiding Bobby's eye. 'If you're quiet. Don't forget, we're working in here and work needs quiet. One little peep and it's back to baking bread with Mary in the kitchen.'

Florence nodded. 'We'll be quiet, won't we, Jess?'

'And when Uncle Charlie comes home, we can play Magazine Spy School,' Jessie said gleefully, thrilled at being able to expand their repertoire of make-believe games.

'So, will we be having a children's page next month?' Bobby asked nonchalantly as she took Reg his mug of tea.

'Aye, we might try it the once and see how it's taken. Not every month, mind.' He picked up the sheet of paper Florence had given him. 'Not a bad story, that, lass.'

Florence, who wasn't accustomed to the Yorkshire habit of understatement, looked rather hurt at what sounded like faint praise.

'I mean to say, it's a right good little story,' Reg said kindly. 'Best we've had, in my opinion. It can go in next month on the children's page. We'll make a proper writer of you one day, Florence.'

Florence looked thrilled. 'Do you mean it?'

'Course I do. Long as you keep working hard at it.'

'And when I'm grown up, could I work for the magazine like you and Bobby do?'

'I reckon so. Put us all out of a job in ten year, most like.'

And that was how the last sceptic at Moorside Farm was conquered. After that, there was no going back. In less than a fortnight, the Parry sisters felt as much a part of the place as if they'd been there all their lives.

Chapter 13

'Florrie, quick, hide!' Jessie screamed. 'He's coming, he's coming!'

Florence gave a little squeak and the two girls ducked down behind the barricade they'd constructed from the Athertons' old tin bath, a couple of chairs, a disused mangle and three cricket bats.

'Now zen, ver are zose pesky Eengleesh gels who gif me zo much trooble?' boomed a man's voice as the door swung open.

Charlie, a square boot-polish moustache painted under his nose and his hair parted at one side, goose-stepped out of the farmhouse. He peered around as if the barricade and its occupants were completely invisible to him. A little curly head belonging to Florence popped up, giggled at him in his disguise, squealed when he started to turn in her direction and popped down again to begin a furious whispering with her sister. Charlie started creeping slowly around the garden, peering into flowerbeds and looking behind the cucumbers growing in the vegetable patch, all the while pretending he couldn't see the barricade right in front of him.

'Did he say "trooble"?' Bobby whispered to Mary, who was watching the game with her as she pegged out the washing.

Mary laughed. 'And "Eeengleesh". He sounds more like Mussolini than Hitler.'

'I'm certain his accent was drifting towards Welsh the last time we played Barricades.'

Mary smiled at the little scene. 'It's good to see a young man who's not afraid to make a fool of himself for children's sakes. I do think it's a crying shame when fathers are too stuffy to let themselves join in the play of their little ones. That's how happy memories are made. I only wish I could persuade Reg to join the fun sometimes.'

Bobby frowned when she noticed a tear sliding down her friend's cheek.

'Are you all right, Mary?'

Mary laughed, putting down her basket of washing so she could wipe the tear away. 'Oh, I'm a daft old lady. It does me good to see them so happy and healthy, that's all. To hear them laugh. All these years knowing we'd never be able to have any more children, that there'd be no grandchildren playing here in our old age, and now... it almost feels like the good Lord has put everything back as it ought to have been. I only wish we could keep them.'

Bobby slipped her arm into her friend's as they watched the children play.

'*Achtung!*' Charlie exclaimed in mock surprise as a sponge sailed past his face from the direction of the barricade. '*Was ist das?* I am under attack, *schnell kartoffeln!*'

There was more furious whispering behind the tin bath, followed shortly by another sponge missile. Charlie tried to dodge, but this one hit him square in the middle. He hammed appropriately, staggering backwards and clutching his chest.

'Reichstag geschenk! I am hit! Ver are zose naughty Engländerin?'

'That's one point to us, Jess!' Florence exclaimed gleefully. 'If he don't catch us before three, we win.'

'Bobby, we need more grenades!' Jessie called.

Bobby laughed. 'Excuse me, Mary. I'm needed for the war effort.'

She picked up a basket containing more sponges and flew over, arms outstretched and humming in her best impression of a Lancaster bomber, to deliver them to the two brave soldiers behind the barricade.

'That was a good shot, Florrie,' she whispered, ducking down with the girls. 'He's getting closer though.'

'We'll get him,' Florence said determinedly. 'Bobby, you throw one. You can get them further than what we can.'

'I think it might be against the rules for grown-ups to help.' She grinned at Charlie over the tin bath. 'But all right. Prepare yourself, Adolf.'

She picked up a sponge and lobbed it at Charlie's head. It just missed, glancing off his ear. Only full hits were allowed according to the rules he'd made up when he had invented the game for them, so it didn't earn the girls a point.

'Ach! Now ze Russians haf joined ze var! Zis iss not fair!' Charlie turned in the direction of the barricade and his eyes narrowed. 'Aha! So zer ist mein enemy.'

'He's seen us!' Jessie squealed. 'Quick, Florrie! We have to grenade him now before he catches us.'

The air was filled with squeaks and giggles as a veritable hail of sponges were thrown in Charlie's direction.

'I am beaten!' he groaned, falling to the floor in the barrage. 'My var ist lost. Ze Engländerin haf defeated me.'

'Again, again!' two little voices demanded as they jumped to their feet. Bobby, laughing, got to her feet too and dusted herself down.

'Well I must say, I didn't expect to find you at war when I got here,' said an amused voice behind her. Bobby turned to see a woman in a Wren's uniform leaning on the garden gate grinning at her, a suitcase at her feet.

'Oh my goodness! Lil!' Bobby went to give her sister a hug over the gate. 'Where did you spring from? I thought you weren't arriving until this evening.'

'I got an earlier train. Your friend the coal man brought me down from the bus stop in exchange for a shilling. I heard the noise and gathered this must be where you were.'

'Bert's put his fee up to a shilling, has he? It wasn't so long ago it was eightpence. You can blame the rising cost of beer for the price hike.' Bobby tapped her sister's arm. 'You ought to have sent word you were going to be early. Charlie could have fetched you down in his trap and saved you getting coal dust all over your uniform.'

'But then I wouldn't have been able to surprise you, would I?'

The Parry girls were staring wide-eyed at this interesting and glamorous new person in the smart, if slightly sooty, navy-blue uniform. Bobby took Lilian's hand to guide her through the gate into the garden.

'Come and meet everyone.' Bobby nodded to the evacuees, who had crept closer to get a better look. 'These are our new additions, Florence and Jessica Parry, who'll be staying at Moorside until it's safe to go back to London – whenever that might be. Girls, this is my twin sister, Lilian.'

Lilian smiled. 'The Parry girls, eh? I heard all about you in Bobby's last letter.'

'What did she say about us?' Florence asked. 'Nice things?'

'She said you were as bright as buttons and very brave, and that you don't always do as you're told the first time. Does that sound fair?'

Jessie put her head to one side. 'That's mostly nice things, ain't it?'

'I suppose it is,' Lilian said, laughing.

'You don't look much like Bobby, Miss,' Florence observed. 'I thought twins had to look the same.'

'Sometimes they do, but not always,' Bobby said.

Jessie squinted at the two of them. 'I think they look lots like each other.'

'No they don't,' Florence said, rolling her eyes at the stupidity of younger sisters. 'Bobby don't wear her hair that way, or make up her face so pretty.'

'They still look the same. Their eyes and things do.'

Mary had approached and was waiting for her introduction.

'I'd certainly not have guessed you were twins,' she said, smiling. 'Or perhaps I would, given time. You look like you go together, for all the differences in your appearance.'

'Now you must be Mary,' Lilian said, holding out her hand. 'From Bobby's letters, I feel like I know you already.'

Mary ignored the hand and drew Lilian into a welcoming hug instead, not minding the soot on her uniform.

'Sorry my husband isn't here to meet you,' she said. 'I sent him into the village to see if he could pick up a little extra off the ration for our supper tonight, knowing we'd have a guest.'

'It's my fault. I should have let Bobby know I was going to be early. I liked the idea of popping up when she least expected it.'

Bobby smiled. 'My sister loves making an entrance, as you can see.'

Lilian glanced around. 'Is Dad not here, Bob?'

'No, he's out with his new friend,' Bobby told her. 'They go walking in the woods most days.'

'That's good. It's healthy for him to be out in the open.'

'Yes.' Something in Bobby's tone must have alerted her sister to the fact everything wasn't as it ought to be, however, and Lilian shot her a look of concern. Bobby shook her head slightly to let her know she'd explain when they were alone.

'We only play this game when your father isn't at home,' Mary said, in an undertone so the Parrys couldn't hear her. The girls were a little distance away now, picking up the sponge grenades with Charlie and putting them back in the basket. 'He doesn't approve of the girls laiking at war, which is understandable given his own experiences. He thinks it's making light of it, and Lord knows it's no joke. Still, I'm convinced it does them good. They've felt so powerless living in London with those evil bombs falling every night, and then there's their father away fighting. Making light of it helps them feel less afraid.'

Bobby nodded. 'Mary's right, it's more than just fun. In their childish way, it gives them a feeling of fighting back.'

'Yes, I can understand that. There's nothing worse than feeling powerless.' Lilian turned to smile at Charlie. 'So, it seems there's only one person I haven't been introduced to yet.'

Charlie had been hanging back with an uncharacteristic air of self-consciousness, waiting to be invited to join them. Bobby flushed as she beckoned him over.

'Um, this is Charlie, Reg's brother,' she informed Lilian. 'I told you about him.'

'You certainly did.' Lilian regarded her sister's suitor curiously. 'Your… friend.'

'Something of that nature.' Charlie looked awkward as he held out his hand, then instantly snatched it back and reached up to rub off the boot-polish moustache he'd momentarily forgotten he had. 'Er, I don't normally look this way. I was… we were… it's a pleasure to meet you at last, Miss Bancroft.'

'Call me Lilian, please,' she said as she shook his hand. She glanced at Bobby. 'After all, we're practically family.'

'Let me take you over to the cottage and show you where you'll be sleeping,' Bobby said hastily, taking Lilian by the shoulders to guide her away.

'What did you say that for?' she hissed as she led her sister to Cow House Cottage.

Lilian shrugged. 'I only meant we were family because I felt like I knew him from your letters, the same as all of them.'

'No you didn't. You gave me a *look*. Charlie noticed it too.'

Lilian smiled as Bobby unlocked the door to the cottage. 'Well, is there any need to be coy? I can read between the lines as well as the next twin sister, Bob. The two of you are engaged, aren't you?'

'We aren't.'

She blinked. 'Oh. In that case, maybe I can't read between the lines as well as the next twin sister.'

Bobby pushed Lilian unceremoniously into the cottage and chucked her suitcase on the bed in her own room, which they were to share for the two days of her sister's visit.

'Is that why he seemed so awkward?' Lilian asked. 'He proposed and you turned him down? I thought you were keen on him.'

'He was awkward because he's been worrying about making a good impression on his sweetheart's sister and you caught him covered in grass stains with a moustache drawn on his upper lip in boot polish.'

'I said I was sorry for not telling you I'd be early, didn't I?' She cast an unimpressed glance around the austere parlour of Cow House Cottage. 'So, have you turned the man down or not? You can't tell me he hasn't asked, the way he was looking at you. I'm not blind.'

'I've turned him down many times, but he's not taken no for an answer yet, thank God.'

'Thank God? So you do want to marry him?'

'I honestly don't know. I mean, I do, but... there's a lot to consider.' Bobby choked on a little sob. 'Oh my gosh, Lil, I'm so glad you've come.'

'Sweetheart, what's wrong?' Lilian folded her into a hug.

'It's just... been so hard. I've needed to talk to you so badly. You don't know how much I've missed having you here.'

'Come into your room and we'll sit on the bed and swap secrets, just as we used to do at home,' Lilian said gently. 'If you show me where everything is then I'll even make us cocoa like Mam used to. Then you can tell me everything that's wrong.'

Chapter 14

Lilian warmed some milk for their cocoa, and when they had a steaming mug each, the sisters went to perch on Bobby's bed. Bobby rested her head on her sister's shoulder as she nursed her drink, imagining they were back in the bedroom they'd shared for so much of their lives in the little house on Southampton Street. She missed the ugly olive carpet and the smell of Lilian's perfumes and creams, but if she squinted, she could pretend they were back at home again and everything was as it had been.

'Now tell me what's wrong,' Lilian said soothingly. 'Is it Dad?'

'No, not Dad – at least, that isn't the main thing, although I am a little worried about him. It's Charlie.'

Lilian bent her head to look into Bobby's face. 'I'm not sure I understand what the issue is. Did he withdraw his proposal after you refused him, is that it? And now you've realised what a big mistake you've made?'

'No. He gave me an ultimatum – he wants a final answer before he leaves for RAF training.' Bobby followed the spiral of steam rising from her cocoa mug with her eyes, watching as it disappeared. 'There's only a fortnight left to make up my mind. It's been tearing me up, Lil.'

'Why? You like him, don't you?'

'I like him.' She choked on another sob. 'I love him.'

Lilian blinked. 'Love! That's a strong word. I could tell you were fond of him, but you never mentioned love in your letters.'

'It's not the kind of thing it feels easy to write down. That's why I begged you to come. I wanted to talk to you in person.'

'Well, here I am,' Lilian said, smiling. 'I'm glad I came, if only to feel a little smug. I told you that you'd fall for a pair of handsome eyes one of these days, didn't I?'

'All right, don't gloat,' Bobby said, smiling too in spite of her tears.

'So if you love him, what's your worry? He loves you, you love him, he's asked you to be his wife. Just say yes and you can both live happily ever after.'

'It isn't that simple. If I say yes then it changes everything for me, Lil.'

'I know, in the best of ways.'

'No. No, it doesn't. I'd have Charlie, yes, but everything I'd planned to do in my life would be pushed aside, because a wife must be a wife first and foremost. And when bairns come along, there really can't be any going back.'

She let out another little sob and Lilian passed her a clean handkerchief from the pocket of her Wren uniform.

'You can't seriously mean you'd consider turning down marriage with the man you're in love with so you can work on that tinpot little magazine the rest of your life,' she said in shocked disbelief.

Bobby had known Lilian would find it hard to understand her reasons for turning Charlie down. Her sister never had been able to grasp why Bobby was so determined to make it as a reporter, and even less so on a tiny country publication like *The Tyke*. For Lil, as for most of their girlfriends, love and romance conquered all – they had Hollywood to thank for those rose-coloured spectacles, Bobby reflected bitterly. The idea a woman would choose her job over the opportunity to have a home and family was utterly alien to them, and try as she might, Bobby never could get them to understand – not even her own twin sister.

'It isn't a tinpot little magazine,' she said. 'I mean it is, but it's my tinpot little magazine. It's important, Lil. You should see some of the letters we get, from soldiers serving overseas and people who've lost their homes in the bombings.'

'What sort of letters?'

'Letters that... I don't quite know how to explain it, but *The Tyke* represents home to them in a world that feels like it's gone mad. Nothing's certain any more, the most awful things are happening, and nobody knows what tomorrow will bring. The magazine reminds them there was a gentler, better world before all this – one that belonged to them. It gives them hope there can be again.' She lifted her head. 'I'm a part of bringing them that hope. Yes, it matters to me, just like your work with the Wrens matters to you. We might not be winning the war here but we're giving people something to keep on fighting for, in our small way.'

Lilian looked unconvinced as she picked up her cocoa from the bedside cabinet. 'All very noble, I'm sure. But you'll be an old maid long after the war ends, Bobby. Your precious magazine isn't going to keep you warm at night, is it?'

'Being an old maid might not be so bad, if I've got the means to keep myself.'

'You can't mean that. You must want a family.'

'Must I? Do I have to want something because you want it, or because most women do, or because I'm expected to?'

'I watched you playing with those little girls today, Bobby.'

Bobby sighed. 'You know, the two weeks since they came have been quite wonderful. We've really felt like a family here. Even Reg has loved having them. In a way, it's made the situation with Charlie so much harder.'

'How?'

'I've always liked Charlie's company. He's fun and he makes me laugh. He stops me taking life and myself too seriously. Last month, we were sitting on the bridge together under the moonlight and I thought that if we could just be that way forever… perhaps if we married and it remained just the two of us, I could have Charlie and my career too.'

'If you didn't have children?'

Bobby nodded. 'Charlie didn't seem like the sort of man who was cut out to be a father. He's too fond of fun and freedom. Of a life without responsibilities.'

'Could *you* live with that though?'

She laughed bleakly. 'The way the world is now, the last thing I'd want to do would be to bring a child into it. Who knows what future there might be for them? A life under the Nazis… it doesn't bear thinking about. I thought that if Charlie and I were careful about things…'

'So it would be a celibate marriage?' Lilian said, laughing. 'If he agreed to that he'd be one man in a million.'

'I wouldn't expect that. There are other ways, aren't there?'

Lilian lowered her voice. 'French letters, you mean?'

'I suppose so, yes.'

'Those things don't always work, Bobby. Trust me, I know enough girls who've found that out the hard way.'

'Well, it's a moot point now anyhow. The Parrys coming made me realise that in spite of what I'd assumed, Charlie's a natural father. They love him to pieces, and I've never seen him so happy as when he's messing about in the garden with them like he was when you arrived today. I couldn't deprive him of the chance to have little ones of his own, even if he did agree to it.'

'Do you think he would have agreed?'

'I don't know. Perhaps.' She swallowed another sob. 'He loves me very much, Lil. I don't know why when I'm such a cross, fractious thing with him sometimes, but he does.'

'Aww, Bob.' Lilian put her arm around her sister and gave her a squeeze.

'And then there's the other worry,' Bobby said. 'That I'll choose Charlie, give up on everything I've been working for here, and then... then I'll lose him. Be left to raise a child alone without him.'

'Not everyone who goes to war doesn't come back. Most will, I hope.'

'It's the air force, Lil. I wish it was the army, or even the navy. I wish he'd volunteered for ground crew instead of flying fighters. It's terrifying to think of him up there in the skies with the Luftwaffe trying to shoot him down.'

'How long is the training? Six months?'

'I think so, but they can cut it short if they're desperate for pilots.'

'Well, maybe the war will be over before he's ever asked to fly a mission. You never know.'

Bobby was only half-listening. 'Even those men who do come home aren't always the same,' she said quietly. 'Some lose limbs, like Reg. Some lose their minds, or part of them. Like—'

'Like Dad,' Lilian finished for her. 'What do you think you'll do, Bobby?'

'I don't know. I really don't know.' She looked up. 'What would you do if you were me?'

'I'd run over to that farmhouse right away and say yes,' her sister answered without hesitation.

'Not what would you do if you were you. What would you do if you were me?'

Lilian paused before answering.

'All right,' she said. 'Here's my very sensible and Bobby-like answer. I'd speak to that grumpy editor of yours and tell him that his brother had made me a proposal.'

'He knows that already. He asked me outright if Charlie had proposed and I said he had.'

'Well, then he won't be surprised if you ask him to be honest with you about what your future with the magazine might look like if you were a married woman and a mother. I know it's unusual, but he might be willing to keep you on. He's fond of you, isn't he?'

'In his way, but he's very traditional. He still hasn't fully adjusted to the fact I'm not a man. I know he's embarrassed whenever he sends me out to talk to people.'

'At least then you'd know. Mary might speak up for you too, mightn't she? Does she have a lot of influence with her husband?'

'More than anyone. They're a very attached couple. Still, Reg can be stubborn, especially when it comes to his notions about how things ought to be done.' Bobby sighed. 'Not to mention that he'd be disappointed in me.'

'For getting married?'

'Yes. Even more so for marrying Charlie. He values me as a sensible, hard-working sort, and I promised him when he took me on that I had no thoughts of marriage. Whereas he thinks his brother's a work-shy thrill-seeker – not entirely unfairly, although he has some nobler qualities that Reg rarely acknowledges.'

'It's still the best plan I can come up with.' Lilian tilted her sister's head up to look into her eyes. 'Or you could take my original advice and say yes now, then just take what comes. All the bylines in the world will be small comfort to you when you're seventy with no grandchildren to cheer you in your old age.'

Bobby shook her head. 'Why does society make it impossible for me to have both? It isn't fair.'

'Life rarely is,' Lilian said, buffing a thumbnail unconcernedly. The injustice of a woman's lot never troubled her in the way it did her twin.

'So, what about you?' Bobby said, wiping her eyes and sitting up. 'Are you still on the hunt for a husband?'

'I'm not exactly hunting. Let's say I'm keeping my eyes open,' Lilian said with a smile.

'Why the sudden interest in matrimony? I thought you'd be having far too much fun with all those handsome naval officers down in Greenwich to settle on just one.'

She shrugged. 'I suppose I've just reached an age where I'm ready, you know? It isn't only you I'm concerned about having a lonely old age.'

Bobby smiled. 'Well, if we both end up old maids then we can always keep each other company. I'm not too worried about you though.'

Lilian was holding up her left hand and turning it this way and that, as if trying to imagine a ring on the third finger. 'We'll be twenty-four next month. That's an age to make a girl stop and think. Did I tell you Bess Slater is engaged to be married now?'

Bobby blinked. 'Bess is engaged?'

Of all their old schoolmates, Bess was the one Bobby would have bet on as being the last to marry, if she married at all. She was one of those girls who was said to have a 'lovely personality' by the kinder folk of her acquaintance but had been described in less pleasant terms by cruel girls at school, who had taunted her for her plump figure, poor skin, thick spectacles and shy, awkward manners. Still, while the bullies might have seen a lovely personality as being an unattractive girl's runner-up prize, Bess had genuinely been a very sweet, warm person. Bobby was surprised to hear of her old schoolfellow's engagement, but she was pleased that at least one man had been open-minded enough to discover Bess's hidden charms.

'That's wonderful news,' she said. 'I'll write Monday and congratulate her. Who's the lucky man?'

'A soldier she met in the ATS.' Lilian smiled. 'They're both sergeants, which made for an interesting announcement in the paper. "Sgt Slater and Sgt Jenkins would like to announce their engagement."'

'So she's the last one.'

Lilian nodded soberly. 'Last apart from us. When Bess Slater steps up to the altar, that's every one of the girls in our class married. I never thought it would be me and you bringing up the rear.'

'No,' Bobby said. 'At least, I never thought it would be you.'

'I'd better pull my socks up then, hadn't I? It would be nice to find myself walking down the aisle before twenty-five comes around.'

Bobby laughed. 'That's if you can find someone Dad approves of enough to give you away to.'

'That'll be half the battle, certainly,' Lilian said with a smile. 'I don't think I've had a boyfriend yet that he's taken to. He disapproves of your Charlie too, I presume?'

'I usually get a stern word if Dad finds out we've been spending time alone together, but he does it more because he feels it's his responsibility to keep me on the straight and narrow than because he disapproves, I think. Actually, he and Charlie rather get along.'

Lilian laughed. 'That's a rarity. Another thing to add to the yes column in your "reasons to marry Charlie Atherton" list.'

Bobby shook her head. 'I still can't believe you're thinking about marriage. I thought you'd at least want to enjoy your time with the navy. Aren't the officers very handsome?'

Lilian smiled dryly. 'The problem is they know they are. A girl has to watch herself. It's hard to monitor weather conditions when a pair of wandering hands might appear at any minute.'

'You like the work though?'

'It can be challenging, but I enjoy feeling as though I'm doing something. It's like Mary said when she was talking about those two evacuees of hers playing at war. There's nothing worse than feeling powerless when something as big as this is happening.' She lowered her voice. 'A few of us were sent to London last week for a training day. Bobby, you wouldn't believe it. It's like another world.'

Bobby felt a sense of foreboding. 'Do you have to tell me?'

'Would you rather not know?'

'No, I… I ought to know, I suppose. What was it like?'

'Devastating,' Lilian said with feeling. 'You remember how Lingard's looked after the bombing last year?'

Bobby remembered. All that had been left of the once-busy Bradford department store after a night of heavy bombing had been a bare, blown-out shell.

'How could I forget?' she said quietly.

'Imagine that but for streets and streets. Shells that were once homes and shops; whole areas flattened to rubble. The bombs fall nearly every day, Bobby – the Germans never let up. Siren after siren. The people still living there are made of stern stuff, but some of them look like ghosts. I would too if I had to live like that.'

Bobby thought back to the day the two evacuees had arrived. That haunted, shell-shocked look in their eyes.

'Do you think it will ever end?' she asked, snuggling closer to her sister.

'I don't know. I wish I could say differently but I really don't know.' Lilian lowered her voice further. 'I'd never dare say it aloud to the other girls down in Greenwich but I know we're all thinking it. We're losing the war.'

'We can't be. The newsreels…'

'The newsreels and the papers tell us what they think we need to hear. Dressing up the little victories to hide the big defeats, just like they did with Dunkirk.' She scoffed. '"Keeping up morale", for all the good that's going to do us if Hitler comes out on top. I've heard there's almost nothing left of Coventry. I'm scared to death, Bob. Scared of what will happen if we lose.'

'It makes things like boys and romance seem sort of insignificant, doesn't it?'

Lilian shook her head. 'Not to me. When you're living in fear for your life and you don't know what tomorrow might bring, romance seems like the most important thing there is. After all, this might be my last chance to enjoy it. Eat, drink and be merry, Bobby, for tomorrow we die.'

'I do worry about Charlie.' A plane flew overhead, and Bobby glanced up fearfully as the drone grew louder and then faded above them. 'I'd promise to marry him or whatever he liked if it would only keep him here and safe,' she added vehemently.

'Would it keep him here? He didn't have to join up.'

'I don't think anything would keep him here now. He feels very strongly about doing his duty. Even if it did, in his heart, he'd resent me for stopping him from going. He'd say he didn't, but I know he would.' She sighed and swung her feet off the bed. 'I ought to make a tea for Dad for when he gets home. Mary's invited us over for supper, but he's always famished when he gets in from his walks with Pete.'

Lilian stood up too. 'Let me make it. I've missed cooking for the old man.'

Bobby smiled. 'He'd like that. Come on, I'll show you where things are.'

They went to the kitchen. As Lilian hunted in the pantry for ingredients, Bobby lit the stove.

'What's he like, this new friend of Dad's?' Lilian asked while she rummaged among the tins and jars.

'Pete's… good for him in a lot of ways. Gets him out of the house, stops him feeling useless or neglected. His nightmares are less frequent now, and he's swapped his whisky for beer. He's more in the present than I've known him since we lost Mam. Honestly, moving him out here with me might be the best thing I ever did for him.'

'Yet you still sound worried,' Lilian said, poking her head out of the pantry to give her sister a stern look. 'What aren't you telling me, Bobby?'

She sighed. 'This friend… he's kind of the local spiv. He's a poacher mostly, but I've heard talk about other schemes. Forged petrol coupons, black market cigarettes… the sort of thing the government are coming down hard on these days.'

'Dad isn't involved with that, is he?'

'He never goes out with Pete but that he doesn't come home with a rabbit or a fish – even a pheasant sometimes. It's good for him in one sense because he's contributing to the household, which helps him feel he's still the head of it, but I worry about him getting into trouble. It's private land, Lil.'

'I doubt he'd get into too much trouble for the odd rabbit, would he? I should think that's common enough out here in the countryside. Surely just a rap on the knuckles and a fine of a few quid.'

'Perhaps. I do worry Pete might drag him into something worse though.'

'You worry too much, Bobby,' Lilian said firmly. 'If a bit of poaching is helping him with his demons, I'd say that's far preferable to letting him sink into the state he was in back in the winter when we nearly lost him. You've got enough to think about without worrying over things that may never happen.'

'Yes, that's what Mary says.' Bobby forced a smile. 'Well, let's cheer up. I've been dying to have you visit for ages. I can't wait to show Silverdale to you. I know you'll fall in love with the place, just like I did.'

Lilian, however, looked far from convinced. 'Hmm. It looked dull enough to send me to sleep when I walked through it earlier.'

'You won't have seen the best parts yet. It's a beautiful place, and it's got a character all of its own.'

'If you say so,' Lilian said doubtfully. 'So what have you got planned for us tomorrow?'

Bobby pulled a face. 'I'm so sorry. I ought to have told you before you came, but I have to work.'

'On a Sunday?'

She nodded. 'There's a farming show in Kiltford that's the biggest event of the year round here. I had to practically beg Reg on my hands and knees to let me cover it. I can't let him down.'

Lilian shrugged. 'Well, perhaps I could come too.'

Bobby laughed. 'You? It'll be muddy and smelly. Full of noisy animals.'

'It doesn't exactly sound like a fun time,' she agreed, wrinkling her nose. 'Still, I'm only here for two days and I want to spend as much time with my little sister as possible. I'm sure I can bear it for a few hours. Besides, I'd rather like to see you at work.'

Chapter 15

Robert came home that afternoon with a brace of grouse, which Mary cleaned and baked into a pie for their supper. Lilian expressed herself impressed and pleased at the change in both his mood and appearance since the move to the countryside, which gratified Bobby. She did believe that moving him out here with her had been the right thing to do. Her father's night terrors, bouts of heavy drinking and general mental state had improved greatly since. However, she felt a faint guilt about removing him from his old home in spite of that. The country air was good for him and he loved this place, but Robert Bancroft was still a Bradford man born and bred. He'd grown up among those sooty mill chimneys and crowded terraces. His few remaining relatives and the friends he'd made at the mill in which he'd worked since he was a boy of fourteen were all there, and although he rarely spoke of his hometown, Bobby knew there were times when he missed it enormously. She had felt even guiltier when he'd taken up with Pete Dixon and started spending his days trespassing on private property while he stripped the land of its game.

So she was pleased when Lilian told her how improved he appeared to be, with the hollowness gone from his cheeks and a healthy spark in his eye after a day in the open air. And after all, did it really matter if Topsy and other local landowners lost the odd bird or rabbit, now that her dad was happy and well for perhaps the first time since her mam died? If it helped him to feel less like a burden on his family, as he'd once told her he feared he was becoming?

That night the Athertons, Bancrofts and the two Parry girls enjoyed a delicious meal of grouse pie together, then they spent a contented evening at Moorside listening to the wireless and playing board games. Afterwards, Bobby's father slept like a baby with nothing stronger than cocoa inside him. That was surely worth a couple of pounds' fine if he ever should get caught.

–

The morning of Kiltford Show dawned bright, crisp and clear. Bobby awoke to an unaccustomed warmth in the air, and a depression on the other side of the bed where her sister had slept the night before. This was explained when she ventured into the kitchen and discovered that Lilian had lit the fire in there and was boiling the kettle for their morning pot of tea.

'I wondered when you were planning to show a leg,' Lilian said when her sister joined her. 'I've been up for an hour. Now I've got into the habit of military timekeeping I can't seem to get out of it, even on leave.'

'We ought to have you stay more often,' Bobby said with a yawn. 'I'm not used to waking up warm. Let me make the tea, though, Lil. You're the guest, you know.'

'I'm not a guest. I'm a daughter of the house. I ought to earn my keep.' She pointed an imperious finger. 'Sit, young Bobby.'

Smiling, Bobby dragged a seat from the kitchen table over to the fire.

'Is Dad still asleep?' she asked.

'No, he's up. He's gone to the outhouse.' Lilian filled the pot with hot water and left yesterday's tea leaves to brew as best they could now they were on their fourth service. 'I didn't want to start the breakfast without talking to you. Do you eat here, or do you pool rations with the Athertons?'

'On working days Mary likes us all to eat together, but on Sundays she and Reg go early to chapel so I usually make a round of toast each for Dad and me.'

'All right, I'll slice some bread and you can toast it on the fire while the tea brews.' She took out half a loaf and started slicing.

'Do you get good grub at your billet?' Bobby asked, reaching for the toasting fork propped by the fire.

'Better than we got as civilians. There's not much meat in it though. I suppose that's the same everywhere. That grouse pie last night was a real treat.'

'Mmm. Shame it was illegal grouse pie.'

Lilian put a finger to her lips as the door opened and their dad entered, looking rather comical in his dressing gown and boots. He stooped to take them off so he could swap them for his slippers, which Lilian had placed by the fire to warm for him.

'Morning, Dad,' Bobby said. 'Lilian's made us tea.'

'Aye, she's a good lass.' He went to pat Lilian's shoulder before he took a seat on the other side of the fire to start putting on his slippers. 'It's nice to have you home again, love.'

Lilian smiled and bent over his chair to kiss the top of his head. Their father wasn't a man who found it easy to be demonstrative, so when he expressed affection for them in word or deed, they knew that he meant it.

'So are you coming around to the Silverdale way of life, Lil?' Bobby asked. 'Perhaps we might see more of you now you know what's waiting for you here.'

'I'll always be a townie but it was rather nice last night, sitting by the fire playing cribbage with the children,' Lilian said, passing her a slice of bread to toast. 'Reminded me of when the boys were small. Mind you, I'd be bored out of my wits if every day was like that. What do you do for fun around here?'

Her dad shrugged. 'Go to t' pub. Play dominoes.'

'I mean, what do the young people do?' She glanced at Bobby. 'I hope Charlie takes you somewhere more exciting than the village pub for a game of dominoes when you go out together.'

Bobby speared the slice of bread her sister had handed her and held it to the blaze in the hearth. 'There's the Nuvic, the cinema over in Settle. Charlie bought a little pony and trap so we don't need to rely on the bus to get us there.'

'Huh,' their dad muttered. 'You're at the place a bit too often for my liking. That lad keeps you out far too late at night, Bobby. Folk'll talk.'

Bobby had heard this a thousand times and ignored him. 'There's a dance hall there too, and a concert hall,' she told Lilian. 'And sometimes there'll be a hop here or in one of the other villages, in a barn usually. They're a lot of fun.'

Lilian curled her lip. 'A barn dance? How very rural. Doesn't it stink?'

'You get used to how things smell out here. Actually, I quite like the smell now.'

'Really? You like the stench of cow dung when your young man takes you dancing?'

'Maybe "like" was the wrong word, but I feel sort of safe when I smell it. Like I'm where I ought to be.' She smiled awkwardly. 'That sounds mad to you, I suppose.'

'Utterly potty.' Lilian sniffed the air. 'This place smells bad enough. You don't share it with a horse, do you?'

'It's probably a hundred years since Cow House Cottage was used for animals, but there does seem to be a lingering smell,' Bobby said. 'Some of that's from Charlie's surgery though. Every day after he's been working in there, the whole place smells of chemicals and wet dog. But you—'

'You get used to it. Yes, I know.'

Bobby smiled at her father. 'We'll soon talk her round, won't we, Dad?'

'We'll give it our best try,' he said jovially. 'Coming to t' show, are you, our Lil?'

She pulled a face. 'Yes, I said I'd keep Bobby company. Apparently a country reporter's work is never done, even on the day of rest. Just what I want to do with my precious leave: look at the back ends of sheep all day long.'

'You asked to come,' Bobby pointed out. 'Besides, it isn't only about the animals. It's the social event of the year out here. Everyone goes, from the villages miles around. You'll enjoy it, I promise.'

'I am quite interested to see you doing your job, although I bet it'll take me until next week to wash the smell off me.' She glanced at their father. 'Are you going as well, Dad?'

'Aye, meeting Pete up there for a few pints later,' he said. 'You two girls look after yourselves in that mob, all right? I hear them farmers can be a rough lot when they're full o' beer. If there's any trouble, come find me.'

'It's all right, we've got a chaperone,' Bobby said. 'Reg is coming too. He was worried about me going there alone.'

However, when Bobby and Lilian called at the farm-house for Reg to drive them over to Kiltford in his car, it was Mary who met them at the door.

'I'm sorry, girls,' she said, pulling an apologetic face. 'Reg can't go to the show with you after all. He turned his leg on the stairs this morning and it's giving him a lot of pain. I've put a mustard plaster on it and told him in no uncertain terms that he's going nowhere today but bed. Do you think you'll be all right making your own way there? It's only a two-mile walk.'

'Of course,' Bobby said. 'If we walk there then I can show Lilian some of the countryside on the way.'

'Charlie will be around to look after you once you arrive. He's on his way already with the bairns. They were very excited to ride there with him in the trap.'

'Our dad's going too. Tell Reg not to worry and look after his leg.'

'Just a moment.' Mary took a folded piece of paper from the pocket of her apron. 'He told me to give you this note. Instructions on what to do when you get there, I think.'

Bobby opened it and read the terse, Reg-like inform-ation scribbled in his handwriting.

> *Get prices fetched by championship beasts in sale ring and names of breeders. Minimum three quotes from winners. Reporters' tent if you need a rest.*

She smiled as she tucked it away. 'Thanks, Mary. Tell him it'll be attended to.'

They started walking up the rough track into the village. Lilian grimaced as she stepped in a present that had been left for them by a passing sheep.

'Why is everyone so concerned about us having a man to look after us at this thing?' she asked Bobby as she wiped her shoe on a patch of grass. 'Are farming shows really as debauched as all that?'

'I've never been to one before, but I'm sure it's just Reg making a fuss. He's always worrying I'm going to get into trouble if he sends me out on a story.' She put on Reg's gruff tones and thick Dales accent. '"This is man's country, lass. No place for a slip of a city girl. Hrumph, hrumph, hrumph."'

Lilian laughed. 'Well, then today's your chance to prove to him you've got what it takes to do a man's job, isn't it?'

'Obviously I'm sorry his leg's bad but it does work out rather well for me,' Bobby said. 'If I can stand my ground long enough to get him a good report, he's bound to be impressed.'

They started crossing the old packhorse bridge. Lilian stopped halfway to look out over the beck. The banks were covered in glorious wild flowers as far as the eye could see: daisies, buttercups, clover and forget-me-nots creating a riot of colour. She breathed their fragrance deeply.

'I can't deny it's a bonny place,' she said. 'Still, I'm sure I'd be bored to death here in a week. Only one cinema and you have to ride there in a trap! How do you live, Bobby?'

Bobby shrugged. 'I'm not like you. Dancing and films are fun now and again, but I rather like a quiet life. Mind you, there's a lot more going on behind the closed doors of Silverdale than you might guess from looking.'

'Such as?' Lilian asked as they started walking again.

'Oh, there are all sorts of delicious scandals to keep our housewives gossiping,' Bobby said, smiling. 'Mabs Jessop was seen walking out with Timmy Doyle last week, although everyone knows that he and Laura Bailey were as good as engaged. And then there was the incident of the prize tup Laura's father hired last autumn, when their neighbour Tot Hector was caught smuggling it out to service his yows on the sly. The families have been at war ever since, and Mrs Hector positively snubbed Mrs Bailey at the WI bazaar in the church hall last week.'

Lilian laughed. 'I only understood about half of those words, Bobby.'

'You soon learn to speak sheep farmer when you live here. Anyhow, there's been plenty going on since the warmer weather came, what with the evacuees arriving and all the walkers and campers coming from the towns for their holidays. Not to mention the airmen's hospital that's going to be opening soon at Sumner House. There's an RAF training school ten miles away too – we sometimes see the cadets in their uniforms at the dance hall in Settle. I suppose it doesn't seem much to you with your exciting war work and all, but things aren't so sleepy here as you might have imagined.'

'So it seems,' Lilian said, but Bobby sensed she was just trying to be polite. Lil had made her mind up that the countryside was sleepy and dull, and nothing her sister could say was going to convince her otherwise. Bobby tried not to feel too disappointed at her twin's lack of enthusiasm for her new home as she pointed out the main path through the village.

'We'll go this way,' she said. 'Then I can give you a tour of Silverdale itself.'

They wandered through the village, Bobby pointing out the church and the chapel, where people were spilling out after the morning services; the Golden Hart; the village green; the wishing well where she'd first caught sight of Charlie. If she was hoping to see her sister go into sudden raptures about the place, however, then Bobby was destined to be again disappointed. Lilian looked interested in a detached way to see the place that was her father and sister's new home, but for all that she admitted it was a pretty, charming little village, she didn't seem particularly excited about it. And yet Bobby had seen her practically swoon over a sweet little hat she coveted, or the latest silver-screen romance being reported in the fan magazines she liked to read. Only the peak of Great Bowside in the distance sparked a little interest when Bobby pointed it out.

'I've never seen a hill so big,' Lilian breathed, her awed gaze drifting to the summit.

'Technically it's a mountain, not a hill. Impressive, isn't it?'

'Very.'

'The source of our beck is all the way up there,' Bobby told her eagerly, pleased to have found something that could impress her. 'After heavy rain, it comes thundering down like a waterfall – we can even hear it at Cow House Cottage, although luckily we're far enough away not to have to worry about flooding. It's one of my favourite places to walk.'

Lilian stared at her. 'You've climbed an actual *mountain*?'

Bobby laughed. 'Is it so hard to believe? I've really developed a taste for exploring the fells. There's a tiredness and hunger that comes from a day out walking, breathing the mountain air... I don't quite know how to describe it but there's nothing like it. The meal you have when you come back down tastes like the best, most satisfying meal you've ever eaten, even if it's nothing but bread and cheese, and though your body's a mass of aches and pains afterwards, the sleep you have that night is the most restful you'll ever experience.'

'I wouldn't like to climb the thing but it's very nice to look at,' Lilian said as her gaze rose again to the peak. 'Have you really been all the way to the top?'

'No,' Bobby admitted. 'I've only been as far as the little shepherd's hut two-thirds of the way up. But Charlie's promised to take me right to the summit now the days are long enough – I mean, before he goes off to training. He says there's nothing like the view from the top, especially at sunset.'

'That would be a romantic place for a proposal,' Lilian said with a dreamy sigh. She glanced at Bobby. 'Or to accept one.'

'Please, let's not talk about that.' Bobby gave her arm a squeeze. 'Today I just want to enjoy spending time with my sister, with no worrying about boys and all the trouble they bring. We can talk about it at bedtime.'

'Did Reg say there'd be other reporters at the show?'

'There must be, since there's a special tent for us. The local newspapers usually carry a report on the bigger farming shows. This isn't one of the really big ones, but it is one of the few that are still going ahead. Most have been postponed for the duration.'

'Is Don coming to write it up for the *Courier*?'

Bobby shook her head. 'He'd have said in his last letter if he expected to be in the area. I suppose he'll send the cub, since it's a Sunday. Freddie, I think the new boy's name is – they seem to finish nearly as soon as they start these days, with the call-up. It's a shame. I'd have liked to have seen Don.'

'Did he send any interesting news from home?'

'Not especially. He suspects from the general improvement in his dress and grooming that Tony's on the hunt for a new girl, worse luck for some poor lass. The lad who was the cub when I was a typist there, Jem, was shipped off overseas last month, and his dozy replacement Len left to take up a better-paid apprenticeship somewhere else. As for the *Courier*, it sounds as though it's going from strength to strength. I knew it would with Don at the helm.'

Lilian smiled. 'You're proud of him.'

'I am,' Bobby said fondly. 'He started to feel almost like an older brother when I was working there, and he was a sort of mentor to me as a reporter too. Don's a good newspaperman. I'm glad to see him doing so well for himself.'

'You don't regret leaving the paper? It could have led to big things for you if you'd stayed. He might have made you deputy editor one day.'

'Yes, he hinted at that.' Bobby's gaze drifted again to the flank of Great Bowside, looking lush and green in the youthful morning sunlight. Her mouth twitched with a smile. 'But… no. I miss the boys at the *Courier*, but I don't regret leaving. This was always where I needed to be.'

Chapter 16

It was a pleasant walk through verdant woodland to Kilt-ford Show, which took place across several farmer's fields in the shadow of a huge limestone crag. Bobby couldn't enjoy the walk as much as usual, however. They'd barely gone half a mile when her sister started complaining about pain in her feet.

'I told you to wear sturdy shoes,' Bobby said as they stopped for the third time in five minutes so Lilian could rub her ankle.

'These are the sturdiest shoes I own. Funnily enough, there isn't much need for hiking boots in Greenwich. How far is it now?'

'Another mile. I'll find you somewhere to sit down when we get there. Hopefully this reporters' tent will be open to relatives of reporters too.'

'We don't really have to walk all the way back after-wards, do we?'

'Lil, it's two miles.' Bobby registered her twin's horri-fied expression and sighed. 'I'll see if there's anyone local who might be able to give you a lift, all right? Charlie might be willing to make two trips in the trap.'

Bobby got a surprise when they reached the show-ground. Of course she'd been told the show was the biggest event of the year here, but everything was done on such a small scale out in the countryside compared to at home that she hadn't been quite prepared for the size of it. Dozens of tents and marquees filled the fields under the crag, with fenced-off areas for the beasts, and the air was ripe with the scent of farm animals. One field was filled with parked cars, carts, wagons and charabancs, and Bobby noticed Charlie's little trap amongst them. Boxer was grazing nearby with a few other horses. There had been a surge in the popularity of horse-drawn transport in rural areas since the petrol ration was introduced.

'Reg said the show had been cut back this year because of the war so Lord knows how big it usually is,' she whispered to Lilian. 'It looks like Bowling Tide fair.'

'And it smells like a neglected privy,' Lilian murmured back. 'I wish I'd remembered to bring a clothes peg for my nose.'

'Oh, stop complaining.' Bobby scanned the fields, which were thronged with people. 'I don't know how we're going to find Charlie and the girls in all of this.'

The answer to that, as usual, was to look for chaos and work your way to the centre of it. The two women hadn't ventured very far into the showground when they heard an almighty row near an enclosure containing a group of sheep. One of the animals, a huge thug of a tup who looked more bulldog than ovine, was standing in the centre of the enclosure looking annoyed while a tiny collie pup ran around his feet, yapping noisily. Meanwhile, a farmer was causing serious damage to his Sunday best as he tried to catch the little dog, getting splattered with churned-up mud. A child had climbed on to the enclosure fence and was waving a rope lead at the dog while shouting, 'Come, Ace! Ace, you naughty puppy, come here!'

'That's Jessie,' Bobby said in disbelief. 'What on earth is going on?'

'Come on.' Lilian started pushing her way through the crowd that had gathered to watch the spectacle, Bobby following.

Eventually they managed to fight their way to the enclosure fence. Florence was there, looking rather frightened.

'Florrie, what's happening?' Bobby asked. 'Where's Uncle Charlie? And whose dog is that?'

'He's ours,' Florence said in an anguished tone. 'Mine and Jessie's. And he won't come back to us, Bobby. The farmer says if we don't catch him quick then he'll get one of the stewards to fetch a policeman.'

'Yours? How can he be yours?'

They were interrupted by Charlie, who appeared at that moment from somewhere in the crowd.

'I got dog biscuits,' he panted, patting his pockets. 'These ought to get him.' He took one out, stuck his arm under the fence and waved it tantalisingly at the little dog. 'Here, Ace! You'd like this, wouldn't you? Come on, boy, come and get it.'

The dog stopped when he caught a whiff of the food. He looked torn for a moment, unsure whether he'd rather have a dog biscuit or an enclosure full of sheep to play with, but eventually, he deigned to edge closer to Charlie's hand so he could give the biscuit a sniff. As soon as he was within grabbing distance, Charlie seized Ace's scruff and pulled the dog towards him under the fence.

'Quick, Jessie,' he said. 'Put his lead on him before he dashes off again.'

Jessie clambered down from her perch on the fence to slip the rope lead around Ace's neck, then cuddled him to her.

'You are naughty, Ace,' she chastised him, wagging a finger. 'If you're to be my dog, you mustn't run off like that and you must always come back when I call you.'

'He's my dog too,' Florence said. 'May I give him his biscuit please, Uncle Charlie? He did come back to you to get it.'

'All right, here you are,' Charlie said, handing her the biscuit. He frowned sternly at the dog. 'Not that he deserves it, the little... blighter.'

The crowd had dispersed now the entertainment was over, seeking new thrills elsewhere on the field. A very muddy, very angry farmer left the sheep enclosure and strode over to the little group.

'By rights I ought to call t' coppers on thee, young man,' he told Charlie, jabbing a finger towards him. 'That's an offence, that is. Out-of-control dogs worrying my sheep.'

'He's just keen, that's all,' Charlie said in conciliatory tones. 'He's only a little sheepdog. There's a lot he still needs to learn.'

'Tha's lucky he weren't shot,' said the farmer, folding his arms across his chest. 'What did tha think tha were playing at, letting a young 'un like that off his lead wi' all these beasts about?'

'We didn't let him off, Mister Farmer,' Jessie said. 'He slipped out of his lead. We'll be careful from now on, promise.'

'Huh. "From now on" don't help my distressed tup, does it, little miss? Judges are on their way round and t' poor owd lad shaking like a leaf thanks to this here pup o' thine.'

The beefy tup didn't look particularly distressed to Bobby. As he pawed the ground, he resembled a bull more than a sheep – one getting ready to charge. However, Charlie nodded in sympathy with the farmer.

'You're right. We should have kept better watch over the pup,' he said soothingly. 'You have my unreserved apology, and I'll be happy to compensate you if necessary.'

It was hard to resist Charlie when he made the effort to charm. The farmer's scowl softened slightly, and he glanced at the two girls making a fuss over their puppy.

'Aye, well. Happen there'll be no need for that,' he said. 'Londoners, are they?'

Charlie nodded. 'Evacuees. They were bombed out of their home.'

'I'm right sorry to hear it.' He turned to the girls. 'Take care o' that there whelp of thine, eh? Instincts are all right, any road. It's just discipline he needs. He's t' makings of a little champion if ye two put time into his training.'

Jessie beamed at him. 'We will.'

'You'll let me buy you a drink later to say sorry on Ace's behalf, I hope,' Charlie said, putting out his hand to the farmer. The man looked at it for a moment before giving it a shake.

'Aye, I'll be around t' beer tent after auction's done. Mind how you go, young man.'

'And lo, peace was restored,' Charlie said when the farmer had gone, smiling at Bobby and Lilian. 'I ought to have been a politician, don't you think, ladies?'

'Lil, can you stay with the girls a moment?' Bobby said. 'I need a private word with Charlie.'

Lilian nodded, and Bobby put a hand on Charlie's elbow to guide him out of earshot of the children.

'Where on earth did the dog come from, Charlie?' she asked in a low voice.

'Ah. Yes. I thought you might ask about that.' He looked guilty. 'Well, when we arrived, the girls wanted to watch the sheepdog trials on the show field.'

'And they enjoyed them so much that they kidnapped one?'

'Not quite,' he said. 'They loved watching, Bobby. Some of the dogs had been trained and handled by kids. You remember Maid, that bitch of young Tess Armitage's we tended to on New Year's Eve? Tess was here with her. She took a red rosette. Grand little sheepdog she's turned out to be.'

'I don't understand what that has to do with our evacuees.'

'Jessie was really taken with how Maid and Tess worked together. She said how much she wished she had a dog of her own to train.' He rubbed his neck. 'And, um… after the trials, there was a sale of dogs and puppies…'

Bobby shook her head slowly. 'Charlie, you didn't. You didn't buy the girls a dog.'

'I got a good price on him. Mrs Armitage gave me ten bob off to pay me back for seeing to Maid. He's a half-brother of hers from the same sire.'

'It isn't what you paid for him that's the problem, Charlie.' She lowered her voice. 'Reg is going to blow up. Two children, two adult dogs and an energetic sheepdog puppy in the house – what do you think he's going to say when you get home?'

'Something about magazine production needing peace and quiet, I imagine,' Charlie said with a grimace. 'Closely

147

followed by a homily on what an irresponsible, wayward loafer his little brother is. How could I say no though? Those little girls have lost everything, Bobby. Their home's gone, their mother's gone, and I know they're worried to death about their father away fighting. They've got attached to me over the past few weeks and I'll have to leave them soon too. Having a dog to train will give them something to focus on instead of worrying about the war.'

'And when they go back to London?'

'We can worry about that when it happens. It might be a long time until it's safe again.'

Bobby sighed. 'Charlie Atherton, sometimes I think you might be the biggest, sweetest idiot ever to grace the face of the planet.'

'Thank you. I think.'

'And I suppose you want me to help you talk Reg round, don't you?'

'Would you?' he asked hopefully.

'No. This is your mess and I'm not going to dig you out of it.' She gave him a quick kiss. 'But if it's any consolation, I'm sure he'll let the dog stay once he's told you off. He's as soft-hearted as you are when it comes to the bairns, as much as he tries to hide it.'

'I hope you're right.'

Bobby glanced at Lilian, who was crouching down with the girls while they tried to teach Ace his first trick. 'I'd better say goodbye to them and go find the reporters' tent. I am supposed to be working today, not trying to get you out of your latest scrape.'

'All right, I think you've lectured me enough for now,' he said with a smile. 'How's the other Bancroft twin finding country life?'

Bobby laughed. 'It smells bad and it's painful on the feet, she tells me. It's a shame, but I can see I'm never going to be able to make a convert of her. Twins we may be, but Lil's a townie right to the heart.'

'I'm surprised she wanted to come with you today. A farming show doesn't exactly sound like her idea of a good time.'

'Well, she's only here until tomorrow. It could be months until we see each other again, so naturally she wants to spend as much time together as possible.'

'You must miss her.'

'More than I knew,' Bobby said with a sigh. 'Come on.'

They went back to join the little group.

'Bobby, watch,' Florence said gleefully. 'See what Ace learned to do.'

Bobby smiled. 'Go on. I'm watching.'

Florence held out her hand to the little dog. 'Paw,' she commanded. After staring a moment, Ace lifted his foot and placed it on her palm.

'He's a corker, ain't he?' Jessie said proudly. 'It was me said we ought to name him Ace, after Ace the Wonder Dog. We're going to teach him ever so many things, Bobby.'

'Uncle Charlie says that for every new trick Ace has learned when he comes home on leave, he'll tip us each sixpence,' Florence added.

Bobby smiled at him. 'Did he indeed? Uncle Charlie is feeling generous today.'

'At the rate this little one's learning, I can see I'm going to have to be prepared for imminent poverty,' Charlie said with a laugh. 'Say goodbye to Bobby and her sister, girls. We'll take Ace to watch the horses in the gymkhana, shall we? Make sure his lead is nice and tight this time.'

'Ooh! Horses! Yes, please,' Jessie said, jumping to her feet. 'And then may we see the cows?'

'If you like.'

After spending a lifetime in a world of brick and concrete, the menagerie of farm animals was as good as a zoo to the two Londoners.

'Try not to buy them a pony, won't you, Charlie?' Bobby said.

'Very funny. We'll see you both later.'

Charlie and the girls headed to the field where the gymkhana was taking place. Meanwhile, Bobby enquired of a steward where they might find the reporters' tent. He looked rather bemused – people often did when they were confronted with the novel idea of someone who was both a reporter and a woman – but he pointed out a marquee and they made a beeline for it.

'I can't believe your Charlie bought those two little girls a puppy,' Lilian said as they walked, simpering rather. 'I hope that when I fall in love, it's with a man who does things like that.'

Bobby shook her head. 'It was a ridiculous thing to do. His brother's going to throw a fit when they go home with a dog.'

'Oh, come on. Don't pretend you didn't think it was sweet.'

'Just because I think it's sweet doesn't mean I think it's a good idea.' She sighed. 'That's just Charlie all over. He'll do anything to put a smile on someone's face, but he so rarely remembers that actions have consequences. Then when consequences inevitably happen, he looks around him helplessly like a schoolboy who needs his mother to get him out of trouble. Well, this time I'm not getting involved. It's high time he grew up and learned to fix his own messes.'

'Aren't you being rather hard on him?'

Bobby relented slightly. 'All right, perhaps I am. It was a kind thing to do, and the girls looked so happy. It will be good for them – they're going to feel quite bereft after Charlie goes. Still, as much as I might love him for it, he shouldn't have done it on the spur of the moment like that. It'll be Reg and Mary who have to care for the little thing when he leaves for the RAF in a fortnight.' They'd reached the reporters' tent now. 'Hopefully there'll be a bench or two inside. You can sit and rest your feet while I venture out into the fray.'

Chapter 17

The tent was quite crowded, with a strong odour of tobacco and beer. It was barely midday, but some of the men in there already seemed quite well-oiled – and of course those present were nearly all men. Some stood talking, a few sat around smoking on forms at the side of the tent and a handful waited in line to use the field telephone that had been set up for those with imminent deadlines to phone their stories through to colleagues in the office. Bobby noticed only one other woman present, whom she recognised: a reporter from the *Leeds Mercury* she had met while she was covering the assizes during her brief time as a reporter for the *Courier*. The woman, Miss Shadwick, rolled her eyes in an expression of female solidarity before pushing through the crowd to join them.

'Miss Bancroft. Hello,' she said, giving her hand a vigorous shake. 'I didn't realise you'd be here. I was sure I'd already spotted someone from the *Courier*.'

'I'm not with the *Courier* any more,' Bobby told her. 'I'm reporting for *The Tyke*.'

'Is that a newspaper? I've not heard of it.'

'No, it's a rural magazine. For Yorkshire and the Dales. Our offices are nearby.'

'Oh,' Miss Shadwick said, with the faintest trace of pity in her tone. 'I'm sorry, I had no idea.'

'Um, this is my sister, Lilian,' Bobby said, anxious to change the subject. 'Lil, this is Miss Barbara Shadwick from the *Mercury*.'

Lilian nodded a greeting. 'I hope it's all right for me to be in here when I'm not a reporter. Bobby said no one would mind.'

Miss Shadwick laughed. 'I don't suppose any of the men will be in a condition to object. If I remember last year, most of them were staggering drunk by two o'clock. My bottom was black and blue by the time I got home, and when it's not the reporters' hands wandering, it's the farmers'. Honestly, some of these country shows are like the last days of Pompeii. I don't know why the beer tent has to be open from dawn until dusk.'

'My editor warned me they could be a bit raucous,' Bobby said. 'I thought he must be exaggerating.'

'Don't you believe it, dear.' Miss Shadwick nodded farewell to them. 'I ought to go and speak to a few of those exhibiting before they're too drunk to be coherent. Good luck in the jungle, ladies.'

When Miss Shadwick had left, Bobby looked around her, unsure what to do. Interested male eyes had already swivelled to observe her and Lilian. One middle-aged gentleman of the press with a rumpled necktie and some-what lecherous smile – and she used the term 'gentleman' very loosely – even looked like he was in danger of approaching to speak to them. Bobby fished her notebook and pencil from her bag, along with her press card, and held them in front of her like a shield.

'How are your feet?' she asked Lilian, edging closer to her sister in the sea of slightly swaying male bodies they now found themselves in the midst of.

'Killing me. There's a blister on one big toe and I think I might have turned my ankle rather badly. It's starting to swell up.'

'Well, there's somewhere to sit, at least.' Bobby gestured to the forms at the edges of the marquee. 'I really don't want to leave you here alone though, even though I ought to get out there and speak to people.'

'I'm not particularly keen on the idea myself,' Lilian said, looking warily at the gangs of men sending curious looks in their direction. 'Still, I don't think I can walk any further, Bobby. I need to take the weight off my ankle before it swells any more.'

'Ladies,' a friendly voice behind them said. 'A pleasure to see you both here.'

Bobby turned around, scowling as she prepared to rebuff whichever over-familiar reporter had had the nerve to approach them, but she relaxed when she saw who it was.

'Tony,' she said, beaming at her old colleague from the *Courier*. 'You know, I've never been so pleased to see you.'

He took the cigarette from his mouth and grinned at them. 'Looks like it's my lucky day. Not one but two Miss Bancrofts for me to squire around.'

'I don't need any of your squiring, thank you,' Bobby told him. 'My young man's here somewhere if I need an escort.'

'Caught yourself a man at last, did you? What is he, a farmer?'

'Never you mind. Anyhow, I'm here for work, not pleasure.' She raised her eyebrows. 'You know, like you're supposed to be?'

He shrugged. 'I've done my work. Finished ages ago, if you must know.'

'You can't have. The show only started an hour and a half ago.'

'So? All Don really wants is a list of who was here. No one cares about these things except the farmers who're at them. All you need to do is put their names in the paper so they all buy a copy, add a couple of sentences about shorthorns or longwools or whatever the breeds are called, and you can spend the rest of the afternoon in the beer tent. Why do you think I volunteered to traipse all the way out here on a Sunday? Time and a half and a full day's pay for half an hour's work.'

'I see you're still as lazy as ever,' she said with a dry smile.

He blew a column of blue smoke from his cigarette. 'I prefer to think of myself as efficient.'

She sniffed the air. 'What on earth are you smoking, Tony?'

He took out the pungent cigarette and looked at it. 'Some Egyptian brand. All I could get. There's not a Capstan to be seen in the shops with this damn fag shortage. Still, you get used to them after a bit.'

'Didn't Don say you were to get names and quotes from all the prizewinning breeders in the sale ring?' she asked, thinking of her note from Reg.

'He said. Thing is, the *Courier*'s not out while Thursday, is it? I can copy the winning breeders' names from one of the dailies. That lass from the *Mercury* will have them all typed out for me in tomorrow's edition.'

Bobby shook her head, half irritated with Tony on Don's behalf and half impressed at the sheer commitment of the man when it came to shirking work. 'You know, Tony, if you put nearly as much effort into your writing as you do into trying to avoid work, you'd be editor of *The Times* by now.'

'Too good for 'em, love.'

Bobby rolled her eyes at Lilian. 'You remember Tony Scott, of course.'

'He hasn't changed a bit,' she said, smiling at Tony.

Tony flashed her what he probably believed to be a charming smile in return before turning his attention back to Bobby.

'I hope you're not going to be telling tales about my little arsenal of tricks to Don, Bob,' he said, his Egyptian cigarette wobbling at the corner of his mouth while he spoke. 'You don't need to be editor's pet any more now he's not paying you.' He glanced at Lilian. 'You know, Lil, it was me that gave your sister her start in journalism.'

'You mean you let me write your pieces for you while you took your girl to the pictures on the newspaper's time,' Bobby said, laughing.

'Got you where you are today, didn't it?'

'I like to think my skill as a writer got me where I am today, but you can have a small share of the credit.'

'Well, are you going to tell tales on me to our mutual friend back in Bradford?'

'No, Tony. For old time's sake, I'll cover for you,' Bobby said with a resigned sigh. 'After all, why change the habit of a lifetime?'

He grinned. 'You're a trump, Bobby. I've always said so.'

Bobby glanced around the tent. Tony wasn't an ideal chaperone for young women, especially in his cups – he wasn't drunk yet but he wasn't exactly sober either, and she knew he had a soft spot for Lilian. Then again, he was an improvement on the other men in the tent:

more flirtatious than lascivious, plus he was an old friend. At least, Bobby corrected herself, he was sort of an old friend, insofar as she couldn't help liking the man despite his many flaws. Definitely the lesser of two evils – Lilian would be unlikely to be bothered by anyone else if she was seen in company with a man.

Lilian was looking quite pale now from the pain in her ankle, which Bobby could see had swollen significantly under her stockings. Her sister needed to rest, Bobby needed to work, and she was certain Lilian could handle a little flirting from the likes of Tony Scott.

'If you've really finished making notes, Tony, then could you do me a favour?' she asked.

He lit another of his smelly cigarettes. 'Depends what it is, doesn't it?'

'Something you'll be only too happy to help with, no doubt,' she observed dryly. 'Can you stay with our Lilian while I go out and speak to some people? She's hurt her ankle and needs to rest it, but I don't want to leave her here alone with this drunken rabble.'

'So you're going to leave me alone with this drunken rabble instead, are you?' Lilian said, laughing as she nodded towards Tony.

He grinned at her. 'Your lucky day, eh?'

'You don't mind, do you?' Bobby said to Lilian. 'I'll be as quick as I can, but I have to do a thorough job or Reg will never send me on another assignment like this again. I had enough trouble convincing him I could do it.'

'It's fine, Bobby. Tony's a friend, isn't he?' She smiled at him. 'I'm sure he'll take good care of me.'

'That's what worries me,' Bobby said, giving the man a censorious glance.

'I might even be persuaded to buy you a half of mild from the beer tent, Lil,' Tony said, taking her arm.

She laughed. 'Ever the charmer.'

'All right. Well, I'll leave you both then.' Bobby flicked to a new page in her notebook, then cast a last, worried look at her sister. 'You're sure you'll be OK though?'

'Oh, don't worry,' Tony said. 'I'll behave myself, Bobby. I'm not entirely addicted to hedonism, despite what Don thinks.'

'Hmm. Just make sure you're a gentleman, that's all.'

'Aren't I always?'

'No.' She turned to Lilian. 'I'll see you later. Keep out of trouble, the pair of you.'

Lilian rolled her eyes. 'Yes, Mother.'

Bobby watched Tony support her sister to a bench and sit down beside her, then left the tent with her notebook in hand.

Now she was left alone to do the job she'd been assigned to do, she wasn't quite sure where to start. There was another round of sheepdog trials just beginning: brace trials this time, where the dogs worked in pairs to round up their charges. The dogs' handlers looked rather focused though, and Bobby wasn't sure they'd welcome the distraction of a reporter on the hunt for quotes. Besides, Reg had specifically told her to get details of the livestock taking prizes in the sale ring. The ring was hard to miss, right in the centre of the largest field with a big crowd gathered around it.

She wandered among the tents and enclosures while she made her way there, scribbling down some of the breeds on display. Once upon a time, before her move to the country, Bobby had naively believed that a sheep was a sheep. However, it didn't take long when you lived among farmers to learn that there were a hundred different types and breeds. There were Herdwicks and Swaledales, Cheviots and Lonks. There were gimmers and shearlings, tups and yows. There were a hundred combinations of breeds, sexes and age categories. Bobby could easily fill her notebook with lists of sheep alone, and she hadn't even reached the dairy section where the cows were gathered yet.

The attitude of the journalist from the *Mercury* she'd spoken to earlier had had time to fester now. Bobby frowned at a lamb she was writing notes about as she recalled the way the woman's lip had curled when she'd mentioned the sort of publication she worked for now. Miss Shadwick thought Bobby had traded her job at the *Courier* for something lesser. Of course she did – all news-papermen sneered at other types of publication, especially those they thought of as 'rural'. Bobby knew her friend Don Sykes, editor of the *Courier*, felt the same. Although he supported her choice to leave her promising career with the paper and go back to work at *The Tyke*, he'd never understand it. Nor did Tony, even though he was hardly what you'd call committed to his own career in journalism.

That was different though. Don and Tony were her friends. And was Barbara Shadwick really so much better off where she was? The *Mercury* didn't even give her a named byline. Her columns for them were always headed 'from our woman reporter', because God forbid the readers were tricked into believing they were reading the work of a man and affording the writer some respect for their skill. She wasn't Barbara Shadwick at all as far as her career was concerned; she wasn't even 'our country correspondent' or some such respectable title; she was merely *the woman reporter.* At least when Bobby wrote for *The Tyke*, her pieces had her name at the top of them. Anyhow, it seemed to Bobby that it might be nice if the small number of woman reporters there were in this county could show each other a little support, especially given the attitudes they encountered from male colleagues.

It seemed like most of Silverdale was at the show, either showing their animals or among the crowds of merrymakers. All the men were in their Sunday best, watch chains polished to a high shine and glistening in the sun, while their wives and daughters wore their brightest, most cheerful summer frocks. Bobby greeted friends and neighbours as she passed, and they smiled benignly at her. A brass band played in one part of the ground and a team of Morris dancers performed in another.

Many people had brought the whole family along, some with three and even four generations. Bobby observed infants carried in arms and great-grandparents in their eighties as she walked across the ground. As well as the animals on show, there was a merry-go-round for the children, and one elderly groom was giving pony rides for a penny each. Farmers' wives sold home-grown vegetables, preserves and cakes. Mingled with the smell of the animals was the fragrance of tea and hot oatcakes for sale from the refreshment tent, and, of course, the mellow, hoppy scent of ale. It was hard to miss the beer tent, which was one of the busiest on the field as farmers headed there from the show ring to celebrate their sales.

Bobby was speeding up to pass it as quickly as possible, more willing to heed Reg's warnings about the bad behaviour of drunken farmers after her experiences in the reporters' tent, when she pulled up short. Pete Dixon was one of the men standing around outside the tent with a pint of beer in his hand, although there was no sign of her dad with him. The old man he was talking to was swaying slightly, but Pete didn't look drunk. As she watched, Bobby saw him surreptitiously slip a small piece of paper into the other man's hand, evidently in a way designed not to be noticed. When Pete drew his hand back again, there was a ten-shilling note in it. It was all rather cloak and dagger. After hesitating a moment, Bobby approached him.

'Afternoon, Pete,' she said.

He turned around, smiling warmly when he saw who it was. He didn't look like a man who'd been caught doing something he shouldn't, but then he rarely did – that was why he was so successful as a poacher. He could be caught red-handed by a landowner with a couple of hares over his shoulder and still swear his innocence like a choirboy. From the corner of her eye, Bobby noticed Barbara Shadwick not far away, her eyes occasionally flickering towards them as she scribbled something down in her notebook. When Miss Shadwick had finished what she was writing, she hurried away in the direction of the reporters' tent.

'Rob's lass, isn't it?' Pete said pleasantly. 'Young Bobby.'

The man Pete had been talking to regarded her suspiciously.

'Are thee that lass from t' paper?' he asked.

'That's right,' Bobby said.

'Hm.' Unconsciously, he put one hand over the pocket where she'd seen him hide the slip of paper he'd paid ten shillings for. 'Pete, I'm off to t' dogs. Sithee, lad.'

'Aye, ta-ra, Adam.'

The man shot Bobby another worried glance before he left.

'Is my dad not with you?' Bobby asked Pete.

He laughed. 'He's around t' place somewhere. Helping me build a country fit for heroes to live in.'

'How do you mean?'

'Oh, just a little joke between the two of us. You'll stay for a drink, I hope. I'm sure he'll find his way here before long.'

Bobby never knew what to make of Pete Dixon. His manners with her were pleasant, polite and always appropriate. He was probably about forty, rather personable, and by all accounts an attentive husband and father when he was within the bosom of his family – even if he did provide for said family through largely illegal means. He had a reputation in Silverdale as a rogue, yes, but also as a man who'd do anything for anybody, always the first to offer a favour to a neighbour if they needed one. And yet something in his eyes left Bobby unsure whether she ought to allow herself to like the man. His mouth might be all smiles and warmth, but his eyes were cool, intelligent and calculating, like a cat's. Bobby never quite trusted what might be going on behind them. This was why it worried her when she knew her dad was out with Pete.

'I'm afraid I can't,' she said, rather grateful to have an excuse not to hang around. 'I'm working today. Writing notes for a piece on the show.'

He glanced at her notebook. 'Oh aye, for that little paper of yourn. Your dad's right proud of you, you know.'

She perked up a little. 'Is he?'

Pete nodded, swallowing the last of his pint. 'Never stops telling me about this clever, hard-working daughter of his, and t' other lass an' all. In the Wrens, isn't she, your sister?'

'Yes, she is.'

'Good for her. Important work they do.'

'Could you tell my dad when he comes that our Lil's in the reporters' tent with a swollen ankle?' Bobby asked. 'I need to find somebody with a vehicle who could take her back to Silverdale later. I thought he might know of someone.'

'Me and my missus can take her back if you want. She'll have to ride in t' back of our wagon wi' three bairns and a dog, mind.'

Bobby smiled. 'I think she'll take anything rather than try to walk. Thanks, Pete.'

She was about to go when she hesitated.

'Um, I was just wondering, if you don't mind me asking… what was that you were selling before?' she asked.

He frowned. 'Selling?'

'Yes. I saw you give a piece of paper to that man, and then he gave you ten bob.' She smiled uncertainly. 'Sorry. It isn't really any of my business. I'm just nosy, that's all. Well, it's my job to be – not that I'm asking in any sort of professional capacity,' she added hastily, remembering the worried look on the other man's face when he'd run away from her.

Pete smiled and lowered his voice. 'All right, I reckon if your old man can keep a secret then you can too. I'm running a book on t' prizewinning beasts over in the show ring. I wouldn't be living up to my reputation if I didn't make a few bob out of today some way or other, now would I?'

'Oh.' Bobby felt relieved, although she wasn't sure why. 'No, I suppose not. Um, did my dad…'

'He put five bob on Paul West's Lonk tup,' Pete said. 'Do you fancy a flutter yoursen?'

'I'd better not while I'm on the magazine's time, but thanks anyhow.'

He smiled. 'Happen you thought I was selling military secrets over here, hey?'

She allowed herself to laugh, reassured that there was nothing more nefarious going on than a bit of illicit gambling. 'Yes, I'm sure there's ever such a lot of fifth column action going on around Silverdale.'

'Don't you worry, love. There might be plenty round here who think I'd sell my own mother for the right price, but even I draw t' line at selling my country. I'll let your dad know you were looking for him when he turns up.'

Chapter 18

When Bobby eventually trudged home after a long day spent meticulously noting down names and getting quotes, she found both her sister and her father back at Cow House Cottage. Lilian was sitting in the armchair with her foot elevated on a stool, listening to *Hi, Gang!* on the Forces Programme, while her dad read the paper. Bobby was pleased to see he was home early rather than joining the raucous celebrations that had spilled over into the pubs after the show.

'I'm glad you both got back all right,' she said. 'Did Pete bring you?'

'Not me. Tony persuaded the reporter from the *Shipley Gazette* he hitched a lift from Bradford with to help a damsel in distress,' Lilian said. 'Tony accompanied me back too. Supported me into the house and everything. I've been home for hours and my ankle feels a lot better for the rest. It was only twisted a little, I think, not sprained.'

'Tony discovered a store of chivalry at the bottom of his third pint, did he?' Bobby sank wearily into a chair. 'I hope he looked after you properly, otherwise I'll be writing him one of my famous sternly worded letters.'

'Actually, he was rather sweet to me,' she said, smiling. 'I mean, he's an incorrigible flirt, but I knew that of old.'

'You should've come to find me,' their dad said, folding up his paper. 'I don't like you girls hanging about wi' that young nowt Tony Scott. He had a bad reputation back in Bradford. I'd have got you home.'

'Tony's not so bad,' Lilian said. 'He stopped any of those drunken old men trying it on with me – actually defended my honour when one of them tried to get friendly while he was out fetching us both a drink. I'd have been a sitting duck for them with my ankle out of action.'

'Didn't Pete pass on my message, Dad?' Bobby said. 'I bumped into him outside the beer tent and asked him to let you know Lil was hurt and needed a lift.'

Their dad shrugged. 'Probably forgot. He's had other things on his mind today.'

Bobby smiled dryly. 'You mean the illegal book he was running on the prizewinners, I suppose.'

He glanced at her curiously. 'What do you know of it?'

'Oh, he was very frank when I caught him taking bets. Owned up to it like a man.' She caught his worried look. 'And yes, he did tell me you'd put a bet on too.'

'Happen you're going to lecture me about it now, are you? It's only gambling, Bobby. Bit o' fun, that's all.'

She sighed, leaning back and closing her eyes. 'No, I'm not a complete stick-in-the-mud. I know men will have their fun at these feast days and there are worse ways to enjoy yourself. I just worry you'll get into trouble, Dad. It is against the law, unlicensed gambling.'

'Betting on farm animals at a few bob a time? I doubt they'll clap us in irons for it.' He took a note from his pocket and held it out to her. 'Anyhow, my luck was in today. You can add this to t' housekeeping. Call it my wages.'

Bobby stared at it. 'Ten bob?'

'Aye, that's right – I won a quid on my little flutter today. There's ten for you from my winnings, five for Lil to treat her friends down south and I'll keep five back to stand Pete a pint or two tomorrow night for the tip he gave me on that tup.' He looked pleased with himself. 'Not bad for an afternoon's work, eh, girls?'

'No. I suppose not,' Bobby said, staring at the note in her hand. Ten shillings was certainly going to be a help on her low salary. And yet somehow, it worried her.

'You ought to be careful what you let this Pete Dixon drag you into, Dad,' Lilian said. 'Poaching the odd bird is one thing, but it sounds like he's running all sorts of fiddles.'

'Oh, Pete's a sound lad,' their dad said, picking up his paper again. 'He knows what he's about, and so do I. We aren't bairns, Lil.'

–

Bobby was too tired that night for much bedtime conversation with her sister. The visit ended far too soon, with Lilian leaving the next morning to head back to Greenwich. Bobby had hoped that her twin's presence might help her find the answers to what she now thought of as The Charlie Problem, but when her sister left again, she felt just as confused as ever.

Time ticked on, with Charlie's leaving date growing ever closer. Every night that Bobby wasn't on duty at the ARP hut they spent together – either playing with the two Parry girls outside the farmhouse in the warm, mellow evening sunlight, holding on tight to each other at the cinema in Settle, swinging each other around the dance hall or sitting with the rest of the family by the fire at Moorside. On Sundays, they would pack a picnic and head up into the fells for a walk, although Charlie still hadn't kept his promise to take her right to the summit of Great Bowside before he left.

The time they spent together in those last two weeks was some of the happiest of Bobby's life. They kept their pact not to mention either marriage or the war, and for a little while she could forget about Charlie leaving and the awful choice she had before her. It felt like they were just an ordinary, happy pair of young people in love, with no war and no adult cares to spoil their time together. Whenever a voice whispered in Bobby's ear that it couldn't last – that a choice had to be made one way or another, and soon – she squashed it down. Because why shouldn't she enjoy these last moments in her lover's company? Why shouldn't she savour his kisses and hold his body close when they danced, the way young sweethearts had done for centuries? This was her last chance. Whatever choice she made, Bobby knew that after this she never could be just a young woman in love again.

And then… there were only three days left.

'What's ailing thee, lass?' Reg said to her one day as they worked. Bobby had been typing up her report on the show for the next issue, but her mind had wandered and she found herself staring out of the window at the birds soaring overhead in a glowering steel-grey sky.

'Hmm?' She roused herself. 'Sorry, Reg. I was… daydreaming.'

'Don't pay you to daydream, do I?' He squinted at her. 'Sleeping all right, are you? You look tired.'

'I'm OK. I had a late shift in the shelter last night.'

'Well, look after yourself. Wrap up warm. You could catch your death sitting in that tin hut.' He smiled as the door edged open and a little black-and-white muzzle appeared. 'Heyup, here comes trouble.'

It was true that Mary and the girls were under strict instructions from Reg not to let Ace into the parlour while he and Bobby were working. It was also true that no amount of strict instructions could prevent the little puppy from sneaking in, since Reg rewarded him with a dog biscuit from his desk drawer whenever he appeared.

Ace approached Reg's desk, wagging his tail hopefully, and Reg picked him up to sit on his lap.

'Escaped again, have you, Mischief?' he said, letting the dog lick his cheek. 'Don't know how I was ever talked into letting you stay. That brother of mine's a menace. This place gets more like a home for waifs and strays every day.'

Ace blinked at him, and Reg, smiling, gave him the biscuit he'd been angling for.

There'd been a big improvement in Reg's mood since the evacuees had come, Bobby had noticed. He smiled now – sometimes as many as three or four times in a day. Occasionally he even forgot to pretend to be grumpy. And as angry as he'd been with Charlie when he'd brought Ace home from the show, one look at how the girls' faces shone while they played with the little dog had melted the man, just as Bobby had predicted it would.

She'd been waiting to find Reg in a good mood before she brought up the subject of Charlie and the answer she still owed him. She did so now.

'Reg?'

'Mmm?' Reg put Ace the Wonder Dog (Junior) down on the floor and he scampered off to find Barney or Winnie. The two aged wolfhounds were far too mature and sedate to want to play his puppy games, but nevertheless he lived in hope.

'Um, it isn't long now until Charlie leaves, is it?' Bobby said, tapping her pencil nervously against the desk.

'Aye, I know. And?'

'And, well, I told you he'd made me a proposal.'

He glanced at her. 'You're not trying to tell me the pair of you are planning to get wed soon, are you?'

'No. Perhaps. What I mean to say is, I don't know. I wanted to ask what you thought about it.'

'I've told you what I think. Happen as a wife you'd do the lad good. You're a steady, hard–working sort with a sensible head on your shoulders. Whether our Charlie would do you the same amount of good as a husband is what worries me.'

'I don't mean about whether we're right for each other.' She paused, looking at the ink that, no matter how hard she scrubbed, would stain the edges of her fingernails. 'I've… made up my mind about that.'

'Well if you've made up your mind then you've no need of my opinion, have you? Just tell me when you've decided whether you're leaving or not so I can dig up a new reporter from somewhere.'

'That was what I wanted to talk to you about.' She took a deep breath. 'Would I have to leave? If I said yes to Charlie, I mean.'

'You'd have to leave when you pair were hitched, naturally.'

'You say that like it's a fact. I could be married to Charlie and still do my job, couldn't I?'

He laughed. 'You what?'

'Well, couldn't I?' she persisted. 'No one expects Charlie to leave his job if he gets married.'

'Charlie don't have a house to keep.'

'I keep a house already, Reg. I keep house for me and Dad, and I have shifts most nights at the ARP shelter, but

I still manage to do my job every day. I don't see why it should be any different if I was married.'

'It's always different when women are married.'

'Why?'

He took up his stick so he could approach her desk.

'Look, lass, I'm not saying it's fair,' he said, adopting a gentler tone. 'It's the way of the world, that's all.'

'Why does the world have to be that way?' She felt a sob bubbling up in her throat and choked it back. Reg would only be embarrassed if she gave in to emotion.

'Because it can't work any other way, if we want to keep making new people and bringing them up to be good ones.' He sighed. 'You're a good writer, Bobby. I wouldn't want to see that go to waste. If you wanted to write bits for us as a freelance once you've a couple of bairns under your belt, I'd always be happy to consider them. But you can't think you can bring up a family and work for me too.'

'I could find a way. If you'd only compromise a little, I could make it work.'

He shook his head. 'You're deluding yourself, lass.'

'No I'm not,' Bobby murmured, although she wasn't quite sure she believed herself any more.

'You'll marry, then in a few months, you'd find a little one was on the way,' Reg said. 'That's how it happens, mostly. The next year it'd be the same again, and probably the year after that, until soon you've got a pack of bairns hanging off your skirts. You're wrong if you think I can pay you enough to hire a nursemaid for them.'

'We'll have Charlie's salary too.'

'Huh. Until you found his wage for the week had gone on a horse or into the till at the Hart,' he muttered. 'Do you think I'd send you out there getting stories when you're in the family way, Bobby? A woman reporter finds it hard enough to be taken seriously out here as it is, and you'd have your health and the health of the babby to consider. And what about after it's born? Do you think I'd watch my brother's bairns left to fend for themselves with some half-interested minder so you can play at newspapers here with me?'

'It wouldn't be that way. Lots of mothers doing war work leave their children with minders nowadays – they have to, when there aren't enough men left to fill vital jobs. My sister-in-law leaves her littlest with an elderly neighbour every day now so she can go out to work making parachutes.'

'But you aren't doing war work, are you?'

'That doesn't mean what I do isn't important. At least, it's important to me, just as it is to you.'

'It's a woman's lot, Bobby. Motherhood's both her punishment and her reward. Nowt to do but embrace it.' He gave her shoulder a sympathetic pat. 'I know it's not what you want to hear, lass, but it's the way it is – the way it's always been. And while everyone round here thinks there's nowt matters more to me than the mag, there's one thing that does: not seeing bairns of my own flesh and blood neglected because their mother would rather collect bylines than have a happy husband and children. Happen you might like to bear that in mind when you're deciding what answer to give our Charlie.'

He limped back to his desk, and Bobby knew there was no point saying anything else. That was the end of the conversation. Lilian's suggestion that she throw herself on Reg's mercy had failed, and the choice she'd always known in her heart that she'd be forced to make had been laid out plain in front of her. She could have her job, or she could have Charlie. She couldn't have both.

–

That evening, Bobby was on duty in the ARP shelter, wondering if it was time to make another round of the village. There was rarely anything for her to do there, but it at least helped her warm up. The cocoa in her Thermos flask had long since gone cold, yet she still nursed her tin cup in both hands, trying to suck some warmth from it. It was a wet, chilly evening for early summer – 'backendish', as Yorkshire folk called it – with thick fog in the air and a steady, driving drizzle.

The hut was a dark, damp, dismal little place: a temporary structure of corrugated metal, lit by a dimmed oil lamp. There was nothing inside but a single chair and a small table, on which was laid out the tools of the warden's trade: a little pamphlet titled *Basic Training in Air Raid Precautions*, a wooden rattle to be used in the event of a gas attack and a first aid kit. There was also an unused and neglected stretcher propped against the wall, mould starting to spread over the canvas. Bobby was sure it would have come in very handy during the air raid that was never going to happen. They were so far from the cities that even on a foggy night like tonight, a Luftwaffe pilot would have to be very lost and confused indeed to drop his load out here.

The wooden rattle always sent a chill down her spine when she looked at it. What a terrible thing a gas attack on civilians would be! It made her think of her father, who had lost comrades in a mustard gas attack at Ypres in the last war. He rarely spoke of it, and never without turning his colour. It was a painful, gruesome death, he said – worse than anything else he'd witnessed out there. And now little children skipped to school with their Mickey Mouse gas masks in boxes over their shoulders, too young and too innocent to understand that human beings could ever be responsible for such atrocities.

She peered at her watch in the gloomy light of the dimmed oil lamp. It would be half past eight before she could hand over to the next warden on duty, and it was now barely a quarter to. Didn't the minutes drag!

Bobby jumped when someone knocked at the door. A moment later, Charlie's head appeared around it.

'Charlie,' she said, smiling. 'You know you're not supposed to be here when I'm on duty.'

'This is a special occasion. I've got something exciting to show you.'

'Well, be quick. I have to go make my rounds.'

'Here, come outside and see. It's still light.'

'All right, for a moment then.'

She followed him outside into the drizzle. To say it was 'still light' was rather stretching the truth. Yes, it was daylight – in the long days of double summertime, it could sometimes feel as though the sun never went down – but in the thick fog, driving drizzle and heavy cloud cover, it might as well have been night. Still, Bobby could see better outside than in the dull light of the hut's oil lamp. Charlie started unbuttoning his overcoat.

'Well, what do you think?' he said when he'd removed it, putting on the forage cap he'd been carrying under his arm. 'Aircraftman Atherton at your service. Am I handsome or aren't I?'

'You are both handsome and modest,' she said as she ran her eyes over the brand-new RAF uniform. 'When did you get it?'

'Today. The greatcoat's going to be waiting for me when I get to my digs. Oh, and look what else I got.'

He took a pipe from his pocket and put it in his mouth, striking a pose.

Bobby laughed. 'You look like J.B. Priestley.'

'I needed to complete the costume, didn't I? All those flyers smoke pipes. I haven't quite got the hang of it yet, but it'll come to me.' He took it out of his mouth again to grin at her. 'So, how about a kiss for the brave fighter pilot from his best girl?'

She glanced around. 'Just one. I am on duty.'

He took her in his arms to kiss her. Afterwards she stayed there for a moment, breathing him in. The lingering pipe tobacco and the new uniform meant he smelled different from the Charlie Atherton she knew. This Charlie smelled like a man going to war.

'You are very handsome,' she murmured, touching her finger to the eagle badge on his shoulder. 'I just wish the uniform didn't mean… what it has to mean.'

'None of that gloomy talk. Not tonight. Nothing can upset me tonight.' He took a note from his pocket. 'Look at this. All for us, to be spent on nothing but pleasure.'

'Oh my goodness, a fiver?' she said, staring at it. 'Where did you get it?'

'Pete Dixon gave me a tip on a horse. I like to see it as a sign that my luck's changing.'

This reminded Bobby of her conversation with Reg earlier, when he'd warned her that she wouldn't be able to rely on Charlie's salary once they were married. She often wondered what Charlie would be like as a husband.

His love of a good time, his often impulsive behaviour – buying Ace for the children being a case in point – were some of the reasons she loved him, but they worried the more sensible part of her brain.

'What's wrong, Bobby?' Charlie said when he felt her shiver, holding her back so he could see her face.

'Oh, nothing. Just remembering something your brother said to me. I'll tell you about it another time.'

'We're fast running out of other times. Only three more days.'

'I know.'

'So, are you going to let me take you out on the town after you finish your shift? I don't have many chances left, and since I'm flush with cash and looking – though I say so myself – devastatingly handsome in the new uniform, it seems only right that I should share my good fortune with the girl of my dreams.'

She smiled. 'And for just one night we'll shut out the world, forget the war and dance in each other's arms until dawn?'

'You read my mind, Bobby.'

'Is it safe driving Boxer in this fog?'

'We'll be all right. He knows his way to Settle by now, fog or not.'

'I think I could be persuaded, if you don't mind waiting while I change into something more suitable at home.'

'If you insist, although I'm rather partial to a girl in uniform myself.'

One of the planes from the airbase flew low overhead, making Bobby jump.

'Are you all right, Bobby?'

'Sorry,' she said, smiling awkwardly. 'I never can quite get used to them flying over. Every time I hear one, I worry for a moment it's one of theirs rather than one of ours.'

'Well, if it was then you'd finally have a chance to use your whistle,' Charlie said, giving the string around her neck a flick. He looked up to follow the sound of the bomber. 'They're very low. Bad visibility to be flying in. I'm surprised they haven't all been grounded until this fog clears.'

'I suppose once they reach the mountain they'll loop around and—'

But Bobby never got to finish her sentence. As she spoke there was a muffled crash from the direction of Great Bowside, as of distant thunder.

The next moment, the mountain was on fire.

Chapter 19

She stared at Charlie. 'Oh my God!'

'Christ, Bobby, they've gone down!'

Great Bowside was no more than a hazy silhouette in the fog but they could see the flames and plume of smoke emanating from just below the summit quite clearly. The plane had crashed at high speed into the mountainside.

'What do we do? Are they dead? Oh God, Charlie, what do we do?'

Charlie stared, horrified, at the blaze on the mountain. 'The base will know it's down if the men were in radio contact, but we ought to let them know exactly where the crash happened. Then when visibility improves, I suppose they'll send a plane to look for survivors and recover the bodies.' He closed his eyes. 'Those poor men, Bobby.'

'But it could be morning before the fog clears enough for it to be safe to fly. If they wait that long there might not *be* any survivors. Their radio must have been destroyed when they went down. Even if they're conscious, they won't be able to contact their base.'

'After a crash like that, it's highly unlikely there would be survivors anyhow. The plane must have hit at some speed to burst into flames that way.'

Bobby watched the pillar of smoke drifting up from the mountainside, stunned momentarily into inertia. Then she dashed into the hut for her wooden rattle. A second later she was running towards the houses that flanked the village green, shaking the rattle wildly and blowing her whistle, making as much noise as she possibly could. Charlie ran after her.

'What are you doing?'

'We have to get up there and see if anyone's still alive, Charlie. We at least have to *try*.'

People started to appear on their doorsteps, regarding her with puzzled expressions. The crash had sounded so much like distant thunder that on an inclement night no one would have thought anything of it unless they happened to have been looking in just the right place at the right time, as Bobby and Charlie had been. Already the fire on the mountain had died down to a dull, hazy flicker, barely noticeable through the fog unless someone knew where to look.

'What's to do?' old Louisa Clough demanded, taking her clay pipe from her mouth. 'There's noan an air raid, is there, Miss Bancroft? I didn't hear nowt.'

Stanley Henderson had also come to his door to see what all the fuss was about. 'It'll be that Arthur Egerton rolling home drunk wi' his bike light not dimmed again,' he said with a laugh. Mrs Egerton, in the house next door, glared at him.

Bobby raised her voice. 'Listen to me, everyone! We need as many fit, strong men as possible for a rescue party. There's been a terrible accident.'

Gil Capstick frowned. 'What's up, Miss?'

'One of the bombers from the base – it's gone down up on Bowside. We saw it, Charlie and I. The weather's too bad for their base to send a plane for them. If there are people alive up there, it's up to us to get them down.'

Stanley peered towards the mountain, squinting. 'Reckon she's right. Summat's on fire up yon, any road.'

'Right.' Gil snatched up his coat from a hook by the door and came out to join them. 'In that case, I'll make one in any rescue party.'

'A crash on t' mountain, eh?' Mrs Clough said slowly, puffing on her pipe. 'There'll be none on 'em walking home after that, lass. It's a death sentence.'

'But we have to try, don't we?' Bobby said. 'Could you all go back to bed and rest easy if there's even a small chance there could be survivors?'

'Nay, not I.' Stanley came out to join them. 'I might not be young but I'm lish yet. I'll make another.'

He was followed by Arthur Egerton from the house next door and some of the other men.

'It's five miles up and same back again,' Mrs Clough said. 'Three-hour climb up in t' dark, fog and rain, and then you've to get down wi' a body. Reckon tha can carry grown men five mile down a mountain at night-time, does tha, Arthur Egerton? That's if there're any on 'em left alive, which I doubt.'

'Better than I could go to sleep knowing I never went up to find out,' Arthur said stoutly.

'Well, happen I'd better fetch t' owd man if rest o' thee are fool enough to go up there,' Mrs Clough muttered, turning to seek out her husband Wilfred elsewhere in the house.

Bobby smiled gratefully at the men who'd volunteered.

'Thank you all,' she said. 'There's no time to waste. Gil, can you run to the ARP shelter and fetch the stretcher that's there? There's only one though. How many are in a bomber crew?'

'It was a Wellington that went down – Mark IC, most likely,' Charlie said. 'That means six men.'

'I've a couple o' strong poles and an old tarpaulin out back that I could stitch up into summat,' Mrs Egerton said. 'I'll need a good half an hour or so to make it strong enough to hold a man, mind.'

'I'll fetch thee some blankets,' her neighbour Mrs Henderson said. 'If there are injured men to come down, they'll need wrapping up warm.'

'That's good thinking. Thank you both,' Bobby said. 'Stan, Arthur: you and Gil can go on ahead with the stretcher from the hut, and the oil lamp, blankets and first aid kit. Two to bear the stretcher and one to take turns relieving them when they get tired. Three more can follow when we've another stretcher.'

'Oil lamp? What about blackout?' Stan said.

'Oh, bugger the blackout. There are lives at stake here. I'll take responsibility.'

'What if there's more survivors than we've got stretchers for?'

'I doubt that,' she said quietly. 'I'll try to get us more though. The worst injured are to come down first, all right?' She glanced around the villagers. 'Does anyone here have a telephone?'

'Fred Midgeley's on t' phone, but he's away selling his beasts in Skipton,' one of the women said. 'Tha'll have to go up to t' Black Bull.'

'Moorside's nearer.' She turned to Charlie. 'Charlie, I need you to take Arthur's bike – I'm sure he'll be happy to loan it – and ride home as quickly as possible to use Reg's phone.'

'All right. Who am I phoning?'

'The police, I suppose. Hopefully they'll be able to contact the airbase and let them know where the plane went down. When you've done that, phone Topsy Sumner-Walsh.'

'What can Topsy do?'

'I want you to find out from her what facilities there are at the big house now for injured men. They've been fitting it up as a hospital for the last six weeks so there'll be beds, at least, and hopefully bandages and stretchers. Tell her to pack up whatever she can find that might help – pain relief drugs, dressings, iodine, stretchers – and drive them here. And tell her she and Mrs Hobbes are to prepare to receive their first patients.'

'Right.'

'I reckon she can't just take that stuff from t' hospital, even if it's her house,' Arthur said. 'Belongs to t' Ministry, don't it?'

'It's an airmen's hospital and there might be injured airmen on top of that mountain,' Bobby said firmly. 'I'll take responsibility for that too, as duty warden, and if they want to throw me in jail for it, they can – better that than leave people to die. And Charlie, you'd better ring Dr Minchin over in Smeltham and let him know he's needed here.'

'He'll not make it up Bowside at his age, Bobby.'

'No, but he can wait here to treat any men we bring down. Get Reg here too with the Wolseley – that'll have to be the ambulance to get them to Sumner House. After that, I want you to raid your surgery for supplies. Pack up any drugs you think might help, put on your walking boots and meet me by Troy's field.'

'What are you going to do?'

She gazed at the summit of the mountain. The flames were gone but a plume of black smoke still rose into the sky, eventually dissolving into the fog. 'I'm going up there with you. I've got my boots and socks in the hut.'

He shook his head. 'Bobby, don't be ridiculous. You can't go up there in this fog. Let the men handle it.'

'It's my responsibility, Charlie. I'm the warden on duty. Besides, I'm the only person with first aid training who's young and fit enough to make it to the top.'

'I'm a vet. I've got all the medical knowledge that's needed. You don't know the route to the summit, it's a ten-mile walk, it's foggy and dark and… well, there might be things up there that'll upset you. In fact, I'm sure there will be. You wait here and manage the rescue parties, or go to Sumner House and help Topsy and Mrs Hobbes prepare the hospital.'

'Charlie, I'm going up. If I'm slowing you down then you can go on ahead but you're not going to talk me out of it.'

'I didn't think I'd be able to.' He smiled. 'You're some girl, Bobby Bancroft.'

'Never mind that. Just go.'

He gave her a peck on the cheek, mounted the bicycle Mrs Egerton had wheeled out for him and headed in the direction of Moorside.

Chapter 20

What followed was the longest night of Bobby's life, or at least it felt like it.

Charlie must have pedalled like he was attached to a motor getting to Moorside and back. It was less than three-quarters of an hour later when he met Bobby at the stile that led to Troy's field – the quickest route up on to the flank of Great Bowside – with a satchel over his shoulder and a cloth bag in his hand.

'Here,' he said breathlessly, handing her the cloth bag. 'Your dad fetched these from your room for me. Some slacks, a jumper and your big coat. I had a job to talk him out of trying to climb the mountain himself. Stubbornness obviously runs in the family.'

'You shouldn't have wasted time. I've got my boots.' Nevertheless, Bobby was grateful to have something sturdier than her denim ARP coat and thin stockings to wear while tackling the five-mile walk to the summit. Charlie, too, had changed, she noticed. His RAF uniform had been put away, and he was in warm clothes suited to the climb ahead of them.

'Turn around then,' she said. Charlie obediently looked the other way while she pulled the slacks on under her skirt and shuffled out of it. She stuffed it in the cloth bag along with her jacket and felt hat and hung it on the field gatepost to be picked up later. Then she pulled on the jumper he'd brought for her.

'What else did you bring?' she asked while she changed.

'Splints, bandages, antiseptic ointment and some aspirin. Minchin's going to pack up his Gladstone bag and wait for us in the village in case anything stronger is needed, and Topsy's raiding the hospital for supplies.' The fog had cleared very slightly, although the drizzle persisted, and he cast a worried look up at the mountain. 'Do you really think there can be anyone alive up there, Bobby?'

'Only one way to find out. If we hurry, we might be able to catch up with Gil, Arthur and Stanley. They've got no medical knowledge and no supplies other than what's in the ARP first aid kit. They could do with our help.'

Charlie had a bicycle lamp from which he'd removed the cover designed to keep it blackout-compliant. It still wasn't very bright, but it provided light enough. He held it aloft to illuminate their way as they began the ascent.

Far from slowing Charlie down as she'd feared, Bobby found herself naturally taking the lead, despite her companion knowing the fells far better than she did. Blinded by drizzle and fog, she slipped frequently in mud and stumbled over rocks, and once even managed to plant herself face-first in a peat bog, but still she didn't let herself lose pace. It felt like she was being driven by some hitherto unsuspected force within her. Someone had survived up there, she could feel it! But anyone who'd been in that crash must be badly injured, and the villagers were racing against the clock if they were to get him to medical aid in time.

'Steady on, Bob,' Charlie panted. 'If you're going to set that speed, you'd better take the bag with the bandages and things and go on ahead. I can't keep up with you.'

'No, we need you. You're the closest we've got to a doctor.' She slowed a little. 'Don't dawdle though. Lives might depend on it.'

'I've never seen you like this before,' he said, casting her a slightly awed look. 'You're a wonder, Bobby – a true natural leader. If the RAF knew what was good for them, they'd take you in place of me. I was useless tonight until you took command.'

She couldn't help smiling. 'Thanks. But don't slow down. You can tell me how wonderful I am when all this is over.'

'Every time I think I know you, you surprise me with something new. Have you always kept such a cool head in a crisis?'

'I've never had the chance to find out before.' She paused. 'Except... the day my mam died. I didn't keep such a cool head then.'

'You were a little girl, weren't you?'

'I was fourteen.' She laughed bleakly. 'Fourteen, and soon to be the woman of the house – me and Lil together. I completely lost control. Smashed the big mirror in my mam's room, raged and kicked like a spoiled child. And then... I pulled myself together. I had to, for my brothers. They were only bairns. Dad had gone into a world of his own, and Lil needed me. After that, I felt like I could deal with anything. Not that I was actually tested until today.'

He squeezed her arm. 'I was very proud of you, Bobby. All those men looking lost and helpless, and there's my girl ordering them about like she was born to lead. You could have been a general in another life. In fact, if you ever decide to stand as our first woman prime minister, you'll have my vote.'

She laughed. 'Lady Astor would never allow it. Save your breath now, Charlie. There's a long way to go.'

'When I promised to take you to the summit, this wasn't at all what I had in mind,' Charlie observed grimly, grasping at a patch of heather to steady himself as he slipped in mud. 'What do you think we'll find at the top?'

'I don't know.' She shuddered. 'Nothing that's going to give us very sweet dreams.'

–

It was nearly three hours before they reached the site where the plane had come down. Once they got near, they were able to follow the pungent, oily smell of smoke. The crash had been only just shy of the summit: if the plane had been flying a little higher, even by a few feet, it would have cleared the crest and the airmen might even now be safe back at their base. Bobby could feel a blister coming up on one red-raw heel, but she did her best to hide her limp from Charlie so he wouldn't try to persuade her to slow her pace as they drew nearer.

Only a wispy silver mist now remained of the fog, and the drizzle had started to ease. When they drew close enough, they were able to make out what was happening at the site. There were the remains of the once-mighty Wellington, one wing half-shattered and the fuselage smashed open like an egg. Smoke billowed from a huge crack in the centre. A little way away was a smaller hunk of metal and glass, another part of the plane that looked to have come free from the rest of the wreckage – the rear gunner's turret, perhaps? Bobby couldn't make out if there were any men – bodies – in the wreckage from this distance, but she could see one man leaning against what she'd assumed was the gunner's turret, and another stretched out flat at his feet. The man leaning against the turret appeared to be alive, at least. She could see his head swaying slightly. Just off to one side were the three men who'd come up from the village, their heads together as if in conference.

'What the hell are they doing standing around?' she whispered to Charlie. 'That man's hurt! Why aren't they giving first aid, or getting him on to the stretcher? He'll catch hypothermia if they don't at least put a blanket over him.'

'Perhaps they're not sure how to move him. From the angle of his legs, I'd say they're both broken.'

'Let's hurry then.'

They practically ran the rest of the way. The scene became clearer as they drew closer. Bobby noticed Charlie's eyes open wide when he caught sight of something, then his expression set. She felt his arm firm around her waist, guiding her in the other direction.

'Bobby, don't look,' he said in a grim voice.

'What?'

'Don't look at the fuselage. Just keep your eyes fixed on Gil, Stan and Norman.'

'But why—' She stopped when her gaze was inexorably drawn to the carcass of the Wellington, and she closed her eyes in horror. There was something black, shrivelled and smoking hanging out of the crack in the fuselage… something the same shape as a man…

Charlie squeezed her tightly around the waist. 'Keep being brave, old girl. We're here to save lives. It's too late for that one.'

Bobby nodded and forced her eyes open again, focusing her attention on the rescue party.

Gil gave a low whistle of relief as they approached. 'Now, here's our Miss Bancroft. She'll know what to do.'

'Huh,' Stanley Henderson muttered. 'Wouldn't have bothered getting up out of my chair if I'd known. Damned waste of time.'

'What is it?' Bobby asked. 'Why are you all standing around? Why don't you help those men?' Close up, she could see that both the airman leaning against the gun turret and the other one stretched at his feet were alive, although only the man sitting up was conscious. He was muttering to himself in a state of delirium, while his comrade-in-arms lay almost as if dead. However, his chest rose and fell in a shallow pant. The man lying prone had been bleeding heavily from the stomach, although it had now started to clot. One side of his face was burned so badly that it was hard for Bobby to look at it.

'Listen for thissen,' Arthur Egerton said bitterly. 'Listen to him muttering there. They're lucky we didn't finish 'em off when we got here.'

Bobby bent down by the man to listen to what he was murmuring in his delirium.

'*Boże ocal nas,*' he was whispering to himself, his eyes rolling to the whites as his head lolled from side to side. '*Boże, proszę. Jolka, Jolka!*'

She stared up at the rescue party in disbelief. 'German? They're *German* airmen?'

'Aye, they're German all right,' Stanley said, spitting the word. 'Them as killed young Billy Wilcox. Them as killed my brother Georgie in t' last lot. We ought to leave 'em here to rot.'

Gil shook his head. 'We can't do that, Stan. They're people, aren't they?'

'Thou're too young to remember t' trenches,' Arthur said. 'Murdering hun bastards is what they are. The enemy is what they are. Nowt more, nowt less.'

'Well, now they've crashed, they're prisoners of war,' Charlie said firmly, collecting his wits enough after the shock to join the debate. 'That means they have rights under the Geneva Convention. And I for one am not going to leave men on a mountainside to die, German or not.' He threw his bag of medical supplies over his shoulder and started to approach the wounded men.

'Oh no you don't, son.' Arthur grabbed one of his arms, with Stanley taking the other to hold him back.

'Get off me, can you? They're prisoners, for God's sake!'

'They're spies for t' Führer.' Stan nodded to the smoking fuselage. 'That's one of ours, that plane is. They're in RAF uniforms and flying one of our bombers. Spies aren't protected under no convention. They're to be executed.'

Charlie scoffed. 'But not by you, Stan Henderson.'

The two men were both farmers, burly and strong, but Charlie was used to wrestling meaty animals in his work and he had some muscle too. He made another bid for freedom and succeeded in shaking the older men off.

'If tha helps that Jerry bastard, folk'll know of it,' Arthur warned him in a low voice. 'Does tha want 'em saying tha's a traitor, eh, Charlie?'

'Don't be absurd. No one's going to call me a traitor for saving a man's life. No one I give a damn about anyhow.'

Bobby, who was still crouching on the ground by the gunner's turret, turned around when she felt something touch her. The injured man had put his hand on her arm.

'Wait,' she said to Stanley and Arthur, who looked like they were about to make another attempt to keep Charlie restrained. 'This one's coming out of it, I think. He wants to tell me something.'

'Jolka,' the man whispered, pressing his fingers into her arm.

'You said that before. I'm sorry, I can't understand you.' She tried to remember any simple German that might allow her to communicate with the delirious man. 'Um. *Non sprechen Deutsche.*'

'Yolker. That's German for spy, that is,' Stanley announced knowledgeably. 'Remember it from army days. See, he's confessing.'

'Oh, do be quiet,' Bobby said impatiently. 'I can't hear what he's saying.'

'*Nie. Nie niemiecki,*' the man whispered. '*Polski. Polski.*'

'I can't understand, I'm sorry,' she said again.

Charlie cast a glance at his antagonists. 'Forgive me, gentlemen, but wouldn't your really top-notch German spies usually be able to speak English?'

'*Nie niemiecki. Polski,*' the man said again, looking at Charlie. With a great effort, since he looked like he was about to faint, he summoned a few more words. 'Polish. We… are… Polish.'

'Polish!' Charlie shot Norman and Stan a look of triumph. 'They're Free Polish airmen, you bloody fools. They're on our side. Now are you going to stand aside and let me do my job? We've lost enough time as it is.'

Stanley rubbed his neck. 'Polish, are they? Is tha sure? Sounded a hell of a lot like German to me.'

'Sort of thing a spy would say, I reckon,' Arthur muttered, but he sounded like a man whose pride wasn't yet willing to let him admit that he'd been wrong. Charlie pushed them aside to examine the men, who were both now unconscious.

'High fever,' he said, holding one hand against the forehead of the man sitting up against the fuselage and then doing the same for his comrade. 'This one sitting up has broken both his legs and has a concussion, and his friend's taken some metal shards to the stomach – nasty wound, as well as the burns to his face and a broken arm. The rain's done us a service keeping the wound clean and cooling those burns, at least. I'll bind the broken limbs with a splint before we take them down. Aspirin ought to bring the fever down a little, but what they really need is for us to get them to a doctor as fast as we can.' He glanced at the man stretched out on the ground. 'This chap's barely clinging on.'

'And… in the plane?' Bobby said, unable to bring herself to look at it.

'No hope for them, I suppose. But you're right, we have to be sure.'

Charlie squared his shoulders and stood up, his jaw setting at the thought of the gruesome task ahead of him.

Arthur Egerton glanced at Stanley, who nodded.

'Tha had best stay here and see to these two, lad,' he said quietly to Charlie, putting a hand on his shoulder. 'We'll go.'

'Could you do it?'

'We were in t' trenches, weren't we? Do thy job and let two old soldiers do theirs. There's lives at stake.'

Charlie hesitated, then nodded. The two farmers went to explore the wreckage of the plane while he administered aspirin to the unconscious men.

Gil squinted down the hill. 'There's men coming up: three on 'em. They've got another stretcher.'

'Oh, thank God,' Bobby said.

When Stanley and Arthur came back from examining the fuselage, both looked pale, with grim, set expressions. Stanley shook his head.

'No survivors,' he said. 'It's just these pair. Patch them up as best tha can, veterinary, and let's get them down to yon hospital.'

Chapter 21

Getting the Polish airmen down the mountain safely was no small task. First the rescue party had to wait for Charlie to splint and bind the broken limbs and apply iodine to the wounds of the most badly injured man before dressing them. When this had been completed, the wounded had to be loaded very carefully on to the stretchers without causing them further damage. Bobby and Gil covered them with a couple of blankets each. The man who had spoken to Bobby earlier was now trembling, although he remained unconscious.

'Could be the fever, or he might be showing signs of hypothermia,' Charlie said, eyeing the man with concern. 'I've got nothing to give him other than more aspirin. We need to get him to the doctor.'

'It'll be three hour at least afore we're back in t' village, Charlie,' Gil said.

'I know. Tuck the edges of those blankets in tight so they're properly swaddled up, all right?'

Bobby was examining the other man by the light of the bicycle lamp.

'Charlie,' she said in a low voice. 'I don't think he's breathing.'

Charlie came over and took the man's wrist, then brought his ear close to his mouth.

'He's not dead but the pulse is very faint,' he said. 'He is breathing still but only barely. We need to get him down as soon as we can to have any chance of saving him. Both are critical but this one's near death.' He glanced at Gil and Stanley. 'Stan, me and you are likely to have the best combination of strength and speed. We'll take the worst one down and Gil, Wilf, you come along to relieve us. Arthur, you and the other men follow with his mate.'

'What about me?' Bobby asked.

'You're not strong enough to bear a stretcher but you're the nimblest on your feet,' Charlie said as he and Stanley lifted the stretcher. 'You'll be our scout, Bobby. Take the bicycle lamp and go on ahead – get back to the village as fast as you can. Tell old Doc Minchin we're coming down with two survivors. Explain what happened and what their injuries are in as much detail as possible so he can prepare. My guess is that the less injured man is the rear gunner, who would have been thrown clear when the turret broke off. The other who was thrown might be either the pilot or the navigator. The men in the belly of the plane weren't so lucky, unfortunately.'

Arthur nodded soberly. 'I reckon that's right, from what Stan and me saw in there. It's pilot and rear gunner we mun have here.'

'Anything else?' Bobby asked Charlie.

'When you've given the doctor his instructions, take a bike to Sumner House and let the two women waiting there know what to expect,' he said. 'They'll appreciate someone who can take command, if you've any strength left by then. I'll meet you there with the patients.'

'Right. Good luck, gentlemen.'

Bobby shot off down the hill, overruling the pain from her blistered heel. She had expected Charlie to assign her a safe but essentially useless job suited to her sex, such as mopping the men's brows as they descended, and was rather gratified to instead be sent on as scout. It made sense to have someone go ahead to speak with the doctor, and Charlie was right; she was the lightest on her feet. If she'd been in charge up there, she would have done the same.

She made much better time descending the mountain than she had ascending it. Bobby might never get her clothes clean again, or indeed herself, but by using the mud to her advantage, she was able to half-walk and half-slide back to Silverdale – often on her bottom rather than her feet.

It was strange, she reflected as she righted herself again after another slide, how she and Charlie had seemed to change places once they reached the top of the mountain. When the plane had gone down, Charlie had looked rather panicked and helpless, and she had intuitively taken charge of organising the rescue party. But when there were injured men to attend to, the skill and compassion that served him well in his career as a vet had naturally given him the authority. It had taken the two of them working together to save lives tonight – if, indeed, they had saved them. She thought of the injured pilot, his pulse weakening by the second, and quickened her pace still further.

She didn't know how long it took her to get down, but she supposed it was a little under two hours flat, which she was sure ought to be a record. By the time she clambered over the stile in Troy's field, exhausted and aching, she was limping badly. She had blisters on both heels and several toes, one ankle was swollen, and she'd torn her leg quite nastily on a clump of gorse she hadn't seen in the darkness. She was also trying desperately not to think of what she'd seen on the mountainside: the smouldering corpse of one of the aircrew, hanging from the plane wreckage. But still her inner motor kept her going, determined to finish the job she'd been assigned, and she didn't slow down as she ran the last quarter of a mile to the village green.

Despite the lateness of the hour – or the earliness, since it must now be morning – most of the village seemed to be gathered there, waiting to catch a glimpse of the rescued airmen should any have survived. Blackout rules had been put to one side on this night of crisis, with lamps glowing dimly here and there, and items the villagers had collected were piled up on a table someone had brought out: blankets, clothes, tinned food, even gramophone records. It made Bobby smile, in spite of her worry and the pain in her feet and leg. They'd wanted to help and they hadn't known how, so they'd shown their concern in the most Silverdale way possible.

Hands reached towards her as she made her way through the crowd to where Reg's Wolseley was parked.

'Miss Bancroft, what's to do?' someone demanded, grasping her shoulder to stop her progress. 'Any survivors?'

'Nay, there can't have been,' another man said. 'Bad crash, it were. You can still see t' smoke, look.'

'Two survivors,' Bobby panted, shaking away the hands that were trying to claim her attention while she struggled to get her breath back. 'Free Polish aircrew. The men are bringing them down. I have to find the doctor.'

Reg and Mary were both by the car, as was her father. It was he who spotted her first.

'Bobby, lass.' He pushed through the crowd to pull her to him for a rare embrace before guiding her back to where Reg and Mary were. 'We've been worried to death about thee. What's happening then? Where's rest on 'em?'

'Coming,' she said. 'They're coming down with two survivors. Dad, I must find the doctor. Have you seen him?'

'Aye, he's here somewhere. I'll fetch him.' He disappeared into the crowd.

'Oh, now look at you,' Mary said in dismay, taking in Bobby's mud-fouled clothes and the bleeding scratches on her leg that were showing through her torn slacks. 'And you must be near dead with tiredness. You'll come back to Moorside when you've spoken to the doctor and let me clean up that nasty cut.'

Dr Minchin, the doctor from Smeltham, appeared from out of the throng with her father. 'You're the young lady who was asking for me?'

She nodded. 'Bobby Bancroft. I've come on ahead from the rescue party.'

'And what's the situation?'

'There are two survivors from a Free Polish bomber crew. One is the rear gunner. The gun turret of their Wellington was blown clear in the crash. Two broken legs, no significant wounds visible, high fever and concussion. In and out of consciousness but delirious, and possible hypothermia,' Bobby said, reeling off the information as quickly as she could so as not to waste precious time. 'The other man we believe is the pilot. He's in a bad way – near death. Only barely breathing, weak pulse and a nasty open wound full of bits of metal in his belly, plus one side of his face is badly burned. His arm is broken too. He hasn't recovered consciousness.'

'That's for the best. He'd be in terrible pain if he did,' the doctor said. 'What's been done for them so far?'

'Charlie bound the broken limbs with splints and gave them aspirin for the fever. The pilot's wounds were cleaned with iodine and dressed. That's all.' She grabbed his arm, feeling her head start to spin. 'They'll need morphine, Doctor, lots of it.'

'They certainly will, and if the pilot has a stomach full of metal then he'll need a surgeon as soon as possible. Where is the nearest telephone, please?'

'My house,' Reg said. 'I can drive you. I reckon we'll be back in good time for when the men get down.' He glanced at Bobby. 'They'll be a fair bit behind you with the stretchers, I suppose?'

She nodded. 'I doubt they'll be here for at least an hour yet. I could make out their lights when I reached Troy's field quarter of an hour ago. They couldn't have been much beyond the shepherd's hut.'

'Our Charlie all right, is he?'

'He's fine.' She summoned a weak smile. 'You'd have been proud of him, Reg. There was a little battle up there that I'll tell you all about some other time, but he took charge of the situation like a true brother of yours.'

'Now will you let us take you home, Bobby?' Mary said. 'You've done all you can here and it's nearly two in the morning. You need a bath, a bandage for your leg and some rest. Reg can drive us when he takes Dr Minchin.'

Bobby could feel herself sagging. Exhaustion was starting to catch up with her, now she was still. A hot bath and warm bed had never sounded more appealing. But she couldn't let herself rest yet. There was still a lot of work to be done.

'Later, Mary,' she said. 'I need to get to Sumner House and wait for the men. Topsy's there, isn't she?'

'Aye, she drove over with some stretchers and bandages in case they might be needed, then said she'd go back to make up beds for any survivors.'

'She's going to need help.' Bobby winced as she accidentally put her weight on her bad ankle. 'I'll stay with her until I've seen it through. I couldn't rest now anyhow.'

'Well if that's the case, I'm coming with you,' Mary announced in a tone that brooked no opposition.

'There's no need. Go home in the car with Reg. I can borrow a bicycle to get me there.'

'I'd far rather make myself useful. If nurses are needed I've some experience, even if it is rather out of date. I was a VAD in the last war for a short time, you know, until our Nancy came along. Besides, you're in no state to ride a bicycle.' Bobby should have known Mary would instantly notice the limp she'd been trying to disguise.

'What about the children?'

'They're fast asleep. Reg will be home before they wake,' Mary said. 'He can drive us to Sumner House after the doctor has made his telephone call, then he can come back here to act as ambulance.'

–

Mary insisted that she be allowed ten minutes while the doctor telephoned a surgeon friend in Skipton to fill a Thermos with coffee. Bobby was impatient to be off to Sumner House, anxious to be doing something useful, but she also knew it would be some time until the two airmen would arrive there so she tried not to fidget. Mary poured her out a cup as they rode to the hospital in Reg's car and the reviving brew perked her up significantly. By the time Reg left them at the top of Sumner House's drive, she felt ready to tackle the next part of her unexpected nocturnal adventure.

There was a large bell rope by the door, which Bobby pulled.

'I wonder when the men will get here,' she said to Mary while they waited for someone to answer. 'I suppose it will be another half an hour at least before they reach the village, and then the doctor will want to give them emergency treatment before Reg brings them over.'

'At least an hour, in that case,' Mary said. 'I'm very glad I made that coffee. Is Dr Minchin's surgeon friend on the way?'

'Yes, he told him to come here directly.'

The door opened, and Topsy peered out into the darkness.

'Charlie said you'd come,' she said, smiling with relief. 'Thank the Lord. We've been like lost souls here, waiting for we don't know what.' She threw her arms around Bobby for a hug. 'But oh, you're filthy!' Topsy held her friend back in horror when she realised the state she was in, then cast a worried glance down at her own nice things. 'What on earth have you been doing, Birdy?'

'Climbing a mountain.' Bobby gestured to her companion. 'You know Charlie's sister-in-law Mary, of course. She's come to help too.'

'Of course.' Topsy looked rather dazed as she ushered them inside. 'You're not telling me you climbed to the top of that big mountain in the dark?'

'That's exactly what I am telling you.'

'But darling, whatever for?'

'Because there were men up there who might have needed my help,' Bobby said, a little impatient with her friend's customary exuberance after the night's ordeal. She looked around the panelled hallway, trying to remember which door led to which room and wondering where the beds for the patients might be.

'Yes, but I mean, surely there were men from the village who could do that,' Topsy said.

'I was the warden on duty when the plane came down. It was my responsibility to lead the rescue party.'

'Where are we taking the patients, Topsy?' Mary asked.

Topsy pointed to a door that Bobby vaguely recalled led to the main hall, which had been used as a dormitory during the hall's short tenure as a school for evacuees. 'That's to be the ward, where the beds are. Maimie's in there making them nice for the men. We've made up six.'

'We'll only need two,' Bobby said, pushing past her to examine the arrangements.

'What about the others?' Topsy asked, following her.

'Dead. Four killed and two survivors, with one critical.' Her voice almost sounded like someone else's as she spoke. She never would have believed she had the ability to talk of death in that cold, clinical manner. 'That one, the pilot, might not make it through the night. The other we can save, I hope.'

She opened the door to the main hall. There were two rows of narrow metal beds facing opposite each other in pairs, creating an aisle down the middle. Three pairs had been made up with sheets and blankets, ready for patients. Maimie Hobbes, Topsy's former nanny, was fluffing up the pillows on one of them when Bobby approached her.

'We'll only need two of the beds, Mrs Hobbes,' she said.

She shook her head sadly. 'I was worried you might tell me that.'

'I know. But let's focus on the lives we can save.'

'When will they arrive, these two men?'

'Not for at least an hour.' Bobby was racking her brains trying to remember a newsreel feature she'd once seen about military hospitals. 'Mary, you said you were a VAD in the last war. Where did you nurse?'

'In a hospital out on the coast, until I discovered I was pregnant with Nancy,' Mary said.

'And when men have broken limbs, do they have them strapped up? I'm sure I remember some newsreel footage where they had metal frames around the bed so they could suspend the plaster casts from a chain.'

'Yes, that's right. Keeping them elevated helps with pain and swelling.'

'Well, these men both have broken limbs. Topsy, are there any of those sorts of frames here?'

Topsy frowned. 'I did see some metal poles and things in the library, and chains too. I suppose that must be what they were for, but they weren't put together.'

'Then we'll have to figure out how to put them together. Mrs Hobbes, Mary, can you bring them here, please?'

They nodded and left to fetch them.

'What about me? What job can I do?' Topsy asked brightly. 'You know, you really ought to be a matron or something, Birdy. You're so deliciously bossy.'

'What about sterile surgical clothing? Is there any here?' Bobby asked. 'White coats, caps, masks – that sort of thing?'

'There's a box of whites over there.' She pointed to a large chest pushed against the wall.

'Then I suggest we all put coats on, if we're going to be needed as nurses tonight – or, I should say, this morning.'

'Must we? They're for men: terribly shapeless and ugly. I tried one on, just for fun, and I looked an absolute fright.'

Bobby took Topsy's shoulders and looked sternly into her face. 'Topsy, there's a man coming here whose guts have been ripped open by flying metal and who has had the skin half-burned off his face. I don't think you want to get his blood on your pretty clothes, do you?'

Topsy's eyes widened. 'His skin burned off! Lord, that sounds awful! Did you really see that up there?'

'Yes,' Bobby said quietly. 'It was a terrible thing to witness. He… might not make it here. He was at death's door when we found him. But if he does, we must be ready to help him in any way we can. You haven't done your VAD training yet, have you?'

'Well, no, but I've been reading a lot so I'd be ready. I took a book from the library here, all about medical instruments and what they're used for, and another about how to dress wounds and things. Maimie let me practise my bandaging on her.' She giggled. 'She looked like an Egyptian mummy just risen from the crypt, Birdy.'

Bobby could imagine the type of book Topsy had been reading. Calm, clinical descriptions of the right way to make a sling or apply a dressing, aimed at Girl Guides probably, with lots of neat little diagrams where both patient and nurse were smiling happily. Nothing about the horror of being faced with a man whose life was ebbing away with his stomach sliced open and half his face looking like something less than human. How was her friend going to react when she saw what Bobby had seen by the glow of an oil lamp earlier in the night, except this time in the cold, unforgiving glare of an electric bulb?

'Is there an operating theatre?' Bobby asked.

'It's not quite grand enough to be called a theatre but there's a surgery,' Topsy said. 'In the south parlour. There's an operating table in there, and a basin and all that type of thing.'

'There's a surgeon on his way from Skipton. When he comes, show him in there so he can see what he's got to work with.'

'What will you do? You look like you're ready to collapse, Birdy. I can give you the key for the cottage if you want to rest awhile.'

'No. No, I can't rest – not until it's done.' She pressed a hand to her forehead. 'But... could I please use your telephone?'

Chapter 22

Topsy showed Bobby into the room that had previously been the office of the headmistress responsible for the evacuees' school. It would be assigned to the hospital matron now, Bobby supposed, or whoever was to be in charge of the place. Wearily, she sank into a chair at the desk, picked up the receiver and spoke to the operator.

'Bradford 5726, please,' she said. 'Donald Sykes.'

Of course, he might not pick up. It was three o'clock in the morning. Bobby felt a wave of guilt, slightly fuzzy at the edges from the exhaustion, about the fact she would also be waking Don's wife Joan and their young daughter Sal. Still, she needed to speak to him. She wasn't sure why exactly, but she knew she needed to.

The phone rang for a little while before there was any answer.

'Hello?' a grumpy, sleep-slurred voice said at the other end.

'Don, it's me.'

'Bloody hell, Bobby! You'd better be dead or in prison if you're waking me up at this time.'

'Not quite. I've got a story for you – a good one.'

'Huh. What story would I be interested in from the back end of nowhere?' he muttered. 'It's not even rightly our patch.'

'You'll want to cover this, I promise.'

'Bobby, at three in the morning, I'm not sure I'd want to cover it if you were calling to tell me you'd had a telegram containing Hitler's personal surrender.'

'This is big enough for the nationals to be interested in, Don; I'm sure it is. A bomber crew came down in the fells tonight – I saw it happen. Six RAF cadets from the airbase ten miles away.'

There was silence while he took this in.

'All right, I'm listening,' Don said grudgingly.

'You've got your pencil?'

'There's one by the phone.'

'I was on duty at the ARP hut when it happened. A Vickers Wellington went into the side of the mountain in thick fog and burst into flames.' She paused while the journalist part of her brain fumbled for a detail. 'Mark… IC. The crew were all Free Polish – four dead and two survivors. A rescue party from the village hiked up to the summit with stretchers to bring them down.'

'You saw them brought down, did you?'

'No, I went up with the rescue party. I'm at Sumner House now, Sal's old school. It's been fitted up as a hospital – it hasn't officially opened yet but there are facilities to care for them here.'

'You went up? How far was it?'

'Ten miles there and back.'

'Ten miles! You climbed ten miles up a mountain in the dark?'

She shuddered. 'It's not the climb that's going to haunt me; it's what was waiting at the top.'

'That took some guts, lass.'

'It doesn't matter. What I did wasn't important.'

Don's voice softened. 'Bobby, are you all right? No offence, but you sound… well, a bit tipsy. Your speech is slurring.'

'I'm exhausted, Don. I've been pushing myself to keep going all night and now it's catching up with me.'

'So let me get this straight. In the past few hours, you've witnessed a plane crash, climbed a mountain, rescued two injured airmen… and then the first thing you think to do when you get a moment to yourself is to telephone me. At three in the morning, I might add.'

She gulped. 'I thought… I thought you'd want to know about it right away so you could run it in the next edition.'

'The hell you did. This isn't really about a story, is it? What's wrong, Bobby?'

Finally, Bobby gave in and let the tears she'd been holding back gush out. She was so tired, so very tired, but how could she ever sleep again? Every time she closed her eyes, she saw that smoking body in the plane. And the man stretched out on the ground, the man with half a face…

'I… had to talk to you, Don,' she sobbed. 'I… I had to talk to… someone who wasn't Silverdale. Someone who isn't part of it all. I can't break down in front of them – not until it's over. They all look at me, expecting me to be strong. Make decisions.'

'All right, I'm here,' Don said gently. 'Let it all out. Have they got any medicinal brandy at this hospital?'

'No.' She sniffed. 'I don't think so.'

'Well, see if you can find some and have yourself a glass. It'll help. Do you want to tell me about what you saw?'

'The men in the plane… were all dead. One of them… I could see it where there was a crack in the fuselage. It was horrible, Don. Just black and smoking and… dead. And the other man, one of the survivors – he was younger than me and… the skin on half his face had been burned off. It made him look like… it's awful to say, but he looked like a monster or… or something from a horror film. Every time I close my eyes, I see it again in my mind.'

'I'm sorry, Bobby. I wish I was there to help.'

'Now I know what my dad sees when he wakes up screaming,' she said in a low voice. 'Now I know why he has to drink to forget. And it made me think… it all made me think…'

'What did it make you think?'

'About how I'd manage if…' She shuddered. 'I don't want to talk about it over the telephone.'

In the distance she heard the muffled toll of Sumner House's doorbell.

'That's probably the surgeon who's driven over from Skipton,' she said. 'I have to pull myself together. I'll be needed soon. Are you in the office tomorrow?'

'Yes. Why?'

'I think… I'd like to come home.' She dabbed at her eyes with the lucky handkerchief Charlie had given her the first time they'd met: the one with the horseshoe and his monogram embroidered in one corner. 'I'm sure Reg will give me the day off after what happened tonight, and there are a few things I need to sort out with the house and our lodgings for Bowling Tide. If you're working, I can come into the office and give you an eyewitness account. Assuming you're going to run the story.'

'I'll run it.'

'And if you've got time, I'd really appreciate some advice. There's something personal I'd be grateful for a man's perspective on.'

'Come near the end of the day and we'll take you over to the Swan for a game of darts, just like the old days. You can tell me what's on your mind at the pub, if you can manage it without blubbering.'

'I'll be all right by tomorrow. Thanks, Don.'

—

The surgeon, Dr Lazenby, arrived with a reassuringly large bag of tools and medicines and was shown into the surgery by Topsy. Bobby met them there to answer any questions he might have about the pilot's injuries, then she went down to the cottage with Topsy to change into some loaned clothes and get cleaned up while Mary and Mrs Hobbes put together the metal frames that went over the beds. After that, there was nothing to do but drink coffee and wait. Her throbbing head had sunk on to her shoulder when, an hour later, she was shaken awake by Mary. Topsy was dozing in her chair, and Mrs Hobbes had returned to the cottage to rest for a little while in case they needed to take shifts later on. A gramophone had been installed in the room earlier in the evening, and Topsy had brought some records from the cottage. The low, dreamlike hum of chamber music had filled the air as Bobby drifted into a shallow sleep, but it was silent now.

'I heard Reg's car outside,' Mary said in a low voice. 'You go see what's what. I'll wake Topsy and tell the surgeon to be ready.'

Bobby nodded and got to her feet.

There was a thin dawn light silhouetting the old Wolseley when she emerged from the house. Bobby blinked as her eyes adjusted. It wasn't Reg who was getting out of the driver's side but Charlie, looking pale and hollow-eyed after his night's work. Dr Minchin got out of the passenger-side door.

There was a figure laid on the back seat. Bobby looked up at Charlie, who answered the question in her eyes.

'It's the pilot. He's clinging on still.'

'Then get him inside, quickly,' she said. 'Dr Lazenby, the surgeon, is ready to operate in the south parlour. Topsy will show you both the way, then you can drive back to the village for his comrade.'

Bobby held the front door open for the men as they bore the injured pilot inside on his stretcher. Topsy and Mary were waiting anxiously in the hallway to show them to the surgery. Topsy, Bobby noticed, had now donned the sterile white coat and cap she had been so set against earlier.

'Oh my goodness,' Topsy whispered when she caught sight of the man's injuries. 'Is he… he isn't…'

'He isn't dead – at least not yet,' Dr Minchin told her. 'Lord knows how he's still with us after what his poor battered body has been through tonight. Which way, young lady? There isn't time to waste.'

'Oh, the poor boy,' Topsy said, her gaze lingering over the burns on his face. 'He must be in terrible pain.'

'Not at the moment. He's full of the morphine I injected into him. Which way to the surgery?'

Topsy drew her gaze away from the man and pulled herself together. 'Come with me.'

Bobby followed them to the south parlour, where Dr Lazenby was waiting. He was a no-nonsense Scotsman with a shrewd expression and kind eyes who didn't flinch while he examined the man's wounds with medical detachment.

'Not much I can do for his face other than dress it,' he said when he'd taken a good look. 'These burns need a specialist – pray God the RAF can come through with one. But it's the metal in his guts that's the more immediate risk to his survival and that, at least, I can deal with.'

'Anything I can do, Archie?' Dr Minchin asked.

He shook his head. 'No, Dick, you're better placed tending to his comrade until the cavalry arrives from the airbase. I assume they've been notified we have two of their own here.'

'My brother went home to telephone,' Charlie said.

'Good. Then they ought to have personnel on the way very soon, I would have thought.'

'In that case, the most helpful thing I can do is probably to set the gunner's broken legs,' Dr Minchin said. 'Charlie, we ought to get back quickly and fetch him. He was starting to come around when we left.'

Charlie nodded, and they hurried away.

Topsy, Mary and Bobby lingered uncertainly, not sure what to do. Bobby's gaze kept returning to the injured man. The burned side of his face did indeed look monstrous, but on the other side he was a sensitive-looking young man of perhaps twenty-one or twenty-two, with a head of cherubic blond curls. Somewhere he had a mother and father, probably. Perhaps a sweetheart, or a wife. She closed her eyes and said a silent prayer that the doctor would be able to help him. His breathing was so shallow now that she could barely hear it.

Dr Lazenby looked at the women while he washed his hands. 'Any of you ladies done any nursing?'

'A little, but my skills must be rather out of date,' Mary said. 'I spent a few months in the VAD in the last war.'

'I've been accepted to the VAD too, but I haven't done the training yet,' Topsy said. 'All I know so far is from books.' She looked at the man on the operating table. 'But I'd very much like to stay and try to help him, please.'

'You know the names of the instruments? What they look like?'

'Oh yes, I've read all about them,' Topsy said eagerly. 'Maimie, my friend, has been testing me on them.'

'I'm afraid I don't have any nursing,' Bobby told him. 'Only basic first aid training.'

'All right, I suppose I shall have to make do with what I've got.' He nodded to Bobby. 'You go help Dick Minchin with the other chap. You other two ladies, ster-ilise your hands, put on these masks and prepare to do as I tell you for the next couple of hours.'

Chapter 23

Bobby, feeling rather aimless after her dismissal from the operating room, went outside to wait for Charlie and Dr Minchin to return with the second patient.

She looked at her watch, an old one she'd been left by her mother, but it had run down. What time was it now? She must have been dozing for a while before Charlie turned up with the pilot. Four o'clock? Five?

The sun was rising over the fells now, staining the sky pink. Still there was a black cloud where the plane had crashed though. Bobby shuddered when she thought of the four bodies abandoned up on the mountain. They'd have to be recovered, of course. Their loved ones would have to be told. Probably their families had felt they had been safe for the time being, away from the fighting, flying routine training missions. They wouldn't be prepared for the telegram about to turn their worlds upside down.

And still the birds sang and the lambs bleated in the distance, like none of it mattered. The drizzle and fog that had wrought such terrible consequences the night before had disappeared, replaced with blushing skies and morning dew. This morning, the summer felt wrong. It felt like an affront.

Reg's car soon appeared, driven once again by Charlie with Dr Minchin in the passenger seat, only this time it was the rear gunner stretched out in the back. Bobby showed the men inside with their patient and guided them to the empty ward. The man on the stretcher was conscious again, free from his previous delirium, and he had stopped trembling. His face was white and drawn where it wasn't blackened with soot, but he managed a weak smile for Bobby as she walked by the side of his stretcher.

'I have seen this face in a dream,' he murmured to her while she helped the men get him on to one of the beds. He shook his head, as if to clear it of fog. 'No. Not a dream. A nightmare. But you… you were not a part of the nightmare world. You were kind.'

'Pay him no mind,' Dr Minchin told her. 'He's full of morphine. I doubt he knows truly what he's saying.'

'You spoke to me on the mountain,' Bobby told the man while the doctor started unpacking items from his bag. 'I came to help you. You spoke to me in Polish.'

'The mountain.' The man pressed his eyes closed. 'That was my dream. I dreamed they… that they were all dead. Is it true?'

Dr Minchin put a hand on her shoulder. 'Don't excite him,' he said in a low voice. 'He needs to be kept calm. Best to break the news when we know the outcome of the pilot's surgery.' Bobby nodded.

'But I pulled Tadeusz from the flames,' the man murmured to himself. 'I had only strength for one. And then… the rest is black.' He blinked blearily at Bobby, his consciousness starting to drift as the morphine did its work. 'Jolka?'

'Jolka…' Bobby looked at Charlie. 'He said that on the mountain too. When he touched my arm. Stan thought it meant "spy", but I could tell that wasn't it.'

'What is Jolka?' Charlie asked the man.

'*Żona*... wife. My wife. My Jolka.' He fell back against the pillows, exhausted by conversation, and his eyes closed.

'It's for the best that he's unconscious,' Dr Minchin said. 'Now we can attend to those broken legs. Charlie, you know how to mix plaster for a cast – it's no different for two-legged patients than it is for those with four. Young lady, I'd like you to cut these bandages into strips approximately four inches wide and three feet long. We'll soon have our friend here as comfortable as we can. This one, at least, ought to make a full recovery with a few months' rest. He'll be reunited with this wife of his in no time.'

Charlie gave Bobby's hand a firm press before they got to work.

–

Two hours later, Topsy came in to join them. Bobby had once again been dozing, sitting in a chair beside the wounded gunner's bed while Charlie and the doctor applied casts to the man's broken limbs, but she woke instantly when she heard someone come in.

She could see at once that her friend had been through a life-changing ordeal of her own tonight. Topsy looked more grown up, somehow, as if what she'd seen in the operating room had aged her immeasurably in just a few hours. Her blue eyes were filled with pain and pity; her white coat covered in blood. But her jaw was firm, and there was a hard, determined expression on her pale face that Bobby had never seen there before.

Bobby was both surprised and impressed at how her friend had rallied tonight, at the end when she was really needed – she had expected Topsy to plead off nursing duties in the surgery within half an hour. But she'd been unfair to her. For all her sheltered upbringing and indulged, charmed life, Topsy Sumner-Walsh clearly had the makings of a fine nurse in her soul. She'd looked into the burned face of the pilot without a trace of either horror or disgust; only compassion.

However, there was no time to talk about such matters.

'What news, Tops?' Charlie demanded. 'The pilot, is he—'

'Alive.' Topsy removed her bloodied coat and sank into a seat by the bed opposite. 'Dr Lazenby is stitching him up now. Mary's helping but he said I could go.'

'And the surgery was successful?' Bobby asked.

'We probably won't know for a little while, I'm afraid,' Dr Minchin told her.

Topsy nodded. 'That's what Dr Lazenby said. The injuries are very bad and the next twenty-four hours are going to be critical, but he's removed all the metal and he said there's no sign of any infection. The man might never walk again though. Dr Lazenby says some of the metal damaged his spine.' She closed her eyes and let her head sag back. 'I wish I knew his name. The poor boy.'

'His comrade mentioned it earlier when he was conscious, I think,' Bobby said. 'It was a Polish name – I can't quite say it the way he did, but it sounded a little like Thaddeus.'

'Thaddeus.' Topsy smiled slightly. 'I'm glad I've got something to call him other than Pilot. It creates a sort of bond, helping to save a man's life.' She pressed her fingers into her eyes and let out a sob. 'Oh God, I hope it is saved. It can't all have been for nothing.'

217

They were interrupted by a clattering outside the house, as of several vehicles arriving at once.

'Ah,' Dr Minchin said with a satisfied smile. 'There's our cavalry at last. The RAF must have sent some men out.'

The RAF had sent more than men. When the four of them went outside to greet the newcomers, they found three Austin Tillys containing various air force personnel, including two doctors and several WAAFs with medical experience. These, they were told by the young, pleasant and slightly pompous officer who seemed to be in charge, were going to take over nursing duties until a permanent hospital staff could be engaged.

'You people have done an excellent job here, considering,' the young man, Wing Commander Phelps, told them in a mildly patronising tone. 'Stuff of the silver screen, that rescue mission from the village, from what I've heard. Anyhow, we'll take over from here. Jolly handy, this hospital being ready to go.'

'You will tell us how they get along, won't you?' Topsy asked anxiously. 'We'll be allowed to visit? When they're well enough, I mean.'

'Well, I'm not sure about that. This is a military facility, you know. We can't have civilians wandering around the place willy-nilly.'

She drew herself up. 'It's also my house. I happen to be Lady Sumner-Walsh.'

This had an effect. At least, the young officer deigned to remove his cap for her.

'We'll see what we can do, er… your ladyship,' he said. 'For now, our priority must be getting these men well. Now, if you'll excuse me.'

He started to leave, but Charlie put a hand on his arm.

'Wait,' he said. 'The men on the mountain, the ones who didn't make it…'

'The ATA is sending a plane out to recover them. My commanding officer will be writing to their families this morning.'

'Why were they flying in that terrible fog? Why weren't they grounded?'

The man gave him a sharp look. 'That really isn't something I can talk about with a civilian.'

'I'm not a civilian, I'm RAF. At least, I will be the day after tomorrow.'

'Nevertheless, I'm afraid it isn't a matter I'm able to discuss.'

'The two who were brought down – can you tell us their names?' Mary asked. 'We'd very much like to know.'

Charlie nodded. 'Surely that's the least you can do, after we saved their lives.'

'I suppose there's no reason you shouldn't be told,' Phelps said, with an air of magnanimity. 'Flight Lieutenant Tadeusz Nowak was the pilot. His comrade is Sergeant Piotr Zielinski, the rear gunner – both Free Polish, like the rest of the crew. Now I really must get on. Thank you all again for your service.'

He strode away without looking back.

Mary sighed. 'Well, that was quite a night, wasn't it? I never thought I'd have cause to use my nursing skills again on anyone other than Reg. Now I'd say it's high time we were all at home and in bed.'

'I know I won't be able to sleep,' Topsy said, stifling a yawn. 'I wish they'd let me stay and help. I want to know what happens to my pilot.'

'There'll be time for that later. You've been through hell tonight, Topsy – we all have. Now you're to go back to the cottage for a cup of cocoa and some rest, on my orders. Mrs Hobbes will take care of you.'

'Do you want a lift back to Smeltham?' Charlie asked Dr Minchin.

'I'll get a lift with Archie Lazenby when he's done here,' the doctor said. 'He's going my way.'

'Thanks for everything you did tonight.' Bobby shook the man's hand. 'You and Dr Lazenby both. They'd have died without you.'

'That's the job. You do it when you need to and hope everything turns up for the best.' Still, he looked rather pleased. 'Goodbye, young lady. You know, you really ought to consider a career in nursing.'

'She ought to consider a career in the Cabinet,' Charlie said with a smile. 'You've got no idea of all she's done tonight, Doc.'

Bobby flushed. 'I didn't do much.'

'Yes you did. By rights, we should be bearing you home on our shoulders like the conquering hero you are.' He rubbed his right shoulder, wincing. 'Except I don't think mine will stand another load today. I feel like a wizened old man.'

'I'll draw a mustard bath for you when we get back to Moorside.' Mary nodded to Reg's car. 'Let's go, shall we? The girls will be awake wanting to hear all about our adventures, and your father will be pacing the floor until he has you back safe, Bobby. Of course Reg will grant you a day's holiday, unless he wants to have me to answer to.'

'It all feels like a bit of an anticlimax, doesn't it?' Charlie observed to Bobby as they climbed into the car.

'How do you mean?'

'Well. The heroic dash up the mountain, getting the men here, the emergency surgery. And then we're sent

220

home by some snooty officer with a pat on the head like a pack of Boy Scouts.'

'I don't think he meant to be snooty,' Mary said. 'He's just that type.'

Bobby smiled. 'What were you hoping for, Charlie? A fanfare and a parade? Maybe a medal or two each?'

He started the car. 'Honestly, I'd have been happy with a round of jam on toast. It's hungry work, carrying men down mountains.'

'Reg will be hungry too, no doubt, and the children,' Mary said. 'I'll make us all a breakfast as soon as we get home. Then it's bed for everyone.'

Bobby shook her head. 'Not me. I couldn't sleep – not after that. Besides, I've got an appointment. I'll need to go for the bus shortly after breakfast.'

'An appointment? But you must be exhausted, Bobby.'

'I am, but it's not the kind of exhaustion that's going to let me sleep.' She shuddered. 'I have to keep busy. Otherwise I'm only going to dwell on… things.'

'Where are you going?' Charlie asked.

'I'm going to see Don Sykes in Bradford.'

Chapter 24

Despite Bobby feeling certain that she would never be able to sleep again after the things she'd seen the night before, there was only so much the human body could take before nature stepped in with a firm hand. In fact, she'd fallen into a deep enough sleep on the train from Skipton to Bradford that she almost missed her stop. Thankfully the Lord in his mercy had granted her a dreamless sleep, free of torturous images of the things she'd seen on the mountain, and she was at least partially refreshed when she stepped on to the platform at Forster Square station around midday and went to board a tram for Southampton Street.

Her first visit was to the family home, to speak to the woman responsible for supervising the soldiers billeted there and ensure everything was as it ought to be. There were some minor repairs needed to the roof, which she made a note of and promised to attend to. Then she paid a visit to some old neighbours, including Clara Stockwell, the woman two doors down from them who ran a boarding house. Clara gave her a warm welcome, commenting on her improved looks since she'd left for the country, although Bobby was sure she must look like a walking ghost after her exploits of the night before. Clara also confirmed she had set aside two rooms for them for Bowling Tide week: one for her father and Jake and another for Bobby and Lilian. Once she had completed her duties as a sister, daughter and landlady by proxy, Bobby was able to give her attention to the true purpose of her trip: a talk with Don at the *Courier* offices.

When she arrived, she was disappointed to find Don wasn't there. Only Tony was in the office, caught in the rare act of doing some work.

'Oh. Hello,' Bobby said when she walked in. As a former employee, she felt she was still entitled to the privilege of entering without knocking. 'Where's Don?'

'God knows. At the barber's, probably, making himself beautiful for you. He said we could expect you this afternoon.' He glanced up. 'You look shocking, Bob. Have you been out on the tiles all night or something? You must've been dancing up a storm to be limping like that.'

'Tony, come on. Don must've said where he was going.'

He shrugged. 'Said he was off to pick up some chips. We've you to thank for that, I suppose. He never goes out to fetch me food.'

'Oh Lord, I'd kill for some chips,' Bobby said with a heartfelt sigh, instinctively helping herself to her old chair. 'I haven't eaten since yesterday. I couldn't manage a bite of breakfast this morning and there was no time to stop for dinner.'

Tony left off tapping at his typewriter and lit a cigarette, clearly exhausted by his exertions. 'That little magazine running you off your feet, is it?'

'Something like that. You can hear all about it when Don comes.'

'You ought to learn to relax a bit, Bobby. Enjoy the finer things in life. It'll put you in an early grave, working like a dog all the time.'

She smiled. 'You mean I should be more like you.'

'Maybe. I'm happier than you anyhow. You might take a leaf out of your sister's book. She doesn't let life weigh her down, does she? Knows how to have a few laughs.'

'Well, Lil's not me.' She glanced vaguely at the papers spread out on her old desk. 'Whose are these? Jem's?'

He shook his head. 'Jem's gone, Bob.'

'Oh. Yes.' She ran a hand over her forehead. 'I forgot. Sorry, I'm very tired. What's the new cub called? Freddie?'

'No, I mean Jem's *gone*.' He took his cigarette from his mouth, looking sober – an unusual occurrence for Tony. 'His mam phoned Don with the news a fortnight ago. Killed in action.'

Bobby stared at him. 'No. He can't have been.'

'Sorry, Bobby. There's a lot I'll joke about, but not that.'

'But… he was so young,' she said helplessly. 'He was only eighteen, Tony.'

'Good lad he was, too. It's not right, is it?' He exhaled a wreath of smoke and watched it thoughtfully. 'Not right at all.'

Bobby felt lightheaded for a moment. She hadn't expected bad news to be waiting for her in Bradford. All she'd wanted when she came back was to find everything the same as when she'd left: the comfort of her old life and her old friends after a night of drama, just for one day. And now…

She could picture Jem's face vividly. Honest, boyish, innocent; quick to blush when his older male colleagues made a ribald joke or teased him about girls. He'd been a sweet boy, devoted to his mother and sister. It wasn't fair. And what had happened to the men in the Wellington hadn't been fair; or to Billy Wilcox; or to any of the boys and men who wouldn't be going home. Damn this bloody war! Damn it to hell.

It was a little while until either of them felt inclined to speak again.

'What are you working on?' she asked Tony a little shakily after some time had elapsed, anxious to establish normality again.

'Hmm?' He glanced at the sheet of paper on his typewriter. 'Oh. It's a story I picked up at that show I saw you at.'

'You're only just writing up the show? It was weeks ago.'

'I wrote up my list of animals and all that dull stuff the next day. This is something the Shadwick lass from the *Mercury* put me on to. I could tell she had something hot under her bonnet when she came rushing back to the reporters' tent all fluttery and got in the queue for the phone. Turned on the charm for her and she soon spilled. The *Mercury* hasn't run it so I suppose her editor must've warned her off – probably worried about a libel case if her evidence isn't up to scratch – but Don encouraged me to follow it up. I've been researching it for weeks.'

'What is it?'

'Oh, it's juicy stuff. It's not just Kiltford Show either.' He cast a satisfied look at the story in progress on his typewriter. 'Illegal meat raffling, at farmers' markets and shows all over that neck of the Dales. I couldn't get anyone to give me names but a few of the farmers must be in on it, along with some local racketeers who've been running the show. They've been rearing and slaughtering pigs on the sly without telling the Ministry of Food. Then, rather than selling the meat on the black market, they raffle it off for ten bob a ticket at the local shows – easier to hide it that way. The Ministry's going to have their heads if they get caught. Magistrates are coming down hard on unlicensed pig dealing these days.'

'Big fines?'

'Hundreds. I'd reckon on a prison sentence for a racket on this scale though.' He looked pleased with himself. 'I could make my reputation with this, Bobby. Wish I could pin down some names. Everyone knows it's going on but no one seems to be talking.' He looked at her hopefully. 'Don't suppose you've heard anything? It's in your patch.'

'Such as what?'

'Anyone tried to sell you a raffle ticket for a ham or a side of bacon, anything like that?'

She shrugged. 'Sorry, Tony, can't help you.'

A bell had started ringing at the back of Bobby's brain, but she was too tired to make a connection. Her thoughts were interrupted by Don's arrival, accompanied by the welcome scent of hot chips.

'Are those for me?' she asked, eyeing the packets under his arm hungrily.

'Some of them.' He tossed her a newspaper-wrapped packet. 'Chips and scraps with extra vinegar, the way you like them. I even got some for you, Tony, as a reward for attempting hard work for the first time in your life.'

'A scholar and a gentleman,' Tony said as he held up a hand to catch the packet Don threw him.

'What is this foray of his into actual work, Don?' Bobby asked, tucking into her chips. She'd missed the ones from the local chip hole. The chips in Settle weren't quite the same somehow. She'd missed the teasing banter of her old colleagues too.

'Your guess is as good as mine,' Don said as he sat down at his desk.

Tony shrugged. 'Maybe I'm turning over a new leaf. I'll need to impress any potential wives with my industri-ousness and earning potential, won't I?'

Bobby laughed. 'So that's it. You're wife-hunting again.'

'Well, I'm not getting any younger. Makes you think about your life, turning thirty. Besides, this was too good a lead to ignore.'

Don watched her as she ate her chips. 'You look all in, Bobby. Were you up all night?'

'Apart from the half an hour I managed to sleep on the train, yes.'

'Why on earth did you come all the way over here instead of getting some shut-eye? You could've given me your eyewitness report by phone, you know.'

'I don't know. I just wanted to be somewhere… familiar. I wanted to be at home.' She sighed as she nibbled on a chip. 'This is nice. Like old times.'

Tony smiled. 'I knew you'd come back to us eventually.'

'Well, don't get too used to me. The *Courier*'s a nice place to visit but I wouldn't want to live here.' She looked at Don. 'Tony told me about Jem. Why didn't you say in your last letter?'

'It felt a bit cold, putting it in writing. I thought you'd rather hear in person.' He looked sober. 'Poor kid.'

'How's his mam?'

'Shot to pieces. You know she doted on the lad.' He folded up the rest of his chips for later. 'How old were the men who survived the plane crash?'

'I don't know yet, but quite young. The rear gunner looked twenty-five or twenty-six, perhaps. The pilot was even younger – younger than me. No more than twenty-two, I'd guess.'

'Family?'

'The gunner had a wife. I don't know about the other boy. He didn't regain consciousness while I was with him.' She rubbed her arm. 'I don't even know if he's still alive. It was touch and go after his surgery, the doctor said. Once the RAF arrived, they shooed us out like the meddling civilians they obviously thought we were.'

Don took up a pencil and licked the end. 'Well, what can you tell me that I don't know already? Names?'

'Only of the survivors, but you'd better not print them before the families have been informed. Besides, they're Polish names. I can barely pronounce them, let alone spell them.'

'Tell me the story from the beginning then.'

'I was on duty at the ARP hut when I saw the crash,' she began.

'In your uniform?' Tony asked.

'Obviously. Why, what has that to do with anything?'

He grinned. 'Nothing. I just like to imagine it.'

'Ignore him,' Don said. 'Was it only you who saw this crash?'

She flushed slightly. 'No, Charlie was with me – the village vet.'

'Your sweetheart?'

'My... friend. We heard a Wellington flying low in the fog and wondered that all the training crews from the base hadn't been grounded when the visibility was so poor. The next thing we knew it had gone into the side of the mountain and burst into flames. That was when I ran into the village and sounded the alarm. A few of the men offered to join a rescue party and up we went.'

Tony raised an eyebrow. '*You* went up?'

'I was the warden on duty. It was my responsibility to coordinate the rescue party.' She shuddered. 'I don't regret it, but… there are things I wish I hadn't seen.'

'Did you see the bodies of the men who were killed?'

'One of them. Only it wasn't really a body – not any more. And one of the men, the pilot, had some horrific injuries. I won't forget his face in a long time.'

And yet Topsy had barely flinched, although Bobby had needed to force herself to look at the poor man's burned face. She had always thought of herself as the strong one out of the two, but her friend had really proven her mettle last night. People could surprise you.

'This is good stuff, Bobby,' Don said, scribbling away. 'I can already see the headline – "Dales village in daring mountain dash to rescue wounded airmen".'

'Just please don't mention me.'

'What time was this?'

'Gosh, I don't know. I suppose it must have been about midnight when we got to the summit, or a little earlier perhaps. It had felt like night for hours, with the weather being so bad. The fog was a real pea-souper, and you could barely see for drizzle driving into your eyes.'

Don looked up from his notes. 'Doesn't sound like weather to be flying in. Do you know why they weren't grounded?'

'No. Charlie tried taking the officer who showed up to task about it, but he wouldn't tell us anything, of course.'

'Well, what happened when you got up there?'

'There was a bit of a battle. Two of the men who'd gone on ahead with the stretcher were veterans of the last war. One of the injured was delirious, speaking Polish, and they thought he was a German spy. They tried to stop Charlie from treating him, but the man recovered enough to tell us they were Free Poles. Then I went on ahead to speak to the doctor while the men brought the injured pair down the mountain. Sumner House has been fitted up as a hospital, although it hasn't been opened to patients yet, so we took them there and a surgeon from Skipton operated on the pilot to remove the metal shards from his belly.' She pressed her palm to her forehead, feeling dizzy as she remembered that hellish night. 'Reg's wife Mary and Lady Sumner-Walsh acted as nurses, and I did the same for the doctor who tended to the other man. And that's the end of the story. After that, a lot of Tillys turned up full of RAF people and they took over. I don't know how the men are now, but the gunner, at least, is expected to make a full recovery.'

Don had stopped writing and was staring at her. So was Tony.

'What is it?' she said.

'Nothing. I'm just impressed,' Don said. 'Hell of a brave thing to do, Bobby.'

Tony nodded. 'Never would have thought you had it in you.'

'I would,' Don said. 'But I'm still impressed. Are you sure you don't want a mention? "Lady ARP warden mounts life-saving Dales rescue mission" is a decent headline too.'

'Please don't. I really didn't do anything except tell people there'd been a crash. It was the doctors and Charlie who saved the lives, and the men who carried the stretchers down. My part of it wasn't much more than waving a rattle about.'

'You're being modest, clearly. But if it's going to embarrass you then you can remain a nameless warden who sounded the alarm.'

'Thank you.'

'Personally, I think our heroic former colleague deserves a drink after all that,' Tony said, standing up. 'Are we going to play darts? I'll buy you a half as your reward, Bobby.'

She laughed. 'How brave do I have to have been for you to make it a pint?'

'With the price of beer these days? Nothing less than being dropped in the heart of Germany would do.'

'All right, since Bobby's here we can finish early,' Don said, standing too. 'Freddie's out covering a WVS jumble sale, but he knows to come and find us at The Swan if we're not in the office.'

Chapter 25

The Swan was the same as ever: a lively, merry city pub filled with workers of both sexes enjoying a drink after the toils of the day were over. It made a change from the Hart with its sombre, mostly male patrons sipping their pints in near silence. Bobby hadn't realised how much she'd missed the place.

The new cub – Freddie – was lounging against the bar with a drink in his hand, flirting with the barmaid, when they arrived. He was only seventeen, but it was clear he was as unlike shy, bashful Jem as he could be: confident, charming (at least, he clearly thought so) and with an eye for the girls. He smiled lazily at Bobby when she approached with his two colleagues to be introduced.

'Hullo,' he said to her. 'You must be the fragrant Miss Bancroft. I say, thanks for the holiday. Don says it's in your honour that we're finishing early today.'

He took her hand and kissed it, something she supposed he'd seen at the pictures and thought looked effective. She laughed and drew it away. 'All right, sonny, don't get cheeky.'

Tony pushed the boy with his shoulder.

'I told you before, Freddie, you're too young for that Errol Flynn stuff,' he said. 'Girls can't take it seriously from you. Stick with me, kid, and I'll give you the benefit of my years as a ladies' man.'

'If you'd been listening properly, Valentino Junior, you might remember that I didn't say you could finish early,' Don told Freddie sternly. 'I said I might dismiss you early. How long have you been here? You ought to have come back to the office if you finished that job with time to spare.'

'I've just got here, I swear! This is my first drink.'

The barmaid rolled her eyes at Don, clearly indicating this to be a fib.

'All right, we'll talk about it in the office tomorrow,' he said. 'You and Tony go have a game of darts. I need to have a word with Bobby.'

Bobby smiled as she and Don made their way to their usual table. 'So now you've got two lady-killers on your staff, have you?'

'That boy is the bane of my life. A juvenile delinquent with the sexual appetite of the Roman emperors. He's going to earn himself a thump from a jealous husband one of these days, especially with Tony acting as his mentor. That ought to knock some of the swagger out of him.'

'You must be paying him too much if he can afford to drink beer at that speed.'

'More than he's worth, the lazy little beggar.' He sat down, and Bobby pulled up the chair opposite. 'Well? What was all that on the phone this morning about needing advice?'

'Tell me about you first.' She nodded to his face. 'Moustache is gone, I see.'

'Aye, I got permission from the wife to shave it off. I managed to convince Joanie I was never going to be Clark Gable, no matter how hard I tried.'

'And Sal's still at home?'

'We decided not to evacuate her again. Seems unlikely there'll be any more bombs on Bradford. We'd rather have her here with us than off with strangers.' He looked uncharacteristically shy. 'We might have something to announce in six months' time as well.'

'Oh my goodness!' She clutched at his arm. 'A baby? Is Joan pregnant?'

'Keep it down, lass. We don't want to announce ahead of time – you're the only other who knows, apart from the doctor. We've tried for so many years, and Joanie's thirty-eight now. There are a lot of risks for a mother that age.'

'I know, but… Don, I'm so happy for you. I know how much you've both always wanted another.'

'Aye, well.' He looked bashful, and a little proud. 'We'll see what comes. But if anyone can do it, it's my Joanie. She's a hardy mare.'

Bobby laughed. 'You say that so proudly.'

'Greatest compliment I can pay her, trust me. She'd say the same.' He took a swallow of beer. 'How about you then? Do I get to hear the crisis?'

She sighed. 'I'm not sure I even know where to begin.'

'If it's man trouble, you should know you're talking to the wrong person.'

'Why? You are a man, aren't you?'

'Last time I checked. That doesn't mean I'm equipped to counsel young women about their love lives. You'd be far better off confiding in your sister or some girlfriend. Even Tony would probably do a better job than me. It's nigh on fifteen year since Joan and me were courting, and there wasn't much to that except I asked and she said yes.'

'My sister doesn't understand. No one does, really. It's ingrained in people that women ought to want a husband first and foremost. They stare at me like the world's most unnatural creature when I say there are other things I want out of life.'

'All right, tell me what it's all about then.'

Bobby sipped her half-pint of beer meditatively. 'The thing is, it isn't really about my love life. I mean, it is, but… it's about everything. My life, my job, the war. All those things go together, and they've become so tangled up in my mind that I don't even know where to begin unravelling them.'

'Start from the beginning, Bobby. If I've got any advice worth a damn you're welcome to it, but I'm not promising anything.'

'I've been walking out with a young man in the village. Reg's brother Charlie.'

'The vet you mentioned?'

She nodded. 'Although he's leaving to start training as a fighter pilot the day after tomorrow.'

'Well? Is he serious about you, this boyfriend?'

'Very. He's asked me to marry him countless times, but I've always put him off.'

'Why's that then? Not keen?' Don asked, sipping his beer.

'As keen as I'm ever likely to be on someone.'

'What's so special about this lad? Not like you to have your head turned by young men.'

'Charlie's… different,' she said with a slight smile. 'He doesn't brag and bully like a lot of them. He respects me and my work. He treats me like an equal, and he never patronises or dismisses me the way so many men do. And he's fun – stops me taking myself too seriously.'

'No mean feat, eh?' Don said with a laugh.

'That's what Lil always says. But if I say yes, I'll have to give up my job, won't I?'

'That's the usual way. Still, there are married women journalists.'

'Whose bairns have grown, maybe, or can afford a nanny for them. And even then… Reg spelt it out plainly to me when I asked if there was any chance he'd consider keeping me on. He won't employ a married woman reporter at *The Tyke* – still less one who's married to his brother.'

'I'd have a job for you at the *Courier*.'

She stared at him. 'You'd have me back?'

He shrugged. 'Why not? You could have a family of twelve and it'd still be less disruptive than my cubs getting called up every few months.'

'The war won't last forever.'

'I used to think women weren't meant for the news-room. Since you left and I got stuck with two randy newspapermen who'd rather flirt with pretty girls in the pub than work, I've come to appreciate the good points of the gentler sex. Besides, you were a bloody good writer.' He swallowed a mouthful of beer and wiped some foam from his upper lip. 'Not that it matters because you won't come back.'

'Won't I?'

'Course you won't. Nothing and nobody's going to claw you away from that daft magazine you love – God knows I've tried my best. I wonder Reg hasn't learned to set a bit more store by you by now. He won't see commitment like that in anyone else he takes on.'

'He's a man of his time. He thinks there are jobs for women and jobs for men, and the job of a woman who's a wife and mother is exactly that.'

'And that's why you've turned down this young man of yours, I suppose.'

'I haven't turned him down yet. But I promised him an answer before he leaves, one way or the other.'

'When does he leave?'

'The 7th of June.'

'That's this Sunday.'

'I know. Only two days left.' She stared into her beer, watching the wisps of froth swirl on the surface. 'I think I know what that answer has to be. I didn't until last night. But I wanted your opinion.'

'What for? Affairs of the heart really aren't my forte, as I said before.'

'This is an affair of the heart and the brain. It isn't just about Charlie – it affects my entire life. And… well, I respect you. I don't have any other male friends I'd feel comfortable talking to about it.'

'All right, if you're going to butter me up,' he said, smiling. 'What was it about last night that made up your mind?'

She sighed. 'It never was only about the magazine or giving up my job. There was always that worry about Charlie going off to war – that I might lose him. When I thought about being left alone as a widow and mother, it terrified me.'

'Yes, I should imagine it would.'

'I suppose at heart I'm nothing but a selfish coward. There are women bravely waving off husbands and sweethearts all over the country, because they know that winning the war is a higher cause. But when I thought about it happening to me… I wasn't sure I could be that brave.'

'This is a little hypothetical, isn't it? Most of the men who go to war will come home safe and sound, I suppose.'

'But a lot won't. What about the men in the plane last night? What about Jem? They're not coming home. Thousands of men aren't – and there could be thousands more again before we see the end of this thing. The ones who do come home might not be the same as when they left.'

Don took out his pipe and started stuffing it with tobacco. 'Ah. That's it, isn't it? It's the men you saw in the plane.'

She lowered her gaze and nodded. 'Whenever I close my eyes, I see them,' she said quietly. 'The smoking body in the plane and the pilot with half a face. They weren't even part of the fight; they were only training. That could have been Charlie. They could all have been Charlie.'

'But they weren't Charlie.'

'Not this time.' She swallowed a sob. 'We're losing the war, Don. Planes are being shot down every day.'

'Things look like they're getting better. There's not been a blitz on London for weeks.'

'Hmm. And why do you think that is? Germany can't have run out of bombers.'

He shrugged. 'Demoralised, perhaps. They suffered heavy losses in the last attack. Hess has given himself up. Maybe the tide of the war is turning.'

'That might be what the powers that be want us to think, but I don't believe it. It's too sudden. If Göring's called off the Luftwaffe for the moment then it can only be because his boss has got something worse up his sleeve for us,' Bobby observed darkly. 'If I know Charlie's out there, how can it not haunt me – especially if we start a family together? Every time I shut my eyes, I'll see a burning body in a plane. Only after he's gone, the body I see won't be a stranger; it'll be the man I love. The father of my children. I'll go mad with it.'

Don smoked his pipe in silence for a few minutes.

'I wish you hadn't gone up that mountain, Bobby,' he said at last.

'So do I. But I needed to, all the same.'

'So you're going to turn him down, are you?'

'I have to,' she said quietly.

'You couldn't ask if he'd agree to a long engagement and wait until the war's over? No bairns to consider then, and you'd keep your job – at least until the knot was tied. Might be long enough for Reg to reconsider.'

'I don't think that's very fair, do you? Who knows how many months or even years it'll be until the war ends?' She shivered. 'Or what the world might look like if we lose.'

'You really believe that's the best decision for you and this lad?'

'It's the fairest. The best thing I can do for him is set him free.'

A small sob escaped. Don patted her hand somewhat awkwardly.

'Then why do I sense that isn't really what you want?' he asked.

She blew her nose on her handkerchief. 'There are many things I want, Don. I want the war to end tomorrow and the world to go back to how it was before. I want all the men away fighting to come home safe and whole to the people who love them. I want to make a success of my job at *The Tyke*. And yes, I want to marry Charlie Atherton. I want to wake up every morning lying next to him, and to protect him from the German guns. But only one of those things is something I can actually have.' She looked up at him. 'Am I right?'

Don smoked his pipe. It was a little while before he answered.

'When you lay it all out like that, I can see why you feel that's the only choice you can make,' he said.

'That wasn't what I asked.'

'No, but it's all the answer you'll get from me. Right and wrong are matters for you alone.' He looked at her. 'Just don't write yourself off, that's all. Things change – these days they seem to change hour by hour. There might be a time you'll think and feel differently about marriage.'

'It wouldn't matter if I did. If I don't marry Charlie Atherton, I sure as hell won't be marrying anyone else,' she said fervently.

'Aye, you say that. Keep an open mind, that's all. Things that seem clear to us one day can have a habit of looking different once the light changes.'

'I can't imagine how things could ever look any different. I wish they could.' She sighed. 'I don't know how I can bring myself to tell Charlie.'

Chapter 26

It was late in the evening when Bobby arrived home. Her head was throbbing with exhaustion and thoughts of the terrible task that lay ahead of her. How she wished she could wake up tomorrow with the burden removed from her shoulders, and the prospect of a Saturday night spent dancing in Charlie's arms as she had on so many Saturday nights before. How she wished everything could just be fixed somehow, as if by the wave of a good fairy's wand. How she wished to God the war could be over!

She frowned as she reached the bottom of the track that led down to Moorside. Reg and Mary didn't keep late hours and must surely be in bed by now, and yet she could hear music. The tinny tinkle of an old piano… was it coming from Cow House Cottage? It sounded louder and more vivid than anything that might be playing on their old wireless set. And someone was singing too: a deep baritone Bobby vaguely remembered from the dim and distant past, singing along to the tune of 'It's a Long Way to Tipperary'.

She had a surprise when she entered the parlour. Charlie was in there, sitting at the old piano that Mary had brought down from the attic at Moorside the day the Parrys came to stay. Someone had screwed the legs back on and it had been squeezed into a corner by the fire.

Her father stood beside it, singing while Charlie played. Bobby hadn't heard him sing since her mother was alive.

The piano was out of tune and her father's rich, deep voice – out of practice for so many years – quavered on some of the notes. Still, it was a homely little scene. For some reason Bobby found herself rather tearful, and she turned away from the men while she unslung the gas mask box from her shoulder and removed her coat. She didn't want to interrupt while they were singing.

Her dad smiled at her when he'd finished. 'Here she is at last. We've been waiting up for thee, lass.'

Bobby knew when her father lapsed into the familiar 'thee' of her early childhood that he was in a nostalgic mood. She went to give him a kiss.

'What prompted the sing-song?' she asked.

'Oh, I don't know. Charlie called round to see if you'd come home and there were nowt but Sandy and that bloody organ of his on t' wireless again. We decided to make our own entertainment. Got this old instrument fettled while we waited for you.'

'You sounded grand, Dad. Just like old times.' She'd been avoiding looking at Charlie, but she turned to him now. 'You too, Charlie. The pair of you could go into music hall together.'

Charlie laughed, standing to greet her. 'Well, the piano needs a good tuning and the pianist probably needs a kick in the rump for letting himself get so shockingly out of practice. Still, it was nice to give the old ivories a tickle again.'

'I never knew you could play.'

'I'm a man of many talents, Bobby.'

She smiled. 'So I'm learning.'

'We've had a rather jolly time, singing some old favourites. I found a book of music on the shelves at Moorside. How was your friend Mr Sykes?'

'He was... helpful.' Bobby kicked off her shoes and flexed her toes, which were still suffering from her hike of the night before. 'Was there a reason you were both waiting up for me? I'd love to join the party but I'm dead on my feet, I'm afraid. I need to get to bed.'

'Charlie's heard some news,' her dad said, nodding to him. 'Of your Polish pal over at big house.'

Bobby was alert now. 'Which? The pilot?'

Charlie nodded. 'Topsy telephoned. It's good news, Bobby. He isn't out of the woods yet, but the surgery seems to have been a success. His fever's subsided and the RAF doctors believe he might have turned a corner.'

'Oh, thank goodness,' she said with a sigh of relief. 'And the other man – the gunner?'

'He's awake and able to hold a conversation, although he needs to rest frequently. Topsy visited with a basket of books and good food for the two of them, sort of a Red Cross parcel.' He smiled. 'I imagine she made a pest of herself for as long as it took to get that toff officer to let her visit the men. No one says no to Topsy.'

'I'm so glad they're going to be all right,' Bobby said fervently. 'If it had all been in vain, after everything we went through...'

'I know.'

'Was that all you wanted to tell me?'

'No, I had some slightly less life-or-death good news from Reg as well. He says you might as well make a long weekend of it now you've had Friday off work and take tomorrow morning too. I think Mary made him feel that a single day off was a little stingy as a reward for the woman currently being hailed as Silverdale's most heroic resident.'

'Oh, thank goodness,' she said with a sigh. 'I feel like I'll die if I don't sleep for at least eight hours.'

'Did you have to go to Bradford today?' her dad asked.

She averted her eyes. 'I needed to talk to Don. It... wasn't something I felt I could put off.'

Charlie came over to peck her cheek. 'I'd better go home so you two can get some sleep. You look exhausted, Bobby.'

Bobby glanced at her father to see if he was frowning at Charlie taking such a liberty as to kiss her in front of him, but his expression was more benevolent than disapproving this evening. It must be the effect of all that singing, she supposed. Her dad had always loved to sing when her mother was alive. Bobby remembered the two of them warbling Christmas carols together at the old family piano, she and Lilian sitting on the top clapping their little hands in time to the music. But that had been a long time ago.

'I'll see you to the farmhouse,' she said to Charlie. 'That's if my dad doesn't mind.'

Her dad gave her a magnanimous nod. 'Don't be out there too long, mind.'

'I won't. I'll be back in a minute, Dad.'

She followed Charlie outside and closed the door behind them. It was dark, but she could just see his face illuminated by the chink of light that escaped from the broken plaster in one of the cottage's window slits. Now they were alone, he looked rather sombre.

'Thanks for sitting with Dad tonight,' she said. 'I can see he enjoyed himself with you.'

'I thought he might be missing you. I was too.'

'He loves to sing – or at least he used to. When my mam was still with us.'

'He has a fine voice. Shame to hide it under a bushel.'

Charlie looked as though he was going to take her hand for a moment, then he seemed to think better of it.

'That was good news about the airmen,' Bobby said, casting about for another topic. The conversation felt strained and awkward now they were alone, as if the answer she still hadn't given hung over them like the sword of Damocles.

'Yes. Topsy was thrilled that "her pilot", as she calls him, looks like he's going to pull through after all.'

'I'll visit them myself next week if I can get that officer to let me in.' She hesitated. 'Look, Charlie—'

'Don't, Bobby.' He sounded sad, but also sort of resigned. 'Not now.'

'We only have one more day.'

'Then let's have one more day.' He took her hands in his now and pressed them tightly. 'One last Saturday, just for us. We'll dance and we'll hold each other and we'll kiss and then... then afterwards you can tell me what you've decided. Please.'

'All right.'

'Thank you.' He kissed her cheek – just the lightest touch of his lips, as if she'd been brushed by a passing butterfly. 'I'll meet you here with Boxer at two o'clock, after I've finished handing over to the vet in Smeltham. Goodnight, Bobby.'

She watched him head back to Moorside. Something about the way he walked seemed different. His shoulders slumped slightly, and his gait wasn't so full of bounce and confidence as it usually was. Perhaps his body was still recovering from carrying the pilot down the mountain the night before. Or perhaps it was something else that weighed him down.

When she went back into the cottage, her dad was waiting for her.

'You see? I wasn't long, was I?' she said, forcing a smile.

'Are you and that boy planning to get wed or what, our Bobby?'

Bobby was rather taken aback at the abruptness of the question. While her dad often gave her stern warnings about being cautious in her relations with boys, he'd never asked her outright before what Charlie's intentions towards her were.

'What makes you think he's asked me?' she said.

'He damn well ought to have by now, with all the time he's been spending with you,' he said. 'Besides, I'm not deaf. It's all over t' village that he's after getting you down the aisle. Glad to know he's honest, at least.'

'I... no. No, I'm not going to marry Charlie.'

He squinted at her. 'Why not then? You see him enough.'

'Why? Did you want me to marry him?'

He shrugged. 'You could do a lot worse. Rather Charlie than someone like that nowt Tony Scott who you were always hanging about with in Bradford. Besides, everyone can see you're keen on t' lad.'

She sank into a chair, feeling light-headed. 'I'm not going to get married, Dad. Not to Charlie, certainly not to Tony, and probably not to anyone else either.'

'You'd better think about wedding someone while they'll have you, my lass. I won't always be around to provide for you, you know, and you aren't getting any younger.'

Bobby felt it best not to point out that it was she who provided for him these days. They lived mostly on what she earned, plus what little her siblings could send home out of their wage packets to add to the family coffers. All her dad was able to contribute was the odd lucky gambling win and some poached game.

'I can provide for myself,' she said instead.

'Aye, and be an old maid with it.'

'Yes, I suppose so. Is there so much shame in that? There are worse things to be, although sometimes it feels like I'm the only person in existence who truly believes that.'

'Worse things to be but not lonelier things to be. No husband, no bairns... it's not what your mam would've wanted for you. Nor what I would neither.'

'I wish everyone would stop being so bloody concerned about how I'm going to spend my old age and leave me to worry about myself,' she said impatiently, turning her face away from him.

'Watch that mouth, young lady,' her dad said sternly. 'Folk are concerned because they want to see you happy and looked after. Folk as care about you, that is.'

'Sorry,' she said in a softer tone, turning back. 'I didn't mean to swear. I know you want what's best for me, Dad, but I'm not a child any more, am I? This is a choice I have to make for myself – and I have. I'm doing what I feel is for the best, for me and for Charlie.' She got up and went to give him a kiss. 'I really do need to sleep now. I've barely closed my eyes for two days. You ought to get to bed too.'

Chapter 27

Bobby was tired enough that no dreams came that night, for which she was grateful. She slept the sleep of the dead for nearly twelve hours before she was woken by a knock on her bedroom door.

'Dad,' she mumbled when he looked around it, trying to focus her sleep-filled eyes. 'What time is it?'

'After ten.'

'Ten!' She pressed a palm to her forehead. 'I'm so sorry. You must have been freezing.'

'I'm not entirely helpless, you know, our Bobby. There's a fire going in t' kitchen grate.' He looked rather proud of himself at having achieved this feat.

'Did you eat? You should have woken me.'

'I reckoned you needed your sleep. Don't worry, I made myself a bit o' toast.'

'I'll get up and make some tea. Just give me half an hour to make myself presentable.'

'No need to rush for my benefit. I'm meeting Pete over in Dunrigg in a bit so I'm heading out. Market day there today. If I see owt worth bringing back for tea, I'll pick it up. I promised Jessie and Florrie some red apples if I could find 'em.'

Bobby smiled, pleased to hear he was going to be contributing to the family table through legal means for once. 'They'll be thrilled if you can. Apples are terribly expensive these days, though, Dad. Pippins have gone up to tenpence a pound.'

'Ah well, if it makes the bairns smile. I've got a few bob to spare.'

'Do you want me to make you some sandwiches?'

'You take your time getting up. I've wrapped up some of that leftover potato pie that were in the pantry to take wi' me, and a bit of malt loaf. Ta-ra, love.'

Bobby was glad when he had left her alone with her thoughts. It had taken her brain a little while to surface from the deep dark of her night's sleep, and she hadn't immediately been able to place the mingled feeling of guilt, depression and dread that settled on her as soon as she was conscious again. Once her dad was gone, however, it came back to her. It was today. Today she had to give Charlie her answer. Today she had to witness the pain and hurt in his eyes when she finally told him that no, she couldn't be his wife. Would it break his heart? Would he ever be able to forgive her? She was sure she would never forgive herself.

And yet she knew she had no choice. The men on the mountainside, the ones who hadn't made it and the ones who had, had finally made her mind up for her. That night, she had stared into the face of death and it had changed her irrevocably. She couldn't let herself love a man who every day was in danger of ending up like the men in the plane; not now she'd seen what that truly looked like. She couldn't bring children into a world so frightening and uncertain, with a father they might lose any day. The torture of constantly knowing that today could be the day she got the telegram – or that Charlie might come home to her mutilated, tortured and in pain like the poor Polish pilot – would drive her mad.

Sometimes there'd be a little whisper of hope. *If the war was over*, it said. *If the war was over.* There were still her worries about her job and motherhood, and everything else that she feared might happen if she married Charlie Atherton, but the only thing in life that was truly insurmountable was death – death and the fear of death, which coloured everything. But the whisper was a false friend, because stark realism told her that the war showed no signs of being over. There was no instant happy ending coming to her aid, and if Bobby allowed herself to hope otherwise then she was a fool. If the war ended tomorrow, it would mean Britain had been defeated, and what then? If it didn't end tomorrow, who knew for how long afterwards it might rage? When the last war had begun, there had been hope it would all be over by the Christmas of 1914. Four years later, when the armistice was finally signed, thousands had been killed – millions. Not to mention those like Reg and her father, wounded both physically and mentally, who had never been the same since. She would be beyond naive to think this war might not follow the same path.

Bobby thought for a moment about going over to the farmhouse to talk over the choice she'd made with Mary, but she knew her friend would only try to dissuade her. Mary had sent a husband of her own off to war, waving him away on at least one occasion when she knew she must be carrying his child. When that husband had come home maimed in mind and body because of his experiences and their child had been lost, Mary had grieved, of course… but then she'd carried on. Bobby couldn't tell her friend what she was feeling in the wake of the Bowside crash. She felt ashamed of herself because she couldn't be stronger, the way other women showed themselves to be.

She felt guilty for being unable to accept that king and country had a greater claim on the man she loved than she ever could. Yet she felt that way all the same.

She wondered what would happen to Charlie, afterwards. It was the first time she'd really thought about it. Of course, he'd never found himself short of friendly female company – charming the birds from the trees was something that had always come naturally to him. No doubt there'd be plenty of pretty WAAFs at the RAF school in East Yorkshire where he was to do his training. Perhaps he'd be sad for a little while. He might believe his heart was broken. Still, he'd rally, Bobby was certain. Perhaps the first time he came home on leave, the space she'd taken up in his heart would already be occupied by a fresh idol.

Bobby wondered if she really believed this, or if she was only trying to make herself feel better about the pain she knew she was going to cause him. Except it didn't really make her feel better at all. It made her feel far worse.

There were still a few hours until she was due to meet Charlie for their date – their last date. Bobby decided to fill the time with a walk up to Newby Top Farm to see her friend Andy Jessop and his family. He'd have heard the gossip about the rescued airmen, no doubt, and be grateful to have the story first-hand from someone who was there. Bobby wasn't particularly keen to go over the events of that night again, but nor did she want to sit around the cottage fretting about Charlie.

Andy was very interested in all the news she had to bring him, as she'd known he would be, and Ginny was so impressed with Bobby's part in the rescue that she absolutely insisted she take home a good-sized ham she'd been curing in the larder. Bobby tried to refuse such a generous gift but the kindly old Daleswoman refused to take no for an answer, and so Bobby found herself walking back down to Silverdale with a basket containing the wrapped ham hooked over her arm.

And Ginny wasn't the only one who seemed anxious to press gifts on to her. She was passing the bakery when Molly Craven, the baker's wife, beckoned her inside.

'Me and t' owd man thought you might like to take this home for your supper, Miss,' she said, handing over a little package. 'Wi' our compliments, o' course.'

Bobby lifted a corner of the paper to see what was inside. It was a small seed cake, still warm from the oven. When she lifted it to her nose, it smelled sweet, moist and rich, like the cakes they'd had before the war.

'Molly, this is very generous of you,' Bobby said. 'You must let me pay for it.'

'Oh now, don't be daft. I reckon after what you and t' rest on 'em done for them poor injured boys, a little treat wi' your cup o' tea is least we can offer.'

'Honestly, I barely did anything. All I did was wave a rattle and shout. The men who carried the stretchers did the hard work, and the two doctors.'

'Aye, we all heard what you did. We heard that it were you got them organised to make a rescue party when there were some as would rather have stayed cosy by t' fire, and it were you who stopped men being left for dead when the rest decided they mun be t' enemy. Gil Capstick's been spreading the word.'

'It was me the gunner spoke to and told me they were Free Polish, but there's no great achievement in that. I was the nearest to him, that's all. Charlie did more than me.'

'And we've a little treat for him too when he comes by. Now you mustn't insult us by refusing it, Miss.'

Bobby knew there was no point arguing further after this. The refusal of a gift of food was an unforgivable offence in Silverdale.

'Well, thank you, it's ever so kind,' she said. 'The cake's going to be a wonderful treat for my dad and me. We're very grateful.'

'Let's say it's on behalf o' them lads who'd noan be alive now if it weren't for you.' Molly gave her a knowing smile. 'Happen you might let young Charlie know we've a treat for him when you see him. The two o' ye never seem to be far apart these days.'

'Um, yes, I will. Thanks again, Molly.'

No matter where Bobby went in the village, it was the same. When she stopped at the butcher's to pick up their meat ration, there was an extra packet of sausages kept under the counter for her. Lizzie ran out from the Golden Hart to let her know there was a jug of beer for her and her father behind the bar whenever they chose to claim it, with the compliments of the establishment. Mrs Clough, who was pegging out her washing, dashed inside to give her a block of cheese she'd saved out of her ration. Bobby half-expected Jos the blacksmith to emerge from his workshop when she passed by and start piling horseshoes into her arms.

When she eventually mounted her bike to cycle back to Moorside, her bicycle basket was brimful of hams, cakes, sausages, cheese and other goodies. Bobby was a little worried she might be stopped by a policeman and arrested for smuggling black-market goods.

Back at the farmhouse, Charlie was leading Boxer from his stable to hitch him up to the little trap he used for getting around in.

'What's all this?' he asked, nodding to the overflowing bicycle basket. 'Did you discover cornucopia, the horn of plenty, when you were out on your walk this morning?'

'I'm not quite sure,' Bobby said, still feeling a little dazed by people's generosity. 'Everywhere I went, people kept giving me things. I didn't want to take them, but they got very offended when I tried to turn any of it down. They seem to think I'm solely responsible for bringing those airmen down from Bowside.'

'And so you are. I told you you'd be a hero today, didn't I?'

'But I didn't do anything. The men from the village brought them down, and you and the doctors treated them. All I did was raise the alarm, that's all.'

'You gave us leadership. Without you, no one would have known what to do or where to go. It's a skill to keep your head in a crisis like that – one not many people have. You ought to stop playing down your part in it.'

'I just feel like such a phoney.'

'Well, you're not. So stop being so daft.' He finished hitching up Boxer and patted the pony's flank. 'I'm certainly going to miss you, old lad.'

Bobby rested her bike against the wall of the stable and approached to give Boxer's nose a stroke. He whinnied appreciatively.

'What will happen to him?' Bobby asked quietly. 'When you go, I mean.'

'Reg is keeping him on. He's going to struggle to keep the Wolseley running when they cut the petrol ration again next period, and besides, the bairns are fond of the old boy.' He turned to look at her. 'If you've ever got a sugar lump to spare then save it for him, eh? Tell him it's from me.'

His tone was light, but Charlie's eyes held a different expression than Bobby had seen there before. Perhaps it was because he was about to go to war, or perhaps it was because of what he'd seen the night they rescued the airmen. Perhaps all of them who'd been there that night looked different now than they had before: Topsy, Charlie. Her. Did her eyes hold that same sad, haunted look?

She could have stood anything except those eyes, looking at her, filled with so much pain.

'Oh God, Charlie,' she whispered.

The next moment she was in his arms, shaking with sobs while he covered her in kisses.

'Hey. It's all right,' he whispered.

'It isn't. Everything's... changing. It feels like nothing will ever be the same here again. Like there'll never be joy again. The world feels so dark.'

'I know. I feel the same.'

'Aren't you terribly afraid?'

'I thought I was afraid before, but I don't think I really understood what I had to fear until Bowside. I remember waking up in the night hearing your dad scream. Now I understand what he must have seen in his dreams.'

'You can hear Dad from the farmhouse?'

'Sometimes. Reg has nightmares too, at times. I suppose all those old soldiers do.' He held her back. 'But every storm has an ending, Bobby.'

'Does it?'

'It has to.'

She pressed her face against his chest, breathing in his scent as she let the tears she'd held back for too long flow. 'I love you very much, Charlie. And I'm sorry, I'm so sorry.'

'Not now.' He lifted her face and kissed her softly. He kissed away the tears on her cheeks and at the corners of her eyes, and then he kissed her lips. 'One more day with joy in it. Just one.'

'You know, don't you? You already know what I'm going to say.'

'I knew the moment I saw you at the hospital, after we came down from the mountain with the airmen.' He kissed her again. 'But don't say it. Don't say it until you say goodbye. Just dry your eyes, put on your best dress and let me take you dancing one last time.'

–

The last night with Charlie was like every night they'd spent together condensed into one. Everything was the same only more so. When they ate fish and chips together under the arches in Settle town centre, they tasted better than they ever had because they were the last fish and chips. Charlie's arms, when he spun her around the dance hall that evening in her best blue crepe dress with the sweetheart neckline, felt warmer and stronger than ever before. The two young lovers held each other more tightly than ever, knowing that tomorrow they'd be lovers no more.

But every storm must come to an end, Charlie had said, and so, too, must the sunshine. The last night had to end, and it did so when Charlie helped Bobby to dismount from the trap outside Cow House Cottage at midnight.

'Here you are, Cinderella, home safe and sound,' he said, smiling. 'I'd better put Boxer away before he turns into a mouse.'

'Charlie…'

He took her in his arms.

'Not yet,' he whispered. 'When you say goodbye.'

And he kissed her like he never wanted the kiss to end. But it did.

Chapter 28

The big goodbye took place in the garden of Moorside Farm the following morning. Charlie looked bashful as he came out of the house in his smart new uniform, freshly pressed by Mary. He was to catch the bus from the Black Bull to the station in Skipton, and from there he'd make his way to his billet in East Yorkshire. The family had lined up to say goodbye to him.

Mary was standing next to Bobby. She glanced down at her left hand.

'What is it?' Bobby said.

'Nowt. Only I thought, after the two of you went out last night, happen I might see summat new there this morning.'

'Then you were wrong,' Bobby said quietly. Mary looked at her, eyebrows raised, before falling silent.

'Now then, young man,' Bobby's dad said, stepping forward to shake Charlie's hand vigorously in both of his own. 'Got your Brylcreem packed, have you?'

Charlie laughed. 'Been buying it by the gallon, Rob.'

'Well, lad, good luck up there. Steady as she goes for your first few flights.'

'I'll be earthbound for a while yet. I understand there'll be eight weeks of solid square bashing before they let me anywhere near the Tiger Moths they use for training.'

'Buy the other lads a round on me when you get there, eh?' Rob said, pressing a note into his hand. 'Mind how you go, Charlie. Looking forward to another sing-song when you're home on leave.'

'That's generous of you. Thank you.'

Bobby cast a concerned look at the note Charlie was tucking into his pocket. Her father seemed to be very free with his money lately. He'd come home from the market yesterday with a basketful of apples for the girls, biscuits for the dogs, and some little treats for her and Mary too. It could only mean he'd been gambling again. She wasn't sure if that was better or worse than the poaching, but if Pete was running it then it was certainly just as illegal. That worried her.

The two evacuees went up next to say goodbye, following a little push from Mary. Ace bounded over with them, walking by Florence on his lead.

Jessie immediately threw herself at Charlie and burst into tears. Florrie, however, seemed to be sulking, folding her arms and looking the other way while her lower lip wobbled.

'Now, Jess, none of that,' Charlie said gently, crouching down to give the sobbing Jessie a hug. 'I'll be home on leave in no time at all, I promise.'

'But… we won't have… any good games till you come back,' the little girl sobbed.

'Don't be daft. Bobby's still here, and Reggie and Mary. They know all sorts of good games. And you've got Ace to play with, and Barney and Winnie, and Boxer to go for rides on. I say, won't your dad be impressed when he visits on leave in a fortnight and you can show him all the tricks Ace has learned?'

This seemed to mollify Jessie a little. She drew a sleeve over her nose, much to Mary's horror, who immediately rushed forward to press a clean handkerchief into the child's hand.

'I wish you could stay and meet Dad, Uncle Charlie,' Jessie said.

'I do too, but there'll be other times for that. And you and Florrie can write and tell me all about his visit, and about how the animals are doing and the new games you've made up. So I shall feel almost like I'm here after all. And I'm going to give you the most important job of all while I'm gone, because you're the only one I trust to care for Boxer for me. Can you do that?'

Jessie looked pleased. 'Oh yes, I can look after him all right. I know when he's to be fed, and how to rub him down and all like that.'

'I knew you did. You've been a good little learner.' He took a coin from his pocket and pressed it into her hand, lowering his voice to a whisper. 'Here's two bob. Don't tell Mary you've got it and you can spend the whole lot on spice.'

Mary, who had clearly heard this, was wise enough to look the other way and pretend she hadn't.

With one child appeased, Charlie turned his attention to the grumpy-looking Florence.

'I've got another two-bob bit here reserved under the name Florence Parry,' he said coaxingly.

'Don't want two bob.'

'Well, what do you want?'

Florence sniffed. 'Want you not to go to the war,' she muttered. 'Why is everyone always going off to the stupid war?'

'Because if we didn't, the bad people would win.'

'Why've you got to go, though, Uncle Charlie? There's lots more people could go instead.'

'And all those people have got other people who don't want them to go. But they have to, all the same.' He beckoned her over. 'Come on, say goodbye properly. I know you wouldn't let me leave without a hug, would you?'

Florence gulped and threw her arms around his shoulders.

'Be brave, Florrie,' he whispered. 'I need you to keep an eye on things here and tell me how everyone gets on. Jess is too little to write me letters all by herself. You're the writer in the family, isn't that true? Published in *The Tyke*, no less.'

Florrie nodded. 'But you'll come back soon?'

'As soon as ever I can. And don't forget you'll have your father here to visit before long.'

'Will you bring me a present from the war?'

'All right. What would you like me to bring for you?'

'Will you bring me… a German helmet?' she asked hopefully. 'Louis Butcher in my class has got one his grandad brung back from the other war and he let me hold it.'

He laughed. 'If I'm in a position to get my hands on a German helmet, it might be some time until I can bring it home. But I'm sure I can find something you'll like.'

He pressed the two-shilling piece into her hand and gave Ace a stroke of farewell before standing up to say goodbye to Mary.

'Well, Mother, it seems you're to be rid of me at last.'

'Oh, Charlie, don't joke.' She put her arms around him. 'Now stay safe, and write to me as soon as you get there safely, and be sure to wear clean underwear if they send you up in a plane because you never know, and—'

'—and don't talk to any strange men, make sure to eat my crusts so my hair will curl and always say please and thank you,' he said, laughing. 'I still remember the speech you gave me when you packed me off to school.'

'Oh, you're a daft 'ap'orth. I don't know how any lass has the time of day for you.' She clipped his ear, then pushed his head down so she could kiss his crown. 'You just be careful out there, that's all. You're a good boy.'

'That's not what you usually say.'

'Well, happen I'm feeling generous today. You'll be missed around here, our Charlie.' She beckoned Reg over. 'Your brother's got something he wants to say to you as well.'

Reg limped forward to join them, looking awkward. He held out a hand stiffly for Charlie to shake.

'Mind how you go, won't you, little brother?' he said. 'Can't say as I understand why you're doing it when you've no need but it's a brave thing you're doing all the same.'

'Thanks, Reggie.'

Mary nudged her husband.

'Oh. Right.' He took something from his pocket that sparkled in the summer sunshine. 'This is for you. Father's old pocket watch. Given to him personally by none other than Lord Kitchener, who was his commanding officer at Omdurman – that's the story he used to tell, at any rate. He gave it to me when I shipped out last time round. Happen it might bring you good luck, eh?'

Charlie stared at it as if mesmerised. 'You're giving our father's watch to me?'

'I know he'd want you to have it.' He glanced at Bobby, who nodded slightly. 'And I wanted you to know, before you go… I'm right proud of you, lad. Not just for what you're doing now. What you did the other day, bringing those poor wounded men down from Bowside and fighting off those old fools who'd have left them up there to die – the whole business took guts I never knew you had. You've the makings of a fine man in you, Charlie, and I'm sorry if it's taken me too long to say it.'

Charlie turned away for a moment. Bobby could see he was touched and struggling with emotion.

'That means a lot to me, Reggie,' he said in a choked voice when he'd managed to get himself under control. He slapped his brother on the back. 'You know, old man, I'm actually going to miss you.'

'Aye, well, let's not overdo it, eh?' Reg said with a smile.

Charlie turned to look at Bobby. Reg gave a signal to Mary, who took charge of the children, and the rest of the household tactfully disappeared inside to let them say their goodbyes in private.

There didn't seem to be any need for words. Everything important had already been said. They just came together and held each other tight, and for the last time, Bobby breathed in the scent of him.

'You'd better give me your answer before I go,' Charlie whispered after some time had passed.

'Do I need to?'

'I'd like to hear it. It's been a long time coming.'

'I'm sorry, Charlie.' She swallowed a sob. 'I'm sorry. I can't.'

'I'd wait for you, you know. I'd wait if the war lasted for fifty years.'

'It wouldn't be fair to ask you.' She pressed her eyes closed but the tears still leaked out. 'People must be mad to be making plans like marriage and families, now. How can they put down roots and talk about a future when tomorrow... tomorrow might not even come? When there might not be a free world for their children to grow up in?'

'Because they need to,' he said quietly. 'To give them the promise of a tomorrow that's worth fighting for. I know you don't feel the same way as I do about it, but there it is.'

'No. But I do love you.' She let him go to look into his face, not caring what state her mascara was in. 'I'll never love anyone else, I swear it.'

He smiled sadly as he brushed a tear away with one fingertip. 'You will though.'

'I don't want to.' She felt almost angry at the suggestion. 'I won't.'

'I wish it were true, for my own selfish sake.' He planted a soft kiss on her cheek. 'Please don't write. It'll only hurt. Let Mary do it.'

She felt her heart sink, realising that with this last request she was truly losing him from her life. 'All right. If it's going to give you pain.'

'Take care of yourself, Bobby Bancroft. Try to find joy in whatever you choose to do with your life. If you ever change your mind and think you could find it with me, you know how to reach me.'

And he was gone.

Chapter 29

A couple of weeks later, Bobby was again stuffing envelopes with back numbers of *The Tyke* at her desk. Usually she was sluggish with this sort of work, not relishing the dull task, but since Charlie had left, she found the repetitive action somehow soothing. As she let her hands mechanically fill the envelopes, her eyes and her daydreams followed the birds that soared above the fells and disappeared into a slate-grey mid-June sky.

She thought of Charlie and wondered what he was doing right at this moment. At least for now she knew he was safe. He'd told her there was nothing but parading and drilling for the first eight weeks of training, so he couldn't be in the air yet. Not that that stopped her imagination from constructing the most terrifying scenarios whenever she allowed her mind to wander to the memories of what had happened on the mountainside.

Mary had had one letter from Charlie since he'd gone. Bobby had watched her open it. For some reason, the envelope with its RAF censor stamp had sent a jolt through her. The officialness of it made him feel so very far away.

He had sounded jolly and happy in his letter, apparently settling in well and making friends among the other recruits he had been billeted with. He'd asked after everyone at home, including her father – everyone except her. The omission filled Bobby with a flat, empty ache, as if something had been scooped out of her insides.

The first Sunday after Charlie's departure, Bobby had asked if she might be allowed to accompany Reg and Mary to chapel. She wasn't a regular churchgoer and nor was she a Methodist as the Athertons were, but it was Charlie's faith and she had wanted to say a prayer for him in his own place of worship. She knew the Dalesfolk who worshipped there would be welcoming to her, although she was an Anglican; there was little sectarian rivalry in the village except of the good-natured variety, usually enacted on the cricket field during the annual Church vs Chapel summer friendly. When the congregation had fallen to their knees to pray, she had done so likewise, clasping her hands tightly as she pleaded with God to keep Charlie safe. She poured into her prayer everything that was filling her heart, with all the intensity it deserved, but so many prayers of that nature must be drifting up to heaven at the moment that Bobby feared hers might get lost in the throng.

'Got summat a bit more interesting than envelope-stuffing for you if you've had enough for today, lass,' Reg said, looking up from his typewriter. 'There's a story I want for the August number that only you can get for me.'

'Hmm?' She pulled her gaze from the birds flying outside the window and gave him a vague smile. 'Oh. That's all right, Reg. I'm happy to do a bit more.'

Reg eyed her with concern for a moment before pushing himself to his feet with his stick and hobbling over.

'What's up then?' he asked, not standing on ceremony as usual. 'Still pining for the boy, are you?'

'No,' she said. 'I miss him, naturally. But I'm all right.'

'You're not all right. You look tired and low in spirits.'

'I've not been sleeping so well, that's all. Please don't worry about me.'

There was a noise outside the room, as of something being dragged. Captain Parry was due to visit them for a few days' leave on Sunday – the day after tomorrow – and Mary was all of a fluster as she cleaned the house and prepared Charlie's old room for him. Her efforts weren't assisted by the 'help' she was receiving from Ace. The little puppy was contributing to proceedings by running around her in circles and barking his head off whenever she rearranged the furniture, which he clearly considered a species of wooden sheep.

'Your old man tells me you do nowt these days except work or sit in that tin hut down in the village,' Reg said to Bobby, ignoring the noise outside. 'Don't sound like much of a life for a young lass.'

'Well, did you think I could just bounce back?' Bobby asked, frowning at him. 'Take two weeks to mourn and then skip off with some other young man to go dancing? That isn't the way it goes, Reg – not for me, at least.'

'You turned the lad down, didn't you?'

'That doesn't mean I didn't care for him. I did, a great deal – I do still.'

'Aye, I know.' He patted her shoulder. 'I miss him too. Don't tell him, though, eh? It'll only make him cockier.'

She smiled sadly. 'I couldn't anyhow. He's forbidden me to write to him. Says it'll only hurt.'

'Look, Bobby, if you've said no to Charlie for my benefit, because of what I told you about your future here—'

'I didn't.' She sighed. 'My job was a consideration, yes. God knows I don't want to leave *The Tyke*. My work on the mag is the most important thing in the world to me, besides family. But…'

'But?'

'It was really the men on the mountain who made up my mind. Now is no time to be marrying and starting a family. I could never get Charlie to understand it but… would you want to bring a child into a world like this?'

'I did bring a child into a world like this,' Reg said quietly. 'And she was gone just when I had hope she'd be growing up in a better one.'

'Yes, I suppose you did. I'm sorry, that was a thoughtless thing to say.'

'Well, happen you made a sensible decision. Our Charlie never could see further than the end of his nose, and you're right, if we can't claw our way back and win this thing then the world'll be no place for bairns. It's up to those of us with a longer range of vision than my brother to make the hard choices, I suppose.' He took the envelope she was holding out of her hands and put it down on the desk. 'What you ought to do is throw yourself into your work. That'll get you sleeping at night again.'

'I am working, aren't I?'

'Filling envelopes. You need to be using that brain of yours. Where's the Bobby Bancroft who badgers me endlessly to send her out getting stories, eh?'

Bobby smiled tightly. 'She's on holiday.'

'Aye, very funny. Well you'll go out to get me a story this afternoon, whether you want to or not. I spoke to her ladyship on the phone this morning to arrange for you to visit Sumner House. That young Polish pilot's in good enough fettle for visitors now, I'm hearing. I want you to frame yourself up there and find out how him and his mate are getting on after their ordeal, plus anything else interesting they can tell you. Get some quotes if they're willing to have them in print.'

'You mean you want me to write up the Bowside crash for *The Tyke*?'

'Damn right I do. I'm not going to waste an eyewitness on my own staff, am I?' He stomped back to his desk and gave her a censorious look as he sat down again. 'I noticed they had a big piece about it in the *Courier*, including several details only someone on the spot would've known about. Ran straight to your pal Don Sykes with it, didn't you?'

'Well, it was news. It's not the sort of thing we usually carry in *The Tyke* so I didn't see why not. Besides, I only really gave him the bare bones of it.'

'And now I'm asking you to give me the meat of it.'

'People before things?'

'Right.'

She squinted at him. 'You're not doing this for my benefit, are you? Trying to stop me brooding?'

'I wouldn't sacrifice precious paper rations just for that, would I? The stuff's like gold dust nowadays.'

She smiled. 'Well, that I can believe.'

'It'll do you good, though, all the same. Get you out and about again.' Reg leaned back in his chair. 'It's got all the ingredients for a great little story, I reckon. We can include names of all the aircrew now the families have been informed, as long as the survivors consent. I know you've got the skill to capture all the suspense and emotion that must've been present when you were there in the thick of it, which is more than Don Sykes can do. For once, Bobby, this is a story only you can write.'

She grimaced. 'I'm not sure I want to live it again. I see it often enough in my nightmares.'

'It'll help,' Reg said as he picked up his blue pencil. 'Trust me. Write me a piece and put everything into it. It'll help you exorcise it.'

'Do you do that?'

'I have done. Keep it all in journals, so I don't have to keep it up here,' he said, tapping his temple with the pencil.

'You mean your memories of what happened to you in the last war?'

'And what happened to me after,' he said quietly. Bobby knew he was talking about losing Nancy.

'It really helped you?'

'Didn't make it disappear but it was a type of relief.' He gave a dry laugh. 'Mary keeps on at me to write them up into something for publication. My memoirs, if you please. *Memories of a Yorkshire Nobody*, I could call them.'

'Why don't you? I'm sure they'd be fascinating. You've got the skill.'

'Because they're mine, that's why. Last thing I want is strangers picking through them, turning up their noses at this and that.'

'Yet you want me to write about what happened on Bowside for strangers to read.'

'That's different. People need stories like that in a time of war; stories about working as a team, bravery, over-coming the odds. Shows them what's best about people at a time when human nature can seem bleak and cruel.' He looked at her. 'But I'm not going to make you if you're uncomfortable about it. Up to you one way or the other.'

Bobby thought about the two men who'd been brought down from the mountainside. Would they want their stories known? They were foreigners, and people could be funny about foreigners, even those on the Allied side. If they'd experienced prejudice in the past, they might just as soon prefer to keep themselves to themselves. They would still be grieving for their fellow airmen who hadn't survived. On the other hand, Reg was right – a mountain dash to save lives against the odds was exactly the sort of morale-boosting story that it did people good to read.

'I'll go, since Topsy is expecting me,' she told Reg. 'I would like to visit the men and see how they're getting along. But I'll only write about it if they agree, all right?'

Reg smiled. 'You know, lass, sometimes I wonder who's editor around here.'

'It's only fair, isn't it? It's their story really, not ours.'

'I suppose you've got a point. Go along and see them. Then, if they're willing, you can write it up for the August number.'

Chapter 30

When Bobby called for Topsy at the cottage in the grounds of Sumner House, she discovered her friend wasn't there. Mrs Hobbes answered the door, dressed up ready for her after-dinner pint at the Hart. She had her bright-red umbrella under her arm and her best cloche hat on her head: the one extravagantly decorated with assorted highly coloured feathers from exotic birds. The thing was quite notorious within the village. Norman was tucked under her arm, looking underwhelmed at the prospect of accompanying her. Mrs Hobbes's plan to find him a wife from the female geese who frequented the beck by the pub had so far been unsuccessful, largely thanks to her spoiled pet's selfish and cantankerous nature. Nevertheless, his mistress cooed over Norman like he was the fluffiest of lap-dog puppies.

'Topsy's yonder at the house,' Mrs Hobbes told Bobby in her faint Scottish lilt when she enquired after her friend. 'She's up there every day now, helping them to nurse. Seems she's a rare talent for it. I never would have believed she could have the patience, myself.'

'But she hasn't done her VAD training yet, has she?'

'Aye, she's managed to talk them into letting her do her training on the job, so to speak. I suppose they found it hard to say no, it being her house and all. I think a friend of her father's who's high up in the RAF might have had some words on her behalf too.'

'How many friends did Topsy's father have, Mrs Hobbes?' Bobby asked. 'They seem to be in positions of power all over the country.'

Mrs Hobbes smiled tightly. 'Well, young lady, that's Eton for you. Still, it's doing her good, the nursing – you'll see for yourself shortly. If you go up to the house and tell them she sent for you, I'm sure you'll have no trouble getting in.' She looked down at the goose under her arm. 'Now say goodbye to your friend Miss Bancroft, Norman, and we'll see if you can get along any better with your courting today.'

After Bobby had given Norman's head a wary pat, much to his evident disgust – 'friend' was rather an over-statement of their relationship – she took the path up to the house. When she reached the front door, she pulled the bell rope. A middle-aged woman in a grey nurse's dress and red cape soon appeared. This, Bobby assumed, must be the matron.

'Um, good afternoon,' Bobby said. 'I'm looking for Lady Sumner-Walsh. She sent for me.'

The woman looked her up and down suspiciously. 'Civilian, are you?'

'Yes, but I was hoping I'd be allowed to visit the two patients you have here. I was part of the rescue party who brought them down.'

'I understood all of the rescue party were men.'

'They were, apart from me. I was the air-raid warden on duty when the plane crashed – Roberta Bancroft. I organised the rescue party and went up with them. Lady Sumner-Walsh can confirm that.' She fumbled in her handbag. 'Here. Here's my identity card, if you need to make sure I am who I say I am.'

She felt it best not to show her press card as well, in case the matron felt the need to consult her superiors before letting her in. The snooty Wingco Bobby had spoken with before hadn't seemed overly keen on admitting civilians, and if the RAF brass who ran the place knew that she was a journalist then they'd be even less likely to grant her visiting rights.

The matron deigned to smile as she checked Bobby's identification. 'Well, I suppose it was too much to believe that men might be able to organise themselves into a rescue party without any female intervention. Since you're a friend of the patients, I think you might come in for a visit, Miss Bancroft. Topsy is with Teddy. She's reading to him, I believe.'

'Teddy?' Bobby said as she followed her inside.

'The pilot, Lieutenant Nowak. His friends in this country call him Teddy.'

Bobby walked beside her to the ward. The house seemed to be bustling with medical and RAF personnel, although as far as she knew, there were still only the two patients from the crashed Wellington here.

'You look like you're preparing to receive more men,' Bobby observed to the matron.

'We're expecting a further eighteen patients from else-where in the country. They're being sent here for the air,' the matron informed her. 'This place was always intended to be more of a sanatorium for convalescing patients than what you might call a hospital, although the Lord had other ideas when He placed those two young Poles here. It must have been divine providence that there was a medical facility so close by and that they were lucky enough to have someone observe the crash after their radio cut out. They'd have died otherwise.'

'It's a shame divine providence didn't stop them crashing in the first place, since their four friends weren't so fortunate,' Bobby muttered, half to herself.

The matron gave her a look. 'We don't hold with that sort of godless talk here, young lady.'

'Sorry.' Bobby put a hand to her head. 'That was an unnecessary remark. I've been under a lot of strain lately.'

The ward looked a little different from the last time she'd been in. The bed next to the gunner's was now occupied, presumably by the pilot; the metal frames around both beds had been fitted with white curtains to give the men privacy when they chose it. These curtains were closed currently, but this didn't stop Topsy shooting out from under one as soon as she heard her friend arrive. She made a beeline for Bobby across the ward.

Bobby saw at once what Mrs Hobbes had meant. Her friend did look improved, in both appearance and mood. She might have expected to find Topsy wan and tired after long days nursing, dealing with gruesome injuries, but the work seemed to agree with her very well. She was positively blooming, bursting with a new sense of purpose. She was dressed in her new nurse's uniform, looking sweet and rosy in a blue dress, white apron and cap.

'Birdy, you're here at last.' Topsy gave her a tight hug. 'Where on earth have you been all this while? I've been waiting and waiting for you to visit the boys.'

'Sorry. I've been… things haven't been good. Besides, I thought they might not be well enough for visitors.'

'You're not any ordinary visitor though. You were the one who saved them. Piotr's been asking all about you and I as good as promised you'd come to see them.'

The matron nodded to Topsy. 'I'll leave you to supervise your friend. You know which areas are out of bounds, Topsy. Visits to the patients are to be kept to no more than an hour, remember.'

'Yes, Matron,' Topsy said dutifully.

The woman disappeared, leaving them alone together.

'She was frightfully strict when I first came,' Topsy said in a confidential tone. 'Gave me a terribly dull lecture about how I wasn't to think I was above the other nurses just because I owned this place or because of who my father was, and a lot of other rot I hardly remember. Still, she's not a bad old stick once she decides she's going to approve of you after all. I believe she rather likes me now I've shown her I'm willing to roll up my sleeves and get stuck in.' Topsy took Bobby's arm to lead her out of earshot of the patients' beds. 'Charlie wrote to me.'

Bobby laughed bleakly. 'Did he? Then that makes one of us.'

'I suppose you miss him awfully, do you, darling?'

'Yes,' Bobby said simply. She didn't have any energy left to dissemble, and there seemed little purpose in it.

'You are going to marry him, though, aren't you? You couldn't have meant it when you told him no. It was all a ruse, I suppose, to make him more madly in love with you than ever. Or was it to test him, to make sure he couldn't have his head turned by any of the WAAFs on the base?'

'If I hadn't meant it, Topsy, I wouldn't have said it.'

Topsy frowned. 'But I don't understand. You love him, I can tell. Doesn't your father approve? Or is it because he's just a poor vet?'

These were strong motives for refusing a suitor if you were a member of the Sumner-Walsh family, Bobby supposed, but it had never occurred to her to consider Charlie's financial status as a factor in turning him down, or even her father's approval.

'It's a little more complicated than that,' she told Topsy. 'I'd rather not talk about it now, if you don't mind. It'll only upset me. How is your pilot doing?'

'Oh, Birdy, Teddy's an absolute dear,' Topsy said, grasping her two hands. 'He's only twenty-two, and he's sensitive and handsome and very, very brave. His family are all in Poland, living under the Nazis – can you imagine how ghastly? He came to England to study at one of our universities and then of course the war happened, and when it was clear we were going to need all the aircrew we could get, he dropped out of his degree and joined up. He doesn't know anything about where his family are now but he's so worried about them. His great-grandfather was a Jew, he told me, although they've done their best to keep their ancestry covered up. Of course they have no idea he's been so badly hurt, or that he nearly died in the crash.'

'Have the doctors been able to help him?'

'He's been given a skin graft on his face, which is healing now. He's lost the sight in his right eye, though, and he's paralysed from the waist down – probably permanently, the doctors say.'

'Oh, the poor man,' Bobby said feelingly.

'Of course that means he'll never fly again, but the wound in his stomach is getting better nicely,' Topsy said. 'He's in a lot of pain, poor boy, but he so rarely complains. I only wish I could persuade him that the crash wasn't at all his fault, but being the pilot, you know, he feels responsible.'

'Whichever officer sent them out in that weather ought to feel responsible,' Bobby said, scowling. 'No pilot could have been expected to see where he was going in all that fog. It was shocking negligence.'

'I know. Teddy doesn't talk of it often, but I know he feels guilty about it. I try to reassure him but he only pretends to believe me, I think.'

'What family does he have in Poland? A wife? Children?'

She shook her head. 'Just his mother, father and two little sisters. I'm glad he isn't married, for I'm sure I'm in danger of being a little in love with him myself very soon. I've made him my particular pet, because he does need such a lot of care and the nurses here are very busy getting ready for the new patients who are to arrive soon.'

Bobby smiled. Topsy was always a little in love with someone but it was hard to take her passions seriously. Like a hummingbird flitting from flower to flower, she soon craved fresh nectar.

'Well, may I meet this marvellous young pilot of yours?' Bobby asked. 'The first time we were introduced, he wasn't in much of a condition to chat.'

'Oh yes, you must! Come over with me. He'll be thrilled, because naturally I told him all about you and how he owes his life to you.'

'He owes it far more to you and Mary, since you helped Dr Lazenby to operate on him. But I'd very much like to meet him.'

'Then you shall.' Topsy took her hand to lead her to Teddy's bed, where she drew open the curtains.

The man in the bed was lying in a half-doze, but he opened his uncovered eye fully after the curtains were drawn. The other eye, and in fact the whole other side of his face, was covered by a bandage where the new skin had been grafted on. Bobby felt a surge of relief that the monstrous burns she'd found it so hard to look at the night of his rescue had been covered, then instantly berated herself for such an unworthy sensation.

The man was so heavily bandaged that he seemed almost half-mummy. As well as the dressing on his face, his stomach was tightly wrapped from navel to armpits – so thickly that the jacket of his hospital uniform hung open – and one of his arms was chained to the bedframe in a cast. But despite his injuries, the boy smiled pleasantly at his visitors. His one visible eye was very handsome. It was dark, sort of dreamy and poetic, as if his mind was filled with beautiful things. Although, supplied the more cynical part of Bobby's brain, the dreamy expression could just as easily be from his last dose of morphine.

'Teddy, this is the friend I told you about,' Topsy informed him gleefully. 'My friend Birdy, who went up the mountain with the men who brought you down. She's going to be modest in a minute and do everything she can to talk her way out of it, but she was really the mastermind of the business.'

The man held out his hand to her. 'It seems I have a lot to thank you for, Miss Birdy.'

Bobby laughed as she took his hand and pressed it. 'It's plain Roberta Bancroft, I'm afraid. Only Topsy calls me Birdy. But you're very welcome to call me Bobby, Lieutenant.'

'And you are very welcome to call me Teddy. Nearly everyone does, you know.'

'I'll bring another chair and you can sit with us, Birdy,' Topsy said. 'Teddy was teaching me a little Polish before he dozed off. I thought it a rather ugly language the first time I heard it, but the way he speaks it sounds quite beautiful.'

Teddy watched her go. Bobby thought she detected a certain wistfulness in the man's expression.

'She is something quite special, your friend, is she not?' he said. 'When I woke, all was white. The bed was white and the doctors were white and the pain that blinded me, even that seemed to be white. Then this Topsy came like an explosion of colours to blow the white away.'

'She does rather feel like that, doesn't she?' Bobby said, taking Topsy's chair.

'You are not married, Miss Bancroft. Bobby.' Her name felt strange in his accent, but she rather liked how exotic her homely English 'for short' sounded on his lips. 'Do you work?'

'Yes, I'm a...' She paused, wondering if the word 'reporter' was one that would translate well into his native tongue. 'A sort of writer, for a magazine. Actually, it was my editor who asked me to visit today, although I'd planned to anyhow just as soon as you and your friend were well enough to see me.'

He laughed. 'A magazine editor? Are we so interesting here?'

'Very much so,' she said, smiling. 'My editor thinks the story of how we brought you down the mountain might boost morale – I mean, it might give people hope. Survival against the odds and all that.'

'Hope.' He closed his eyes for a moment. 'Yes, I suppose it may. Yet it does not seem so fortuitous to me. It should not have happened. I should not have allowed it to. And now... my friends are gone, and I am... I am something other than I was.'

'No one could have seen a thing in those weather conditions,' Bobby said soothingly. 'You should never have been sent out in them. What happened wasn't your fault.'

'So says your friend too. And yet it feels differently in my heart.'

He made an effort to reach for a glass of water by his bedside. Bobby passed it to him and he took a few groggy mouthfuls.

'I am sorry,' he said when he'd relieved the dryness of his throat. 'We all need hope in these times. I myself should like a little hope, if you know where there is any to be bought. Of course, if you feel our story will help people to hope then you ought to write it as your editor says.'

'Thank you. I'll... try to do it justice.'

He smiled sleepily at her, although each curve of his lips was accompanied by a wince, as if it gave him pain. He seemed like a man in whose nature it was to smile frequently and who had forgotten for the moment that he shouldn't.

'Piotr told me of you,' he said slowly, his speech slurring as the morphine began to overcome him. 'He told me there was a woman on the mountain. I told him he must have been delirious. A woman on the mountain! I said it was the face of the Madonna he must have seen as he hovered between life and death. The Madonna does not wear lipstick red like cherries, he told me. Nor does she wear a scent that smells of peaches and honeysuckle. He said he thought at first he was seeing his wife, but he knew when he woke up in the hospital and you were again there that it wasn't so.'

'Jolka. He called me by her name.'

'Yes, Jolka. He talks a lot of Jolka, this wondrous Jolka, but I have not met her. She will be coming here soon.' Teddy seemed fatigued with the effort of conversation, and he sagged back against his pillows. 'He is a good man, this Piotr. When our plane came down, it was he who pulled me from the flames and saved my life. Sometimes, alone in the night, I could wish he had left me there, but all the same, he is my brother.'

'I know,' Bobby said softly.

'You must write of this in your magazine. Write of Piotr Zielinski, who saved my life, so all may know of it.'

'I will.'

'Perhaps it may find its way even to my family in Poland one fine day.'

Topsy came back with another chair and sat down beside Bobby.

'Oh, you've tired him out, Birdy,' she said, looking at the weary man. She softened her voice. 'Teddy, my love, would you like us to leave you?'

'No, stay a little longer,' he murmured. 'It does me good to hear you. The nights are so silent that I like to hear the happy talk of healthy people in my days.'

'Is it true what he says?' Bobby asked Topsy. 'Is Piotr's Jolka coming to visit?'

She felt a lot of curiosity about Piotr, the gunner, and about the wife he had momentarily mistaken her for on the mountain. Teddy had been unconscious when he came down and it had been Topsy who had helped with his surgery and been here when he woke up, so in a way, it felt that he belonged to her. Piotr, however, had spoken to Bobby on the mountain, and she felt a certain ownership over him likewise.

'That's right,' Topsy said. 'Not to visit but to stay. She came up from their home in Warwickshire to see Piotr as soon as she received the telegram from his commanding officer explaining what had happened. A day or two after she went home, I had a letter from her asking to be allowed to telephone me. You'll never guess, Birdy.'

'What will I never guess?'

'You know the darling little painting we have in the cottage over the fireplace, of my father's old hunting lodge by the lake in the woods? It's not one of the grand oil paintings from the house that we took to furnish the place but a little one that stole my fancy in an art shop in Leeds – I recognised at once that it was my father's lodge and so of course I had to have it. Well, who do you think painted it?'

'I couldn't begin to guess.'

'Then I'll tell you. It was Jolka!'

Bobby blinked at her. 'You mean Piotr's wife is a painter?'

Teddy's eyes were closed but he was listening, not sleeping, and he nodded.

'Very talented,' he murmured. 'Very celebrated. Ah, you should hear Piotr boast!' He laughed softly. 'Oh, to be the doting husband of a fond wife.'

'It seems she and her husband stayed in this area for a little while when they were newlyweds freshly emigrated from Poland three years ago,' Topsy went on. 'That was when she painted Father's lodge. We had a lovely long chat on the telephone. She said how inspiring she'd always found this part of the country to be, and she asked if there was any place here that she could rent – somewhere she could concentrate on her painting and where she and her little boy could be close to Piotr. Well, the lodge itself is vacant now since the previous tenants moved away so I said she was welcome to it at half the rent I charged the old tenants if she painted me something lovely to remember them all by. She and the baby are moving in next week, and then when Piotr is well enough he can be moved there to convalesce.'

'That's wonderful,' Bobby said. 'I'm sure it will help his recovery to have his family with him. He sounded quite devoted to his wife. I hope I shall get to meet her.'

'Would you like to see Piotr?' Topsy asked. 'One of the nurses wheeled him off to be bathed half an hour ago. I have to meet Dr Fisher in the dispensary shortly for a lesson on how to mix the diamorphine doses, but you're welcome to wait here until they bring Piotr back. Don't worry about Matron if she starts giving you some of her looks. She's all bark and no bite.'

'I'd like to speak to him very much.'

Topsy glanced at Teddy, who seemed to be fighting against sleep. 'I think we ought to leave him now, don't you?'

'I wish you would stay with me, Topsy,' he mumbled.

'If I stay then you shan't sleep, shall you, naughty boy? I'm sorry, but I am a nurse, you know, and I must be a little strict at times. You're weak, which means you need to rest so you can heal. Besides, I have an appointment in the dispensary in five minutes.'

'You will come back afterwards?'

'I will.' She smiled fondly at him. 'Don't worry. I'll be here when you wake up.'

He reached for her hand to press it. 'Do you promise?'

'I promise. You, me and Piotr can listen to *Record Time* on the wireless before I go home and you boys can teach me some more rude words in Polish.'

284

Bobby smiled. 'So it's rude words he's been teaching you, is it?'

Teddy laughed. 'Only the purest of my mother tongue, I swear to you, Bobby. The blame lies all with Piotr.'

'Topsy's right. We ought to leave you to sleep.' She stood up. 'You gave us all quite a fright when we brought you down the mountain, you know. You really are lucky to be alive.'

'So I understand.' He closed his eyes. 'I wish my crew had been so lucky – or else that I had been so cursed.'

Chapter 31

Bobby didn't have to wait very long for Piotr to reappear. She had no sooner drawn the curtains around the now sleeping Teddy's bed for him and taken a seat in a vacant chair opposite Piotr's little cubicle when a nurse pushed the injured gunner into the ward in a wheelchair. He recognised Bobby at once and waved jovially.

'Is this your wife, Sergeant?' the nurse asked him when Bobby stood and approached them.

Piotr laughed. 'I made the same mistake myself once. No, although I believe they wear the same scent. This is my rescuer – a Miss Bancroft, Topsy tells me.' He smiled at her. 'And she is very welcome. Nurse Enid will just throw me back into my sickbed, Miss Bancroft, then I shall be ready to receive you.'

She smiled. 'I think after all we went through together, you might call me Bobby.'

'If you call me Piotr, then it shall be done.'

'I will, only I don't think I can say it quite the way you do.'

The nurse laughed. 'This is why I still call him Sergeant.'

'Ah, it is easy,' Piotr said dismissively. 'It is merely the Polish of your English Peter. It is Pyohtrr. Py*oh*trr, with all the weight in the middle. You must practise now we are to be friends, Bobby,' he told her solemnly, and she laughed.

'Pyohtr,' she attempted. 'I can't make the R out right.'

'A good first attempt. With practice it will soon come.'

The nurse, Enid, opened the cubicle curtains, and, with Piotr's permission, Bobby assisted her in getting him back into bed. Then the nurse left them alone.

Piotr seemed a cheerful soul now he was free of the concussion and delirium that had marked their previous encounters. While his countryman's expression had been filled with a sensitivity and sadness that Bobby suspected had been there long before the crash on the mountain, Piotr's face was filled with laughter and merriment. She wondered what a man with two broken legs, who'd recently suffered the horror of seeing four of his friends killed in that terrible way, had to be merry about. Piotr Zielinski seemed to draw his cheerfulness from some inner source, wherein he kept an unlimited supply.

'This is a fine place to convalesce, is it not?' he asked her, gazing around at the oak-panelled walls and oil paintings of Sumner House's main hall. 'I feel like the lord of the manor in my bed here, with all these pretty nurses to wait on me. Still, I had far rather be at home.'

'Your friend Lieutenant Nowak told me that your wife will soon join you here.'

He smiled. 'Yes, my Jolka. Soon I shall be able to go to her in the little home she has arranged for us, and the doctors will come to poke and prod at me in the bosom of my own family. I cannot tell you how I long to sit my boy upon my knees again and tell him old stories, Bobby.'

Bobby smiled. 'I should think he's a fine boy.'

'He is. He is all his mother's, for which I am grateful. I should have hated him to be like his worthless father. All the talent and charm are from Jolka, although I am told often that he has my eyes. The same shade of green. His mother teases us that we are left by elves.'

His eyes were indeed a very vibrant shade of green, closer to emerald than Bobby had ever seen before.

'What age is your little boy?' she asked.

'Just two years old, and as fine a fellow as ever breathed. His name is Tomasz, although since he was born an Englishman, we like to call him Tommy.'

'Why did you leave Poland?'

He turned away, looking serious. 'Poland was no place to be a Jew, Bobby, with Germany and the Nazi party so close at hand. Only a fool could not see what was coming. Jolka and I, we did not wish our children to grow up in a world where they were not free – where they would be hounded and persecuted. And so we left.'

'Are you Jewish?'

'I am, although my wife is not. My faith now, however, is Roman Catholic, like my wife's. But my family are Jews.'

Bobby regarded him curiously. She had never met anyone Jewish before. Teddy had told her he was a small fraction Jewish from his great-grandfather, but she didn't suppose that counted. Except perhaps to the Germans.

Piotr smiled. 'You see, on the outside we look much like everyone else.'

Bobby flushed. 'I'm sorry, I didn't mean to gawp at you. I'm not prejudiced, I promise – I never learned to be.'

'When I meet those who are prejudiced, I remind them that the Marx Brothers are also Jews. And who does not like the Marx Brothers? I like Harpo.'

'I like Groucho.'

'Well, Groucho is good also.'

Bobby smiled. 'Sorry if I was rude before. I've just never met anyone Jewish.'

'How do you find us? Are we so very frightening?'

'You're quite charming, Piotr, and not at all frightening.'

'I did not think so. We frighten none but those with small minds.'

'Your family – are they in Poland still?'

He shook his head. 'My mother and brother were all the family I had. They both came with us to England, along with Jolka's father, and here we have made lives for ourselves.'

'I'm glad of it,' she said, feeling genuine relief to know they were out of harm's way.

'As am I. I wish it could have been the same for all Jews in Poland, and all those who will suffer under this evil fascism. Alas, all we can do is keep fighting and hope one day soon all will be free.' He looked at her curiously. 'Now tell me, Miss Bobby Bancroft, how you came to be on top of a mountain when I and my friend Tadeusz lay there dying. I have waited, hoping you might come, so I could ask you to tell me your story.'

She smiled. 'If I tell you my story, will you tell me yours? Before you answer, I ought to warn you that I am here on a job. I'm a writer for a magazine and my editor asked if I'd write an account of the rescue mission. That's if you agree.'

He squinted at her. 'A journalist?'

'That's right.'

'Are you a good journalist?'

'I like to think so,' she said, a little shyly.

'Then I shall tell you my story for your magazine. But you must go first.'

'I didn't do all that much,' she said. 'Everyone seems determined to give me the credit for the whole thing, but all I really did was wave a rattle.'

He raised his eyebrows. 'A rattle?'

She nodded. 'I'm one of the ARP wardens in the village nearby. I was on duty and I saw your plane crash into the mountain at high speed and burst into flames. So I took my wooden rattle that's supposed to be used for gas attacks and I raised the alarm. I organised the men who volunteered into parties to bring down survivors and I arranged for you to be received here at the hospital. That was really all the part I had in it.'

'Not all the part. You climbed the mountain too, to save us.'

'I knew I didn't have the strength to do much good but I felt like I had to go up, since I was the one who saw the crash. And… I needed to see for myself if anyone had survived.' She paused. 'Although often I wish that I hadn't.'

'Ah. You saw, I think. What was in the fuselage.'

She nodded. 'Your comrades… I often think about it. The men in the plane and your friend Teddy, when we first brought him down and his injuries looked so horrific.'

'Such things are not for women's eyes. Nor for men's either, but war makes these things necessary.'

'It wasn't that. I just… I suppose I hadn't realised what war looked like. My father fought in the trenches and he often has nightmares about what he saw out there. When I go to him after another nightmare and I hear him rambling about what he sees in his head… I thought I knew about the horrors of war. But it wasn't until I saw those men that I *really* knew.'

'And now you see it all the time in your mind,' he said quietly.

'Yes.' She cast her eyes down. 'There was a man in my life. A... a sweetheart. He isn't my sweetheart now, but I still care deeply for him. I can't help but imagine...'

'That one day it may be this man you love on fire in the plane,' Piotr finished for her. 'It haunts my dreams also. My older brother is with a Polish fighter squadron, repelling the German planes in the skies over the Channel.'

Bobby wondered why she had told him all that about Charlie; this stranger. Somehow he didn't feel like a stranger, after what had happened on the mountain. He felt like someone she'd known for years and years, almost like Don or one of her brothers. More than that, she could tell he would understand.

'Yet you seem so cheerful,' she said. 'You saw those men in the plane, and all these dreadful things have happened to your country and your people. How do you do it?'

'I am not always happy, but I am always able to keep from being sad for too long. I suppose it is through knowing I have a home to go to, even though I had to leave my country – always while Jolka and Tommy are safe somewhere, there is a place for me. The world cannot feel dark or empty long while my soul is with them.' He smiled at her. 'You must come to us, when I am well enough to join them in Topsy's little lodge. You must come and meet my wife and boy, Bobby.'

'I'd be honoured.'

'Ah, you will be impressed. You will say what a fine boy my boy is and what a clever, talented woman I have married, and the two of you will be excellent friends.

And you will wonder how I tricked such a woman into marrying this clumsy fool Piotr. Unfortunately, I have no answer.' He looked at her. 'When your men from the village believed me to be the enemy and wished to leave me to die…'

'You remember that?'

'I remember, although the world span and I hardly knew where I was.'

'You mustn't be too hard on them, Piotr. They fought in the last war, and lost people in it too. They wouldn't really have left you. We wouldn't have let them anyhow, Charlie and Gil and I, but I like to think their better natures would have overruled their anger in the end.'

'You knew though. That I was not the enemy.'

'Yes, you told me. You managed to tell me you were Polish – in English so I could understand.'

'You knew already, however. Before I told you, you knew.'

Bobby hesitated, thinking back to that night on the mountain. She hadn't understood what Piotr had been saying to her as he'd rambled in what she'd then believed to be German, but his eyes had spoken to her, pleading with her to end the nightmare he was trapped in. They hadn't looked like the eyes of an enemy.

'Yes, I… I suppose I did,' she said. 'Something in your expression, I think. The way you looked at me. It reminded me of my father.'

'And you knew, when you came up the mountain, that men were alive up there. Am I not right?'

She frowned. 'I did have a sort of gut feeling as we went up that there had been survivors. How did you know?'

'I had a feeling as if someone was coming for us. It is peculiar, is it not? I suppose this is what they mean when they say that God moves in mysterious ways.'

'I wish we could have saved you all.' Bobby glanced at the curtains around Teddy's cubicle. She could hear his deep, rhythmic snoring, indicating he was now asleep. 'Your friend thinks the crash was his fault.'

'He does, but he is wrong. He could hardly see in the fog. None of us could.' Piotr scowled. 'It was that fool of a squadron leader who insisted we fly when we knew the fog was forecast. The Luftwaffe do not stop for fog, he said, so we do not stop for fog. And because we are Polish, he chooses us to fly this training mission. Pah! I wonder how he sleeps now, this Englishman.'

'You ought to report him, Piotr. To someone more senior who can investigate.'

'Huh. Probably I would be punished for insubordination for being so presumptuous. Bomber Command do not take the word of a Pole and a Jew over what I have learned the English call their "Old School Tie".'

'But you must, if he's giving orders that are costing men their lives! Who knows but that this might not happen again? This isn't the first time I've seen planes from your base flying when they ought to have been grounded. The others were lucky, but your crew wasn't. The next one might not be either.'

'It is of no use, Bobby. It has been tried before, by others.' He looked at her and his scowl lifted. 'But it is good of you to be concerned.'

'What did happen up there, Piotr?'

He lifted his hand to wipe his brow. 'I have very little to tell for your magazine, I am afraid, Madam Journalist. We were flying, and the wind howled and the radio scratched so you could not hear your prayers in your own head, but the wind did not blow away the fog and the rain that blinded us. Tadeusz took us lower, trying to drop below the cloud so we could get a fix on our position, but still the fog held us. To fly so low over high ground was dangerous, against regulations, but we had no choice. Everything around us was thick and grey like a blanket, and Jan, the radio operator, he shouted to the base that we were lost and we could not see, but only noise came back. A shape loomed in the fog suddenly and Tadeusz turned the nose up, trying to gain enough height to clear it, but it was too late. Too late for us to bail out and too late to change our course. I do not know what happened next, except that when I awoke, I was not in my gun turret but on the ground. I had hit my head when I was thrown and been unconscious a little time, I think. My strength was very small, but I crawled to the fuselage. I do not know if all the men were dead, then, but Tadeusz I could see was alive – if only barely. He had slumped against the fuselage and his face was burned on that side where it rested on the scalding metal, and shards of the wing where it had shattered were embedded in his stomach. I had just strength to drag him away from the plane before the flames spread and consumed him, then I lost consciousness again until you and the men arrived.' He pressed his fingers to his temples. 'If I had only been conscious a little longer, perhaps I could have saved them all.'

Bobby reached out to take his hand. 'I doubt that. Your friends most likely died on impact. The plane hit at some speed. It would have been quick, at least.'

'I wish I knew that to be the case.' He summoned a shaky smile for her. 'You see, it is not only Tadeusz who wrestles a guilty conscience.'

'While the squadron leader who sent you up there drinks brandy and cocoa in bed, no doubt,' Bobby said, scowling. 'I wish you'd reconsider making a report against him.'

'I wish to rejoin the fight, Bobby. I wish to free my country from the Nazi tyrants. I do not want, to borrow an English expression, to be rocking any boats. If I was an Englishman and a Christian by birth it would be different. Perhaps I would be listened to and my complaint taken seriously. But this, I'm afraid to say, is not the case.'

They were interrupted at that moment by the matron, who came over and clapped her hands at Bobby.

'Now, Miss, you ought to be long gone,' she said, tutting. 'An hour, I said. You must have been here an hour and a half already. The sergeant here needs his sleep just as much as his comrade, even if he is in better shape.'

'Oh, pfft. Nonsense, Matron,' Piotr said, flicking a hand. 'I feel fit enough for the Olympics. I could take a gold medal from Jesse Owens this afternoon, if you would only give me some running shoes.'

'Fit enough you may feel, my lad, but now you're going to take your medicine and have a rest before Cook brings in the evening meal. Say goodbye to your friend.'

'Goodbye, Bobby.' Piotr shook her hand. 'You will come again? Next time we will talk of more pleasant things, I promise. Perhaps you may bring me your magazine to read. I should like to see what it is that you write.'

Bobby smiled. 'I'd like that. Thank you, Piotr. I'd love to come again.'

'And do not forget your promise,' he said, jovial once more as he waved farewell. 'When I am well enough to be at home, you will come to visit and meet Jolka and

Tommy. The doctors say it may be less than six weeks until I can leave. And then we shall all be as jolly as if the war was already won, yes?'

'I'm looking forward to it very much.' And she was surprised to find, after the depression she'd been languishing in since Charlie's departure, that this was true.

Chapter 32

'What are you up to?' Bobby's dad asked her when he came back from a Sunday morning out to find her sitting in the parlour at Cow House Cottage, writing in her notebook. 'Writing your life story?'

'No, I'm writing a draft of that article Reg sent me over to Sumner House for,' she said without looking up. 'The one about the crash.'

He started unbuttoning his coat. 'You're not working on a Sunday, lass?'

She shrugged. 'There's precious little else to do. It's too hot to be out in the sun for very long. At least it's cool in here.'

'You've been spending far too much of your time working since that Charlie Atherton went to war.'

She smiled. 'I seem to recall that before he went to war, you were always lecturing me about spending far too much of my time with that Charlie Atherton.'

'Still, you know what they say about all work and no play.'

'You've been working on a Sunday too, haven't you?' She nodded to his shoulders. 'I take it you haven't suddenly developed a hunchback.'

He shrugged off his coat and dislodged a dead hare that had been draped across his back. 'A man's family needs to be fed, even on the Lord's day.'

'You'd have been better off coming to church with me and the girls than going out poaching.'

'You're making a right old habit of that these days, aren't you?'

'The Parrys ought to have someone take them to St Peter's, since they're not rightly Methodists. Besides, I feel like I need it these days. You know, since…'

'Since your young man left.' He sighed. 'I suppose I should've kept it up, after your mam died. I was angry, I reckon, when we lost her. Didn't have much to say to Him upstairs. Happen I'll come along with you next week.'

She nodded to the hare swinging from his fist. 'To confess your sins?'

'Nay, it's no sin to keep your kith and kin fed. It's a man's job. He'll take my part on Judgement Day, lass, don't you worry.' He took the hare through to the kitchen to string it up in the pantry, then came back and took a seat by her. 'Why's Reg working you on a Sunday this time then?'

'He isn't. I started it of my own accord.'

'What for?'

She shrugged. 'Keeps me from brooding. Besides, we'll have little peace around here after Captain Parry arrives this afternoon. I should probably take advantage of the quiet.'

'Girls making big plans for his visit, are they?'

Bobby laughed. 'Aren't they just? They're planning to show him the whole of the Dales in the two days he's here, from the sound of it.' She glanced down at the writing in her notebook. 'It wasn't only that though. I felt like I wanted to write it.'

'Why's that?'

'Reg said something about… he said if I wrote it, it might help me come to terms with what I'd seen on the mountain. And he was right; it has helped. Partly it was talking to the two survivors and hearing their stories – they've both been strongly affected in their different ways, but sharing experiences with them and knowing they understood made me feel like I wasn't alone. And then writing it down… I suppose it's helped me think through everything I saw and felt that night. Not that it makes it go away – I don't think I'll ever stop seeing it in my mind's eye. But I can cope with it better than if I tried to just push it down inside of me and forget.' She smiled at his blank expression. 'I know it sounds daft, but honestly, it does help. You ought to try it.'

'Nay, I'm no writer, lass. You get that from your mother's side.'

'It isn't about writing something that's good. It wouldn't be for anyone to read but you. What helps is the process of summoning it up in your brain and sending it out through your fingers. It doesn't exactly bring peace, but it does bring relief of a kind.'

He turned away from her. 'Last thing I want to do is go through all that business again, Bobby.'

'But you already do go through it, Dad,' she said gently. 'It can't do any harm, can it? And you never know, it might help.'

'Sounds like quackery to me. Sort of thing them psychotic doctors get you doing when they think you've a few screws loose. Load of modern nonsense.'

Bobby sighed and put down her notebook. She hadn't had much hope but it had been worth a try.

'All right, it's up to you,' she said, standing. 'I only thought it might help.'

He looked up at her. 'Where are you off now?'

'I thought I'd go over to Moorside to see if Mary needs me to help her with her preparations. Then I'll probably wait there to greet the visitor. I doubt the girls will let me leave until I've been introduced to this legendary Captain George Parry. Will you come?'

'Aye, I'll come in a bit when you two biddies have stopped your flapping.'

'All right, I'll see you there.'

It was a hot, sunny afternoon in midsummer – exceptionally hot for the time of year, with the temperature into the seventies even up here in the high country. Bobby could hear voices from the garden when she emerged from the cottage, so she made her way around the farmhouse to investigate.

Mary was standing at the washing line, smiling indulgently while she watched the girls having a game. She beckoned Bobby over when she spotted her, indicating she should be quiet.

It was a comical sight that met her in the garden. The old tin bath that served as many different things in the games of the two Parry girls had been filled with water, and from somewhere, an old blackboard on a stand had been found. The two little girls were sitting cross-legged on the grass in just their slips and knickers, wet through and struggling to stifle their giggles, while Reg stood soberly in front of the blackboard.

'Now then, Miss Florence Parry,' he said sternly to the child, tapping on the ground with his stick. 'This is your last chance to answer a question correctly, otherwise it will be another dunce's ducking for you.' He took a piece of chalk from his pocket to write a question on the blackboard. 'What is the opposite of a dog?'

'Ooh, I know, sir!' Jessie's hand waved in the air, but Reg ignored it.

'Um, is it a cat?' Florence said with a giggle.

'Incorrect.' Reg pointed to Ace, who was sitting on the grass looking hopefully at Mary – it was around the hour she would usually give him his dinner. 'Clearly, opposite of a dog is a Mary. Prefect Jessica, escort Miss Parry to the bath for her dunce's ducking.'

Solemnly, Jessie took her sister's arm and guided her to the bath. Florence squeaked as she jumped in, then started splashing water at her sister.

'May I be ducked too, please, Reg? I mean, sir?' Jessie asked.

'Ducking is a punishment, not a privilege, young lady,' he said. 'You will be ducked if you fail to answer this question. What is irrelevant?'

'Um, it's a word that sort of means where something isn't important?'

'Wrong. It's a large grey animal with a swinging trunk that you might see at the circus. In you get with your fellow dunce.'

'How did this happen?' Bobby whispered to Mary.

'I'm not entirely sure. They were all hot and bothered when you brought them home after Sunday school, and they kept badgering to be taken out for a paddle in the beck. I said I was fair thrang with getting ready for their dad's visit and I had no time to take them laiking, but that I'd fill the bath with cold water for them so they could have a mess about in that.'

'Where did the blackboard come from?'

'Oh, it's some old rubbish that's been sitting in the cellar for Lord knows how long – since our Charlie was a scholar, probably. When they caught sight of Reg taking it to be chopped up for the fire, they begged for a game with it. He was awkward about joining in at first, but he knows they've been missing Charlie so he gave it his best try.' She smiled. 'Do you know, Bobby, I think he might actually be enjoying himself? I never realised he remembered so many of his schoolboy jokes.'

It made Bobby laugh to see Reg in the role of school-master. It just suited him; Charlie couldn't have done as good a job. He was pretending he hadn't seen her, but she saw the side of his mouth flicker in her direction.

'It's a pity to interrupt their game, but their father is due soon,' Mary said. 'Reg is going to drive up and collect him from the bus stop. The girls ought to get themselves dry and into their good clothes to greet him.' She clapped her hands for attention. 'All right, bairns both big and small, I'm afraid it's time to get ready. Florrie, Jessie, up to the attic to get yourselves dry and dressed. Reg, you ought to be setting off.'

'You heard Mary,' Reg said to the girls. 'Quick march and upstairs with you both.'

'Aww.' Jessie stuck out her lip. 'But Florrie had more dunce's duckings than what I did.'

'We can play it again on another hot day. You need to smarten up for your father.'

'Come on, Jessie,' Florrie said. 'We want to look nice for Dad. And maybe he'll play Ducking School with us too, when he comes.' They scampered off upstairs.

Mary approached her husband to kiss his cheek before he left. 'Well done, Reg,' she said quietly. 'I never would have believed you had it in you.'

He rubbed his cheek where she'd kissed him, casting an embarrassed look at Bobby. 'Ah, well. Lot of daftness but it makes them smile. I'll be off then, Mary. Get kettle on, eh?'

When Reg had left to start the car, Bobby followed Mary into the kitchen.

'Can I do anything to help?' she asked.

'Aye, you can read me our Charlie's latest letter while I get the tea things ready,' she said, handing her an envelope from the dresser. 'I should imagine you're anxious to hear all his news.'

'A letter from Charlie? I'm sure I never saw Gil bring it.'

'Came on Friday morning.' Mary raised an eyebrow. 'Watching out for it, were you?'

'No. I just… I usually see him bringing the post when I come over for breakfast,' Bobby said, flushing. She wasn't prepared to admit that she listened near the door every morning at post time to hear whether Gil was paying the farmhouse a visit with fresh letters. 'Haven't you read it already?'

'Yes, but I can stand to hear it again.'

Bobby opened the letter and started to read it aloud.

'"My dear Mother. I wonder if I've been gone long enough for all of you at Moorside to forget me, or do you miss me a little still? It seems so long since I left that in taking up my pen to write to you, I feel much as Rip Van Winkle must have done on waking from his century-long sleep. At any rate, I feel about a hundred years old. My body is broken after all the cross-country runs, parades and drills I've been put through in the past fortnight. The drill sergeant is a horrid, shrivelled dwarf of a man named Murdoch. He has the same hooded, despotic eyes shared by both Joe Goebbels and my fourth-form Latin master – or perhaps that's only how I see the little sadist in my mind after flogging myself half to death on an eight-mile run yesterday. I thought we country vets were generally fit, healthy specimens, but I see now what a broken-down wreck I've let myself become. At this rate, I doubt I'll survive long enough to make it into the air. I'll be dead of fatigue long before the Luftwaffe have a chance to put me down."'

Bobby paused, and Mary looked up from making the tea. 'Anything wrong?'

'Sorry. I just don't like it when he jokes about things like that.'

'No. I don't consider myself prone to superstition but it does feel a little like tempting fate. Still, you know Charlie – he can't help but be flippant about the most serious of things.'

'I know.' She looked down at the letter to read on. '"And so you may tell Reggie that he was right after all and I truly was a great idle loafer who ought to get more exercise, which will absolutely make his day. Other than the news of my poor broken body I have not much to tell, except that Smithy – the friend I wrote you of with the painfully Liverpudlian accent – is on at me to keep him company tonight at the flicks, since the WAAF he's had his eye on refuses to go with him without a girlfriend along to chaperone. He assures me the girlfriend is very pretty and jolly and so forth, and that I shan't regret going as her escort, but of course he would say that, wouldn't he? I shan't be at all surprised if she turns out to be forty-seven with only three remaining teeth. Still, like a loyal pal, I said I would go along. I do hope Captain Parry's visit is everything the girls are hoping for. Tell me how it goes off when you write, and also any news of the Polish airmen. My love to Florrie and Jessie, and to you and

Reggie and Rob, and all at Moorside. Until the next time, your devoted foster son, Charlie. PS Please could you send a couple of Erle Stanley Gardners from my bookshelf in the cow house? I'm famished for want of thrilling reading material here."'

'Well?' Mary said when Bobby had finished reading.

Bobby smiled sadly. 'He missed me off again.'

'He said love to all at Moorside. That includes you, I suppose.'

'But he mentioned everyone else by name. He even mentioned my dad.'

Mary left the tea and put an arm round her.

'He's hurt, Bobby,' she said gently. 'He loved you very much and you threw him off. How did you expect him to feel?'

Something about her friend's use of the past tense, 'loved', felt like a hot knitting needle in Bobby's side.

She looked at the paragraph about Charlie's date and laughed bleakly. 'He seems to be recovering quickly.'

'Oh, don't be daft. He's doing a favour for his mate, that's all, the same as this lass is doing a favour for hers.'

'Mary, it's Charlie. You know how he is with women. They fall for him when he isn't even trying – probably even more so now he's in uniform.' She sighed. 'The date must have happened by now, if you had this letter on Friday. She's probably in love with him already.'

It wasn't beyond the realms of possibility that Charlie's charm might produce an instant effect. Had he held this new flame tight against him in the darkness of the cinema, as he'd once held Bobby? Had he kissed her with the same passion and urgency that Bobby had once been proud to feel could be inspired by her and her alone?

'If you ask me, he put that in on purpose to make you jealous,' Mary said, catching her dejected expression. 'He knows I'll let you read the letters. Probably there never was any date at all.'

Bobby pressed her eyes closed. 'No. No, I'm glad he's taking out girls rather than sitting in his digs pining for me. I mean, I ought to be glad. I told him he should move on and not wait for me to change my mind.'

'And yet you wonder why it still hurts,' Mary said gently.

'I know why it still hurts. I just wish it would stop.'

'You are a funny old thing, Bobby. Here's happiness right within your grasp – it isn't too late, I'm sure. All you've to do is reach out for it, and instead you shove your hands firmly into your pockets.'

'You told me you understood why I'd turned him down.'

'From a head point of view, I understand. From a heart point of view, I can't fathom it at all.' Mary looked at her curiously. 'I always believed there was nothing harder to say no to than love, once it happened. You're a strong young woman to be able to do it.'

'A strong one and a foolish one. Isn't that what you're thinking?'

'I'm thinking no such thing. But I know it isn't a choice I could have made for myself if Reg and I were you and Charlie. You know, I was asked that same question by a man who loved me while all the world went mad around us too. And I'm very glad, all told, that I was too weak to say no instead of yes.' There was the sound of Reg's car pulling up outside. 'Here's our guest arriving. Bobby, can you fetch the girls from upstairs? I'll set the tea to brew.'

Chapter 33

In fact, Bobby had no need to fetch Florence and Jessie, who came thundering down the stairs as soon as they heard Reg arrive back with their father.

Captain Parry was a tall, somewhat gaunt man of about thirty-five, spruce and clean in his uniform, with thick red hair like his daughters' and whiskers to match. When Reg first showed him in, this hero of Dunkirk looked very much the English military gentleman: stiff and guarded in expression, with manners of the old school. However, his standoffish air altered at once when he caught sight of his two daughters running down the stairs to greet him. All formality disappeared as he threw open his arms and the pair of them barrelled into him, almost knocking him off his feet.

'Well, this is truly a welcome fit for heroes,' he said, laughing breathlessly.

'Daddy, you have to come and see Ace,' Florence said, tugging his sleeve, while at the same time, Jessie said, 'We've made up lots of new games, Daddy. You need to come and play with us.'

'I'll demand a proper hug from each of you before I do either of those things, which you ought to give like dutiful daughters.' He crouched down so he could draw them to him, looking slightly damp of eye as he planted a kiss on each little crown. 'I'm not sure you realise how much I've missed you both, my little red-headed rascals.'

'We missed you too, Daddy,' Florrie said. 'Lots and lots. Now please will you come and see Ace? Uncle Charlie bought him for us.'

Mary intervened at this point. 'Girls, your father's had a long journey. I think the least you might do is let him sit down and have a cup of tea in the parlour before you start demanding dogs and laiking from him.'

'Laiking means playing,' Florrie told her dad with a knowledgeable air. 'They talk English different here. Reg says it's what you call a *dialect*.'

'Daddy, come on.' Jessie took his hand. 'I'll show you the parlour.'

'I can fetch the tea things,' Florrie said eagerly. 'Mary lets me bring in the tray if she carries the pot.'

Smiling, Captain Parry allowed himself to be led into the parlour by Jessie. Mary went back to the kitchen with Florrie for the tea things while Reg and Bobby followed him through.

The captain glanced at the desks, typewriters and stacks of magazines that took up most of the space on one side of the parlour, but he was too polite to make any observations. Jessie pushed him unceremoniously into an armchair and immediately clambered up into his lap. Since there were only armchairs enough for three, Bobby sat at the chair behind her desk.

'This is where Reg and Bobby make their magazine,' Jessie told her father as she snuggled under his arm, evidently relishing the role of guide. 'Sometimes they let me and Florrie help with it too. Florrie had a story in it. Oh, but you ain't to tell her I said so because it's meant to be a big surprise when she shows it to you.'

The captain raised an eyebrow at Reg. 'Is that right? We have a published writer in the family?'

Reg smiled as he took a seat opposite the captain. 'I'm not allowed to either confirm or deny that. Your daughter insisted it be kept a secret until you were here and she could show you in person.'

Florrie came bouncing in with the tea things, the mugs rattling on their tray as she struggled to restrain her exuberance. No sooner had she put them down on the table than she was bounding towards the door again.

'Dad, I'm going to get Ace,' she announced. 'He's in the attic. We hid him there so's he'd be a surprise.' She disappeared without waiting for a response.

Captain Parry looked rather windswept at the barrage of talk and children.

'What is this Ace, Jess?' he asked his younger daughter. 'A pet?'

'He's our puppy,' Jessie told him proudly. 'Ever such a clever puppy, Daddy, just like the real Ace – I mean Ace the Wonder Dog, from the pictures. That's who we named him after. Uncle Charlie bought him for us and we're training him to be a proper sheepdog.'

'But you don't have an Uncle Charlie.'

'I know he's not our really proper uncle like Uncle Jack is but we call him that because he sort of feels like an uncle, all the same.'

The captain looked helplessly at Reg.

'Charlie is my younger brother,' Reg said. 'He can be rather… impulsive. He bought the girls a border collie pup at one of the local agricultural shows so they wouldn't grieve too much when he left for the RAF. Of course, we don't expect the dog to go back to London with you.'

Jessie shuffled round to look at her father. 'But we wouldn't leave him behind, though, would we, Dad?'

'One thing at a time, Jess,' he said, planting a kiss on her forehead. 'At the moment we don't have a home for ourselves, let alone pets. Besides, the city's no place for a country dog.'

'Yes, but he's our dog! Please say we can keep him.'

'We'll talk about it another time. It could be a long while until we can go back to London.'

Mary came in with the teapot and started pouring out the tea. 'Did your train journey give you much trouble, Captain?'

'George, please. We're not in barracks now,' the captain said with a smile. He looked different when he smiled – warmer, and far less serious and formal. 'You might even call me Ginger if you like, as the chaps do.'

Mary laughed. 'Oh, I couldn't possibly do that. But I'd be very pleased to call you George. Did you have any problems getting to us?'

'There were the usual delays for bomb damage on the line and so forth, but we made good time, considering.' He took the cup of tea she handed him. 'Thank you. Jessie, you had better hop down so I don't scald you.'

Jessie did so.

'I'm going to fetch Barney and Winnie,' she said. 'You have to meet them as well as Ace, even though they're not our particular dogs. Oh, and Daddy, you must meet Boxer too.'

'Another dog?'

'No, he's our horse.' She puffed herself up. 'Uncle Charlie left me especially in charge of him.'

'Boxer can wait until tomorrow. He's certainly not going to fit in here,' Mary said with a laugh. 'I'm sorry, George. We've got quite a menagerie, as you can see.'

Jessie disappeared to go find the big dogs, leaving the adults alone.

'Ah, it does them good,' the captain said. 'They seem to be blooming since they arrived in the countryside.'

'Aye, it's a good spot for bairns here,' Reg said. 'Fresh air, outside play and wholesome food. That's what you need at that age to grow up strong.'

'I quite agree.' Captain Parry put down his tea, looking earnest. 'And I wanted to say how grateful I am to you both, how very grateful, for giving them a home here. I wasn't sure what would become of them after we lost our own home – I only knew they had to be removed from the bombs at once, before I lost the last two things I had to love on earth.'

'Had you or your late wife no family?' Bobby asked. 'They spoke of an aunt.'

He looked at her. 'You are… the daughter of the house, perhaps?'

'Um, no,' she said, flushing. 'More a sort of… employee of the house. Bobby Bancroft. I work on the magazine with Reg.'

'Oh yes, I recollect the girls mentioning a Bobby in their letters. I'd rather got the impression you were a man, I'm afraid.'

Reg laughed. 'Don't worry. It's happened before.'

'Bobby's very much a daughter of the house in spirit, if not in fact,' Mary told the captain. 'The girls didn't care much to live with their aunt, I think, George.'

'No,' George said, scowling as he picked up his tea. 'Their Aunt Sadie is the wife of my younger brother –

not family by blood, and only barely by marriage with the way she… but I shouldn't speak ill of a lady. She's been unhappy in her marriage, and the fault wasn't all on her side. Suffice it to say she doesn't care much for the company of children. I was very grateful when you wrote to me that you would be willing to give the girls a home for the duration. The Luftwaffe seem to have gone quiet over London for the moment, but you never know when they might be back.'

'Florrie and Jessie are certainly welcome to stay for as long as they need a home,' Mary said, rather eagerly.

The captain was silent for a moment.

'When I was rowed from the beach at Dunkirk with a bullet through my shoulder, I remember thinking to myself that I must survive this,' he said quietly. 'I must because one day the war would be over and I could go home to my girls. And now, if I should go and search for that home I so longed to return to, I should find nothing left of it except rubble. But I am glad, at least, that the girls have found a place they can feel is their home for as long as it might be necessary for them to stay here. You are very kind.'

'It's pleasure for us as much as duty. Reg and I have no children or grandchildren of our own. We've loved having them stay, haven't we, Reg?'

Reg nodded. 'I wasn't always keen on the notion of taking in evacuees, but Florrie and Jessie feel like a part of the place now. And of course, you're welcome to stay with us whenever you have leave, George.'

'They certainly seem happy here. I'm glad. I ought to have sent them away before now but one hears such horror stories of host families in rural places, with evacuees being put to work in the fields like farmhands. I dreaded where they might end up.'

Florrie and Jessie came running back in at that moment. Florrie had Ace under one arm, wriggling ineffectually to free himself, and the copy of *The Tyke* she'd contributed to in the other. Jessie, nearly invisible behind a sea of grey fur, was driving Reg's wolfhounds ahead of her like a cowhand.

'These are the big dogs,' she said. 'This is Winnie – she's a girl – and Barney is her brother. They're old so they don't do tricks or anything, but they're nice to cuddle with.'

'This is Ace,' Florrie said, dropping him unceremoniously into her father's lap. 'Ace, give Dad your paw.'

Ace only blinked up at this new human, looking as windswept as George did himself. Mary laughed.

'It's starting to feel rather crowded in here, isn't it?' she said. 'I shall go and listen to the wireless set in the kitchen while I prepare the evening meal. Perhaps when the place is free of dogs there might be a little more room for me.' She left the parlour.

'He can do it, honest, Daddy,' Jessie said, frowning at Ace. 'He's just scared because you're new. But he can do a whole five tricks now, and he knows three different games to play. When he's got used to you, he'll show you.'

'I'm sure he will,' said the dazed-looking captain, scratching Ace behind the ears.

Florrie stepped forward now with an open copy of *The Tyke*, looking proud. 'Now look at this, Dad. Read it, and I'll bet you can never guess who wrote it.' She kept her finger over the name at the bottom while he perused it.

Their father knew enough to feign ignorance until he had read the story and praised it to the skies.

'Now guess who wrote it,' Florrie demanded.

'Well, I'm sure I can't think.' He looked at Bobby. 'This young lady, perhaps.'

Bobby laughed. 'I'm afraid you're greatly overestimating my skill as a writer, Captain Parry.'

'In that case, I suppose it must be this gentleman,' he said, indicating Reg. 'I can't imagine anyone else it might be.'

'It was me!' Florrie exclaimed gleefully, unable to contain herself further. She drew her finger away so he could see the name.

'Ah, you've made this to play a trick on me, haven't you?' he said, smiling. 'For shame, Florence Parry, when it's months since All Fool's Day.'

'Honest, it's not a trick. I really, truly wrote it. Ask Reg if I didn't.'

George looked enquiringly at Reg, who confirmed the truth of it with a nod. 'Best thing we ever printed, I reckon. I said it before and I'll say it again: give the lass ten year and she'll do us all out of a job here.'

They were interrupted at that moment by Mary rushing back in, making an entrance that could only be described as dramatic. Her face was red, her hair a little dishevelled, and her features twitched with emotion.

'Mercy, Reg, you must come quick!' she said, flapping her hands at her husband. 'All of you, come into the kitchen right away!'

Reg pushed himself to his feet with his stick and went to her. 'What is it, our lass? You look all of a fluster. Is there a fire?'

'No. No, it's not that. Now, on the wireless… they've done it, Reg!'

314

Reg looked alarmed. 'Who's done what? Come on, Mary, out with it.'

'The Germans, Reg! They marched on Russia this morning.'

Chapter 34

Bobby's father joined them in the parlour soon after, having heard the news himself on the wireless over at Cow House Cottage, and the three men stayed up late into the night doing what men always like to do on such occasions: smoking, drinking beer and turning over every possibility, every angle, everything that might go wrong and everything that might go right, now that the war had gone in a new direction. Gramophone records were played in the background, those with a rousing, patriotic theme being favoured. All in all, there was something of a festival atmosphere in the air as the folk at Moorside heralded the end of Russian neutrality.

Mary had long since dozed off in her armchair. Jessie was curled in her father's lap with Ace, while her sister had pulled a cushion over to sit at his feet. The girls had been allowed to stay up late in honour of their father's visit, and it was now long past their usual bedtime. Jessie was doing her best to force her eyes to stay open, knowing that giving in to sleep would mean it was to be bedtime at last, but Bobby could see the little girl was fighting a losing battle and Florrie wasn't far behind her. Ace was already fast asleep, twitching as he dreamt of errant sheep.

Bobby, on the other hand, was finding the war talk quite fascinating, although she contributed little to it – this was a topic where men rarely welcomed a woman's views, especially when the men concerned were all old soldiers. She listened intently, however, and weighed it all up in her mind.

'Well, of course it means the end of the war,' Reg announced confidently – not for the first time that evening – before taking a swig of beer from his pewter tankard. 'Fighting on two fronts? Sheer hubris on old Adolf's part to think he can pull it off. He'll be limping back to Berlin with his tail between his legs soon enough, I daresay, just as a certain Corsican upstart hobbled back home six months after he tried the same trick.'

'I wouldn't be so quick to assume the war will be over tomorrow, Reg,' Rob said. 'Still, if t' Red Army can hold out for just three months – four at most – then I reckon tide'll turn for us. We'll have those Nazi buggers beat sooner rather than later.'

Captain Parry was sitting stroking Jessie's red curls, leaning back in his chair with his eyes half-closed.

'I hope you're both right,' he said. 'If the Red Army succumb and Russia falls under Nazi control, it doesn't bear thinking about.'

'The place is impenetrable. As Reg said, it's been tried before without success.'

'But this war isn't like any that's gone before.'

'Ginger, m' boy, you're out of beer,' said Reg, who was in a rare gregarious mood. 'Let me fill your glass for you.'

'Well, I'm really not much of a drinker but a half-pint more wouldn't go amiss. Thank you.'

'Don't get up, Reg. I'll get it.' Bobby left her seat and went to fill the captain's mug from the jug on the table.

'What do you think, Captain, as a soldier?' she asked him as she topped up his beer. She couldn't quite bring herself to call him George, despite his invitation. His rank seemed to suit him. 'Could this really spell the end of the war?'

'If I've learned anything since that warm September morning when Mr Chamberlain came on the wireless and told us there was to be a second German war, it's not to make any hasty judgements,' came the reply. 'I will say, however, that through Hitler's rash action we might gain ourselves a powerful ally – if our government is forward-thinking enough to accept the Soviets as allies. I'm cautiously hopeful.'

'I remember that morning,' Reg said in a faraway voice. 'Heather in bloom and the moors purple far as you could see. Sun blazing. Apples ruddy on the trees, Sunday roast in the oven, and then we'd to face the thought of all that slaughter to come. Wondering if it would be better than last time or if, God forbid, it could possibly be worse. Standing for "God Save the King" as if that might make us feel less helpless, but it didn't.'

'Pray God that now there'll be an end of this,' Robert murmured.

Reg, in the chair beside him, reached over to clasp the man's shoulder briefly. Robert acknowledged the gesture with a nod of soldierly camaraderie.

Captain Parry sighed and sagged back in his chair. 'I'm grateful that my home city, at least, may escape the utter obliteration that many more months of bombing would have effected. The nightly blitzes must surely be a thing of the past now the Luftwaffe's bombers will be needed for the Soviets.'

'Those poor people,' Bobby said feelingly. 'It seems very hard that in celebrating a reprieve for ourselves, we're forced to wish bombs on others. I only hope a few more months will see it through.'

'There are some who believe the Communists are more our enemies than the Nazis. Others believe the opposite. For myself, I can't help feeling that absolutes are never our friend in these discussions.'

'Amen,' Rob said quietly.

'If the Yanks joined us, we could have Jerry licked tomorrow,' Reg said, beckoning Bobby over to top up his beer as well.

'Do you think they will?' she asked.

'Hmm. Not while they think they're safe across the ocean, I reckon. We shall see.'

They were interrupted by a yawn from Florrie, which she tried and failed to stifle.

Bobby smiled. 'I think it must be time for two little girls and their puppy to go up to bed.'

'But we want to stay with Daddy,' Jessie said sleepily, snuggling against him.

'You won't miss anything except more boring war talk,' Captain Parry said. 'Besides, Daddy will be going to bed himself very soon.' He kissed the top of her head. 'Don't worry, my darlings. I'll still be here in the morning, ready to have some romps in the garden and be shown all the sights of this new home of yours.'

'Promise?'

'Promise.'

'Come on, girls,' Bobby said. 'We won't wake Mary. I can put you to bed tonight.'

'Will you sing to us as Mary does?' Jessie asked as she clambered down from her father.

She smiled. 'All right, but you'll need to instruct me.'

Florrie went to tuck Ace under her arm, then they kissed their father and Reg goodnight, leaving Mary to sleep. Bobby took them by the shoulders to guide them upstairs to the attic.

The windowless attic had never been intended as a bedroom. It was rather dark and gloomy, with low-hanging beams that meant it was impossible for a fully grown adult to stand up straight in there, but Mary had made it as nice as she could for the two evacuees. The old mattress they had slept on for their first few nights had been replaced now with a good-sized bed to share, including a warm, fluffy eiderdown, and she had persuaded Reg to repaper the walls with a suitably colourful patterned paper. A couple of night lights made the darkness of the room seem almost exciting as they cast shadows into the corners, like a sort of smugglers' cave.

The girls were already in their nightdresses. They climbed into bed, with Ace eschewing his basket as usual in order to curl himself in the crook of Jessie's knees on top of the eiderdown.

'Bobby, why are Daddy and Reg and your dad so excited about Russia?' Jessie asked as she snuggled under the covers. 'I couldn't understand all that war stuff they were saying.'

'Well, because a few years ago when we realised there was probably going to be a war, we had hoped Russia would be on our side and it could be won quickly,' Bobby said.

'But they weren't, though, were they?'

'No. Stalin, who is like the prime minister in Russia, signed an agreement with Hitler to say his country would stay out of it. But now Germany has attacked them, the Russians really have no choice but to come in on our side after all. At the very least they'll be fighting the Germans as well, even if they're not officially our allies. That will help us to win the war sooner.'

'Huh. We don't need 'em,' Florrie said, scowling fiercely. 'We can win the war all by ourselves. We don't need no Russians if they go round signing things with Hitler.'

'I know we will win eventually, but the more countries are fighting back against the Germans, the sooner that will happen. And then there'll be no more bombs, and people away fighting, like your father and Uncle Charlie, can come home again.'

'Hm. Well, all right. S'pose they can be in the war with us then.'

Bobby smiled. 'And now you had better instruct me on what to sing, for it's a long time since I had children to put to bed.'

Jessie blinked sleepily at her. 'Did you have some children, Bobby?'

'Are they grown up now?' Florrie asked.

Bobby laughed. 'I'm not nearly so ancient as I'm sure the two of you believe, that I could have children grown and left home.' She tucked their eiderdown tight around them. 'But I was a big sister to two young brothers who had no mother, once upon a time. And one of them, at least, was still small enough to want to be tucked in at night.'

'Where is he now?' Florrie asked.

'Oh, he's grown up,' Bobby said, somewhat wistfully. 'Both my brothers are men now, away fighting in the war. It's a long time since they wanted a song at bedtime.' She forced a smile. 'So you see, I'm rather out of practice. What lullaby does Mary sing to you?'

'Sometimes she sings "Oranges and Lemons", or "Bye, Baby Bunting",' Jessie said. 'But I like it best when she sings "Lavender's Blue".'

'So do I.' Florrie yawned deeply. 'She says that was her little girl's favourite. Her name was Nancy, but she's in heaven now. Do you know it too, Bobby?'

Bobby cast her mind back to her own childhood. Her mother in her pink dressing gown… yes, that's right, and her father too, sitting on the edge of the bed she shared with Lilian. Her mother singing the melody, her father the harmonies… she had almost forgotten.

'Yes,' she said quietly. 'Yes, I think so. "Lavender's blue, dilly dilly, lavender's green…"'

'That's right,' Florrie said happily. '"When I am king, dilly dilly, you shall be queen."'

Bobby smiled. 'I remember. Close your eyes now and I'll sing it.'

She sang the lullaby softly to them. Jessie was breathing the deep, rhythmic breaths of someone in deep sleep before she reached the final verse.

'Night night now, darlings,' she whispered. She planted a kiss on the sleeping Jessie's head, then went to the other side of the bed to do the same for Florrie. She thought the child was asleep likewise, but her eyes blinked open as Bobby bent to kiss her goodnight.

'Bobby?' she whispered sleepily.

'Yes, my love?'

'If the war does finish because of Russia, are you and Uncle Charlie going to get married?'

'Now why on earth would you think that?'

'I think he'd like to. He looks at you sometimes like someone he wants to get married to.'

Bobby laughed. 'How does that look?'

'I don't know, sort of silly and grown-up. But he's really nice though, and he's good at games and he likes dogs and children, and he always shares sweets and he's got a horse of his very own. So if you did want to get married, I think you should marry Uncle Charlie because no other men are as good, except my dad but he don't want to get married again.' Florence paused. 'And Reg is good as well, because he made up Ducking School and he makes a magazine, but he's much more old than you and anyhow he's married to Mary already. So really, it ought to be Uncle Charlie.'

She smiled. 'Well, thank you for the advice. I'll… bear it in mind.'

Florence shuffled up in bed. 'I bet you miss him lots now he's gone, don't you? More than we miss him, even.'

'I certainly wish he was at home again.'

'See?' She sounded triumphant. 'That proves you should marry him, because you miss him when he isn't there.'

'All right, that's enough of that talk. You're too small to be thinking so much about grown-up things like marriage, Florence Parry.' Bobby kissed her forehead. 'Lie back down and go to sleep now, sweetheart. You want to be wide awake tomorrow so you can show your father all of Silverdale.'

'OK. Night night, Bobby.'

When Bobby crept back downstairs, she didn't immediately rejoin the men in the parlour. Instead, she went into the kitchen and leaned against the table with the heels of her hands, drinking in the darkness and silence and solitude.

It had been a strange day. Writing her piece about the airmen who'd survived the plane crash. Watching the girls reunited with their father, and the love and joy in his eyes when he'd held them against him once more. The changing path of the war. The lullaby she'd crooned to the children that had evoked so strongly memories of her own childhood when both parents had been alive, and of tucking Jake in when he'd still been a little boy of ten who was grieving for his mother. She felt tearful, for some reason, and oddly hollow. Or not hollow exactly, but more sort of… drained of life force, like the emotions of the day had wrung her out.

And she thought of Charlie. She tried not to, and she especially tried never to think of what married life might have been like with Charlie – ever since that day in the shepherd's hut when she'd awoken in his arms and thought what a wonderful thing it might be to wake there every day. It was nothing more than a good way of torturing herself to give in to those daydreams. Still, she couldn't help her thoughts turning that way now. That could have been her and Charlie, putting bairns of their own to bed at night, singing them lullabies in a duet just as her own parents had once done for her and her sister. Her mother and father had loved each other very much, and although money had never been plentiful, working days were long and her father's mental state always shaky, Bobby had had a mainly happy childhood – until her mother had fallen ill, at least. The sort she'd have liked to provide for children of her own, if there were to be any. Putting the little Parry girls to bed tonight had made her realise all too strongly that – in spite of the war, the uncertainty of the world's future and everything she wanted to do with her life and career – she did really want to be a mother.

Could Reg and her father be right? Might the Russians now see off the German aggressors and the war come to an end in a matter of months? Just six short weeks ago, the bombs had rained down on London night after night with no sign of letting up and the end of the war had been nowhere in sight. After today, everything was different. And perhaps Charlie would be coming home and—

She blinked as the kitchen light was switched on. Reg had appeared at the door, leaning on his stick.

'You're here, are you?' he said. 'What're you doing standing about in the dark?'

Hastily, she dashed away the tear that had leaked out while she had been musing unseen. 'I just needed five minutes to myself before I came back in to join you. It's been a funny sort of day.'

'You might as well have gone back to your barn. It'll be bed for everyone when your father and the captain have finished their drinks. Heads are nodding left, right and centre in there.'

'You like him? The captain?'

'Aye, he's a true gentleman – I mean the sort of gentility that comes from nature, not wealth and high breeding, which to my mind is the only kind worth reckoning. An affectionate father too. I'm glad of it, for the bairns' sake.' He carried the empty beer jug to the sink and glanced at her as he rinsed it under the tap. 'All right, are you?'

She took out her handkerchief to dab her eyes. 'I'm just being soft. The girls asked me to sing them a lullaby that my mam used to sing to me. It brought back a memory I'd lost long ago.'

He turned to face her. 'Happen you're thinking what it might feel like to sing your mother's lullaby for little ones of your own one of these days, eh?'

She frowned. 'I… the thought might have crossed my mind. How did you know?'

'I've had my eye on you these past couple of weeks, since the boy left. I reckon I can see what's going on in that brain of yours.'

She turned away. 'I'd really rather not talk about this, Reg. Not with you.'

'Answer me one question, that's all, and I'll let the subject drop.'

'What question?'

'Just tell me this: if the war ended tomorrow and our Charlie came back home for good, and he asked you again what he asked you before, what would you say?'

She stared at him. 'You mean, if he asked me to marry him again?'

'Aye, that's what I said.'

'And your decision would be the same? About my future with the magazine if I was a married woman?'

'Let's say it would.'

She was silent for a moment.

'I'd say yes,' she said quietly.

'I know you would, lass.' He patted her arm as he passed to go back to the parlour. 'I know you would.'

Chapter 35

June became July and July seemed to race along in a blaze of sunshine until it became August, however, and there was still no end to the war in sight. While the Germans had thus far failed to capture Moscow or Leningrad, neither had the Soviets been able to launch a counter-offensive that would decisively flatten their enemy as Reg had so optimistically predicted they might. Aid for Russia became the cause of the moment, and the war machine chugged eternally on.

Time had done little to settle Bobby's mind either, nor had it provided balm to the other organ in her chest that had been giving her so much trouble recently. She tried to put thoughts of Charlie Atherton out of her head – keeping herself busy with work, her ARP duties, visits to her friends in the village and the two Polish airmen over at Sumner House, now a thriving hospital of twenty patients – yet still she thought of him.

She no longer even pretended to disguise her eagerness for his letters. Whenever she saw Gil delivering post to the farmhouse, she hurried over in the hope that if a letter had come from Charlie, Mary would allow her to read it alongside her.

They were a special sort of torture, Charlie's letters. By the time the first week in August arrived, he had reached the end of his initial eight-week training. That meant he would be beginning elementary flying training and might very soon be in the air. Before the Bowside crash, Bobby would at least have felt secure in the knowledge that he was safe. After all, it was only training, with no German guns attempting to destroy him. Now, even the idea of training flights filled her with fear.

Then of course there were his dates. He hadn't mentioned a steady girlfriend but he often seemed to be out at nights, usually keeping company some pretty friend of a pal's girl at the pictures or a dance. It felt like a knife in Bobby's stomach, every time, and even worse was that she knew she had no right to feel that way. Why should she be jealous, when Charlie's current state of carefree singleness was all her own doing? Still, she did feel he might have had the gentlemanly decency to grieve for just a little longer. He could at least have pretended he missed her.

'What do you write back to him, Mary?' Bobby asked one Saturday afternoon when they had perused the latest letter together. 'Do you tell him about me?'

'I tell him about all of us here,' Mary said. 'Aye, you included.'

'I'm almost tempted to go on a date myself, just so that you may write him about it.'

'But you won't, will you?'

She sighed. 'No. You could pretend though.'

Mary tapped her arm. 'Lying is a sin, young Bobby. Now you can hoist your sleeves up and roll out the pastry for this evening's pie, since you're here.'

'I will, but I can't stay long. I need to pack the cases for me and Dad ready for our trip home tomorrow, then I've got an engagement at two.'

Mary raised an eyebrow. 'You mean you actually do have a date?'

'Nothing so exciting as that,' Bobby said with a smile. 'Piotr was released from the hospital three days ago to convalesce at home. He and his wife have invited me to the hunting lodge for afternoon tea. Topsy and the other young airman, Teddy, are to go as well. Teddy is still quite frail, but his doctor feels a trip out will do his spirits good.'

'It sounds a regular party.' Mary handed her the rolling pin. 'What is she like, this Polish wife of Piotr's?'

'I haven't met her, but I have seen her paintings. I must take you to see the one Topsy has in the cottage sometime, Mary. I'm no judge of art – certainly not compared to you – but she seems to have a rare skill as a painter. I understand her work sells for considerable sums.'

'I wonder how she manages, with a child of two tugging at her skirts perpetually.'

'So do I.' Bobby smiled as she rolled out the pastry. 'Piotr's terrifically proud of her. Whenever he talks about her, his chest swells so much that I worry he's going to pop every button off his hospital uniform.'

'They sound like a devoted couple.'

'Yes, they seem very happy together.' She paused, concentrating on making sure the pastry she was rolling was an even thickness. 'The girl Charlie mentioned in his letter today – Ruth. That's the same one he talked about having a date with last time, isn't it?'

'I believe so,' Mary said vaguely.

'Do you think they might be... that she's a steady girlfriend?'

'I really wouldn't know, Bobby. He doesn't say so.' Mary glanced at her. 'He says he's requested some leave though. He could be coming home soon.'

'Yes.'

'What will you do then?'

Bobby shrugged. 'I'll cope somehow, I suppose. I don't want to make things awkward for everyone here.'

'I meant, do you think you might have something to say to him? A different answer, perhaps?'

'It would be ridiculously arrogant of me to assume the question still stood after the way I sent the poor boy packing two months ago.' Bobby flinched as the image of the burning body in the plane rose unbidden in her mind, which it did with unpleasant frequency. 'No, Mary. Even if the question was repeated, as long as there's still a war on then my answer would have to be the same.'

–

After helping Mary with her meal preparations, Bobby returned to Cow House Cottage to pack her and her father's suitcases, ready for their trip to Bradford the following day. It felt like a long time since she'd really been able to get excited about anything, but she was rather looking forward to her week's holiday. Lilian had been home for two days already, staying at Clara Stockwell's boarding house on Southampton Street, and Bobby was eager to join her there. Sharing a room with Lil again, seeing Jake, Raymond, his wife Sarah and their children, the whole family back together... it would be just like old times. In fact, it would be better, because Dad was so much happier and healthier than he had been the last time they'd all been together as a family. She couldn't wait to hear everyone's news: to find out how Lil's hunt for a husband was going; whether Jake was still walking out with Nessie Tate; and how her brother Raymond's daughters, Susie and Rose, were getting on at school. There were old friends to catch up with too, not least the boys from the *Courier* – Don rarely mentioned his home life when he wrote to her, and she was anxious to know how his wife Joan was getting along in her pregnancy.

And then there was Bowling Tide itself. Bobby still remembered the excitement of the holiday week when she had been a child, when all the mills had closed and everyone in the city was in a festival mood. It had started with a parade through the streets, the sound of brass bands filling the air for miles around, and there had always been a big fair in what was known as the Tide Field. The fair had been heaven to a child. There were rides and roundabouts; coconut shies and other games, with sweet things and goldfish for prizes; fortune tellers, and Italian showmen playing musical instruments with gaily dressed little monkeys on their shoulders. Men had taken part in friendly matches in the boxing booths, and charabancs had driven people to the seaside for day trips. Thanks to the war there would be no coach trips to the coast this year, no Italian showmen, and, for the first time, the holiday was to be staggered over the whole month instead of a single week to prevent the textile industry coming completely to a standstill. However, Bobby was sure that even war couldn't quash the spirit of Bowling Tide.

Once she had finished packing, she put on her slacks and walking boots, slung her gas mask over her shoulder and set off for the hunting lodge in the woods that was now inhabited by Piotr and Jolka. The invitation that had arrived from them had said there was no need to be formal or dress up, for which she was grateful. Topsy was taking Teddy and had offered to pick Bobby up in her car as well, but it was a lovely day for a walk in the woods. She was planning to take the scenic route.

It had been a rather uncomfortable July, too hot to be really enjoyable, but now August had arrived the temperature had fallen to something more bearable. Bobby breathed deeply as she followed the beck into the woods, where it widened to become almost a river. The valerian, harebells and knapweed that jewelled the banks gave the air in her lungs a sweet flavour. An imposing grey heron stood stock-still in the middle of the beck as Bobby passed, almost like a statue, waiting for its dinner.

'Oh!' she exclaimed after she had walked about a mile, stopping in her tracks.

It had been very fleeting, just a flash of dazzling sapphire against sun-dappled water, but she had seen it all the same. A kingfisher! Her very first kingfisher. Charlie had told her that August was the best time to spot them, when the adolescent chicks had learned to fend for themselves and were driven from the nest by their ruthless parents. He'd said that when a Silverdale kingfisher deigned to show itself to you, it meant you truly belonged here.

The first line of a poem beloved of her mother came back to her in a rush of ecstatic nostalgia. *As kingfishers catch fire, dragonflies draw flame...* she wished she could remember the rest. The kingfisher had indeed seemed to burn with heavenly blue fire as it flashed by.

Bobby leaned back against a tree. Suddenly her heart was full and heavy; so heavy she felt she would be unable to walk for a moment. The beauty of the shy, fleeting bird and the memory of what Charlie had said overwhelmed her. How she wished he'd been here to share it with her! And now he'd never know, because he had chosen to banish her from his life utterly. She couldn't even write to tell him about the Silverdale kingfisher that had finally sealed her acceptance in her new home.

–

The old hunting lodge sat in attractive leafy surroundings on the bank of a small lake. Bobby knocked on the door, which was soon answered by a willowy woman with thick black hair and lively, intelligent eyes. At her hip she held a red-cheeked little boy, half-asleep, who she bounced absently against her. This woman, Bobby assumed, must be the celebrated Jolka. She liked her at once.

'Ah, now this is the rescuer of my Piotr who he talks to me about so often, I am sure,' Jolka said with a beaming smile. She kissed Bobby on both cheeks. 'You see, I greet you like an old friend, because all are old friends when you are in their debt.'

'You're not in my debt at all.' Bobby looked at the sleeping boy. 'This must be Tommy, I think?'

'I shall tell you what it is. It is a little monkey who has been bothering his poor mother all the morning. I am very glad his father is at home and well enough to take him for spells, or the commission I am working on would never be finished. Now you will come into the back garden, Bobby, where your friends wait for you in the sunshine.'

Jolka shooed her inside like a sheepdog gathering her charges together.

'We had expected you a little earlier,' she said as she guided Bobby through the house. 'I am afraid the tea is already out, but there is plenty left.'

'Sorry. I, um… I saw a kingfisher.' Realising this sounded rather odd, Bobby added: 'You don't see them often here. It was my first sighting.'

'Oh, I should love to paint a kingfisher,' Jolka said with a sigh. 'I know there is no blue in the world that could do such a bird justice, but still, to have the opportunity to try! I wonder what trick would persuade one to stand still.'

Bobby laughed. 'I'm sure they'd be far too shy to ever sit for their portraits.'

In the garden, a pleasant little tea party was taking place. Piotr was sitting in a wicker chair, the crutches he used for getting around leaning against it. Teddy was in a wheelchair, covered in a blanket, while Topsy stood over him, fussing. A cloth-draped table that had been taken outside from the house was laden with sandwiches and other tasty-looking food. In one corner of the garden was an easel and canvas, with a smaller table bearing the tools of a painter's trade standing beside it. It looked out over the leafy lake, where a small, dilapidated rowing boat that had been moored to a jetty bobbed on the surface.

'Ah, and here is our last friend,' Piotr said, beaming. 'Now our party is complete. Bobby, you must sit down and have a glass of the apple drink your friend Topsy brings us. It is quite refreshing on a hot day.'

Tommy seemed to be waking up now, blinking sleepily at these new people in the garden. Jolka took him to Piotr and stood the boy at his feet.

'Piotrek, here is your son,' she said, planting a brisk kiss on her husband's head. 'I will bring Bobby a chair from the house. See that he does not take all of the sweet things from the table before our guests have had a chance to eat their fill.'

Piotr laughed as she disappeared into the lodge. 'You see, Bobby, when he is awake, he immediately becomes my son.'

Tommy was creeping towards the table now, and his father pulled him back.

'You must listen to Mama, Tommy,' he told the child. 'Sweet things are for guests first. Do not try for your advantage because I am no longer able to chase you.'

Bobby smiled. 'He's welcome to my share. I don't really have a sweet tooth.'

'Then you will have a friend in him for life.'

Topsy finished fussing with Teddy's blanket and stood up straight. 'There you are, darling. Now you're tucked in properly.'

Teddy wasn't smiling today, Bobby noticed. In fact he looked depressed, and a little sullen.

'I am really not so weak as all that, Topsy,' he said irritably. 'You make me feel like a child.'

'You know Dr Grant said I was only allowed to bring you if I took special care of you and didn't allow you to catch cold. You've got a lot of getting well to do yet.' She turned to Bobby and folded her arms. 'Well, Birdy, I really oughtn't to speak to you at all. You've quite neglected me lately. I know you had the invitation to the garden party I held last week because I put the envelope through your door myself.'

'Sorry, Topsy. I haven't been in the mood for big parties lately.'

'You ought to do something a little lively with yourself. You're going to shrivel up and grow old before your time if all you do is work. There were scores of people I wanted to introduce you to, and some of the gentlemen were quite wretched when you weren't there after all I'd told them of you.'

Topsy often held these gatherings for her upper-crust friends and she was perpetually badgering Bobby to join them. Evidently, Topsy thought the promise of match-making for her friend with some of the wealthy young men she hung about with would be enticing. However, the last thing Bobby wanted was to be afflicted with posh suitors who would be unlikely to entertain thoughts of marriage with a girl from a Bradford mill family but might well entertain thoughts of other things that hadn't occurred to Topsy's innocent brain. Whenever her friend was throwing a party, Bobby usually found an excuse to be somewhere else.

'I'll come next time if I'm free,' she said, silently determining that whenever it was, she certainly wouldn't be free.

Topsy turned to Teddy again. 'I can hardly wait for you to be well enough to come too, Teddy. We always have such a jolly time.'

'Your friends do not want to be troubled with invalids while they have their jolly times,' Teddy said quietly. 'The sight of me would only dampen their spirits.'

'Oh, nonsense. I've told them all about my pilot and they're just dying to meet you. You shall be introduced as my particular friend and be quite the guest of honour, I promise.'

'I would rather not, Topsy. It is not in my character to enjoy being feted and lionised. You will enjoy your party more without me.'

'Oh.' Topsy, who was used to getting her way, looked rather put out. 'Well of course, if you don't want to come then I won't force you. But I do wish you would recon-sider. I should like to have you there if only for my own selfish sake.'

'I am sorry. I cannot.'

Jolka had now set another chair out. Bobby was about to take a seat when Teddy looked at her.

'Bobby, I wonder if I might trouble you to take me for a turn around the garden before you sit down?' he said. 'I have not yet seen the lake. I do not like to ask Topsy, who must be sicker of my company than she would ever say, but a little conversation between us would be pleasant.'

'Of course, I'd be glad to,' Bobby said.

'Be sure that you don't start making passionate love to her when you're alone, Teddy, or I shall be frightfully jealous,' Topsy said as Bobby took the handles of the young pilot's wheelchair. 'He's the most terrible flirt, Birdy. A hundred times worse than Charlie Atherton.'

Bobby flinched when she heard the name, but she managed a smile at what was evidently supposed to be a joke. 'I'm sure I can keep him at bay. Let's go, Teddy.'

Chapter 36

The lodge had a large garden, prettily adorned with colourful flowerbeds and with a beautiful view of the lake over the back fence. Bobby wheeled Teddy to the garden gate, near to Jolka's easel, and opened it so he could see the view.

The young man wasn't looking at the view, however. He was looking sideways at Topsy, who was playing a game of Pat-a-Cake with little Tommy Zielinski.

'She is quite beautiful, is she not?' he said quietly.

Bobby blinked. 'Topsy? Oh yes, very.'

'She has many gentlemen friends who come to these parties of hers. Many of these Englishmen are in love with her, I suppose. They would wish to marry her.'

'I couldn't say.' Bobby sat by him on the grass. 'Certainly she has no wish to marry them.'

'The man she marries will be quite a man. She is like a butterfly, like a… like a creature made all of joy and life. I never knew someone with so much life as this Topsy.'

Bobby laughed. 'She always says she's going to marry a poor man and become a fishwife or something.'

Teddy smiled. 'She will do no such thing. She will marry a maharajah and become a princess; I am certain of it. She could be nothing less. And if she becomes a fishwife as she threatens, she will be a princess among fishwives.'

Bobby drew her gaze away from Topsy to look at him. 'How long have you felt this way about her, Teddy?' she asked softly.

'I do not know,' he said with a sigh. 'Since the moment I saw her, I think.'

'Does she know?'

'Of course she does not know. How could I speak such foolishness to her?'

'Why is it foolishness? She's ever so fond of you, you know.'

'She indulges me, as she would a child or a favourite pet. Nothing more.'

'I don't think so. She hasn't said anything to me but I believe she cares about you a great deal, in her Topsy-like way.'

'What will I say to her? The doctors tell me I am crippled for life, Bobby. Half-blind, my body broken, I can do nothing for myself. The metal your Dr Lazenby removed from me has damaged my spine so I will never walk again, and so I must be pushed everywhere in a chair, a useless mound of flesh. Perhaps I will never be able to father a child. I am half a man, destined to be a burden on those who care for me. And I am poor; a foreigner. Even this so-sweet Topsy would not look twice at such a man.'

'You don't know that.'

'Huh.' He turned the other side of his face to her: the side that was bumpy, scarred and mottled with skin grafts, from which the socket of his now-useless right eye peeped out. 'Would she lie next to this at night? This monster from a freak show?'

Bobby took his hand.

'You know, when I found you on the mountainside, I found it hard to look at you,' she said quietly. 'The burns on your face looked so horrific that it made me feel quite sick to see them. I'm ashamed to admit that to you, but so it was. But Topsy, she looked straight into your face and didn't even flinch. All she felt was compassion for a man in pain. I'd underestimated her strength, and her compassion too. I think perhaps you do as well.'

'So she would take me for pity?'

'No, but she would take you for love, and I believe she could love you despite all those things you just said.'

He sighed. 'Even if there was a chance she might have me, would I be so selfish as to attempt to tie myself to a beautiful young girl who is so full of life? She would be more nurse to me than wife. I love her enough that I would never suggest such a thing to her. Sometimes when we love, we must make the hard decisions.'

'Yes. I know we must.' Bobby pressed his hand. 'I'm so sorry, Teddy.'

'As am I.'

'I do think you might reconsider. Topsy ought to be able to make her own choice. It isn't a sacrifice to care for someone you love.'

'Would you do so, if your young man came home so maimed and broken? If you knew he could never give you children?'

'I have no young man,' she said quietly. 'But… yes. Yes I would, if it was someone I loved. Not because I was trying to be noble or anything of that nature, but because I'd want to be with him and help to ease his pain.'

Teddy's gaze drifted to Piotr and Jolka. Tommy was sitting in his father's lap, having finally managed to get his hands on one of the cakes from the table. Piotr was wiping the boy's custard-smeared face with a napkin while Jolka cleared away some of the empty plates.

'Now here are a happy husband and wife,' Teddy said wistfully. 'I do not know many men, Polish or English, who would be comfortable for their wife to be the bread-winner while they tend to the baby. Yet Piotr seems quite content with his lot.'

'Do Jolka's paintings really sell as well as all that?'

'Enough to make her a rich woman one day.' He nodded to the easel. 'Look for yourself.'

Bobby stood to examine the half-finished painting on the easel. It was very evocative, with the lone rowing boat in the foreground and the green flanks of the fells rising above the trees behind. There was a quiet, lazy solitude in the summer day it captured; one that seemed far removed from a world at war. The colours were so vivid you could almost smell it.

She was gazing at it admiringly when someone tapped her shoulder. Topsy and Jolka had come over together. Bobby flushed at being caught examining the painting.

'Sorry, Jolka, I hope you don't mind me looking,' she said. 'I couldn't help it. It's such a beautiful painting.'

'Well, it is not yet finished,' Jolka said. 'But I am rather proud of it.'

'This is the commission you're working on?'

'No, this I paint only for myself. I am going to make a present of it to Topsy when we leave.' She looked out over the lake. 'If we ever do leave. This is a perfect spot for painting, and near to Piotr when he returns to his training. Now Fate has sent us here, I have a mind to make it our permanent home.'

'Oh yes, do stay,' Topsy said, clapping her hands. 'You can't leave now we know you. You can have the lodge for as long as you like if it means we get to keep you.'

Jolka smiled. 'Well, I will think it over.'

Topsy turned to the pilot in his wheelchair, and Bobby noticed how he always tried to keep the burned half of his face to one side so she couldn't see it. 'I came over to demand your company, Teddy. We can't make do with only one gentleman over there – or I suppose two if you count Tommy, but he's far too interested in cakes to make a good companion for pretty young ladies. It isn't fair that Birdy should steal you away and keep you all to herself over here.'

Teddy smiled. 'I am ready to come back now Bobby and I have had some little talk, and prepared to be in better spirits. I am sorry if I was sullen before.'

'Don't apologise. I know it must be tiring for you, all of this. I promise I'll be quiet and not annoy you with my silly chatter while you eat your sandwiches.'

'Your silly chatter is my favourite part of the day, Topsy.'

Topsy laughed, looking at Bobby. 'I told you he was a tremendous flirt, didn't I? Are you going to join us, Birdy?'

Bobby looked at Jolka's painting, and then at the view that inspired it. 'I think I'll have a walk by the lake before I come and sit down. I can't help feeling restless today for some reason. I'm not ready to be still just yet.'

'May I join you with my sketchbook?' Jolka asked. 'There are some details on the boat there I should like to study at closer range before I work any more on my painting.'

'Of course, I'd like that. Will your little boy be all right here without you?'

'Oh yes, his father can mind him well enough. He will never notice I am gone – at least, for as long as there are cakes and custard.'

Topsy wheeled Teddy back to Piotr while Bobby and Jolka walked along the silver-pebbled shore of the lake and down the jetty towards the rowing boat.

'It must be wonderful to have such a talent for painting, Jolka,' Bobby said.

'I don't know about talent, but it's a comfort to know I'll always have the means to support myself and my family.' Jolka crouched down by the rowing boat and took out her sketchbook and pencil to capture deftly the detail of its flaking paint.

'Does Piotr mind that you earn more than he does?'

'Why should he mind?' Jolka said absently as she drew.

'Well, because sometimes men can be funny about things like that. They feel it's humiliating to be supported by a woman.'

'Then such men must be fools. To be able to provide for your family and have your children never know hunger is always a blessing.' She looked up from her sketch. 'When I selected a husband, I knew that I would not be willing to give up this painting that I loved. I wanted a man who would not expect this from me. One who could see me as an equal and would be truly a partner in our life together. I was lucky enough to have many suitors when I was a young woman in Poland, Bobby – that sounds rather vain, I am sure, but so it was.'

Bobby took in the woman's slender, willowy figure, her flashing eyes and thick, glossy black hair. 'I can believe it.'

'My family thought I must be a madwoman, to choose a poor man and a Jew to be my husband when I could take my choice of handsome, wealthy young men. But I knew I could only be truly happy with Piotr, because to Piotr I was not merely a woman. To Piotr I was Jolka.'

'He's excessively proud of you, you know. What's more, he loves you a great deal. The first thing I heard him say on the mountain was your name.'

Jolka smiled. 'Yes, he loves me. But more important to me was that he respected me, so that I may love him in return. Many people I know think me hard-headed, I think. I have had to be, because Piotr does not have the hard head for business matters.' She got to her feet again and put the sketchbook away. 'Even so, Bobby, I love my husband very much – as much as any sensible woman can.'

'Aren't you afraid?' Bobby asked as they walked back down the jetty towards the shore. 'I mean when he flies. He was lucky to survive that crash.'

Jolka scowled. 'That foolish squadron leader. He ought to be told he has blood on his hands. He ought to be punished. Piotr will not let me get involved.'

'No, I couldn't persuade him to make a complaint either. Won't you be frightfully worried when he's restored to flight status?'

'I am always worried. But this is Piotr's choice, and it is the right choice. It is the only way that the world can be free again. That Poland can be free.'

'Still, it must haunt you.' Bobby closed her eyes. 'It does me. I can't stop seeing what was up there on the mountainside. What I saw in the plane wreckage and Teddy as he was when we found him, so horribly disfigured and burned.'

Jolka looked at her curiously. 'Piotr tells me you have a young man of your own in the RAF.'

'He isn't my young man any more. But he is someone I care about.' Bobby sighed. 'That was why I had to say no when he asked me to marry him. I knew I couldn't think of him up there in the skies without being tortured by images of him… like the body in the plane.'

'You turned down the young man because you feared he may crash and die in that same horrible way, and then you would be alone?'

'Yes. I knew I wouldn't be able to stop thinking about it. Imagining it.'

'Ah. So now you have refused the man, you no longer imagine it.'

'Well, I… I mean, yes, I still think about it,' Bobby said. 'I still care for him. Very much.'

'You disagree with his decision to join the air force, perhaps?'

'No, I don't disagree. I wish he could have stayed at home, but you're right: the fight for a free world is paramount. I admire him for it.'

Jolka glanced at her. 'Does he respect you, this young man?'

'I believe he does. A lot of men won't take a woman reporter seriously, but Charlie understands why my work matters to me.'

'I see. But because he might die, you would rather not be with this man who respects you. You would be with someone who is not quite so good for you, perhaps, but who will not be likely to die.'

'I don't believe I'll be with anyone,' Bobby said quietly. 'I couldn't feel for someone else what I feel for Charlie.'

'Then you would be alone, and you would worry about the death of this Charlie just the same not being with him as being with him,' Jolka stated in a matter-of-fact tone. 'This choice, I feel, is rather foolish.'

Bobby was silent. Of course, what Jolka was saying was true. She had told Charlie she couldn't consent to an engagement because she would be tortured by visions of him being injured or killed, as the men on the mountain had been. But saying goodbye to Charlie had failed to banish those images, just as it had failed to banish her feelings for him. Two months after she had given him her final answer, Bobby was just as haunted by terrible visions as she had been before. And she was just as in love with Charlie as she had been before – more, it felt like, for having gone so long without him.

She thought of the kingfisher she'd seen earlier. That magical flash of blue flame as it soared and dived…

Jolka didn't speak again until they reached the garden gate, leaving Bobby to wrestle with her thoughts alone. When they arrived at the gate, Jolka turned to her.

'Men are not all good creatures, Bobby,' she said. 'It is not always easy to find and fall in love with one who is worth the falling in love with. Too often they think women are there only to serve their needs and bear their children. They forget we are people with wants and needs of our own. If this Charlie you speak of is truly able to be a partner and an equal to you, he is perhaps one of a rare few. I will not give you advice because your mind can supply you with enough logic of its own. I only state what I have found to be true and hope it might help you to find the right path.' She glanced over at the rest of the party and tutted. 'That monkey Tommy has another cake in his hands. He will be sick before his dinner, I am sure. Let us go to them.'

Bobby, feeling rather dazed, followed her to the group around the table and took a seat next to Topsy. Her friend leaned over to speak confidentially to her.

'Are you all right, Birdy?' she whispered. 'You're very white.'

'I'm… not sure.' She shook her head. 'Topsy, I… I think I might've made the most dreadful mistake.'

'What did you do?'

'Charlie. I should never have… my God, what a fool I've been!' She pressed a hand to her forehead. 'Perhaps it isn't too late. If I write to him, as soon as I get home…'

She trailed off when she noticed Topsy's eyes were now wide.

'Oh, darling, don't you know? I was sure he must have told Mary, and of course I expected she would pass it on to you.'

'Told Mary what?' Bobby felt a grim foreboding. 'Have you had a letter from him?'

'I had one this morning, begging me for a favour when he comes home on leave.'

'What favour?'

'He asked if I could put Ruth up in the cottage for a week. He's keen to introduce her to Mary and Reg before they announce anything officially.'

'Ruth?' Bobby felt dizzy. 'You mean the WAAF he's been out with a couple of times?'

'A little more than that,' Topsy said. 'I'm sorry to be the bearer of bad news, Birdy, but… Ruth's his fiancée.'

Chapter 37

Bobby was silent throughout the journey to Bradford the next day. There was no longer the excitement of anticipation as she prepared to see her family and join the Bowling Tide celebrations. All was tarnished now – not only the holiday but everything.

She had said goodbye to Charlie but she'd never really thought of him as lost... until now. He'd said that if she changed her mind, she knew where to find him, but now he no longer loved her. He had found someone else to fill the space in his heart, just as she'd told him she wanted him to. It was all her own fault.

She had realised too late what it was she really wanted. The Parry girls had shown her how much it would mean to her to have children of her own. Jolka and Piotr had shown her how a woman could be a wife and mother without losing her own soul, if she could bring up a family with a partner who loved and respected her. She had been a blind fool, and now Charlie was lost to her forever.

'You sickening for something, lass?' her dad said as their train arrived at Forster Square. 'You're looking none too well, and you've barely spoken a word since we set off.'

She forced a smile. 'Just a bad night's sleep. I'll have a rest when we get to Clara's, then I'll be fine.'

As always during the festival week, the town was thronged with people. The local pubs were doing a thriving trade, of course, as the usually industrious mill-hands took advantage of their time off. Charabancs passed them on their way to Shipley Glen or other local beauty spots. Bobby could hear the sound of the fairground organ even from here, a mile away.

They waited for a tram to Southampton Street but that too was full of merrymakers on their way to the fair, so they walked. Her father dawdled, saying hello to old friends he bumped into and savouring the sights and smells of his old home. However, Bobby strode along the pavements with purpose. She wasn't in the mood for being sociable. All she wanted was to find Lilian and pour out her heart to someone she knew would understand.

One thing she saw as she walked did catch her attention, however. Nessie Tate, who until recently had been her brother Jake's steady girlfriend, nodded a greeting to her as she passed by. She was with a young man who had his arm around her waist, but it wasn't Jake. On taking a closer look, Bobby realised it was her brother's best friend, Eddie.

It didn't surprise her, therefore, to find her brother in low spirits when she reached Clara's place. He and Lilian were sitting in the communal living room with some other residents, listening to the wireless.

'Oh.' He cast her a listless look. 'Heyup, Bob.'

'That's it? That's all the greeting I'm getting when I haven't seen you since Christmas? Get up and give me a hug, you mardy sod.'

Jake managed a smile as he got up to hug her.

'It's good to see you, little brother,' she said. 'I've missed you.'

'All right, don't start talking soft at me. I'm not Lil. Where's Dad?'

'He was taking ages, saying hello to everyone he met, so I came on ahead.'

She glanced at Lilian, who had stood up too and was waiting to greet her. Her twin looked tired, and a little anxious too. Bobby wondered if her important naval work had started to take its toll.

'Lil, can you show me which is our room?' Bobby asked. 'I'd like to unpack and rest for a while.'

'Of course. Come on upstairs.'

'Is our Jake all right?' Bobby whispered as they climbed the stairs. 'I saw Nessie out with Eddie when I was walking over.'

Lilian laughed. 'Oh, he's not upset about that. He's already got another girl lined up for his favours, he says. It's his motorcycle – he's had to take it off the road. Eddie was supposed to be looking after it for him while he was away but he's been neglecting it since he started walking out with Nessie. Jake says it's going to take him ages to get it fixed up again.'

'I should have known,' Bobby said with a smile. 'He'll cheer up when he starts working on it.'

Lilian opened the door to the room they were to share for the week. Bobby chucked her suitcase down on the bed, closely followed by herself.

'Are you all right, Bobby?' Lilian asked. 'You look washed out.'

Bobby couldn't hold back her emotions any more. She burst into tears.

'Lil, I've been such a fool,' she sobbed.

Lilian sighed. 'More boy trouble, I suppose. All right, I'm here.'

She sat down beside Bobby on the bed and put an arm around her.

'Well, what happened?' she asked. 'Is there a new man on the scene?'

Bobby let her head sink on to Lilian's shoulder. 'No new man. Just the old one, and a big mistake I realised too late that I'd made.'

'You were mistaken about Charlie, you mean?'

'Yes. I thought it would be too painful for me, after what I saw up on the mountain, to know the man I loved could end up like those airmen who were killed. But whether Charlie and I are together or not, I'll be tortured by visions of it just the same. As long as I'm in love with him I always will be, and I'm in no danger of falling out of love with him any time soon. The only difference is that I'm alone and miserable thinking about him with someone else.'

'Then if you feel that way, why don't you tell him? Didn't he say when he left that you should write if you changed your mind?'

'He said that then. But I waited too long, Lil, and now it's too late. He's engaged to someone else – a WAAF called Ruth.'

Lilian frowned. 'That was a very fast engagement. He's only been gone two months.'

Bobby gave a damp laugh. 'It doesn't take girls long to fall for Charlie Atherton.'

'Are you sure he's engaged? Who told you?'

'Topsy.'

Lilian smiled dryly. 'This would be the same Topsy who previously told you she was engaged to Charlie herself when there was no truth in it, would it?'

'Well, yes, but she can't be wrong this time. She said Charlie wrote to her and told her in as many words that he was engaged, and that he wanted her to put his new fiancée up when he comes home on leave so he can introduce her to Reg and Mary. That can't be a misunderstanding, can it?'

'Hmm. No, I suppose not,' Lilian said. 'But you ought to write to him, all the same.'

Bobby looked up at her. 'I can't, can I? He's engaged, Lil. If I throw myself at him when he's preparing to marry another woman, I'll get nothing for my trouble but humiliation.'

'I'd take the chance of humiliation if there was an equal chance of being happy. Supposing he only got engaged to this woman because he thought he couldn't have you? Maybe he settled for her because you broke it off with him.'

'I don't think Charlie would get engaged to someone unless he loved them.'

Lilian looked thoughtful. 'Unless... he had to get engaged,' she said slowly. 'As I said, it happened very quickly.'

Bobby felt a chill run down her spine. 'You don't mean...'

'If she was in the family way. He'd want to do the right thing by her then, I suppose. He seemed like the honourable sort.'

'Oh, I wish you hadn't said that.' Bobby gave an involuntary shiver. 'If that's what it is then I can't write to him, can I? He'd have to marry this other girl whether he loved her or not, and I'd be a pretty terrible person to want to stand in the way.'

Lilian shrugged. 'I only say it's a possibility. It might just as well be heartbreak leading him to make impulsive decisions. You said he was impulsive.'

'What would I say if I did write?'

'Just tell him calmly and rationally what your feelings are and gently hint that if he were to ask you the same question again, he'd get a different answer. You don't need to let on that you know anything about this Ruth. I don't see what's so humiliating about that.'

'You really think I should?'

'I would, if I were you.' She looked up at the sound of the front door being opened downstairs. 'I wonder if that's Dad. I need a word with him about something when he gets here.'

'What is it?' Bobby managed a smile. 'You haven't found a potential husband you want him to give his blessing to?'

'No, nothing like that. It isn't important, really.'

'You haven't got any irons in the fire then, husband-wise?'

'There is a young officer I'm keen on,' she admitted. 'Lieutenant John Cartwright. Handsome, wealthy, and sweet too. I'm waiting for him to ask me for a date, but he's rather shy. At this rate I'm going to have to make Mam turn in her grave by asking him, like some sort of fast woman.'

Bobby shuffled to look at her. 'Let's go out tonight, shall we, Lil? Me and you, just like the old days. I'm so sick of worrying about Charlie and the war, and being unhappy. I'd give anything to forget all my troubles for a night. There's bound to be a dozen dances to choose from in Tide week.'

Lilian massaged her temples. 'I can't tonight. Sorry, Bobby.'

'Are you badly? You do look pale.'

'No. I've got a date, that's all.'

'A date! I thought you were holding out for Lieutenant Cartwright.'

She shrugged. 'A girl has to have a little fun while she's waiting, doesn't she?'

'Who are you going out with? Someone I know?'

'Just a lad I met at the dance hall the night I got back. You won't know him. He's from out of town, only here for the festival week.'

'All right,' Bobby said, disappointed. 'We can go another night. We've got the whole week.'

Lilian swung her legs off the bed. 'I need to speak to Dad. You can write your letter to Charlie while I'm gone.'

'I'm really not sure I ought to write to him, Lil. He's practically a married man, after all.'

'You ought to do something. Otherwise you'll spend the rest of your life wondering "what if?"'

—

Bobby unpacked her case slowly while Lilian was out of the room, turning the problem over in her mind. If Charlie really was engaged, he must surely be in love with the girl. He wasn't the type to settle for anything less than that, she was sure – unless, God forbid, Lilian was right and there was a more urgent reason for the hasty engagement. But it was true that if Bobby didn't let him know how she was feeling, then theirs would forever feel like a story without an ending. If he intended to marry someone else then let him reject her decisively, so there would be no 'what ifs' about it.

'Well? Did you write to him?' Lilian asked when she came back in.

'I'm not going to write a letter.'

'Are you sure? It would drive me mad knowing I felt that way and doing nothing about it.'

'I'm not going to do nothing either. I'm going to send him a telegram.' Bobby showed her the scrap of paper on which she'd written her message to Charlie.

'"Ask me again?"' Lilian read. 'You write for a living and that's all you've got to say?'

'It's all I need to say. He knows how I feel. This tells him that I've changed my mind about marriage, and that if he asks me again, I'll give him a different answer. But I've phrased it as a question because I'm not making any assumptions about whether he will ask again. It's in Charlie's hands now.'

'Well, you know best.' Lilian gave her a squeeze. 'I hope it works out for you, little sister. I'd like to see you happy with him. He suits you.'

'You're right, it would have driven me mad not to at least let him know. I'll take it to the telegraph office now.'

There was a sense of relief that came with sending the telegram, and a certain excitement too. Perhaps it had all been a misunderstanding and there was no engagement, or at least not a serious one. Perhaps she would receive a reply tomorrow – even today if Charlie sent a telegram in return. She had given Clara's boarding house as her return address. And when Charlie came home on leave, she would be there waiting to give him the answer he'd always wanted from her…

On the way back to the boarding house, she stopped at a telephone box to phone Don at the *Courier* offices and ask if the boys there would be free later, since her sister wasn't available that night. The mills were closed but it was still a working day for the newspaper, which needed to get a new edition out on Thursday even in festival week. Tony and Freddie already had plans that evening, Don told her over the phone, but he would meet her in The Swan for a drink after work.

—

'How is Joan?' was the first thing Bobby asked him when they met in the pub later. Like all of the city's drinking establishments during Bowling Tide, The Swan was thronged with people. However, they'd been lucky enough to find a small table to themselves.

'I'd like to say she's blooming, but she's been as sick as a dog for the past three months,' Don told her. 'It was the same when she was having our Sal.'

Bobby smiled as she sipped her half-pint. 'I hope you feel suitably guilty about it.'

'I'll be glad when it's over and done with, for her sake. The quacks reckon the baby's growing strong and healthy though, in spite of her age, so that's a weight off my mind.' He took out his pipe and started filling it with his favourite Tom Long tobacco. 'How's your old man doing these days?'

Bobby thought back to the evening meal they'd all shared at the boarding house. She'd been looking forward to eating together as a family again, but it had been rather a sober affair. Jake was still mourning the loss of his beloved Triumph motorcycle, Lilian had been uncharacteristically quiet, and her father, who had been in high spirits when they'd arrived, had seemed depressed for some reason too. It hadn't exactly been what Bobby would call a holiday atmosphere. She wondered what Lilian had needed to speak to their dad about and if it could have anything to do with his sudden shift in mood.

'All right, I think,' she told Don. 'Country living certainly agrees with him, and he barely touches whisky these days except as an aid to sleep – he drinks beer now instead, and not too much of it. He seemed quiet this evening though. Perhaps he's missed the old place more than I thought.'

Don lit his pipe. 'Or he's already had enough of it. Wouldn't blame him. Bloody hate Tide week, all these people everywhere.'

'How's Tony?'

'Oh, don't talk to me about that idle bugger,' Don said, scowling. 'You know, just when I thought he was experimenting with the concept of hard work for the first time in his career, just when he'd actually managed to impress me, he goes back to being pure, undiluted Tony Scott. He's got another girl on the go to distract him, I suppose. I ought to have sacked that loafer when I took over the paper, but God help me, I couldn't bring myself to do it.'

'How did that story of his work out – the big meat raffling racket he was working on exposing last time I came up? He reckoned it would make his name as a reporter.'

'That's what I'm talking about. He was all excited about it, said it was going to be the biggest thing we'd ever run and he had names, dates, everything, then the next minute he's pulling it. Flat-out refused to let me read the thing or see his notes or anything. Chucked the whole lot in the fire and said we couldn't print it because it would be a libel risk.'

Bobby frowned. 'But it wouldn't be, would it? He said he had some really strong evidence to back it up.'

'What Tony says and the truth are not often the same thing, Bobby, as I'm sure you remember when you spent your days writing most of his copy for him.' He glanced at her. 'You changed your mind about coming back to us yet?'

She smiled. 'You ask that every time I see you.'

'Well, one day I might strike it lucky. I still say you're wasted on that little country rag.'

'And I still love that little country rag.'

'I know, more's the pity.' He laughed, nodding to the bar. 'Speak of the devil. Look who just turned up.'

Bobby turned to follow his gaze, but the pub was too crowded to see where he was looking. 'Who is it?'

'Tony, out on a date by the look of it. I knew he had a girl on the go. Poor cow doesn't know what she's letting herself in for.' He squinted. 'What's this one, a Wren? It was an ATS girl last time. The lad's got a real thing for uniforms.'

'A Wren?' Bobby felt a sense of foreboding. 'Let me see.'

She stood up to get a better look, and her fears were confirmed when she saw the profile of the woman in the navy-blue Wren's uniform that Tony was out with.

It was Lilian.

Chapter 38

Bobby didn't confront her sister right away. Instead she made her excuses to Don and slipped out before Tony and Lil saw her, then waited in their room at the boarding house for Lilian to come home.

There were many things she didn't understand, chief of which was why her twin, who had never been short of attractive, appealing suitors, would want to go on a date with Tony Scott. She knew Tony had always been keen on Lil – every time he saw Bobby, he would enquire after her pretty sister. Of course he was keen on any pretty girl, but he'd made a special effort to single Lilian out. Lil, however, had never shown any romantic interest in Tony. She liked the man, she found him amusing and she smiled when he flirted with her, but Bobby knew she'd turned him down for dates on plenty of occasions before. He just wasn't her type. So why now was Lil out on a date with him – and the even bigger mystery, why had she lied to her sister about it?

It was after midnight when Lilian came in, looking weary.

'Oh. Hello,' she said when she saw Bobby sitting up in bed in her nightgown with her arms folded. 'I thought you'd be fast asleep by now.'

'Good date, was it?'

Lilian shrugged, bending down to remove her shoes. 'It was OK.'

'Is he good-looking, this boy from out of town that I don't know?'

'He's not bad.'

'Financially stable? Good career prospects?'

'We haven't really talked about his work. Have you turned into Dad or something?'

'He smokes those Egyptian cigarettes, I notice.'

Lilian frowned. 'How do you know?'

'I can smell them on you a mile away.'

'Is there a reason you're glaring at me like that?' Lilian asked as she unhooked her stockings and rolled them down. 'I am over twenty-one, you know, Bobby. Well over it, sadly.'

'Don't play innocent with me, young lady,' Bobby said sternly. 'You lied to me, Lil. And I'd very much like to know why.'

Lilian sighed. 'You saw us.'

'At The Swan. I was in having a drink with Don Sykes.'

'I should have known you'd find out from someone around here. Tony won't be able to stop himself bragging about it. He looked as smug as a peacock when he took my arm to escort me into the Palais tonight.'

Bobby patted the bed to invite her sister to join her. 'Why didn't you tell me you were going out with Tony tonight?'

'I was ashamed, wasn't I?' Lilian said, sitting down next to her. 'I mean, it's Tony Scott. He's not exactly my dream man.'

'Then why go out with him?'

'I had to. For Dad.'

Bobby blinked at her. 'For Dad? But Dad can't stand him.'

Lilian sighed again. 'All right, I'll tell you the whole story. Perhaps I should have told you before, but I wanted to deal with this myself. You have all the Dad worry these days.'

'Deal with what?'

'I had a telephone call at my digs from Tony a few weeks ago. He wanted to talk to me about a story he'd been working on. Exposing illegal meat raffles at country shows in the Dales.'

'Yes, he told me about it. Don said Tony pulled the story because he was worried it was a libel risk.'

'It wouldn't have been a libel risk,' Lilian murmured. 'Every word of it was true, and he had more than enough evidence to back it up. Dates, details, even names.'

'Did he tell you the names?'

She nodded. 'Peter Dixon, for one. He was the ringleader.'

'Pete!'

'Yes, Pete.'

'I saw him,' Bobby said slowly. 'I think I saw him at it, at Kiltford Show. A man gave him ten bob in exchange for a piece of paper – I suppose it was a raffle ticket. But when I confronted him about it, he told me he was just running a book on the prizewinning animals. How did Tony know you knew Pete?'

'He didn't, but he knew I knew one of the other racketeers involved. Pete had a partner, Bobby.'

Bobby stared at her. 'Not... Dad?'

'Yes. They were in it together – them and a handful of local farmers who reared the pigs.'

Bobby shook her head. 'No. Dad wouldn't be so stupid, surely. A fine for poaching is one thing, but he could go to prison for selling rationed meat. The Ministry is really cracking down on the black market.'

'I know. And with his other problems, a prison sentence could well kill him.'

'Did you tell Tony that?'

'I didn't need to. He'd already decided to pull the story,' Lilian said. 'That was why he rang me: to tell me he wouldn't want to get Dad into trouble so he was going to destroy it. And he hinted that since I was coming home for Bowling Tide, it might be nice if I met him for a drink and thanked him in person. Tonight was the third time we've been out together since I started my leave.'

'You mean the dirty sod has been *blackmailing* you into going out with him?' Bobby shook her head in disgust. 'I'll bloody kill him!'

'It wasn't like that. He genuinely pulled the story as a favour, I think – for both of us, not just me. He's your friend more than mine, after all. He never suggested destroying the evidence was dependent on me going out with him, but I did feel like I ought to repay the favour.'

'I bet I know exactly how Tony thinks you can repay the favour,' Bobby said darkly. 'Given that he is my friend and you're really only a passing acquaintance, one might have thought he'd contact me about it. He set this whole thing up to get to you, Lil. He's always been keen on you.'

'I suppose you're right. Still, he's harmless enough. He just wants a bonny girl on his arm to show off for Tide week, that's all.' She smiled. 'Actually, I've grown rather attached to him since he took care of me at the show. Not in any romantic way – he's not the sort of man I'd ever fall in love with – but he is a lot of fun. He makes me laugh.'

362

'I knew I never should have left you with him,' Bobby muttered. 'Taking advantage of your injury to worm his way into your affections, just so he could spring a trick like this on you.'

'He really isn't as bad as you make out. He was very sweet that day, taking care of the damsel in distress.'

'Huh. Has he tried anything on with you? I bet he has.'

'Nothing I can't handle.' Lilian gave her a squeeze. 'It's fine, Bobby. Dad's safe, the story's pulled and I've repaid Tony's favour. There's going to be no more illegal meat raffling – at least, none that Dad's going to be involved in. Your big sister's made it all go away and there's nothing you need to worry yourself about.'

'This was what you spoke to Dad about earlier?'

'That's right. I was very gentle about it so as not to humiliate him. I told him I knew what had been going on and that he'd come closer than he knew to being exposed, so if I were him, I'd turn it in before the law showed up on his doorstep. I didn't tell him who my source was though. He saw the sense of it, once I'd emphasised the fines and sentences that are being handed down for black-market profiteering nowadays. I mean, some of the newspapers talk about it as if it's tantamount to treason.'

'So he doesn't know you've been repaying Tony Scott for the favour in dates then.'

'No, and he doesn't need to either. He'd thump the lad if he knew.'

'I'm tempted to thump him myself. At least, I've a good mind to march into the *Courier* offices tomorrow and give him an earache. I knew Tony had the morals of a tomcat but this is low, even for him.'

'Please don't do anything like that. Like I said, he didn't put any pressure on me. He just hinted he'd enjoy my company while I was at home, that's all, and I said I'd be glad to give it. I do like the man so it's not exactly a chore, even if he wouldn't have been my first choice for a male escort this week.' She patted her sister's arm. 'Anyhow, it's all sorted out now, Bobby. If I give Tony my company in Tide week so he can show me off to his friends, the whole thing will be gone and forgotten about again and Dad never needs to be any the wiser. Nothing for you to worry about.'

But despite her sister's assurances, Bobby couldn't help feeling this wasn't going to be the end of the matter.

–

Bobby tried to enjoy the rest of her week's holiday, but Lilian's confession cast rather a pall over their remaining time together. She didn't see nearly as much of her sister as she could have wished while she was out on dates every night with Tony, her dad remained quiet after his confrontation with Lilian, and Jake seemed far more upset about the broken Triumph than was warranted even for someone as motorcycle-mad as her brother. Bobby suspected he was more hurt by Nessie and Eddie's betrayal than he was choosing to let on. As nice as it was to see everyone, to hear their news and take her little nieces to the fair, Bobby found she was approaching the end of the holiday in even lower spirits than when she'd left Silverdale.

Worst of all, there was still no reply from Charlie. She had hoped for a telegram or letter from him within days of sending her own, even if it was only to tell her she was too late after all, but when she left town a week later, there had been nothing. His silence was even more painful to her than an outright rejection. To think that this man, who she'd believed had been deeply and passionately in love with her, now cared so little for her that he couldn't even muster the energy to write and tell her to leave him alone… it hurt beyond anything she could imagine.

She had a single hope: that Charlie had failed to notice the reply address on the communication she'd sent him and there would be a letter waiting for her at Cow House Cottage when she and her father returned home. But when they opened the door of the old barn on arriving back, there was nothing waiting for her on the doormat. She felt her heart sink as her final lingering hope was dashed.

'Owt wrong, love?' her dad asked.

He'd been quiet all the week: not unhappy exactly, but thoughtful. He hadn't mentioned the talk Lilian had had with him, and Bobby hadn't brought it up either. She had been keeping a close eye on him, however, worried his depression over the loss of what he thought of as his job might send him to the bottom of a bottle again, but there had been no noticeable increase in his drinking. He'd been unusually fond towards his family though: gentler and less gruff than he tended to be with them.

'I thought there might be a letter for me, that's all,' she said. 'I'll get the fire lit, shall I? There's a backendish chill in the air today.'

'Aye, well. Every summer must end,' he said, sinking wearily into a chair.

Something in his tone made her follow him. 'Is everything all right, Dad?'

'Everything's all right.'

'Are you going to walk over to the Hart tonight? I'm sure Pete must be missing his dominoes partner.'

'I'd best keep out of his way for a bit, I reckon. Life's easier when we keep oursen to oursen.'

Bobby sighed and sat down in the other chair. 'Dad… why didn't you tell me how you'd been making your money? I mean, with selling illegal meat.'

He sagged back in his chair, looking diminished and defeated. 'Lil told you, did she?'

'Of course she did. Why didn't you tell me what had been going on?'

'Because you'd try to talk me out of it, wouldn't you?'

'We didn't need it. We might not be rich but we've got enough, with the rent from the old house, my wages and what the others send home. You didn't need to risk a prison sentence.'

'A country fit for heroes to live in,' he muttered. 'That's what that old fool Lloyd George told us he was going to build. And what are we now, those of us who managed to survive the trenches? I'm a wreck at fifty-one: unemployable, broken. The war chewed us up and spat us back out like so much rubbish.' He punched the arm of his chair. 'I was entitled to this, Bobby! This country owes me a debt, and if it won't pay it willingly then I don't see why I shouldn't take it from the fat of the land.'

'I know how betrayed you feel, Dad. You went through hell on earth and I don't blame you. But you have to stop now, before this goes any further.' She bowed her head. 'I won't lose you too.'

'Anyone might think you wanted to keep me around. Lord knows why, useless lump that I am.'

'You're not a useless lump.' She stood up and went to kiss the top of his head. 'You're my dad. The only one I've got.'

'At least when I were bringing money and food in, I could feel I was doing summat for the family,' he said quietly. 'Without that, what am I? An old man, crying by t' fireside for the loss of his prime. An irrelevance with nowt left to do but wait to die.'

'You can get another job. You're not really old. There must be plenty of legal ways for you to make money.'

'Huh. Such as what?'

'Well… I can't think of any just at the moment, but there must be. We'll find you something, I promise.'

'I wouldn't get your hopes up, Bobby. I'm too old for a farmhand, and I know nowt about animals other than how to trap 'em the way Pete taught me. I can kid myself we're country folk now, but I've never been nowt but a wool man, good enough to work the mills and that's it.' He patted the hand that she'd rested on his shoulder. 'But you're a good lass for trying to help. What was the letter you were hoping to find?'

'Oh, nothing important. I thought it might be here by now, that's all.'

'Happen it's over at Moorside. I've had my letters end up there many a time.'

Bobby brightened slightly. 'Yes, I suppose it might have gone over there. Do you mind if I go and check before I light the fire? I need to let Reg and Mary know we're back anyhow, and the girls will be dying to see me – if only because I promised to bring them some spice from the fair.'

'Aye, go on. I'm warm enough from t' walk down to keep chill out for a bit.'

Bobby left the cottage, not bothering to put her coat and hat back on. Hope had risen its head again, if only a fractional amount. Her dad was right: it wasn't uncommon for short-sighted Gil Capstick to deliver their post to Moorside on occasion. Perhaps Mary had her letter from Charlie and was keeping it safe for her.

She knocked on the side door, which was opened shortly after by Mary. Bobby was expecting her usual greeting on returning home from an absence, a beaming smile and a warm hug, but Mary only looked a little uncomfortable.

'Bobby,' she said. 'I wasn't expecting you back until tomorrow evening.'

'Yes, we came back early. My dad was anxious to be back in the countryside. I just wondered if—' She broke off, frowning, as Mary glanced nervously behind her. 'Is anything wrong, Mary? You seem out of sorts.'

'I do wish you'd telegraphed to say you'd be early, Bobby.'

'I didn't think there was any need. Why do you—'

She stopped short as a male figure appeared behind Mary. Not the grizzled, slightly hunched figure of her husband, but someone tall, young and handsome. Someone in an RAF uniform.

Charlie.

Chapter 39

'Charlie.' The sight of him almost took Bobby's breath away for a moment; his name when she said it sounded more like a gasp than any intelligible sound.

'He was granted leave rather earlier than he'd expected,' Mary said with an apologetic grimace. 'Only three days. He's leaving tomorrow morning. I was expecting he'd be gone before you and your dad were back.'

'It's… fine.' Bobby forced a smile, trying to get her fluttering stomach muscles under control. 'You didn't need to worry on my account, Mary. We're all sensible people who are quite capable of co-existing in this place without serious consequences, I'm sure.'

'I quite agree,' Charlie said. Mary looked relieved.

'Well, since we're all being civilised, perhaps you and Rob might like to come in for a cup of tea,' she said.

'Is Ruth here?' Bobby was rather proud of herself for managing to say the name without flinching.

Mary frowned. 'Ruth?'

Bobby looked at Charlie. 'Topsy told me you were planning to bring her home with you.'

'Oh. Yes.' He rubbed his neck. 'I was hoping to be granted a week's leave later this month so we could both make the trip, but in the end I could only get these three days at short notice. I'll bring her next time.'

'Who is this Ruth, Charlie?' Mary asked.

Charlie shot Bobby a warning look that seemed to plead for silence. Clearly the news of his engagement had not yet been broken at Moorside.

'Just a friend, Mother,' he said airily. 'I was waxing lyrical about this part of the world and she expressed a wish to see it, so I arranged for her to stay with Topsy when she visits and then we could travel down together.'

'This is the same friend you take to the pictures sometimes?'

'That's right.'

'Um, I ought to go back to the cottage,' Bobby said, feeling awkward beyond belief. Charlie must have received her telegram before he left for Silverdale, yet he seemed determined not to refer to it. 'My father's sitting in the cold, waiting for me to light a fire for him.'

She turned to leave.

'Bobby, wait.' Charlie followed her out, nodding to Mary to indicate that she could go back inside.

'What is it, Charlie?' she asked when they were alone.

'So... Topsy told you about Ruth.'

'That's right.'

'I might have guessed she would. She's a terrible gossip. I'm sorry you had to find out like that.'

'What is she like, this Ruth?'

'She's a lovely girl. Very jolly. You'll like her.'

He looked earnest and anxious, his eyes scanning hers to see what her reaction was going to be.

'I'm sure I will.' She forced a smile. 'Look, Charlie, it's all right. It was bound to be a little awkward, I suppose, but... I'm glad you've met someone new. Genuinely I am. You deserve to be happy.'

'That's really how you feel?'

'Of course.'

'Right.' He was silent for a moment, looking rather sombre.

For a second she thought about mentioning the telegram she'd sent, but she couldn't bring herself to do so. She was too embarrassed. Clearly he was too.

'I have to go home,' she said, taking his silence as the signal that their conversation was at an end.

'Wait. Don't go yet.' He put a hand on her arm.

'What is it, Charlie?'

'I thought, since you were home early... I made you a promise once, Bobby, and I feel guilty that I never managed to fulfil it.'

'What promise?'

He nodded to the peak of Bowside. 'I promised to take you up there to see the sunset before this summer was over, didn't I?'

'You did take me up there.'

'That hardly counts.' He flashed her the old familiar smile, the one she'd missed every day he'd been away, and Bobby felt herself start to melt as she had so many times before.

'There's a nice fire blazing in the parlour at Moorside, and I'm sure Reggie, Mary and the girls would be glad of Rob's company for the day,' Charlie said, sensing her weakening. 'One more fell walk, for old time's sake? It won't be so easy once I'm a married man, you know. I'd like us to be better friends again.'

'I'll have to change into my walking things first.'

He grinned. 'I knew you couldn't say no to me.'

–

Some time later, they were once again striding the lower slopes of Great Bowside with the summit in their sights.

371

Bobby could almost forget everything that had happened between them, forget Ruth, and imagine things had been restored to how they were during their happiest time together. The cuckoo time, when the fells had stretched out endlessly and Charlie's arms had been for her and her alone. She wished he would slip his arm around her waist as he used to, but then she remembered that such wishes were no longer permitted. What a fool she had been in the past to ever have pushed his arm away! She hadn't known then, as she played at being coy, how one day she would long for his touch only to find it was now forbidden.

'I haven't been up here since that night,' she said dreamily.

'I often think of that night.'

'So do I.'

'How are our friends the airmen?'

'Piotr is thriving,' she said with a smile. 'He can walk now, with the aid of a pair of crutches. I was introduced to his wife and little boy just last week. They're well-matched, he and Jolka – truly a partnership of equals. I've never met a married couple quite like them.'

'And the pilot? Topsy's letters are full of him, but she gushes so about those people she decides to make pets of that it's hard to build a proper picture.'

'Teddy's spirits are rather depressed. He's lost the sight in one eye and the doctors say his legs will be permanently paralysed. He feels responsible for the crash as well, and the deaths of his comrades.' She sighed. 'I wish there was something more I could do to help him.'

'The crash wasn't his fault. All training flights should have been grounded until the fog lifted.'

'I know, but he feels that way, all the same.' She scowled. 'And somewhere the squadron leader who was really responsible probably never loses a wink of sleep over it.'

Charlie smiled. 'Oh, I've missed that scowl. Being angry suits you, Bob.'

'No flirting please. Not allowed.' But she couldn't help a half-smile. The shepherd's hut was in the distance, reminding her of the day they'd sheltered there from the storm and fallen asleep in one another's arms.

'I've got some news to tell you,' Charlie said. 'News that even Reggie and Mary don't know.'

'About Ruth?'

'No, not about Ruth.' He sounded impatient. 'Not everything is about Ruth. This is about me.'

'What is it?'

'I've requested to be transferred. To finish my training as bomber aircrew rather than flying fighters. It's bomber crews that are going to be needed now the blitzes are less frequent and the Soviets are holding the Luftwaffe at bay.' He glanced at her. 'It means I can come home to complete my training, Bobby. I've asked to transfer to the training school ten miles away, and I've been given every reason to believe that request will be granted.'

'That ought to be nice for your family,' she said vaguely. 'Will Ruth mind a long-distance engagement, or is she able to request a transfer too? I suppose if you marry soon, that will make it easier for her to join you here.'

'I wish you'd put Ruth out of your head for a moment. It really isn't important where she goes.'

'I imagine it's rather important to her.'

There was silence for a while as they navigated the steepest part of the climb. As the ascent became easier and they neared the summit, Charlie slipped his arm around her waist. Bobby knew she ought to push him away, but she didn't.

'I remember you that night, Bobby,' he said softly. 'Striding ahead of me like a woman possessed, determined to save those men's lives.'

'There's some of the wreckage.' Bobby pointed out part of the plane's fuselage where it had slammed into the rocks. 'It's funny, but it almost seems like a dream now.'

'You told me that was the night you finally decided what answer you were going to give me.' They were at the summit now and he turned her around to face him. 'I never told you that I decided something that night too.'

He drew her into his arms. That wasn't allowed either, was it? But Bobby found she had little power to resist. She felt light-headed, as if she was floating – perhaps it was the altitude. Everything felt like a strange dream. Was she really on top of a mountain with Charlie Atherton, wrapped tight in his arms, watching the sun go down?

'What did you decide?' she whispered.

'I decided that there'd never be any other woman in my life but the one I was with that night. A woman who was kind, and as courageous as a lioness. One who never backed down when she knew she had the power to make a difference. One who showed me what bravery really meant and inspired me to be a better man just so I might be worthy of her.'

Bobby looked up at him. 'Do you mean me?'

He laughed. 'Well I'm not talking about Gil Capstick. I decided that night I wasn't going to give up on you, no matter how long I had to wait. That was the decision I made.'

'But… Ruth. What about Ruth?'

'Ah, yes. Ruth.' He flicked a strand of hair that had come loose from her headscarf out of her eyes. 'I may have a small confession to make.'

'What is it?'

He grimaced. 'There never was any Ruth, Bobby. I mean there is, and she's a nice, jolly sort of girl who appreciates the great outdoors and I really did invite her to come and visit us here if she wanted to. But she isn't my fiancée – just a good friend. I've been twice to the pictures with her and some others only because she's a pal of Smithy's girl. She actually has her eye on a young flight lieutenant, if you must know.'

'But Topsy told me you were engaged.'

'I might have asked her to tell you that, yes.'

She shook her head. 'Charlie, I don't understand.'

'Don't you? It was simply that I wanted to drive you mad with jealousy so you'd realise just how in love with me you really were. Since the tales of all my dates hadn't achieved the desired effect, I decided to take things a step further.'

'You mean the dates you told Mary about never happened?'

'They did – I couldn't lie to Mary – but they only happened so I could write to her about them, knowing she'd then tell you. I never gave up hope that you might change your mind. I didn't know you weren't at home this week – I came home hoping particularly that you would be, so I could see what effect my machinations had had on you and if it was time to have another go.' He looked into her eyes. 'Are you very cross with me?'

'Yes I am. But it'll keep.' She stroked his cheek with her thumb. 'Ask me again, Charlie,' she whispered.

'Kiss me first, in case you say no.'

'I'm not going to say no. But I'll gladly kiss you.'

He pulled her closer, and their lips met in a kiss that felt like their first one all over again.

'All right, if you promise you're not going to say no then this time I'm going to do it properly,' Charlie whispered when they finally broke apart. He let her go so he could fall to one knee, then he took her hand. 'Miss Bancroft, would you do me the very great honour of agreeing to become my wife?'

'We couldn't do it right away. It might need to be a long engagement.'

'When you said you wouldn't say no, I was sort of hoping the alternative answer would be yes.'

She laughed. 'It is yes. Get up out of the mud, you daft lad.'

He smiled as he stood up and pulled her back into his arms. 'As long as it's yes, Bobby, you can impose whatever terms you please. If you want to wait until we're ninety I shan't complain, although our wedding night might be less exciting than I was anticipating.'

'I really shouldn't say yes after the way you tricked me.' She shook her head. 'One of these days, you're actually going to be engaged when Topsy tells me you are and I'm not going to believe her. She's like the boy who cried wolf.'

He smiled. 'Ah, but the next time she gives someone the news I'm engaged it will be true, won't it? I'll let you be the one to tell her, then you can get your own back.'

'When Lilian suggested it might have been an engagement of necessity, my heart nearly hit the floor.'

'An engagement of...' He frowned. 'Oh. I hadn't thought of that.'

'No, I don't suppose you would.'

'If I can manage to resist your charms until we've signed on the dotted line, Bobby, then I'm certainly not at risk from anyone else's.' He fished in his pocket for something and took her hand to slide it on. 'Here.'

Bobby held up her left hand and stared at the sapphire ring on her third finger. 'It's beautiful, Charlie! However did you afford it? Please don't say your horse came in.'

'Family heirloom. It belonged to my grandmother. Mary doesn't know, but I had a talk with Reggie when I came home and I told him I was planning to take one last crack at it. He gave me this to help persuade you.'

'Reg gave it to you? You mean he approves?'

'I believe he does. You know, he's mellowed quite considerably since those two little girls came into his life. It makes me wonder what sort of man my brother might have been if Nancy had lived and he'd never gone to war.'

'It's the exact colour of the kingfisher I saw,' she murmured, moving her hand so the stone glistened in the dying sunlight.

'I knew you'd like it.' He guided her to a flat rock. 'Let's sit and watch the sunset. I've been promising you this moment for a long time.'

Bobby smiled as she sat by him and snuggled into his arms. 'When I saw you at Moorside, I was worried you couldn't have got my telegram – either that or you were too embarrassed to mention it. I've been waiting all week for an answer from you.'

He frowned. 'Telegram?'

'Yes, the telegram I sent to your billet.' She looked at him. 'That is why you asked again, isn't it?'

'I asked because I hoped you might have changed your mind, and because I wasn't strong enough not to ask. I didn't get any telegram. What did it say?'

'It said "Ask me again."'

'Did it? If I'd seen that, I'd have been off to Bradford on the next train before you changed your mind.'

'I knew I'd made a mistake the moment I saw Piotr and Jolka together, and the sort of family life they lead.' She shook her head. 'I really thought the telegram must be why you brought me here.'

'I'm very glad I kept my nerve up enough to go through with it. When you sounded so happy about my supposed engagement, I almost changed my mind. I thought perhaps you'd stopped caring about me.'

'Your machinations nearly had the same effect on me. I'd already realised I'd made a mistake when Topsy told me about your engagement. Then I thought you'd moved on and it was too late. If it wasn't for Lilian persuading me, I never would have telegrammed at all. I'd have left you to be happy with your new love.' She leaned over to kiss him. 'I hope that's taught you a lesson about telling fibs.'

'From now on, I'll be as honest as a magistrate.' He idly twirled a loose strand of her hair around his finger while they watched the sun paint the sky orange and pink. 'What changed your mind, Bobby? You sounded so certain when we said goodbye.'

'Like I said, it was partly Piotr and Jolka. They showed me that there isn't just one type of marriage – that a marriage is as unique as the people in it, and you can still have goals and ambitions of your own even if you are a mother. She's a sort of a bluestocking, which a lot of men would find intimidating, but Piotr loves and respects her for it. And it was partly the Parry girls, making me realise how much I wanted children of my own. But mainly it was something Jolka said to me.'

'What did she say?'

378

'She made me realise… that night we climbed up here, and I saw what I saw in the plane, I thought it would be torture to me to know that the man I loved was up there in the skies. I knew I'd see that burning body in my nightmares and be terrified that the next time it would be you.' She turned to him. 'But that's going to happen anyhow, Charlie. What Jolka helped me to understand was that telling you I didn't want to be with you wasn't going to stop me worrying about you. It wasn't going to stop me loving you. I'll always love you, whether I'm with you or not.'

Charlie smiled and cuddled her closer.

'What about your job at the magazine?' he asked. 'You know, the other great love of your life.'

'Reg wouldn't expect me to leave until I was actually married. After that… I don't know. Don Sykes said he'd always have a job at the *Courier* for me, married or single, but I really don't want to leave *The Tyke*.' She kissed him. 'But I don't intend to lose you again either.'

'You won't. I wouldn't let you.' He drew her closer. 'I love you very much, Bobby,' he whispered. 'One day soon the war will end and I'll come home for good, I promise.'

'Every prayer I say that isn't for you is for the end of this filthy war.' She took his hand and pressed it to her lips. 'I do love you, Charlie. And I'm sorry.'

'No you're not. I can't allow you to be sorry. You've never done anything wrong in your whole life except for loving me.'

She smiled. 'If that's a sin, I'll never feel the need to confess it.'

A joyous silence reigned as they looked down from the summit at the little villages and hamlets in the valley below them, the beck meandering through like a ribbon of gold in the dying sunlight. A sheep occasionally gave a mellow bleat, and somewhere in the distance, a red grouse let out its chuckle call. Elsewhere the storm clouds of war might roll on, but that August evening the Dales were peaceful, calm and serene. Bobby snuggled into her lover's arms, content for the moment to be content. And still the grouse called and the sheep bleated, like the promise of a world to come that would be at peace once more.

A letter from Betty

Hello, and thank you for choosing to read *War Comes to the Dales*, the second of the 'Made in Yorkshire' series. I loved returning to Silverdale to find out what happened next for Bobby and friends, and I hope you enjoyed reading about it just as much.

In this story, I've endeavoured to shine a spotlight on the challenges Bobby faces as a young woman in love but with dreams and ambitions beyond this, as she tries to find a place for herself that encompasses more than the roles traditionally ascribed to women of her time. All this must take place against the backdrop of a war from which even Bobby's idyllic home of Silverdale cannot remain isolated, its residents living under the shadow of what the world of tomorrow may look like for families and their children.

I'd absolutely love to hear your thoughts on this book in a review. These are invaluable not only for letting authors know how their story affected you but also for helping other readers to choose their next read and discover new writers. Just a few words can make a big difference.

If you would like to find out more about me and my books, you can do so via my website or social media pages, which can be found under my other pen name Mary Jayne Baker:

Facebook: /MaryJayneWrites
Twitter: @MaryJayneBaker
Instagram: @MaryJayneBaker
Web: www.maryjaynebaker.co.uk

Thank you again for choosing *War Comes to the Dales*.
  Best wishes,
  Betty

Acknowledgments

My first thanks go to my editor at Hera, Keshini Naidoo. This is the sixth book we've worked on together, and as always, I'm indebted to her commitment to making this story the best that it could be. I'd also like to thank the rest of the team at Hera for all their hard work on this title.

Thanks also to my agent Hannah Todd at Madeleine Milburn Agency for contributing her support and expertise to the Made in Yorkshire series.

I'm also very grateful to my former colleague, ex-*Dalesman* editor Adrian Braddy, who first suggested to me the idea of a story inspired by the founding of *The Dalesman* magazine.

As with the previous book in this series, the story also owes much to the writing of late journalist and author (and another former *Dalesman* editor) WR 'Bill' Mitchell. Bill wrote about the Dales and the unique people who dwell in them in a career that spanned over seventy years, and I am indebted to his interviews with Dalesfolk and memories of times gone by.